THE BEAST AND THE BADASS

Vegas Immortals

A COMPLETE DUET

HOLLY ROBERDS

Cover Design: Holly Roberds
Editors: Theresa Paolo
Sensitivity Readers: The Havoc Archives & Wanika Kiana

BOOKS BY HOLLY ROBERDS

<u>VEGAS IMMORTALS</u>

Death and the Last Vampire

Book 1 - Bitten by Death

Book 2 - Kissed by Death

Book 3 - Seduced by Death

The Beast & the Badass

Book 1 - Breaking the Beast

Book 2 - Claiming the Beast

Scribe & the Sinner

Book 1 - Dying for Death

<u>MONSTER UNDER MY BED</u>

Book 1 - Volume 1

<u>LOST GIRLS SERIES</u>

Book 1 - Tasting Red

Book 2 - Chasing Goldie

Book 3 - Igniting Cinder

Book 3.5 - Hooking Tink

Book 4 - Blackmailing Belle

Book 5 - Feeding Beauty

<u>DEMON KNIGHTS</u>

Book 1 - One Savage Knight

Book 2 - One Bad Knight

To all the Vegas Immortals fans
Let's stay and play in this world a while

BREAKING THE BEAST

THE GOD OF THE DEAD

The elevator descended deeper into the bowels of the hotel, and with each passing moment, my unease grew. The humans didn't know that the Grim Reaper ran the most exclusive hotel on the Vegas strip. And no one knew what I kept in the basement far beneath the massive pyramid of dark glass, high rollers poker tables, and hottest night clubs. My greatest shame. And tonight, it called to me.

As the elevator doors opened, I stepped into a concrete room that extended out to either side. I met with a wall of steel bars, creating a structure similar to that of a zoo, but this held something far more dangerous than any jungle cat. The predator within couldn't be unleashed on this world. I had done my best to keep him content under lock and key, but I could not deny his request when he called.

Despite the harsh lights overhead in the antechamber, the cage gradually sank into darkness, concealing the truth of its depths. A voice called out from the shadows, low and lucid for once. "You came," it said, and a chill ran down my spine.

I loosened my tie, feeling the hot sting of power against my skin. It was wild, untamed, and as volatile as an atomic bomb. "You called," I replied, wary of what this encounter might bring.

As the god emerged from the shadows, hair fell over glinting silver eyes and sharp features. The power sickness surrounding him made it difficult to look at him. It grated against me and stung like lemon juice pouring into an open wound. My eyes burned from the onslaught of energy pulsating off him, but I didn't look away. I knew I had failed him, and it weighed heavily on my shoulders.

He grasped the bars of his cage, flexing muscles built on chaos and destruction. "The blade of bane, Grim. You found the blade of bane," he said, his voice holding a dangerous undertone.

"Vivien did," I replied, already aware of where this conversation was headed and trying to calculate a way to curb the outcome.

He grinned at the mention of my vampire bride. It was a terrible, sinister baring of the teeth. "Ah, the firecracker. We've met." The mirth evaporated from his face, replaced by cold ruthlessness. "Bring me the blade, Grim."

"The blade has bonded to a human, and only she can wield it now." Perhaps the god retained enough reason to understand why I couldn't bring her here. Why I couldn't let any mortal near him.

He cocked an eyebrow and tilted his head. "Then bring her to me."

"I can't do that either," I said, squaring off my stance.

Xander stilled. He seemed unnaturally frozen, staring at me. Power crackled in the room, sizzling against my skin with anger and impatience.

My words came out low and careful. "Xander, she doesn't know how to use it. And she doesn't know how to protect herself. . ."

". . .from me," he finished. His voice became gravelly and raw. "Then bring her to me, Grim. And I'll teach her. And with any luck, she'll only need to learn once."

I turned away from him, running a hand down my face. "We both know your luck is shit," I muttered under my breath. But I owed him. I owed him what he asked, because even as the reaper of death, I couldn't give him what he needed. It was my ultimate failing.

Xander's silver eyes gleamed with warning as he bared his teeth.

"Grim? If you don't, I'll break out of this cage and take matters into my own hands."

The threat hung in the air between us, and I knew he wasn't bluffing. We both recognized he was only in a cage because he let me put him there. As I stepped back into the elevator and the doors slid shut, I couldn't shake off the unease that lingered within me or the burn of his power from my skin. As much as I feared for Miranda's safety, I couldn't deny Xander his wish.

The elevator suddenly jerked to a stop, the lights flickering before going out completely. A cold, malevolent energy filled the air, emanating from Xander.

It was a parting warning. *Bring the girl or the beast will come out to play.*

Miranda had admirably dealt with the problems of gods, but the predator in that cage was far more dangerous than any creature she had encountered. Mortals shouldn't mix with monsters, and the beast I kept contained in the cage was more monster than god after all these years.

I could only hope that Miranda would quickly resolve this situation and absolve me of my ultimate failing. Otherwise, the beast would be unleashed.

Chapter One

THE BADASS

I sank into the hot water, submerging myself in the froth of lavender-scented bubbles. A low, contented sigh slipped out of me. I welcomed the caress of the water around me. Embracing the pleasure of a near-scalding bath was almost painful after the intense week. I was literally trying to melt my worries away.

I'd been waiting for days to find the time to get in my porcelain sanctuary and melt my stress with scalding heat.

Spillover from the supernatural world had twisted my panties into such a tight bunch that I'd forgotten how to breathe properly for days. As if holding my breath would keep the bullshit at bay. There is that saying 'don't hold your breath' for a reason.

I closed my eyes trying not to think about the idiot group of demigods who tried to break into the antechambers below to see Amit, the soul eating crocodile god. Then a half-crazed, scared vampire got loose in the hotel, biting one of my maids where there were a dozen witnesses who had to have their minds wiped. And then there was a clashing of personalities at the check-in desk where one employee ended up relentlessly quacking at the other. That's right. Quacking.

Oddly enough there wasn't a handbook on how to handle immortal chaos, or jackass employees who mock each other in inventively annoying ways.

And yet I am the one who has to lay down the discipline, attempt mediation, clean up the blood, and come down on the dumbass demigods bearing the only weapon that will give them pause.

Not bad for a human, but hell if I didn't need two weeks' vacation on a beach somewhere after all that.

My muscles still fought release, even in the luxurious heat. So, I laid my head back and let out a deep breath, talking to myself in a low voice.

"Nothing needs to be done right now, Miranda. Just relax."

Again, a bigger part of me still wanted to fight it. Since Jamal left for summer camp a couple of days ago, my restlessness had flipped into overdrive.

But I made the serenity of my small bathroom irresistible with candles flickering all around the room. Lianne LaHavas crooned my favorite song, "Midnight," from my phone that I set on the closed toilet lid.

At last, I was lulled into some semblance of peace and relaxation.

I used the towel to dry my hands before reaching for my romance book.

Except my hands reached for an empty spot.

"Dammit," I cursed, rubbing my face. I had left my book and my glass of red wine in the kitchen.

Bubble baths were a self-care ritual I took incredibly seriously. It required all the right accessories from the choice of bath bomb, to the music, to the book.

And it wasn't just any wine sitting in the kitchen; it was a 1992 bottle of Pinot Noir from Celestial Cellars. It had been gifted to me by an actual goddess of wine who appreciated my assistance in training her hotel staff after a series of security breaches. I had tasted it once at my best friend's wedding, and it was the best thing to ever pass my lips.

Adjusting the cap holding up my braids, I sunk deeper into the water, trying to enjoy the bath anyway.

I don't need everything to be perfect to relax.

Who cares if I don't drink that ambrosia right now? I bet leaving it out will aerate it so it tastes even better!

But after I got out of the tub, the moment would be gone. The calm I felt in water didn't typically extend beyond the tub.

I scowled. My fingers flexed and relaxed several times as restlessness coiled through my limbs.

No. I can do this. I can relax without needing things to be perfect.

I sunk a couple of inches deeper, submerging my chin in frothy bubbles, my hands resting on either side of the tub.

My fingers began to tap. Tap, tap, tap on the porcelain edges.

Irritation mounted inside me as I kept envisioning the lone wine glass and book.

Water sloshed violently as I stood up. Yanking my towel off the rack, I wrapped it around me.

I opened the bathroom door, and left the small steamy room into the bracing cold of the rest of the house. Water tracks followed me as I went to grab my targets. I'd deal with the mess later.

With my spoils in hand, I stomped back to the bathroom, but the cool air was already pulling me out of the moment I had created.

A loud, obnoxious electronic beep preceded the house plunging into darkness. Ugh. Another brownout. Thankfully, I had candles lit all over the place, so I didn't lose total visibility, which meant I was less likely to trip and snap my neck.

With my son gone for the next couple of months, I wasn't sure who'd find my naked ass sprawled on the ground. At least we didn't have any cats to feast on the soft bits of my corpse.

Damn, that got way too dark too quick.

The house was way too quiet without Jamal brightening it up. Maybe I did need some kind of pet. A low-maintenance pet, like a guinea pig or a bird. Nah. My level is more like sea monkeys. Yes, that's more like it! I'll raise a hoard of sea monkeys in my kid's absence. When he comes home, he'll discover his mother had become a crazy sea monkey lady.

I tripped on the carpet, wine lurching dangerously to the rim of my glass.

I *really* needed to buy a generator. Maybe I should go get my laptop and −

I spoke out loud to myself, "Nope, you are not going to think about any of that. We are going to relax, goddammit."

A second dip back into the tub was not as nice as the first. The reentry of my cold, wet body chilled the water several degrees. Irritation raked along my insides at the inconvenience. At least I had managed to fill the tub before the brownout.

My beats cut out as my phone rang, and Vivien's face appeared. I scrambled to get up, clawing for my phone before settling back into the bath with a hard splash. Half the bubbles had disappeared from all my moving about. Just freaking great.

"Hey," I said, a little breathless.

"Hiya," Vivien said brightly. She was my best friend and also happened to be a vampire.

It took only that one word to let me know why she called.

"What do you need?" I sighed.

"My dearest, most awesome friend," Vivien said, laying on the syrup in her tone. "What makes you think I need something? Can't I just call to chat with you?"

Silence fell over the phone. I didn't bother to fill it, instead I smoothed a thin layer of pearlescent bubbles over my smooth, brown legs and waited. Waxing my legs at home was a messy, pain in the ass chore, but I didn't like shaving every day. I wondered if my vampire best friend had to shave anymore? Probably not, the lucky bitch.

"Okay, okay," Vivien burst out.

I knew if I waited a scant two minutes, she would crack. I was fairly certain if Vivien tried to hold in a secret for too long, she would explode into a cloud of blood, glitter, and sugar. The things I knew about her sex life alone were as detailed as they were vivid. Not that I minded since her stories of banging her equally supernatural honey were the only sexual thrill I got these days.

"It's not me actually," she confessed. "Here—" she said to someone off before I heard a shuffle.

A male voice came on the line. "Miranda?"

I straightened in the tub so fast, bubbles and water sloshed over the side.

"Mr. Scarapelli." Grim Scarapelli, aka Vivien's husband, aka the Grim Reaper himself. Though his original origins are more ancient and Egyptian, he is the god of the dead, once known as Anubis.

He used to prowl about in a monstrous jackal form and judge souls in the pyramids, but he'd modernized to the times.

Grim now wore expensive suits and owned the most exclusive hotel in Vegas, Sinopolis, a massive pyramid made of dark glass and filled with decadent luxury. He also happened to be my boss.

"Miranda, how many times do I have to tell you to call me Grim?" His voice was smooth as dark chocolate, and though he was my best friend's soul mate, I couldn't deny my attraction to him. But I learned not to take his magnetic effect seriously; every person had a little bit of a death wish. It helped to know it was a supernatural thing, and that I wasn't just a total scumbag.

"How can I help you?" I asked my boss.

There was a pause, and I imagined him pinching the bridge of his nose on the other end, a pose he fell back on when particularly pensive. While I waited for him to answer, I wondered why he didn't call or text me from his phone. It wasn't totally uncommon for him to contact me; I was head of security at his luxury hotel, Sinopolis, the most exclusive and upscale place to be on the Vegas Strip. Then I realized this wasn't business as usual. Going through Vivien meant it was personal.

"I know it's late, and I hate to impose, but there is something I would like to discuss with you."

I was already up and out of the tub with a towel wrapped about my soaking body. "Is it serious?"

"It is of a serious nature, yes," he said, hedging his words. "It's best if we speak in person. Is there any chance you could come to the hotel? Is Jamal at home? I'd be happy to send Timothy over to watch him while we handle our matters."

"I could watch him," I heard Vivien suggest in the background.

"No," Grim and I said in unison.

I wouldn't even trust my best friend with my imaginary hoard of sea monkeys. She'd either get distracted and leave them to die, or get some strange idea stuck in her head like feeding them sugar packets would supersize them somehow.

Translate these propensities toward a child and Jamal would definitely end up worse for wear. Nope. It was best my kid and the woman-sized child stay buddies rather than give her an ounce of power or authority over my spawn.

Pulling my cap off, I ignored Vivien's long whine that followed. A tumble of thin box braids fell down past my shoulder blades to my lower back. "That won't be necessary, sir. Jamal left this morning for camp."

My sweet, intelligent baby boy was eleven years old, and I missed him already.

"He'll be away for some time then?" Grim asked, trying to keep things light.

"Nine weeks," I answered as I finished snapping on my bra. He had been going since he was seven, and while I missed him terribly when he left, he loved the friends he made there. The camp was half focused on survival, and the other half was STEM education. My baby was a budding genius and got a special scholarship to this camp. Not that I was surprised. He got his wicked smarts from his mama. But his absence left me itching for a more exciting life. It sounded like Grim had something for me.

"So, you'll come then?"

I could tell it pained Grim to ask it of me. My pants were already on, and I donned a forest green tank top. This didn't seem to call for formal attire.

"Of course."

"Good, good," he muttered more to himself.

Before I hung up, he said, "And Miranda, bring the blade."

My eyes tracked to my closet. I didn't lower the phone even after the call ended. I kept the Blade of Bane stored in a sheath between my formal dresses and my sweatpants. An unpleasant churning started in my stomach.

Whatever the god of the dead was about to ask me, I had a feeling I already wouldn't like it.

Chapter Two

THE BADASS

"Mirranda, you understand duty," Grim said, swirling a glass of brown liquor while avoiding meeting my gaze. We sat in his penthouse apartment atop the pyramid hotel, surrounded by upscale luxury.

My fingers grip the couch cushion beneath me. I feel like a kid who's been called to the principal's office even though my boss is in unusually informal shape.

Grim's usual pristine black suit jacket was carelessly discarded on a nearby chair, and his shirt was only partially buttoned. As he spoke, his fingers tapped restlessly against his thigh. To my surprise, he was barefoot, his feet planted firmly in the plush white carpet. I couldn't stop staring at them, which unsettled me.

"I suppose I do understand duty," I replied slowly. Needing to do something with my hands, I reached over and straightened a pillow.

Grim and I might share a sense of duty, but I found myself thinking of the person who linked us—Vivien.

Vivien often boasted that I was a badass because I used to be in the Special Forces and because I'm a single mom. But the military was a lifetime ago and being a single parent had made me softer in some ways. Although I would never admit that to Vivien, With Jamal away at camp, I found myself floundering for direction and orders. I enjoyed being her scary, tough as nails friend. Though sitting across from her husband, the god of death, I began to think she had a type she aligned herself with.

"I take my duties seriously," Grim said with a wry smile.

A deep line forms between my brows.

Grim was the god of the dead, and he was comparing our sense of duty.

How many feet of shit was I about to dive into?

I pushed back the cuticles on one hand. "I imagine sorting souls for the afterlife on a daily basis would require a certain level of commit-ment," I said, my eyes dropping back down to his bare feet.

He nodded, expression absent as if his mind was elsewhere.

I wasn't used to hanging out with my boss, and I didn't know why I was there. I moved to pushing back the cuticles on my other hand.

"And when I'm unable to perform my duties, it can...well, it eats away at me. I don't know if you can understand..." Grim said, sounding distracted.

"This isn't a sex thing, is it?" I asked incredulously, unable to believe I even had to ask.

"What?" He straightened and blinked. "No."

I sank back into the couch, relieved. "Oh good, because if the duties were in regard to my friend, I mean, she's kind of your problem now."

Grim seemed flustered. "No, there's no problem. I mean I perform with her just fine. That isn't what—"

I took the opportunity to reach for the glass of red wine waiting on the coffee table for me. It was divine, a testament to Grim's godly taste and wealth. But it wasn't a 1992 Celestial Cellers Pinot Noir, I thought glumly.

Grim rubbed his forehead and chuckled. "I feel I'm beginning to understand why you are so close with my sekhor."

Sekhor was an ancient word for vampire. While Vivien was a bloodsucker, she only had fangs for Grim.

My brain bounced like a strung out, hyper child, waiting for him to tell me why I was here. Again, my eyes fell on his bare feet. So wrong.

I put the glass back down, realizing I'd drained half the glass in one go.

This time Grim caught me staring and looked up at me, as if he was trying to gauge my thoughts. I quickly averted my gaze to his face.

"Yeah, we vibe." My knee began to bounce.

Why wasn't he getting to the point?

Vivien was already a vampire when I met her, and I may have tried to kill her at one point. She suffered from amnesia, having no idea who'd bitten her or who she was. She may have forgotten her name, but no amount of amnesia could downplay her wild, antagonist, and playful personality. She'd been put through the wringer when it came to immortals' business, and after a flood of humans were turned, she was the one dealing with the mess of newly minted bloodsuckers who didn't understand what had happened to them or what it meant.

It was also part of the deal Vivien made with the god Osiris. While Grim took care of the souls of the dead, Vivien shepherded the new vamps as the master vampire. She could control their will and keep them from harming anyone and help them through their transition.

"Right," Grim said, acknowledging mine and Vivien's close tie while setting his drink down as well. "I'm being obtuse. This can all be quite quick and over with." He stood abruptly. "You are the caretaker of the blade of bane. The only one who can wield it, correct?"

The sword lay on the couch next to me. My fingers rested on the hilt, as if needing to assure myself it was there. "Yes."

A jolt of warmth shot through my fingers and up my arm. The sword was like a living thing, humming with a subtle power that fused with me. I caressed the sleek, gold inlaid hilt reverently, feeling its weight and balance. It felt like an extension of me, like an extra arm at times, and I knew it was meant for me and me alone.

Though I didn't really kill a god with it, so much as she threw herself on the sword's edge, not wanting to live anymore. It didn't feel right assisting her suicide like that. If I'd been faster or cleverer, I would have seen it coming and prevented the goddess Bast from ending her life.

Grim stopped in the middle of the room, hands folded behind his back. "I have a formal request of you as the blade's keeper."

"For cripes sake, would you spit it out already? I'm a big girl."

My hand clapped over my mouth as soon as the words escaped me.

Grim's golden brown eyes widened in surprise.

I couldn't believe I just mouthed off to the Grim Reaper. Not that I thought he would kill me. Or maybe a small part of me was all too aware that was a possibility.

I covered my eyes for a moment. "I'm just saying, you don't need to pussyfoot around me."

Grim unsuccessfully tried to suppress an amused smile. "You're right." Then he turned serious again and finally came right out with it. "I need you to kill a god for me."

Before I could even process that, he looked down at his feet before meeting my gaze with uncertainty. "And is there something wrong with my feet?"

Chapter Three

THE BADASS

I artfully dodged the question about Grim Reaper's feet because thankfully there was a bigger topic at hand. Despite him being the god of the dead, Grim was one of the last people I'd expect to ask me to assassinate someone. When I asked for more information, he said it was better we take a short trip to further elaborate on the situation.

Whatever that meant.

My breath hitched in my throat, an eyebrow arching involuntarily when we got on his private elevator and a black button appeared below the column of three buttons like magic. Not *like* magic. It was magic. And I still wasn't totally used to it.

I'd released a small sigh of relief when I noticed he was now wearing slippers. For some bizarre reason, that made me feel a bit better, as if a modicum of order had been restored to my world.

Wherever we were going, it was a place below the chamber of judgement where Grim either led souls to the afterlife or fed the corrupt hearts to a giant crocodile god named Amit. I hadn't been to that level below the hotel, but Vivien had told me all about how it was like stepping into a pyramid chamber in ancient Egypt.

The doors of the elevator slid open with a ding that reverberated in the eerie stillness, putting me on edge. As soon as the doors parted, I felt an intense surge of energy. It was like a live current of electricity had replaced the air down here and enveloped me, making my skin feel raw and overstimulated.

A prickling sensation ran up my spine, cold beads of sweat forming on my forehead. I involuntarily shrank back, every instinct screaming for an escape route from the pulsating power. Ghostly hands formed of pain and sickness traced patterns across my skin.

Grim gave me a concerned sideways glance. "Are you alright? It can be a lot for a human to be this close."

This close to what?

If the god of the dead himself was nervous for me, why the hell was I down here?

To kill a god, apparently. This Wednesday may be one of the weirdest yet, and I've cavorted about with vampires, and gods.

"What has he done?" I asked quietly, before stepping out, showing I could handle it. But could I? Could I really do this? Kill a god? But if he was a threat, wouldn't it be better for everyone? Or was I just trying to convince myself?

A different male voice answered. "*He* has lived too goddamn long."

Something about the voice sent a shiver down my spine. While it had a masculine timbre, there was something unhinged about it. The cadence of his words bounced unevenly, irreverently.

Grim sighed and gestured for me to enter further.

The long, narrow room extended to either side of me. Ten feet in front of me were the bars of a massive cage. Inside the cage was mostly darkness, but the floors and walls in there were concrete like the entrance chamber.

I'm not one to shake in my boots, but I suddenly wished I'd worn flats or maybe heels instead of the lace-up shit-kickers I favored on off-hours because I was shaking in them now. Power pulsed against me, threatening to push me back and out of this place.

"So you are a god of your word, Grim," the same voice said from within the darkness. "Brought the mortal woman to kill me?"

"Is today a good day, or a bad day?" Grim asked in a gruff tone.

There was a trickle of creepy laughter before it halted suddenly.

"I've had worse," the same mysterious voice answered in a dark, bitter tone. "Looks like it's about to get a whole hell of a lot better."

My grip tightened on the hilt of my blade. "I haven't agreed to kill anyone."

Silence fell, and my breath turned shallow. The little hairs on the back of my neck stood straight up as I stared deep into the darkness, but I didn't see anything.

Whoever, or whatever, was in there was dangerous. It was ancient, and it melded into the shadows. The energy filling the room made my body feel strange, and the chaotic swirl made me feel dizzy and nauseous.

I edged closer to the bars, my heart pounding. I needed to see what was inside. Staring harder into the darkness, I tried to detect an outline or any movement, but there was only inky blackness.

CLANG.

A body slammed into the bars in front of me, causing me to jerk back. My heart leapt up into my throat. One moment there was nothing, and now there was a bare-chested man pressed against the bars. No, not a man. A god. A hazy glow surrounded the figure.

Ocean blue eyes captured me like a tracking beam. The air shifted around me as his scent invaded my senses—a potent mix of saltwater and sandalwood filled my nostrils. It was wild, invigorating, stirring a strange warmth within me.

His strong fingers gripped the bars. Wide nail beds. I found wide nail beds appealing. His abs formed a washboard and his navel was halfway to an outie.

Xander was as painfully gorgeous as any god. He had a body built for speed, dexterity, and power.

There were also the hundreds of scars across his chest. Like someone took a knife and sliced his flesh over and over again, leaving behind countless pale lines.

He was dangerous, there was no doubt about that, but there was something in his eyes that made my heart race for a different reason. An unseen thread seemed to weave between us, binding us in an intimate connection. It pulsed like a current, a magnetic pull I couldn't deny. *He's a god, Miranda. You are a mortal. All gods are beautiful and alluring to better sway you to worship them. Don't fall into the trap.*

But his eyes, so intense, unsettle me in ways unfamiliar and uncharted.

The air thickened around me and electric energy raced along my skin, each charge a reminder of the power that was trying to force itself on me. The electricity in the air surged and sparks spat out, sending searing heat through my skin. My muscles tensed as my instinct to flee was overruled—I had no choice but to stay put. I felt a magnetic pull towards him.

My eyes widened as I fought against it, but what I saw in his gaze made me clench my fists in fear. His blue irises bore into mine, trapping me in their depths. Their striations seemed to move and swell like ink spilled in dark choppy waters--threatening to pull me under its cresting wave. I gasped for breath, struggling to keep my head above the overwhelming tide.

They ensnared me, drawing me into their depths with an intensity I hadn't expected.

Breathe, dammit.

While I couldn't pull out of the gravity of his eyes enough to even register the rest of the god's face, I saw curiosity, or maybe surprise, flicker in his gaze.

Don't step back. Do not retreat, Miranda. Remember, you are a badass.

"You won't kill me, then?" he asked in a voice laced with both hate and desperation, his fingers tightening around the bars of his cage.

My heart pounded as I tried to steady my voice, but it trembled slightly as I replied, "I didn't say that either."

I clenched my jaw, my grip tightening on the hilt of my sword. His words wrapped around my mind, twining my fears with my doubts. The power lashing at me added ten tons of weight to my mind and body. The invisible force seemed to crush me from all sides, pressing ever closer, until it felt as if I was surrounded by a sea of darkness. It was like drowning without even being in water.

The god's eyes bored into mine, and I felt like he was peering directly into my soul. The power around him danced like the northern lights, giving me a headache and causing my stomach to churn. It was out of control and...wrong.

"Tell her, Grim, tell her to run that sword right through me," he spat out the words with a maniacal cackle that made my skin crawl. Was he daring me to kill him or begging me to end his torment? I couldn't tell.

This time, I took a step back. His eyes may be the only grounding place to look, but in them, I found madness, chaos, and power.

When Grim spoke, he sounded weary and bitter. "I cannot tell her to do anything, Xander. She is the keeper of the blade. She was entrusted with the weapon, and she decides how it is to be used. But I did bring her here, so you could ask."

Ask?

I hesitated. "Wait, you want me to kill you?"

Xander commanded, "Leave us," with sudden force.

My heart leapt into my throat, but I tried to remain calm and composed. Grim hesitated, and I found the strength to tear my gaze away from Xander to look at him. For a moment, I didn't want Grim to go. He could protect me if I needed it, but as soon as the thought surfaced, I drowned it. I was the keeper of the blade; it was my responsibility. This was my business, and I could conduct it on my own. I gave Grim a curt nod.

"I'll just be. . ." Grim pointed up, and I gathered he'd be in the lobby or his penthouse.

My chest tightened as he started to walk away. Grim murmured as he passed by me, "Don't get too close," then added, "if you can help it."

The elevator dinged shut, and with that, any safety I felt in the room fled. But no, that wasn't true. This god was behind bars, I told myself.

"Why do you want me to kill you?" I asked, raising an eyebrow. My tone was both incredulous and skeptical. This whole thing felt like a bad setup, though I was sure the gods didn't go for candid camera gags. Or. . . I was *pretty* sure.

"Yes," Xander hissed, eyes glowing supernaturally. He shut them tight, his body curved back from the bars while still keeping a grip on them, as if he were trying to regain control. Twisting his head to the side, he looked as if it pained him to push down whatever was trying to force its way up from inside him. When his gaze returned to me, some of his feral had ebbed and it was a little easier to stand so close. A metallic taste filled the air, like an electrical conduit had a short and a surge of electricity passed through.

I tried to lick away the buzzing sensation from the sensitive skin of my lips. "I need to hear you say it."

There was something new in his eyes now. Pain. Deep, endless pain. As if he'd been a man tortured past his limits.

"Why do you want me to kill you?" I asked, raising my chin.

His glare was sharp, but I refused to retreat. I shifted my weight to one leg, adopting a more relaxed, in control stance. I wouldn't budge until I could assess the situation for myself. The ability to exterminate any being was not a light undertaking, and I'd been chosen to be judge, jury, and executioner.

Xander remained silent, choosing to glower at me.

"I know we just met," I began, forcing a calm I didn't feel into my voice, "but let me explain something to you. I don't kill indiscriminately. I have killed before, and I can again if need be. So you called me down here, interrupting my evening, to demand I kill you. Explain why."

It was far from a perfect night. But he didn't need to know that. A smirk twitched at the corner of the god's perfect lips, and my stomach suddenly swam up and down like I was weightless on a powerful ocean wave. That small twitch proved he was exactly like the other gods in one respect, as he was downright gorgeous under all the layers of chaotic power. And that scared me more than anything else. I refused to examine why.

"Bubble bath?" My breath hitched as his lips curved into a predatory smirk. I pressed my hand to my stomach, trying to quell the strange fluttering sensation that was suddenly there.

"How did you become the keeper of the blade?" Xander asked, his fingers caressing the bars in a far too suggestive manner.

Was he...was he *flirting*?

Ignoring the strange jolt of heat that his words sparked, I squared my shoulders. "Does that information matter to you?"

He shook his head, dropping the topic and whatever sensual web he had started to weave around me. "No, I suppose not."

As if it took great effort, the god released the bars of his cage. "I have lived down here for millennia, and I cannot die. The only key to oblivion and my release is in your hand right there. And I'm asking that you help set me free."

Xander's eyes traced the blade as it glinted in the dim light of the chamber. The weight of the weapon felt heavier than usual in my hand, as if it too was hesitant to be used in such a way.

"You're not going to do it, are you?" Xander asked, his voice barely above a whisper. Hope, anticipation, and disappointment all mixed into his question.

His gaze burned into me, the intensity of it causing my skin to prickle. A strange mix of fear and desire rose in my chest, and I found myself leaning closer to the bars without even realizing it. Then a sick wave of dizziness swept over me. The power flowing off his body threatened to sweep me away.

"I didn't say that," I replied, my voice sounding unsteady even to my own ears. "You won't come back," I went on. "You won't return to the cradle of life and respawn in a hundred or a thousand years. You'll truly cease to exist."

His eyes met mine again, surprise evident. "A human knows so much about godly matters?"

I narrowed my eyes. It wasn't uncommon for someone to underestimate me, but I refused to ever get used to it.

Gods could die. When they did, their essence returned to the cradle of life. While I hadn't laid eyes on it, the description Vivien gave me reminded me of one of Jamal's video games that has a respawn point. But instead of instantly coming back to life, they stay there for hundreds, if not thousands of years before they emerge and rejoin humanity.

What I was less clear on was the consequences of them arising too soon. Vivien said it had something to do with being too powerful, or half-baked, like one of her cupcakes. My vampire best friend had a passion for baking, but that passion did not translate into any amount of skill. The cupcakes, cookies, or pastries usually came out burnt to a crisp, salty as the ocean, or a half-melted mess from being undercooked.

And a half-melted, salty god walking among us definitely sounded like a recipe for disaster.

I pulled the sword from the sheath with a sharp hiss. "This human knows how to use her toys."

The blade glinted in the dim light. To my surprise, intricate runes and symbols of ancient power glowed along it. Was it the god's presence powering the sword? I didn't know. But I did know if an immortal died by the edge of my blade, there would be no chance to respawn. It was game over.

Once more, his lips twitched—an action so subtly beautiful that it felt like a physical blow, threatening to topple my carefully constructed defenses.

It was so unlike anything I had experienced before; I couldn't begin to explain it. Grim made me aware of the death wish I held in my soul, but this was a different power. His power, his eyes overwhelmed me, and part of me desired to be swept away. To be taken away from my life and thrown into another dimension where everything was fresh and new, including me. I both craved and feared it.

Despite the thunderous alarm bells in my mind, my feet drew me closer to him.

Xander leaned in closer. "Do it," he hissed, his voice an intoxicating blend of velvet and venom. His eyes blazed with a fire that threatened to combust. "End this eternal suffering."

His words stirred a maelstrom within me, sending a shiver down my spine that somehow ignited a comforting warmth in the pit of my belly. There was something in the way he looked at me, something that made me feel wanted, needed even.

Though my brain was screaming at me to stay back, to keep my distance if I wanted to live, I continued forward until a half foot of space and the bars were all that separated us. I grounded in those deep blue eyes as the energy pulsating off him accosted my body.

"Please, Miranda." His plea came out in a hoarse whisper. The way he said my name clawed at something inside me. "Kill me."

"Why?" I whispered.

Xander's eyes softened, and for a moment, I could see the pain and sadness in them. "Because I have endured eternal pain, because I am tired," he said, his voice barely above a whisper. "Tired of this existence, of this never-ending torment. I want to rest, to be at peace. And the only way to do that is through death."

A wave of sympathy for him crashed over me, but beneath it lay the unforgiving, jagged rocks of my duty. The blade of Bane had been entrusted to me for a reason.

I took a deep breath, steeling myself for what was to come. "I'll do it," I said, raising the sword high above my head.

Xander closed his eyes, and I could see his body tense up in anticipation. I swung the sword down with all my might, the blade singing through the air.

But at the last moment, I hesitated, my hand shaking. The blade stopped just short of Xander's chest, the tip hovering there as if suspended in mid-air.

Xander opened his eyes slowly, and I could see a fathomless depth of despair lingering in their depths. His mouth curled downward in a grimace of anguish, and his entire body seemed to slump with the weight of his resignation. For a moment, we just stood there, the sword still hovering between us. It seemed to fight me, wobbling in my hands. But it was likely just my own nerves.

Electricity crackled between us, and my heart pumped furiously. Our gazes locked as time stood still while I stood in the vortex of his power. The air was heavy with his scent of power, sex, and danger. I was drawn like a moth to flame, knowing if I got any closer, he would scorch me and leave me in cinders. Stranger yet, some part of me wanted to send him to oblivion with a kiss.

His gaze, now hooded, seemed to pierce through my defenses, devouring my unspoken thoughts. They dropped to my mouth as if considering the texture and taste of me.

How long had it been since this underground god had been kissed? Was it as long as it had been for me? Likely longer, though it felt like it'd been a thousand years since I felt the pressure of another's lips against mine.

"Xander?" I asked in a low voice. My palm turned sweaty around the hilt of the blade.

"Yes," he murmured, his body fully pressed against the bars now. As if he were straining to get closer.

"Wish granted."

My blade jabbed into his chest, cutting deep into his heart.

His eyelids flew wide as he grunted. First confusion filled them, as if he wasn't sure what was happening. Then face relaxed, mouth going slack, like he was experiencing immeasurable relief.

I yanked the blade out and Xander stumbled backward, hand gripping the wound in his body. Bright red blood covered his hand. Xander fell to the ground, dead.

The onslaught of abrasive energy disappeared, as if I'd been standing in a nuclear reactor that had been shut off. The silence, the sudden absence of his energy was deafening.

My body was drained, like I'd just been through a battle. I took a deep breath, trying to steady myself. The job was done, but the weight of it remained heavy on my shoulders.

I turned and marched to the elevator, my mind reeling with a mix of emotions. Guilt and regret were already creeping in, as I thought about the life I'd just taken. The elevator doors closed, and I hit the button to go up.

As the elevator ascended, I couldn't shake the unsettled sensation in my gut. I'd just killed a god, and it didn't feel like a victory. It felt like a tragedy. The world had been stripped of a powerful presence, and it felt as though, in fulfilling my duty, I had somehow hollowed out a piece of myself.

Chapter Four

THE BEAST

Oblivion. Bliss. At last. Death swallowed me whole into nothingness, bestowed by the dark angel with the face of a seductress and the scent of bergamot and lavender soap. Her eyes, her eyes were the last, most devastating beautiful thing I'd see.

But then, cold seeped into the skin on my back, and I blinked.

I blinked again, and reality hit me like a ton of bricks.

"Fuck," I grumbled, the ceiling of my cage creeping into my vision, each cold and uncaring line a mocking reminder of my unending torment. My powers buzzed under my skin like a swarm of hornets, their relentless sting eroding the last vestiges of my sanity.

I sat up, gripping my hair as I set my elbows on my knees. Then I screamed. "Fuuuck!"

My cries of despair bounced off the confining bars, creating a symphony of agony as I convulsed, teetering on the edge of sanity. Death had briefly cradled me in her arms, a fleeting respite from my torment. Each shuddering breath felt like inhaling shards of glass, the pain a cruel reminder of the life I was bound to.

I had died, but only briefly. The wound on my chest had closed, and I had healed entirely. I had survived the Blade of Bane, something no immortal had ever done before.

To have come so close to what I wanted so badly made the failure a thousand times more painful.

I blinked back the wetness stinging my eyes, clenching my jaw so hard that I threatened to break some teeth. But they always grew back.

Staggering to my feet, a surge of raw emotion ripped through me, each pulse of my power a white-hot needle threading insanity into the fabric of my existence.. My senses were a cacophony of torment: the sight of my captivity, the taste of stale air, the rough coldness of the bars against my skin – all were sharp, maddening reminders of my reality. I stood at the precipice of my own mind, teetering on the edge of a freefall into the abyss of berserker rage

For once, I welcomed it. I wanted to lose myself to the oblivion of white-hot power searing through my brain, driving me right out of my mind. A roar of agony exploded from me, and the bars of my cage rattled.

Still, my frustration did not tip me over the edge. Hell, my surge of anger didn't even affect the lights. Normally they'd pop, spark, and plunge me into darkness.

Then I noticed it. A bit of my power was gone. It was as subtle as a missing spark from an inferno of power. Yet it was enough to keep me from losing control. A glimmer of hope dared to ignite in the black abyss of my despair.

And I did find oblivion, at least for a little while.

Excitement welled up inside me almost as fiercely as when I learned the Blade of Bane had resurfaced. This wasn't over. No, this was just the beginning. A grin curled on my face just as the elevator opened.

They revealed the impeccable silhouettes of Grim and his aide, Timothy.

Like Grim, Timothy donned exquisite suits, though his were always tinged with an extra flare, reflecting his taste for the theatric. His jet-black hair stood up in a perfectly gelled coif, offset by the deep purple suit he wore.

Grim had kept his tawny colored skin and strong Egyptian

features, while Timothy spent many hundreds of years in China until he adopted Asiatic characteristics himself. We tend to adapt to whatever environment we immerse ourselves in. Down here, I grew pale, not having felt the kiss of the sun for I don't know how long.

Timothy's shrewd eyes narrowed when he saw me.

Grim looked surprised as well. "We thought you were dead."

"Yes, I was here to make plans for the body," Timothy announced in his uptight British accent. He fiddled with the cufflinks on his velvet, paisley suit.

Unfinished business made Timothy anxious. I'd been unfinished business for the past thousand years, and I knew it grated on the both of them. But this was about me.

"Believe me," I said, baring my teeth, "no one is more disappointed than me."

Grim's expression pulled into his usual scowl. "It didn't work."

I grabbed a bar up high. "Oh, it worked, just not how I imagined it would. Send the girl to me again. It turns out she and I might be stuck with each other for a while."

Grim and Timothy exchanged a wary look. When I explained it, I was certain they wouldn't deny me. The god of the dead wouldn't dream of denying someone death.

As I slumped against the cold, merciless bars, a chaotic symphony of thoughts and emotions raged within me. Among the discord, a single melody echoed above the rest - the dark angel, her cat-like eyes burrowing deep into my fractured soul.

She was like an alluring siren's song, and I the dangerous predator lurking in the depths, eager to disrupt her rigid composure.

Her warm, brown skin had a radiant glow that made me ache to touch it. Her hair, woven into intricate braids, flowed down her back like a waterfall of onyx silk ropes.

Miranda's cat-shaped eyes held a fierce determination, warning me not to cross her. They beckoned me, a captivating lure in the dark, tempting me to coax out the fire beneath her icy, no-nonsense demeanor.

She was a warrior at heart. I'd heard there were few warriors left in the world, but she'd been born one. My little badass. Beneath that tough exterior, there was a flicker of vulnerability that only made me more intrigued.

The thought of her provoked a visceral response: a thrilling shiver that rippled down my spine, causing my skin to prickle and my muscles to tense in anticipation. Miranda possessed a magnetic attraction that I couldn't deny. Despite the fact that she had come closer to killing me than anyone else, the idea of being tied to her, even in a dance to the death, was both terrifying and exhilarating.

A sly smile slithered across my lips, the first genuine show of amusement I'd felt in an eternity. I had two things to look forward to: the inevitability of my death and another chance to meet the beautiful woman who would be the author of my demise.

Chapter Five

THE BADASS

Six AM the next morning, I sat at a table by Perkatory, the hotel's café, my hands wrapped around an oversized to-go cup of coffee. I tried to shake off the chill that had settled into my bones, but even the piping hot, bitter liquid flowing down my throat failed to warm me up.

I used to work at Castlegate, a neighboring hotel, where garish colors and boisterous families were the norm. Sinopolis, on the other hand, offered a stark contrast. Here, the onyx marble floors shimmered like a moonlit abyss, while gold accents punctuated the surrounding walls and ceilings like gilded poetry. Amidst this luxurious setting, Grim had created a sanctuary, with lush green plants surrounding soothing indoor waterfalls.

The lobby of Sinopolis resonated with echoes of an ancient Egyptian oasis, reminding me of the grandeur and power of the god I had recently slain. It felt as if the hotel itself reflected his immense power and storied past. How long had he been confined in that cage? Did he yearn for the black sands of his true home?

Perkatory was nestled amidst large, exotic plants, offering a semi-private space within the lobby. It allowed me to be aware of the hotel's activities while finding a much-needed moment of peace and solitude.

But today, I found it difficult to access the serenity I usually found in my morning routine. As I sipped my drink, there was a nagging whisper telling me I had just crossed a dangerous line into the world of the gods, where power and danger were intertwined.

I knew that treading carefully was the key to surviving in this new world, but I couldn't help but feel drawn deeper into it.

Xander's words echoed in my mind, the desperation in his voice as he begged me to end his existence. I knew I had no other choice, but that didn't make it any easier. It wasn't every day that someone asked me to kill them. I hoped it never happened again.

Though admittedly, I felt as though I'd performed an important duty. My job as head of security at Sinopolis gave me purpose, but I couldn't help but feel like something was missing. With Jamal's absence, it was harder to deny I was lacking a certain satisfaction in my life.

My eyes closed for a moment. Xander's face haunted my dreams, and still remained behind my eyelids every time I blinked. The sharpness of his porcelain features, the way he looked at me through the wild hair half covering his eyes, like he was a predator studying me. And there was the way he held himself with an air of confidence and power – it all drew me to him in a way I hadn't expected.

I pushed those thoughts away and opened my eyes, bringing myself back to reality.

A sudden heat wave coursed through me, causing my forest green suit jacket to become suffocating. I rolled up the sleeves, but it didn't help. I wouldn't clip on my nametag until I officially started work for the day, which wasn't for another thirty minutes. I took a deep breath and downed some more coffee, hoping to find some clarity in the chaos that had become my life.

"Morning, Viv," I said, taking another sip.

A petulant groan came from behind me. The auburn-haired vampire wearing blood red lipstick and a tight leather dress dropped into the chair across from me. Vivien put the vamp in vampire. "How do you always know?" she complained.

My lips curved around my coffee cup. I'll never tell.

"Looks like you've got a long way to go before you graduate from ninja school," I said in a lofty tone.

Vivien glowered at my taunt. "Yeah, well, you better watch out for my ninja stars." She made whooshing sounds while miming throwing some at my head.

I snorted. "Like anyone is dumb enough to let you wield anything sharper than a butter knife."

"Eh," she shrugged, "Who needs 'em?" She flashed her fangs at me. "As the only master vampire, the newly turned primarily rely on my diplomatic skills and my ability to control their will if any of them get out of control. Isn't that a laugh? Me using diplomacy."

Vivien had clearly just learned the word diplomacy and was swinging it about as if it were a large appendage between her legs. Good for her.

The usual string of leather was wrapped a dozen times around her neck, hiding the bite of the master vampire who turned her. Thankfully, he was long gone.

Little lines of exhaustion snaked out and around her eyes. They hadn't been there a couple months ago. The beginning of my day was the end of hers, being a night dweller. Weirdly enough, the lack of windows in Vegas hotels made it safe for her to stay up past her bedtime when the sun came up.

"How is it, managing the newly turned?" Vivien had been appointed by Osiris— an Egyptian god so powerful he wasn't on our plane— to be the shepherd of the vampires. When humans were turned, they were scared, hungry, and sometimes reckless. My vibrant, rebellious friend was now in charge of handling all those situations.

She frowned. "A pain in the neck." She rubbed her neck as if someone had tried to bite her. Maybe they had. "But you know what really chaps my ass?"

"Do tell," I asked.

Vivien's fingers curled around the edges of the table. "Grim and I got into an argument the other night, and do you know how he ended it?" Fire blazed in her eyes.

"With sex?" I guessed. That was the usual method.

She waved a hand. "That was later, so yes, but no. That uptight bastard had the gall to hit me with a pillow. Right in the face." Her words came out an indignant screech.

"That bastard," I responded in an even, dry tone.

Vivien stood up, hands still gripping the table. "He thinks he won the argument, but now he's started a war."

The maniacal gleam in her eye should have scared me. The fact that I was only amused probably meant I was deranged as well.

"So have you retaliated yet?"

She settled back into her chair. "Oh, I've got plans. Don't you worry, I've got plans." Vivien might as well have been drumming her fingers together like a James Bond villain. Lord help us all.

"You realize this war you've declared is likely a coping mechanism and distraction from being the only Master vampire, right?" I blinked at her innocently.

Her eyelids flickered as her head tilted. Time was momentarily suspended as she absorbed the weight of the words. The little men running Vivien's brain seemed to freeze up, as if they hadn't considered it before.

When the gears finally began to work again, she sniffed. "So what? It doesn't hurt to indulge in a little play, a little escapism. So I don't have to think about the grief of a vampire who realizes she'll outlive her entire family." A shadow passed over her eyes for a moment before she snapped out of it and put all her focus back on me. "Speaking of immortals, tell me what happened last night."

I squirmed in my seat.

"W-what are we t-talking about, ladies?" Aaron asked. He twirled the third chair around and plopped down in it, handing a blended coffee drink piled high with whipped cream to Vivien. Vampires may subsist off blood, but my friend had a sweet tooth that was out of control.

There were few people milling about the Sinopolis lobby this early in the morning, making it perfect for us to have a mini hang first thing. Our little threesome morning chats had become one of my favorite rituals.

"Grim asked Miranda to kill a god last night," Vivien explained without preamble.

"Way to put me on the spot," I hissed at my traitorous friend.

No one was around to hear the insane summation, and what human would believe us? Still, it didn't settle well.

Aaron's eyebrows shot up. He wore his black smock with the skull design encircled by the café's name. The logo read "Good to the Last Breath."

Aaron brushed the wild mane of blond hair, naturally bleached by the sun, from his glowing, tanned face. Vivien and I agreed he resembled Patrick Swayze from the surfer heist movie, Point Break. When we told him of our conclusion, his blinding white smile nearly cracked his entire face. We noted to be careful not to feed his ego too much in the future.

It didn't hurt that Aaron was an avid surfer from California and an adrenaline junkie. While he wasn't near the waves anymore, he spent most of his time rock climbing, skydiving, or learning to fly a helicopter.

Aaron was also one of the very few humans to know gods, vampires, and more lived among us in plain sight.

"D-did you? Kill him, I mean?" he asked me. Years ago, he got hit in the jugular with a surfboard and was left with a permanent stutter, but it didn't seem to skin a single slice off his confidence. In fact, with speech therapy, his stutter had lessened slightly.

"I did," I confirmed, interlacing my fingers around my cup. Then my phone vibrated against the table. I picked it up to find a picture of Jamal with a toothy smile, arm flung over one of his camp friend's shoulders. Another couple of pictures followed. The counselors led them on a sunrise hike, and Jamal took photos of mountains backed by brilliant purples and shocking oranges as the sun appeared over the horizon.

My heart squeezed hard. I missed my little man, but it was great to see him having such a good time.

"And. . .?" Vivien tried to dig in, forcing me to put my phone back down. "You aren't going to share details?" Vivien's brows furrowed, her eyes scanning my face acting like magnets attempting to draw out my secrets

"Are you okay with it?" she asked in a sincere, low voice.

I shrugged. "I'm fine." Strange feelings rioted in my chest. The replay of Xander's death began to start up again in my brain. A mixture of pain and gratitude etched into his sharp, beautiful features. The unnamed chemistry that lingered in between as he studied my mouth in those last moments.

Aaron and Vivien exchanged a look. "You are definitely not okay," Vivien countered.

Maybe that's because I killed a god, my brain informed me.

Rude. I was just trying to make everything normal. Why was my brain a traitor?

I brushed the thought away like a buzzing fly. "It's fine. Like Grim said, I understand duty. Duty to honor the mantle of Bob's responsibilities."

"Bob?" Aaron asked, rearing back.

"The Blade of Bane," I explained. "Their nickname is Bob."

"Their, not his?" A line formed between Aaron's brows.

"Bob is a nonbinary blade," Vivien chimed in. "So we use gender-neutral pronouns."

Vampire or not, Vivien got me. She went on. "So you respect your duty to Bob to slay gods as fairly as possible. It doesn't mean you aren't shaken."

I was shaken. Killing someone wasn't a small thing, no matter how much I tried to rationalize it. No matter how much he wanted it. It sat heavy in my gut.

A wave of queasiness washed over me, twisting my stomach into knots. I left him there, slumped on the ground. Alone.

In that moment, I longed for some of Vivien's playfulness. If I could combat the trash feelings churning inside me with a light-hearted, err, bloodthirsty pillow fight, maybe I'd feel better. But I left the playing to Jamal. I got a kind of vicarious fun from watching him animatedly play video games or talk about the basketball game he played at school that day.

Between living through him for fun and Vivien for her sex life, I started to wonder when I was living for myself.

You had that bubble bath last night, I tried to argue with myself.

Yeah right. Despite my claim to Xander, my bath time had been far from perfect. I couldn't even wind down enough to enjoy the few minutes I had before I was called to work. I all but leapt at an opportunity to have a mission of some kind.

I'd almost think I needed a vacation, but I wouldn't even know where to go or what to do.

"Miranda, just the person I want to see," a British voice announced behind me.

I knew who it was before I turned. If not for the voice, Aaron's eyes rounded and went glassy as if looking upon a prime A-grade steak. He all but drooled, hungrily.

I twisted around to face Timothy. The man's style was as fierce as it was flawless. Like all the gods, he was painfully beautiful from his high cheekbones to his long dexterous fingers. Timothy tried to keep his dark, narrow eyes averted from Aaron, but the magnetism was always palpable when they got within striking distance of each other. The uptight god and the surfer bro human. I guess opposites do attract.

"What do you need?" I asked. In a few minutes, I planned to head to the security office to start my duties for the day.

"A word, alone." He stressed the last word for Vivien's sake. She leaned back in her chair and sucked vindictively on her frozen coffee, hating to be left out of things.

Timothy studiously ignored both her and Aaron. I gave my two best friends a nod before following the god of literature, science, and wisdom.

He led me across the lobby, ensuring we wouldn't be seen or overheard. Timothy's question came out with a held breath. "We need you to do it again."

"Do what?" I asked.

"Kill Xander."

My heart pounded inexplicably. "I don't understand. He's dead."

Timothy shook his head, lips thinning. "Not exactly. He was for a time, but woke up, revived and healed."

Kaboom. Mind blown. I was surprised I wasn't thrown off my feet, but I managed to stay upright.

"But the blade kills gods, immortals," I stuttered. "How can he be alive?"

That familiar line formed between Timothy's eyebrows as he fiddled with his tie. "Xander is a. . . special case. He is very powerful, too powerful."

That I easily believed. I was shocked to find out my eyebrows and eyelashes hadn't sizzled right off my face in that basement.

"But Xander requests you return today to do it again," Timothy said.

That piercing gaze entered my mind's eye, and I suppressed a shiver.

"Will you do it?" Timothy carefully studied me.

"I don't know what good it will do if it didn't work last night," I said. "And I really don't want to kill two nights in a row, even if it's the same person."

Especially if it's *that* god. Something in me knew it was best to stay far far away, if not for the burn of his power, but because of the magnetic intensity that seeped into my every pore, urging me toward him.

There was a gentle intensity in Timothy's eyes as he regarded me, his gaze now filled with empathy. "It would be a great service to both Grim and me. You can't know what a burden it is to serve the transition from life to death for so long and encounter someone who can't make the same sacred passage. Believe me, you are a benevolent force here."

Aw damn. He was appealing to my feelings. While I liked that I exuded a hard-shell exterior, it served me well in covering up that I had a gooey center. But I'd been through the ringer in the past with Timothy when it came to immortals and end-of-the-world stakes. This classy sonofabitch knew exactly what a softie I was.

"Low move," I growled.

He gave me a weak smile. "So you will?" Without waiting for my answer, he went on. "This takes precedence, and Grim and I realize this, so consider this your primary concern. No need to handle security matters. Javier can handle things for a while."

A spike of panic went through me. While I implicitly trusted my number two, and good friend from the army, I didn't want to be replaced.

"I still need a job."

If I refused to kill Xander to keep my job, would they accept that? Instantly, I knew I couldn't do that. Damn, Grim knew exactly what he was saying when he said I was bound by duty. And I didn't take that responsibility lightly, being the only one with the power to permanently eradicate any god.

Timothy's eyebrows shot up. "Oh, you misunderstand me. You would, of course, keep your current pay and compensation. But seeing as you are handling immortal matters, we view this as no less important than the service you provide this hotel. Far more so, in fact."

Oh.

"If it's all the same, I would like to keep my regular duties," I said.

Timothy seemed confused, so I shrugged. "It didn't take long to kill him. But I still don't understand how he—"

The tablet under Timothy's arm began to chime with notifications, ending our conversation as he whisked off to take care of the entire world, humans and immortals alike.

But I had more questions. Did Timothy intend for me to take the day off or more? It seemed like this could be a lasting situation. And why did they believe I could have any effect on Xander's immortality if I didn't succeed in killing him last night?

I had a feeling the person, or rather the god, who could explain was currently caged and waiting for me to kill him...*again*. A shudder ran down my spine. I wasn't sure what caused it—the prospect of facing his out-of-control, searing power, or my uncertainty about how to handle the way he looked at me, or the way he made me feel.

I clipped on my nametag and headed to the security office. Though I didn't relish the thought of returning, I knew I had to pull myself up by the bootstraps and murder a god tonight.

Chapter Six

THE BEAST

The elevator binged, announcing the arrival of my angel of death. A jolt of feverish anticipation sent spikes of exhilaration through my veins, electrifying the otherwise stagnant air of my cage. I'd been unbearably restless, pacing in the shadows for hours.

"I was beginning to think you weren't coming," I said from where I hid in the darkness.

Gods, she was more alluring than I remember. Miranda's face was tight, full lips pursed together. The muscles of her body grew tighter with each step she took further into my own personal hell. Either she had a rough day, or she was girding herself against the waves of power that arced and flowed off from me like the sun.

If you think that hurts, my little badass, try being me.

An insane titter escaped me. I worked to swallow down the power, not wanting to scare her off. The feral, wild side of me longed to be free of this cage, to unleash my power and show her the full extent of my madness. To explode with all my pent-up energies. But if I shifted or went berserk, I would scare her off. I couldn't afford that.

"I had to go home to pick up this," Miranda explained, lifting the sheathed blade of bane. "I don't typically carry it with me on a normal workday."

She lifted the blade of bane, and a surge of hunger swept through me. I craved death, and she held the power to grant it. My heart raced. The sheer force of her presence unleashed a whirlwind of emotions, cascading over me like a waterfall of exhilaration. I grew dizzy from the thrill of being near my dark angel.

Gone was the athletic goddess of yesternight, in a tank top and leggings that embraced her every toned, muscular curve. Today, she was a figure of authority, clad in the formal armor of her station. The forest green of her jacket made her eyes appear lighter, more luminescent. Or maybe I was hallucinating again?

But I knew underneath her garb, she had a body like a battle-axe. I couldn't forget. That same body danced around my dreams all last night, taunting and tempting me. Beckoning to bend her, break her, claim her until she killed me.

It had been a long time since I had seen such a beautiful woman. Maybe I had *never* met such a beautiful woman. Maybe I had never met *any* woman.

I clenched my fist instead of using the hand to knock sense into my rattled brain.

"Since you've brought it all this way," I said, trying to remain coy. If I weren't in my cage I would have hurled myself at her and upon the blade she held. To contain my erratic desires, I gripped the cage bars so hard they groaned.

Miranda eyed my white knuckles.

Steady, Xander.

Instead of coming closer and stabbing me as she'd done yesterday she asked, "Why didn't it work?"

Oh for fuck's sake. They didn't tell her? They couldn't bother to save me the trouble?

"It did work," I answered.

She raised an eyebrow at the same time she cocked a hip and set a hand on it. I was struck by the amount of sass she packed into that posture. I absolutely loved it.

More more more. Lick her sass, make her yours, my brain singsonged.

Then I remembered yesterday how for a moment I thought she was going to kiss me. I knew the effect I have on humans as an immortal, enough to not take it seriously. Her attraction to me was a byproduct of being a god. But for a heart stopping moment, I almost gave in despite knowing better. I wanted her to close those seductive eyes and surrender those impossibly seductive lips to me.

But then she gave me an even better gift. Death.

"I died for a little while. That's never happened before, no matter what I've tried. I always stayed in perfect consciousness."

Her lips twisted into a scowl, the sass in her eyes replaced by a look of confusion. "They said you had too much power."

I nodded and stretched, leveraging myself against the bars, and a vertebra popped. Miranda's eyes flitted to my flexing arms before returning to my eyes. I knew it must be painful for her to be down here, this close to me. Yet she still put off the relief she'd get from killing me right away to assess the situation. She certainly was unusual.

"Yes, far too much power. But when I awoke after regenerating, some of it was missing. I believe you killed some of it off when you stabbed me."

"Oh," was all she said, her hard gaze back on my face. I flexed my muscles to see if I could draw her attention even if for a moment.

Her eyes swept down my bare abdomen, her mouth parting ever so slightly.

Heat rushed south as I felt something I hadn't in years. Pleasure. My mouth instantly went dry. I was hungry for her. Starving.

Miranda cleared her throat and looked away. Even as she swallowed hard, I knew she wanted me. The crazy god in a cage. Any mortal would likely have the same reaction, but she fought it.

It made me want to push her further until she gave into the desire swirling around her. Let it off the tight leash she had on it.

I was a god. She must want to worship me. But I wanted to worship her. Feel the soft touch of a woman again.

My curiosity and pleasure shattered abruptly, replaced by pain. Buzzing assaulted my brain. I shut my eyes, my head snapping to the side as I braced myself against it. Retreating, I clutched at my ears. I unleashed a primal howl, a vain attempt to drown out the onslaught.

Every nerve vibrated like a tuning fork, the agonizing ache radiating throughout my frame. *No. No. No.*

"It's coming, it's coming, it's..." The words spilled from my lips, a mantra of impending doom, their meaning lost in the cacophony of my spiraling mind.

My muscles swelled as I tried to ground against the wave of pain. The beast wanted to come out. It wanted to rage. Human fingers transformed into long, lethal talons. The world around me pitched and rolled as though I was at sea, the strobing lights a frenzied whirl of color that threatened to consume me until there was nothing left. I carved the claws into the floor, grasping at anything that could anchor me and keep me from floating away in a sea of agony.

"Xander?" I heard a voice call. I forced my eyes open, not realizing I closed them.

Miranda stood inside my cage, then outside of it. She teleported back and forth.

No. Get out of here. I don't want to hurt you.

"Xander," her command sliced through the chaotic fog. I grabbed at the anchor of her authoritative voice and pulled myself toward it.

At last, the tumult eased leaving me shaky and exhausted. As long as I could remember, my flesh had been a battleground of unrelenting agony, leaving me feeling hollow and depleted. I was trapped in a never-ending cycle of suffering. The weight of it suffocates my spirit, fueling a bitter resentment towards a life that seems to revel in my torment.

Miranda had taken several steps back, still well behind the bars. Thank fuck. Both her hands strangled the hilt of her blade. The radiance in her eyes had dimmed, her normally warm brown skin paled several shades.

Fear shone in her eyes. Bitterness swallowed me up as it usually did. I wanted to rip the bars off this cage and impale myself to the wall. Punish myself for losing control.

Good, better she's afraid. It will just give her another reason to run me through.

Still, nausea and disgust filled me. There was no escaping this prison of meat and bone.

Except that wasn't exactly true anymore.

Gritting the words out through my teeth, my voice rougher than before, "I need you to come back here and kill me, every day, until I achieve true death. Based on yesterday, I expect it will take some time."

My eyes were drawn to her sword once more as I sidled closer. Oh gods, I wanted her to kill me, so bad. I could practically taste the edge of the blade.

Please my angel of death. Carve a new fate in my flesh. Cut out the pain from the organ of my heart.

"This is. . ." she seemed to search for the word, "unusual."

I couldn't stop the cackles escaping me then. The sound of my own laughter helped fight off the buzzing in my head. When I finished, I couldn't help but grin at her. Though it probably appeared like I was baring my teeth. "You wield an unusual weapon."

Miranda tipped the blade at me. "Fair point."

Impatient, and unable to wait any longer, I snapped. "Well, do you agree? Will you come down here every day and kill me?"

Miranda's frown deepened. I wanted to lick her cheek up to the frown lines gathered on her forehead. Was that a normal response? I couldn't say anymore.

I bit back the next batch of crazy giggles that threatened to escape me. I needed her focused on the task, not on my crazy. Though the need to climb the bars to swing and rail against them and my miserable fucking existence was overwhelming.

She strode across the room, approaching me with purpose. On instinct, I pressed my chest hard to the bars, so hopeful, I could barely breathe.

Kill me, beautiful.

"Wish granted." Then she stabbed me in the heart for the second time.

In that moment, I fiercely loved her more than anything in my entire damned existence. My lips twisted in satisfaction and pain as they mingled in the most intense manner.

She was so close, I breathed her in with my last breath — bergamot oil and her unique scent — inducing an insatiable hunger. My mouth watered. I almost wished I had a second breath to inhale her one more time.

But that blissful black haze engulfed me.

My last thought was bless the goddess of mercy before me and the invention of bergamot.

Chapter Seven

THE BADASS

Every day after I'd completed my security work, I headed down to the god of the dead's basement, and stabbed a god straight through the heart. Then I went home, poured myself a half glass of red wine and called it a day.

After a couple of days, I'd gotten used to the strange ritual. It had become the new central gravity of my life.

Though I never got used to the feelings Xander aroused in me with his intensity and power.

His cerulean eyes said so much more than his lips did. And if we were speaking the same language, he was saying he wanted the bars between us to disappear along with our clothes.

Usually right at the moment I ran him through, leaving me more than a little confused by the riot of emotions he inspired.

Kill me. Fuck me. Thank you.

A hot shiver raced up my spine. I tried to ignore it. This was a simple job. Nothing more.

While I'd grown use to our strange routine, it was becoming harder to kill Xander. The blade seemed heavier every time I returned. My aim had even failed me. Once I sliced in just to the left of his heart and it took a second strike to finish him off. Embarrassment flooded me, but he never said anything other than the grunt of pain at impact. His expression was only of gratitude and desire.

I was grateful he didn't bring up the mishap.

Nowadays, I brought the blade of bane with me to Sinopolis. I had to keep it on my person at all times, so I started to wear the black duster jacket Vivien gifted me for May twenty-second. She said she probably should have waited for a holiday, but she decided May twenty-second deserved some celebration as well. Yet again, I found myself envious of her whimsical nature.

Vivien said it suited me, and I had to admit that I absolutely loved it. The best part was cheetah print lined the inside of the black vegan leather. She said it was exactly like me. Badass on the outside, extra on the inside.

Considerate friend that she was, Vivien also had a designer add a holster to the inside of the jacket for Bob, so I could hide the sword underneath. No one said anything about my change in attire at work, and I wasn't sure if it was because they were used to strange things happening at Sinopolis, or because I scared everyone.

I asked my number two, Javier, who not only came over from Castlegate hotel with me, but we were also in the special forces unit back in the day. He didn't even look up from the surveillance monitors as he affirmed, they were all, "scared pissless" of me.

Today would be no different. I waved a hand over the buttons of Grim's private elevator to make the secret fourth one appear, and pushed the black circle.

I entered the entry chamber and Xander was there as usual. But instead of his usual positioning, pressed against the bars, eager for me to run him through, today Xander sat further back, mostly covered in shadow. Light from my side of the cage slashed across him, illuminating only his mouth and half of his body. His lean, muscular arms encircled his legs where he sat on the ground.

My ears and face buzzed. Coming down here, still felt like entering a nuclear reactor, but some of the painful sizzle had ebbed. Presumably because I'd been killing off pieces of his power. Soon there would be nothing left to kill.

I'd have nothing left of this except the ghost of his blood on my blade.

Xander still hadn't gotten up.

"Hi," I said awkwardly. Typically, we don't speak. It's enter, stab, leave.

There was a long pause.

"What's in the bag?" he finally asked. Xander's voice seemed raspier than I remember.

In one hand I gripped the blade of bane, and in the other I carried my purple reusable lunch sack. I didn't need two hands to kill him, so I hadn't planned on putting it down.

Wow, I really had adjusted to the weirdness fast.

"Lunch."

I'd planned on walking straight to my car after this and scarfing down some of the food to ease the hunger pains rumbling in my gut.

"Busy day. I missed my chance to eat." I couldn't keep the exhaustion from my voice. One of the high rollers in the poker room got caught cheating, I found a cocktail waitress skimming money because her abusive scumbag boyfriend pressured her into it, and a rock band partied straight through the morning, trashing a hotel room and terrorizing the staff. It had been a lot for one day.

Not that I couldn't handle it. In fact, with Jamal gone, I welcomed the chaos. I could make order of it. Help the waitress, soothe the staff, and kick the ass of everyone out of line. But admittedly, I worked until I was too tense. There would be no Jamal when I went home to lighten the mood, to tell me what cool new stuff he learned today, or put on some ridiculous cartoon and giggle until I had to join in.

At least I had Vivien and Aaron in the mornings to break things up. Though Vivien was busier these days between helping new vampires and plotting Grim's demise by goose down. The great pillow war raged on.

Over a caffeine and sugar, she victoriously recounted how she jumped Grim while he was in the shower. The bedding popped, and he ended up wet and covered in fluff. He'd been displeased, as she put it. If she weren't immortal, I'd be worried for her life.

I really did envy her whimsy.

In the shadows, Xander's outline nodded. "Busy day? Or hard day?"

We didn't talk like this. We didn't talk at all. "Yes," I answered, in the affirmative to both. The admission added an extra ten pounds of gravity to my body. I was bone tired and hungry as hell. I had to readjust my grip, the sword seeming impossibly heavy as well. Or was I getting weaker?

Was I getting weaker around *him*?

The moment of pause between us was heavy and long.

"Me too," he said in a low voice.

I could hear it. His voice sounded like it had been dragged over a long road of gravel and ash. He was either exhausted, in pain, or both.

He gestured to a chair off to the side of me. "Why don't you take a seat and eat something before we get to business?"

I looked at the chair, then back at him.

"I'd prefer you have all your strength if you are going to kill me properly today," he said. My cheeks heated, knowing he referenced my double stab mishap.

Before I could tell him we should just get on with it, my stomach took that moment to emit an obnoxious gurgle. One corner of his lips curved up.

Though I'd rather stab and run, something told me he also needed a moment before we got to business today.

Before he died today.

Yep, my life was really fucking weird.

"Okay," I conceded, and went to settle in the single metal chair against the wall and opened my lunch tote. I pulled out a container of sliced apples. As I chewed, the awkwardness of the situation began to creep in on me. Usually I don't mind silence, but something about it seemed so wrong right now.

"What *is* your job?" Xander asked, breaking the silence and granting my wish. For a moment I wondered if he was a god who could read my mind.

Pickles, pickles, pickles.

Okay, if he could read my mind, he certainly would have reacted to the barrage of pickles spewing from my brain at him. I figured I was safe.

Swallowing my bit of apple, I said, "I work for Grim. I'm head of his hotel security."

Then I wondered if he knew he was at the base of a hotel. Did he know what a hotel was? He said he'd been imprisoned for a thousand years. Maybe he had no concept of time or space.

"What?" he asked.

"What what?" I asked back.

"You have a look on your face, like you want to ask me something."

Pickles pickles pickles pickles.

Nope, guess he really did just read my expression.

"Do you know what a hotel is?" I asked.

He barked out a laugh. It wasn't like his usual broken, crazy laugh that set my teeth on edge. It was sardonic, and I liked it. "Yes, I know what a hotel is."

"Oh." I crunched into another slice of apple.

"You're still frowning," he said.

My hand instinctively reached up to touch my forehead. "Am I?"

"You have more questions."

I did have more questions. He was all but inviting me to ask them. I shifted in the seat, feeling caught between two desires. "Maybe it's better if we keep this professional."

In the darkness he elongated his arms, stretching them out from his body. He never wore a shirt or footwear, only the same dark loose set of pants. Unlike Grim, his feet didn't weird me out. I needed my boss to fit into an orderly box, that included his feet. But it seemed right for Xander to be like this, half naked and feral. In fact, I couldn't imagine his feet being covered by socks or shoes. They were long and attractive.

Inwardly, I cringed. Sweet baby Jesus, did I have some kind of secret foot fetish going on?

"Keep it professional," he echoed in a lofty tone. "Worried you are going to fall in love with me?"

I was the one to smile this time. "Hardly."

He rocked back and then sprung forward up onto his feet with all the grace of some kind of jungle cat. Deft, silent, and positively lethal. A shockwave of unexpected heat hit me.

He sauntered out from the shadows. "Come on, I'm irresistible. Afterall, I'm a god."

"And just as humble as the rest of the gods I see," I taunted. "Real sexy."

Unfortunately for me, I'd taken another bite of apple and when Xander fully came into view, I inhaled a piece, choking hard. Even as I fought for my very life against that bit of fruit, my heart ripped itself up at the sight of him.

I dropped the bag to the floor. Xander looked positively ill. Deep dark circles surrounded his hollowed-out eyes. His cheeks were sunken, and his normal golden pallor was a sickly grayish green. Fresh deep slices decorated his exposed chest. As if a rabid animal clawed at his chest over and over again. His chest was a mess of exposed muscle. Anyone else would be bleeding out from wounds like that.

"See? I take all the ladies' breath away," he said with a wan smile.

I somehow managed to glare at him even as I coughed violently, tiny apple pieces flying from my mouth. If I were vainer, I'd worry about how I looked spewing little chunks. But this was duty, not pleasure. I wasn't here to impress a god. Just kill him.

When I got a hold of myself, I stood. "What happened to you?"

"I thought you wanted to keep this professional?" he taunted, throwing my words back in my face.

Fuck. He had me there.

Xander's sickly smile widened into a grin. "Your glower is even more appealing than your frown."

"I'm not—"

He interrupted. "I'll save the trouble of defending your ire and tell you that I did this to myself." He waved a hand over his grisly chest.

In less than a heartbeat, he'd thrown me off entirely.

As if some magnet pulled me forward, I took several steps closer to his grotesque form. Seeing him like this pained me in a way I couldn't describe. "Why?"

The mirth bled from his eyes and face, leaving something stoney in its place. "Like I said, it's been a bad day."

"I've had a bad day too, but you don't see me taking a razor to my arm," I said, anger vibrating in my voice.

Xander's face smoothed in surprise. "Are you—are you mad?"

Why did it bother me so much to know he'd torn his own flesh open? Was I just taking the stress of my day out on him? Admittedly, a secret part of myself felt like I was letting off steam by going after him.

"Mad you mutilated yourself? You're fucking right I am. I thought you were a god who'd lived for millennia, not a moody teenager who thinks this is the solution." I waved a hand at his wrecked flesh.

Xander's eyes darkened. An oppressive force closed in around us like a pressure cooker, sealing all of the air inside. His skin seemed to ripple before my eyes, as if he were made of liquid that morphed and changed with every breath we took. My heart pounded in my chest like a galloping horse, and my breathing was rapid and shallow as fear slowly flooded my veins. I could almost taste the electricity in the air around me; feel the danger radiating from his pores.

In the blink of an eye, Xander had morphed before me into a scary, unpredictable god. And that was very, no good news for me.

He snarled and leapt onto the bars, several feet above me. The movement was as fast as it was erratic. He craned his neck at an unnatural angle, continuing to meet my gaze. "How dare you compare my pain to that of some pissant little teenager. You know nothing of pain. You sit there with your perfect neat little life and judge how I handle this shitty existence I'm enslaved too? Sweetheart, you don't know what pain is."

Despite my galloping heart and skittish nerves, I couldn't take that lying down. I met him with an unwavering gaze, and took a step toward the intimidating, unhinged god. "You don't know anything about me. You don't know anything about my pain or my life."

He raised an eyebrow, still sneering at me in a way that made my blood boil. Slowly he slid down the bars, coming closer to my level. "You clean your boots every night, don't you?" Neither of us looked down to confirm what was obvious about my footwear. He went on.

His toes touched the floor, hands dropping from the bars. "Not only is your lunch bag neatly written with your address, that food container is also properly labeled with your name."

"What's wrong with that?" I challenged.

Xander shot me a wicked grin that heated up my blood in a totally different way. "From your head to your toes, you are as neat as a perfectly licked envelope. And I can see inside that envelope you shove all your feelings because you are so busy calculating them. Pain means feeling and you work very hard not to feel, don't you?"

I stiffened. That blow landed as true as an axe splitting a log. "Are you calling me a robot?"

"If the tin heart fits, sweetheart," he purred, stretching his arms up and grabbing the bars over his head. His arm muscles flexed. My stomach turned fluttery and weightless in response.

"Do you even know how to have fun?" The tip of his tongue touched his top lip in a lewd manner.

"Do *you?*" I shot back at a loss for words. The way his satisfied grin deepened; I knew I'd said the exact wrong thing.

"Why don't you open the door, come in here and I'll show you." He scanned me up and down with a look so hot my skin burned. The sudden twinkle in his tired eyes told me he was trying to get under my skin.

It took a minute to fully swallow.

"That's right, sweetheart. Come in here and I'll show you how to lose control." He opened his arms in invitation. "I bet we could have some fun. I could split those pretty legs and lick up your yummy slit until you beg me to fuck you. We could go all night, until you have screamed my name so many times you've forgotten your own. I think that could be *fun.*" Slowly, his hand slipped down the front of his pants. His fingers disappeared under the fabric, creeping toward an evident bulge growing in his loose slacks.

My throat turned as dry as a week-old scone, but I still managed to get out the words in my sternest tone. "Watch your language."

Xander's smile was half amusement, half disbelief. "What are you, my mother?"

His hand receded from his pants. Thank god, because it was inspiring far too many images in my head. Ones that made my heart beat faster and generated a liquid heat in my lower belly.

"Maybe that's because I *am* a mother," I shot back. "So I have no problem calling bullshit on someone when needed."

Shock registered on his haggard face, brows climbing up his forehead. "You. *You* are a mother. What are you nineteen?"

My cheeks grew hot. Was I flattered or insulted? Usually, I knew. "No."

He looked at me with renewed interest. "You seem *so* young."

Okay, I was definitely insulted now. I knew I looked damn good, but people tried to underestimate me based on my looks, and youth was one of the many stigmas I had to prove myself against.

The fire gave me enough fuel to push away the strange mixture of arousal to volley back to outrage.

I touched my forehead with the tip of my finger. "Maybe you haven't heard this because you've been a sad old man trapped in a cage, but black don't crack honey. I'll look this good until I'm ninety." If I lived that long. Because this strange banter/fight was more dangerous than I was probably giving it credit.

Sure Miranda, scold a god. Pick a fight with him, this will end well.

A voice in my head assured me, *we can take him*.

At the very least, I should back away out of reach. All he'd have to do is thrust his arms through the bars and snap my neck, rip out my jugular, or. . .or other things he mentioned.

My thighs squeezed together.

Xander's eyes took more of an interest in perusing me from top to bottom. "Black don't crack," he echoed in an amused voice. As if I'd given him a new idea he enjoyed playing with, like a cat batting at a ball of yarn.

His gaze flitted away before meeting mine again. "And what does your husband think of our arrangement?"

Something flashed in his eyes that I couldn't identify. It could have been raw power, or maybe...jealousy?

No that's ridiculous.

"My husband died years ago." I said it as a point of fact, because it was. Jamal was still in diapers when Rashon died serving his country. It hurt. It hurt knowing we'd lost our future, but between both our deployments, Rashon and I never got to know each other on as deep a level as I would have liked. In fact, the pain that should have throbbed in my heart at the thought of him remained silent and still.

"Lucky him." Xander's words were laced with dark jealousy.

Oh no he fucking didn't. What didn't hurt before, suddenly roared to life with pain.

I smacked one of the bars by his head with an open palm. The strike of the cold, hard steel felt good in contrast to the heat of my anger. "You sonofabitch. How dare you say that to a widow."

The god seemed unphased. "I wasn't implying he should be deprived of your wonderful company. I simply meant I am envious of his situation."

Before I could further comment on the inappropriateness of his demeanor, he asked. "How did he pass to the Afterlife?"

The way he phrased it struck me. Since learning Grim was god of the dead, I knew invisible reaper dogs fetched the souls of the dead and transported them to the afterlife. Which meant that's where Rashon went. It was both comforting and unnerving to know that now.

I stuck my chin up. "He died on foreign soil, serving his country."

"A hero's death then," Xander said bitterly.

"What is your goddamn problem?" How dare he make light of the sacrifice my husband made, of the sacrifice his family had to endure?

Xander's body seemed to fill the space around him, and I wasn't quite sure if it was his physical body or his power doing it. "My problem is I have no such luxury as your late husband. My problem is I am stuck in this prison."

My gaze naturally went to the bars.

"Not that prison, sweetheart." He gave me a humorless grin. Trailing his hand over the open wounds of his chest, they traveled down the pronounced muscles of his abdomen before his thumb hooked into the edge of his pants. "This prison."

While he was making a rather gruesome point, I couldn't help but follow the track of his hand too closely. The front of his slacks dipped under his thumb, exposing a vee of muscle that led to his groin.

His 'prison' stirred things in me. Things that threatened my good sense. His lewd suggestions sent them rioting in a way I hadn't felt for years, and I resented it. I prided myself on good sense. But still, my nerve endings strained, wanting to touch his solid muscle, and take his idea of 'fun' for a test ride.

He was oblivious of my sudden shift in mood as his expression darkened with loathing.

"Live a thousand years of power and pain in a cage and let me know what you do then, sweetheart," he growled.

Instead of acknowledging his point or my sudden arousal, I shot back, "Don't call me sweetheart."

He cocked his head to the side. "Again, are you worried about falling in love with me if I call you sweetheart? Afraid you'll believe you *are* my sweetheart."

I shot back a vicious grin as I pulled Bob out from my duster. "This just makes it all the easier to kill you, beast boy."

He neared the bars but didn't press his chest against them like usual. "Beast boy, is it?"

How had our conversation escalated so quickly? Part of me was excited by the way he needled me. Was I always secretly looking for a fight?

Xander puckered his lips and sent me an air kiss. "Then why don't you just do it, my little badass."

I couldn't decide which I hated more: his nickname or the way it made the liquid heat intensify at my center. Bob plunged into the already broken flesh on his chest.

"Wish granted," I said through bared teeth.

I yanked the blade out, and Xander smiled at me. I couldn't help but smile back just before he fell and died...again.

As I gathered up my sack lunch, something light and almost whimsical fluttered in my chest. Like a hoard of butterflies taking flight. The heaviness of the day no longer clung to my body or mind. There was satisfaction from a day of hard work that wasn't there before. From the security work, or killing Xander? That question could fuck a girl up.

But not as much as the excited anticipation I felt at the prospect of killing him tomorrow.

Chapter Eight

THE BEAST

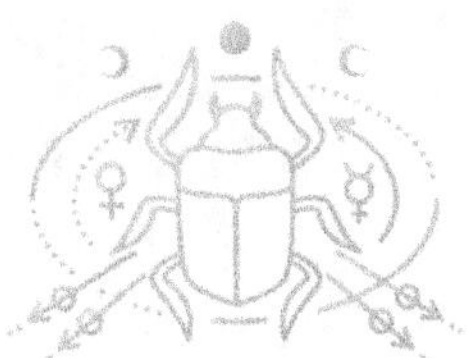

When I woke from my temporary death, the smell of bergamot clung to the inside of my nose. For all these years I'd been obsessed with one thing. Death.

But now I had two obsessions.

Getting to my feet, I smoothed my hand over my chest, over the healed sword wound. I retreated into the shadows of the cage until I reached the back door. Pushing it open, I descended the stone steps to my chambers.

I wanted to see her again. I wanted to breathe her in. I wanted to touch Miranda's skin and feel her warmth. No, fuck that. I wanted her hot and out of control.

I meant what I said. I would be happy to school Miranda in fun, in exchange for her deadly services. That is, if I weren't worried I'd go crazy and kill her.

I shoved down my pants, kicking them away as I grew hard. I followed one of the rocky paths to the pool of water. Slowly, I stepped into the cool water, immersing myself. As soon as I touched it, the water bubbled, heating up from my energy. I sunk in until it reached my chin. My hand fisted around my cock and I groaned.

The fantasy of Miranda falling apart under me played over in my mind as I stroked myself. Could I fuck away her worries, the inner workings of her mind? Could I make her eyes glaze over, and kiss her with such bruising force her already full lips would turn swollen from my abuse? I wanted her screaming and begging, mindless with need.

She'd fight me on it. She'd fight me every step of the way, vying for control and the upper hand. It was her nature. My hand moved faster along my straining, rigid flesh. Pleasure rippled through my spine, gathering in my balls.

Again, I had to question if I was reacting to her because I'd been trapped in solitude for so long. Was this about any morsel of flesh I could get my hands on?

No. I'd seen Grim and the other gods through the years. I'd even met Grim's firecracker of a woman. But next to my angel of death, the sekhor was a mere muted spark.

Miranda was delectable in her own unique way. She shimmered and shone like a diamond and was even stronger than the precious gem.

An orgasm built at the base of my spine as I furiously pumped my engorged flesh. My pleasure wove in with my anger and bitterness. Two fires fueling each other. Dueling for release in my body and release from this existence. And now I felt imprisoned by my need for Miranda. She trapped me in a way I hadn't expected. I wanted her. I wanted her all to myself. A monster taking his maiden back to his lair where I would treat her like a queen. But it would still be a prison and I would still be the beast.

Something crackled at the back of my mind, my senses overloading with power. The water glowed blue from my energy.

I panted as images tumbled through my fractured mind. Tying her up, making her feel as trapped as I was. Before touching, kissing every inch of her soft, luxurious skin. Tasting the bitterness of her scowl, until I coaxed out her sweetness, her screams for more. The world would splinter around us as I thrust home into her inviting body. I'd be surrounded by her strength, grounding her even as her foundation shook to pieces.

A rock shaking roar exploded from me when my release reached its precipice. The lights flickered. I released myself over the edge of the boiling spring.

As soon as I was spent, the vision swirling in my head shifted into a nightmare. Under me, Miranda was no longer a willing participant. Her face was a mask of horror, terrified I would hurt her.

The lights continued flickering, as if scared for her.

This time, another roar, more powerful yet mournful ruptured from my throat. I longed for death more than ever before if only to escape the visions of Miranda's fear and disgust that circled my brain.

I burst from the spring, water surging up with me in a powerful blast. My rational side disappeared as pain engulfed me. Rage and agony pulsated like a pack of clawed demons gleeful to torment.

Then my agony folded over like a piece of paper, again and again, thickening with layers of Miranda's fear, her revulsion of me.

Her sword carved through my flesh over and over again as the landscape shifted into sun baked black sands, then into the searing yellow light of the cradle of life. Tumbling, flying in agony until there was no beginning or end.

But it did finally end. Eventually, I found myself blinking on the floor. My muscles were stiff and frozen. I hadn't died, but I was trapped in a body struck by rigor mortis.

Getting up slowly with great deliberation, I grunted through the pain to stand. I pushed the hair back from my face, taking everything in.

Fuck. My chambers were destroyed.

Usually I could make it to the cage before losing all control, but the episode had come on so quick. I hadn't the wherewithal to get to the barred room. I'd found Miranda carved enough power off me that I couldn't turn berserker even if I wanted to for hours. But the desire I had for her, along with the fear-fueled hallucinations, pushed me over the edge. The thought of hurting her was unbearable.

I limped over to the wall with a control panel. I pressed the button Timothy referred to as "room service."

This is when I would normally wallow in the broken mess I'd created, let myself stew in it. The shadow images of Miranda in pain haunted me like dancing demons, refusing to give me relief. I needed to see her. I needed to know she was okay. That my craziness hadn't somehow stretched out beyond these bars and hurt her.

Miranda would be back tomorrow. I might be on my way out with every thrust of her blade, and I was determined to die like a man, not a beast.

Chapter Nine

THE BADASS

In the elevator, my heart quickened, and a hot flash of excitement possessed me. Our verbal sparring yesterday had opened up something in me. I wanted more. I wanted to talk to Xander more, fight with him more. All day, I'd been thinking about the scarred, broken god and his sharp tongue.

He illustrated a little too well what other things that tongue could do. I dreamt of the image he painted, waking up with a sheen of perspiration on me, and an insistent ache between my thighs. But I didn't have time to give myself any relief.

I didn't need it. I'm fully in control of my baser desires, I told myself. If I was being honest, my being able to hold off my own needs was a point of pride. I only broke down a couple times a year and pulled out a vibrating aide to help me release the sexual tension I'd stored up.

The moment I entered the basement, I knew something was wrong. My arousal evaporated instantly as I dropped into my body, coming into the moment. My hand automatically gripped Bob's hilt. The energy of the room was wrong. It pressed against my bones like a heavy cold cloud. Something crackled in the darkness, a lethal power that could destroy me. My mouth dried and sweat popped out on my forehead, fear flooded my instincts, forming a sour patina on my tongue.

Every nerve-ending shouted at me to back right up into the open elevator and leave. The fragility of my humanity was all too real right now.

"Xander?" I called out. The word came out hoarse. The air grated against my throat with something toxic and raw.

Something panted in the shadows of his cage. But whatever was making the sound couldn't be Xander. It didn't sound human, it sounded like an animal. My eyes tracked the movement of the something in the cage. The outline was so much bigger than Xander's.

Oh my god, had something gotten in? Had it hurt Xander?

The elevator doors closed behind me, and I took a couple steps into the room. He had to be alright. He couldn't be dead. Not until I killed him anyway.

"Xander," I tried to call out again, but it came out even weaker than last time.

The thing inside the cage growled; it was a guttural, menacing tone that emerged from the depths of what had to be a monstrous throat.

Goosebumps broke out on my skin, and ice chilled straight to the marrow of my bones. My adrenaline pumped so hard and fast; I could barely take a breath.

"Xander?" This time it was a whisper.

"Get out." The words ground out like gravel. Then a deep monstrous cry of pain pierced the air. Each sound made me recoil as if I'd bitten on tin foil.

Jesus, it wasn't some new beast, it was Xander in there. I neared the bars, a half inch of my fear melted away. "Xander. What's happening?"

A strange cackling laughter cracked through the air like a whip lashing against my senses. "He's crazy. He's crazy. He's crazy."

I could barely discern it was his voice. The pitch shot up and down like a roller coaster. "Eat his heart. Wet his lips. The trees aren't happy. The trees aren't happy, so we are all angry here. We are blacks and reds and blues. All of us here."

My instincts ripped me in two. I was painfully aware of how much danger I was in. If I valued my life, I'd get the hell out of here. I'd go find Timothy, or Grim maybe. But the other half of me couldn't. His pain, his power was palpable. It grated against me like course sandpaper, but Xander was the one at the epicenter.

Xander's growls and monstrous cries tore at my soul, but I couldn't leave him like this. I forced myself closer to the cage.

His rambling cut off suddenly.

Soft whispers began. All the hairs on my forearms stuck straight up as if someone were speaking directly against them.

"She thinks, she thinks she can. She thinks you won't. She thinks you won't, but you will."

"You will do what?" I asked, carefully. If he came closer, I could kill him and stop whatever this was. Help carve a piece of his power off and release him from this madness.

The whispers layered like a hundred demons, scaring me even more. "She thinks you won't eat her up, yum yum, like a dish of meat in the bowl where the tongue licks and ticks and licks."

I didn't understand. Maybe there was nothing to understand, but I kept thinking if I kept him talking, I could crack the code.

"Xander," I tried to keep my voice from shaking. My hand wasn't nearly as steady. "I need you to come to the bars so I can. . .help you." I had to get through to Xander, to break through the madness and reach the man I knew was still there. The thought of killing him in his current state made my stomach churn, but it was a necessary evil. I would do anything to save him, even if it meant taking his life.

He whined out the words like some metal machine, "The blade doesn't like my blood. The blade doesn't want to bite me."

"Xander," I said softly as if speaking to a child. "Please come here."

A cackle of laughter filled the air, and I had to resist covering my ears in protection. Then it stopped.

A creature slammed into the bars, bursting into supernatural blue light. My mouth parted in a silent scream as my chest seized up.

It was Xander, but not. I recognized only a trace of his likeness. His body had expanded into a massive eight-foot monster. His skin turned into black lava rock but cracks in it revealed a supernatural blue glow that also radiated hatefully from his eyes. Slate gray hair flowed upward as if underwater, defying gravity. The azure glow wafted off the top of his head and surrounded his body like an aura. The power was electric, painful, and I had to close my eyes against the burn.

My skin sizzled.

A massive boom forced my eyes open. The beast in the cage slammed against the bars. Arms reached toward me with massive rocky fists that opened and closed. He was trying to get at me.

Fear paralyzed me. I couldn't sort out all the painful sensations in my body. It felt like I was being irradiated. And Xander's new form made me want to ball up and scream for help. But instead, I gritted my teeth.

The monstrous voice called out my name before he slammed into the bars again. The room shuddered and the lights went out. My stomach dropped out of my body as I was plunged into darkness. Only Xander's blue energy illuminated the room. It wafted out toward me like inviting hands of death.

Hands shaking, I swallowed hard and took a step back. Every primal part of me wanted to scream and run. His ancient uncontrollable power pummeled into me.

I needed to kill him. I needed to kill his power before it hurt me, or anyone else.

Forcing my feet forward, I started toward the beast. The monster slammed against the bars again, his long, muscle roped arms reaching for me. "Miranda."

This time the voice still held all the menace and danger as before, but underneath it, I could swear I heard him pleading with me.

If I got any closer, he'd be able to grab me.

The Xander-monster said he'd eat me up. Would he try to kill me? Every instinct told me he would crush me before licking the meat from my bones. Xander wasn't just powerful, he was out of his mind.

I could leave. Or at least, if the elevator didn't work, I could hide in there until it started working again, then run home with my tail between my legs. Later I'd come back and give him what he wanted, after he calmed.

"Miranda," he pleaded again. That sonorous demonic voice was so sorrowful it ripped at my insides.

The power wasn't only painful to me, it was agony for him. And I couldn't leave him like this.

"Xander," I said, using my best authoritative voice. Blood rushed in my ears so loud, I'm pretty sure I screamed it. "Stop!"

What sounded like tumbled gravel came from his throat, but he stilled. His arms were still outstretched.

I drew closer.

You got this. You got this, a voice softly in my head chanted. For once, my sword felt light and sure in my hands.

When I stepped inside the space between his arms, my alarm shot through the roof. I was in the most vulnerable position possible. I looked up into his illuminated blue eyes and found agony in their blaze. Despite my fear, his arms remained still.

"Kill me," he gurgled.

"Wish granted," I whispered, before thrusting Bob into his chest.

Xander threw back his head, an excess of electric sparks shooting up and out from his eyes. The sparks landed and prickled painfully on my skin. Releasing the blade, I retreated back across the room, fleeing the white-hot energy.

He crumpled to the ground, blue energy dimming where the sword still protruded from his chest. The harsh lights in the room flickered back to life with an audible hum.

Suddenly the explanation for all the mysterious brown outs in the city became clear to me. It was him. He was causing them.

I neared the cage again, needing to retrieve Bob. I crouched down and stuck my arm through the bars. My fingers reached out toward the hilt, but a blackened hand intercepted mine. My heart shot up and lodged itself in my throat as he gripped my hand in his hard, rocky hand. I met his tortured gaze even as the blue blaze faded, turning them human again. Intensity shone from those cerulean depths. "Thank you," he rasped.

His head fell back with a thud. Xander's eyes remained open and sightless. I held his cold, lifeless hand as he fully returned to the shape of a man.

I don't know how long I stayed crouched there with him, but at some point, I became aware of the tears on my cheeks. Xander was dead. For a little while, anyway. But I didn't want to leave him there all alone. His torment, his pain, his gratitude and then relief, they all seared their way into me like a brand.

No one should have to endure that much pain.

The stark reality that he'd been caged down here for millennia, unable to control his power or his pain hit me like a brick in the face. I'd known, but. . .I hadn't truly understood until now.

Eventually, I gently laid his hand down and straightened. My knees were stiff from crouching for so long. I pulled the sword out from his torso, making his body jerk. A sick feeling lurched in my gut. I tucked Bob back into my coat and wiped the tears from my face before heading toward the elevator.

My body started to shake. I needed a bath so hot it could melt my bones. But it wouldn't erase what I saw, what I felt.

I was inside his storm of torment, terrified it would swallow me up. And for a brief moment, I was inclined to let it. Just so he wouldn't have to be in the vortex by himself.

I wrapped my arms around myself, suddenly more scared of myself and my feelings for whatever *this* was.

But no matter what I felt, I had to return tomorrow. I could only wonder, would I face the god or the monster?

Chapter Ten

THE BADASS

"What's wrong, boss?"

I jerked up at Javier's question. He'd turned from the security monitors to face me.

"What? Nothing."

This morning we'd already worked security details for the high roller guests that would show up tonight, as well as helped track down a woman's miniature schnauzer that got loose in the hotel. Everything was perfectly ordinary. Except today I felt zero satisfaction in bringing order to the ongoings of Sinopolis.

Javier's serene eyes studied me closely. With a closed mouth he licked his teeth, causing the small mustache on his upper lip to push out for a moment. Javier was born in Mexico, but his parents managed to get into the US when he was five years old. He never lost his accent though.

More often than not, Javier had a steadying silence about him. It was that steadying silence that got me through our tour in Afghanistan. It was his strong, silent presence that gave me a modicum of strength when Rashon passed and I still had to take care of my toddler. Javier showed up at my door every morning, made breakfast for us, and watched Jamal until I could pull myself out of bed, which for several months, was never before eleven am.

"You steady?" he asked.

It was our code. When shit got rough, too rough, we checked in. The code was sacred and unbreakable. No lies, no bullshit.

Was I steady? After yesterday, seeing Xander like that...it shook me. I could admit that.

Because he scared the shit out of you with his god-likeness?

I'd seen it before. Grim and the other gods all had one. I'd personally seen my boss transform into a massive jackal monster to fight off other gods. So, this should not be that big of a deal.

But it was.

I'd seen Xander completely out of control. I saw his pain, his power, his misery, and it shook me to my core. That's why he was caged.

No surprise when I got home, my neighbor emerged to inform me we'd experienced yet another brownout. She was getting sick and tired of it and went out to buy a generator right then.

My insides quaked as I stepped inside my dark, hot house. Without the A/C the Vegas night heat seeped inside.

How many times had I also been inconvenienced by the brownouts since moving to this area?

But now I knew what the cause of them were. Xander's suffering.

Of course, I'd been terrified of him. Grim was scary but Xander was beyond, what with his power beating on me, trying to sear the flesh away from my bones. The pain had robbed him of all sense and he was an animal.

My fingers slowly curled into my palm as I thought of how long I held his cold, dead hand. I wanted him to wake up. I needed him to wake up.

What if that had been the last blow that took him out?

I realized I knew too little about him. The god I was killing nightly.

I'd wanted to keep things professional, but was I really just trying to protect myself from emotionally attaching to Xander?

The way he groaned out my name in a plea, begging me to kill him, still tore at me.

What had I really gotten myself into? I decided then and there I was going to find the fuck out.

"I'm steady," I finally said to Javier.

He nodded, accepting my answer and the amount of time it took to consider before answering.

The door to our office opened and slammed shut. I was shocked to find Vivien standing there, dark circles under her bloodshot eyes, her back pressed against the door as if barring anyone who wanted to enter.

"What are you doing up? It's daylight?"

While Javier wasn't nearly as entrenched in the business of immortals as I'd been, he'd been privy to Vivien fanging out among other strange occurrences. He handled it like a champ. Which also made it easier for us to work as an effective team in running a not-so-normal hotel.

"I know, I know," she said breathlessly, her eyes wide and wild with fear. "But I'm on the run, and you gotta hide me."

Javier and I exchanged a glance, both of us preparing ourselves for whatever catastrophe was about to come knocking on our door.

I got to my feet and took hold of her shoulders to steady her. "What's happened?"

"H-he was judging someone's soul, and I'd already snuck into his chambers and was in hiding."

My fingers tightened on her. "Vivien, you didn't."

Despite my highest hopes, she nodded her head. "Right as he was about to cast judgement—you know, the part where he whips out his big magic scales and weighs the heart of someone against the feather of truth—I exploded from behind the pillar and swatted him right in the face with a pillow."

I scrubbed my face with my hands while I heard a scoff from behind me. That was the closest I'd heard Javier to giggling.

"It's not funny, Javier," I said. "She's led him right to us."

The small smile on his face vanished.

"What fucking possessed you?" I demanded of my insane friend.

"The need to win?" she shrugged. "And I knew he would have to stay there and finish out the judgement of the soul and couldn't follow me."

"Yeah, not right away. But he'll be done eventually," I said, pointing out the huge hole in her plan. It won't be long before he surfaces from his ancient Egyptian chambers below this very hotel. And when he comes, he'll come hunting for the troublemaker.

Her eyebrows scrunched together, her lower lip popping out as she grabbed me by the shoulders, giving me a slight shake. "I get that now! I didn't think it through. What else is new? You've got to hide me."

I suddenly knew why people got the urge in old movies to slap someone who was hysterical.

The room suddenly got darker, like someone dimmed the lights to fifty percent. My eye caught on the bits of black smoke that seeped in from under the doorway.

"In the utility locker," I said, immediately rushing to unlock it and push aside our sensitive equipment to make room for my friend. It was well over eight feet tall, and was organized in a way that she could easily fit.

Vivien didn't hesitate, cramming herself in. "Lock it behind me," she ordered in a harsh whisper.

"Duh," I said, shutting the door in her face and locking it again.

A knock came a moment before the door opened. I'd only just slipped into my chair as Javier easily became engrossed with our work.

Fear prickled the back of my neck, causing all the fine hairs to stand straight up.

"Where is she?" a low, inhuman voice grumbled.

I swiveled around, my face cleared of any and all emotion.

"Mr. Scarapelli, nice to see you. Are you here to check in on the ongoings of security?"

My boss was already a dark hulking mass in his black suit, but he seemed bigger right now. Black smoke poured off his shoulders as if he was literally seething.

"Where is she?" he repeated.

I casually toyed with my pen. "Where is who, sir?"

"Where is my wife?" he said the last word through gritted teeth.

My eyebrows knitted in apparent confusion. "Why, it's daylight. I imagine she's up in the penthouse fast asleep. She's a vampire."

He opened his mouth as if he were going to yell at me, but then his jaw clicked closed.

Instead, his words came out delicate as glass, like if he bit down on them too hard they'd crunch under the pressure. "I was in the middle of determining whether someone's soul should either be admitted access to the Afterlife or condemned to Amit where their soul would be consumed and destroyed. A very serious matter. When I was attacked by my wife. It was upsetting to say the least. Now please answer carefully when I ask again, where is my wife?"

Javier's face gave away absolutely nothing. As if he'd never done anything his entire life. Like before Grim entered, all he'd been doing was sitting here, since the moment he was born. Not touching anything, just being.

I mimicked his expression.

"Haven't seen her," I said.

Grim continued to scrutinize the two of us, but we stared placidly back.

Finally, he said, "Then can you please explain why there are five reaper dogs currently in this room?"

"What are reaper dogs?" Javier asked.

I turned to him. "They fetch the souls of the dead and take them to the Afterlife, to Amit the crocodile god who eats souls, or to Grim for judgement. We can't see them because we aren't dead."

"I see," he said, nodding his head.

Our conversation was casual and lofty, a contrast to the intensity of the god demanding answers from the doorway.

Javier turned to Grim. "No dead people in here."

Only undead, I thought to myself.

Grim let out a huff, the black smoke having reduced to wisps coming off his shoulders. "As my security team, I expect you to inform me of the location and ongoings of people in this hotel."

He was pulling the "I'm the boss" card. But our duties were to protect the ongoings of operations above ground. His antechamber of judgement was below the hotel and out of our jurisdiction.

"Of course, sir," I acknowledged.

"Always," Javier agreed.

Grim's gaze bounced back and forth between us for another minute before he turned and shut the door behind him. The lights in the room instantly brightened, and it suddenly felt like I could breathe again.

While Grim adored his wife beyond measure and would never truly hurt her, I could only imagine the special brand of revenge he will exact when he finally catches her.

A muffled voice came from inside the utility cabinet. "Thanks guys."

Chapter Eleven

THE BEAST

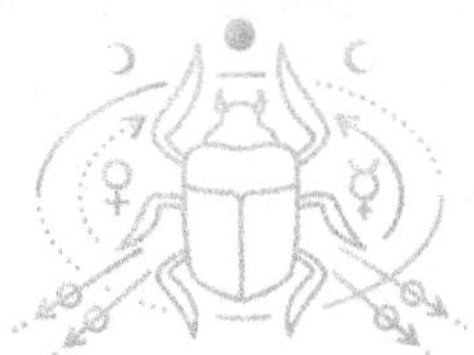

"Who are you?"

I looked up from where I sat in the corner of my cage. After last night, I hadn't expected Miranda to ever return. Yet I dragged my ass into the cage, prepared to make my disappointment all the worse.

Miranda couldn't see me, where I was hidden in shadow. I liked it that way. I liked the shroud around me as I saw my personal angel of death shine under the bright florescent light.

The fierce yet compassionate look in her eye made my breath catch. The badass had returned.

She'd seen me lose control, saw the beast I truly was. It both sickened and disgusted me. I'd never felt this way before. The comings and goings of my sanity and power were what they were. Yet around Miranda, I wanted her to see. . .me. I wanted to be a man around her.

A strange feeling swirled in my chest. It made me feel vulnerable and powerful at the same time. But I was always fucking vulnerable and powerful. Whereas she stood before me, as perfect as any goddess. Dare I say, more so.

"I'm no one," I finally answered.

"They wouldn't put *no one* in a cage. What kind of god are you?"

My earlier thoughts echoed. I wanted to be a man around her. Not a god. But I was what I was.

Pushing to my feet, the usual cold bitterness about my situation spread like an infection from my heart.

"I am the kind of god you should kill." I pressed my chest against the bars.

Miranda didn't move. As the tension thickened, her gaze remained unyielding, a defiant spark igniting within her eyes. She was dissecting every nuance of my fractured being. This mortal was always thinking, always calculating like some kind of threat machine. But I wondered if she ever just *was*. Was there a moment she was relaxed, simply in the moment?

Suddenly I craved to see that. I craved to yank her scheming mind into the present. Make her see me, really see me. No. The god I used to be wasn't good enough. I wanted to *become* something new for her.

"Tell me," she requested in a quiet voice.

It was the softness in her tone that snapped my barrier like a twig.

"I once was the god of the seas and oceans." My words came out hoarse, as they were laden with the heaviness of the past. "I ruled the tides. My most favored was the Mediterranean." My heart squeezed painfully with aching and longing. "I brought balance and bounty to everyone with my oceans."

"Like Poseidon?"

I couldn't keep my lip from curling. "Yes, that is a name I've been called, though I never sported a white beard and trident. The myth spiraled far away from the man," I held open my arms. "Originally, my worshippers knew me as Nun."

Miranda snorted. Her eyes flew wide as she clapped a hand over her mouth. "I'm sorry."

"What?"

"It's nothing."

I scowled. "It's not nothing. You are clearly on the verge of some kind of fit." Her outburst and the way she covered her mouth was highly abrupt.

She shook her head, her palm back over her mouth.

"Miranda." I drew her name out in a dangerous tone.

With great reluctance, she dropped her hand. "It's just I'm surprised you didn't tell me your name was Nun earlier."

I cocked my head to the side.

"Nunyabusiness," she added. The grin on her face was as absurd as it was infectious. She burst into laughter. Waving a hand, she tried to get control of herself. "I'm sorry, that's my son talking through me. Or maybe Vivien. It's ridiculous. I think it's a sign I'm crumbling under all the pressure."

Her laugh. I'd never heard a real laugh from her. It was like being kissed by a thousand butterflies and warmth spread through my lower belly.

I didn't join her, but I watched her, drinking in this new side of her like it was some kind of rare liquor. And I was intoxicated by it.

We fell into silence as her laughter trailed off.

Composing herself, she got back to business. "So Nun, why are you down here?"

The utterance of my true name acted as a catalyst, unleashing a surge of raw, agonizing power that ripped through my body like a bolt of lightning.

I gripped the steel bars to brace myself. The air vibrated painfully around me, threatening to send me over the edge. If anyone didn't need a super charge, it was me.

"Please," I said through bared teeth, "do not use my ancient name. Call me Xander."

I caught a flicker of surprise in her eyes, a subtle widening and a brief parting of her lips, as if my unleashed magic had taken her off guard.

Me too, sweetheart.

Trying to sound calmer and more reasonable, I explained, "The old names still hold power, and as you know, I have an excess of that. In ancient times, whenever gods became too powerful, we were forced to change our name and move to another locale. It upset the balance. Eventually, Osiris forbid any of us from being worshipped." I cracked my neck to the side with a loud snap.

Though now that I think of it, a couple days ago and such a slip would have sent me into a raging blackout. She'd slowly been carving slices off of my power, and with each jab the pain was a little less, and I was a little more in control.

She frowned. "I wasn't worshipping you."

I'll show you how you can worship me, sweetheart.

While I could not take her fealty and prayers, I wanted to make her moan and scream to the heavens as I fell to my knees before her.

My hands slid up and down the smooth metal while thinking of her warm, pliable body. Miranda tracked the movement, her mouth parting slightly. For a moment, I thought I caught a trace of lust in her eyes, but it was gone in an instant.

I dropped my arms and took a couple steps away. "To answer your question as to how I got here, I died of course."

"How?" She neared the bars once again.

"By the hands of my enemy." A snarl sprang to my lips.

"Was he a vampire? A sekhor?"

I shook my head. "He was another god, a sun god. He burned me to death."

"Who was it?" Miranda suddenly asked in a demanding tone. "Is he here? In Vegas? Running one of the hotels while you sit down here and rot in pain?"

When I looked up at her, I saw fire in her eyes. A smile tugged at the corner of my lips.

"No. He's long dead and gone." I nodded to her. "By the very blade you hold in your hand there."

Miranda studied her sword with renewed interest, as if she could see the ghost of my nemesis there.

My tone turned dark as I paced along the edge of my cage. "He was insane, out of his mind, the power hungry son of a bitch. I tried to warn the others, but no one believed me. I told them he would burn everything to the ground until he was the last one standing." I opened my mouth to say his name, but then closed it shut. Ancient names held too much power, even though he'd been vanquished by the very blade I was trying to end my existence on. The irony was not lost on me. It was like he was still here, sending me to my death for a second time. Winning after he was long dead and gone.

"I faced him alone, and we battled. I tried to drown him, he boiled my seas, and in the end, he was the victor."

I fell silent, the echo of my last words lingering in the air. Then, with a sigh, I continued, "But my death was the catalyst for the uprising against him. Timothy regaled me with the events after my godly essence returned to the cradle of life. Gods, fae, and man fought him alike, until he was finally vanquished with the blade of bane."

Miranda had listened intently, but now she asked. "But why are you here? Why are you like this?"

I shrugged. "Like I said, I was killed and returned to the cradle of life. But my repose was cut short. I don't know why. I don't know how. It was far too soon. I had not lain long enough."

Miranda expanded on the issue. "Gods need to lay in there for years, even hundreds of years before they can emerge again."

I nodded. "At first, our energies are too volatile which is why we must rest until we are in control again."

"But Vivien called Grim out from the cradle within a matter of days and he wasn't...out of control. Or at least not after a while."

I stopped my pacing, my heart thumping wildly with anger over the injustice. I knew he'd been revived along with some of the details. "Indeed," I said in a dark voice. "He did not suffer the same effects as me." My words came out crisp and bitter.

"Why?"

I shrugged, trying to bury my anger and resentment in indifference. "Who knows? Perhaps he is more controlled than me. Perhaps I am being punished."

"Is that what you think?" She came within arm's reach.

I stepped back up to the bars again, inhaling her scent. It both calmed and infuriated me. I wanted her. I could never have her, if for nothing other than the fact I was a monster.

"Look at me, Miranda," I said, my words harsh. "Do you see where I am? I am far from any ocean because my simple presence makes them boil. Grim moved to the desert of North America to help sequester me. I am kept behind bars. There is nothing but endless pain and solitude for me. I am not an omniscient god, but I understand punishment when

I'm in the midst of it. Osiris cannot or will not account for my current state. So perhaps some even larger entity rules us all and saw fit to make me suffer. Perhaps my enemy is still somehow pulling the strings on my pain long after his demise. Either way, will you do me the kindness of running me through and giving me a modicum of relief until I am finally dead and gone for good." It was then I realized I'd yelled the last bit.

Miranda's lip trembled as she shrank away from me.

At first, I thought it was my power flaring, hurting her. But no, I hadn't unleashed anything for once. She was simply experiencing some strong emotion. From the look in her eyes, I couldn't guess if it was pity, fear, or maybe disgust. I was a monster last night, but most of all, I hated the bitter creature I was right now. It almost made me long to return to my gnarled, deformed god-likeness so she wouldn't see me like this.

Just as I was about to retreat to the shadows, Miranda stepped even closer. A mere inch separated us. A shaking hand raised up. My brow furrowed as she reached through the bars and ran her fingers through my hair. A hard lump formed in my throat, and it was as if someone tightened screws in my chest. Both sensations loosened at her touch, and I swallowed hard.

Fuck. When was the last time I'd been touched in affection? Had I ever?

A bottomless chasm opened in my chest even as her touch softened the hardest parts of me.

I drew in a shuddering breath as long forgotten sensations overwhelmed me. The warmth of flesh. The unique healing power it possessed when pressed against another's. Immortals may possess magic, but did mortals understand the power of touch?

The soft pads of her fingertips grazed my scalp. The sensation threatened to pull me under, drown me. I could drown in her. In the solace she somehow traced into my mind with the scrape of her short nails.

What would it be like to feel her touch all over? To hold her warm, pliant body to mine? To smooth away the worries from her troubled mind?

Her hand dropped away, and my insides railed at the loss as a deep sadness consumed me from the inside out. It was not meant to be. It could never be. There were only two fates for me. Existence and pain. Or death and oblivion. But Miranda would live.

She withdrew her sword. "Wish granted," she said.

The painful strike of the sword was a welcome sensation after she stopped touching me. And it helped cut up my rush of affection and need for Miranda. I wanted more. So much more.

I couldn't remember the last time I wanted more. I've only wanted less, less breath, less life. But those enchanting fucking eyes made me want to drop to my knees and promise her anything she wanted as long as she touched me again like that, looked at me like this. Like she gave a fuck about me.

Chapter Twelve

THE BADASS

The next morning, I bought a redeye from Aaron — a large cup of coffee with an espresso shot thrown in on top— and sat at my usual table at Perkatory.

Aaron was hard at work, steaming milk and pulling shots for the long line of bleary-eyed guests who stayed up way too late last night, indulging in all their vices.

Vivien wasn't back from her evening yet. I finally broke down and texted our group thread after waiting for ten minutes.

You coming, Viv?

Ugh. I can't today. I'm dealing with the BS.

These days, BS was synonymous for bullshit *and* blood suckers.

What now?

The dot dot dot of her texting appeared for a long time before the message downloaded.

One of the new baby vamps is having an emotional breakdown. I've been here most of the night trying to assure her immortality isn't the worst thing in the world. Hard when she has a husband and kids. Had to hold the bitch back with my vamp powers to keep her from turning them too. Have a dollop of whipped cream on your coffee in my honor.

I swallowed hard. I couldn't even begin to imagine the trauma of being bitten and turned immortal without having a say in it.

But maybe it was for the best she wasn't here. I'd been warring with myself on what or what not to share.

How could I tell her I couldn't help but reach into the beast's cage and touch him? How could I tell her I couldn't figure out the monster, the man, or the god? How could I allow myself to share the excitement and anticipation fluttering in my stomach at the prospect of seeing him again tonight? It seemed so. . .silly? Awkward? Bizarre?

Don't worry about it, I wrote Vivien back. *Take care of baby vamps. That's more important.*

After another dot dot dot. *More importantly, after my shower attack, Grim used his powers to float pillows to surround me before they bombarded me. That sonofabitch. I told him no powers allowed. Though now I'm thinking about mind controlling all baby vamps to attack him with pillows.*

A smile threatened to disrupt the firm line of my lips. Aaron barked out a laugh. People were still waiting for coffee, but he'd clearly read the message on our group thread too. We traded a knowing look across the room. She was crazier than a squirrel's nuts, but we loved her.

The clack of heels against the black marble floors jerked my attention away from my thoughts. A figure rounded the high wall of lush plants. A frothy pink robe, lined in feathers, fluttered all around a woman who looked like a pinup model from the 1940s. Flaxen blonde curls fell in a soft cloud around her perfectly beautiful cream face. The woman was the definition of femininity, and I'd met her before. The goddess, Hathor, otherwise known as Bianca, seemed to be on the hunt for someone or something.

When her crystalline blues alighted on me, I knew she'd found her target. My fingers curled around my coffee cup. Uh oh.

Before I could even guess as to why she was looking for me, Bianca floated into the seat across from me. The air carried her heavenly fragrance, a blend of cotton candy sweetness intertwined with the gentle essence of blooming flowers.

"There you are, Miranda. I'm so glad I found you," she said with a tight smile. The goddess was normally the picture of ease, but there was a tension around her eyes. As if she'd been up worrying all night.

"How can I help you?" I asked, putting my business voice on. Bianca owned the Parisienne hotel further down the strip. This could be a hotel matter, but the twist in my stomach told me it wasn't.

"Miranda," she said my name again as if preparing both of us for what she had to say. "It is urgent I speak with you about your. . .recent activities."

"Recent activities?" My gut clenched as a guilty conscience kicked up. But no. There's no way she could know the feelings I'd been having recently, and there was even less of a chance she would care whether or not I was experiencing some kind of sexual awakening.

Little lines gathered between her eyes as she looked at me in earnest. "Yes. The task Grim has assigned you. It isn't safe."

Something cold snaked through me.

"I'm afraid you'll have to be more specific," I said carefully. Grim and Timothy never told me my job with Xander was a secret, but I'd be damned if I assumed and let something important slip out.

With another tight smile, as if understanding what I was making her do. "Killing Xander," she said, confirming my suspicion for sure. "You have to stop."

"What?"

She shook her head mournfully. "It's my fault you see. I told him. I told him you had the blade. I saw his death. But it was meant to be a warning. You must trust me, Miranda. Under no circumstances should you try to kill him."

I looked away from Bianca, down to my cup of inky black caffeine. "Why not?"

Her delicate hand covered mine, pulling it off my cup, forcing me to look into her eyes. "Because it will bring about the end of the world."

Well fuck me sideways on a rollercoaster.

"What did you see?" I asked, my voice suddenly hoarse. Bianca was an oracle and had visions about the future, but from what I gathered, they weren't always clear or as literal as her interpretations.

Bianca's head tilted as she closed her eyes, like she was sending her vision inward. She wrinkled her brow as if trying even harder to see something. "Chaos. Blinding light."

I slid my hand away from hers to hold my coffee cup again. "No more detail than that."

Bianca frowned. "Miranda, you must take this seriously."

My hackles rose at that. Of all the people she could accuse of not taking things seriously... That was my problem. Hell, my identity. Everything was a dire event that needed me to be the strong leader who cleaned up everyone else's mess. Without Jamal, what little humor and sense of play dried up into a raisin. To insinuate anything else, grated. Maybe I should have been taking a back seat to all the shit, maybe I should spend more time messing around or screwing off. Then I wouldn't be so pissed off by her comment.

Even though it wasn't Bianca's fault she'd hit one of my hot buttons, my blood boiled. "Of course, I'm taking this seriously. But your vision doesn't seem to tie coherently to Xander. How can my killing Xander create what you are seeing? How do you know they are connected at all." I couldn't control the steel edge in my words. She wanted me to take this seriously? I'd show her how critical I could be about all sides in the matter.

Bianca shifted in her seat and looked away, her cheeks flushing. "It's more a feeling. Visions aren't a science."

Trying to calm my tits, I said in a slightly softer tone, "Is there a chance you are wrong?"

Bianca shook her head slightly as if in amazement. "You are so intent to kill him? I don't understand, why?"

I licked my lips, preparing my answer. "Because he is in pain." At her reaction, I realized she knew it too. "Do you want him to be in pain for eternity?"

"No, of course I don't," she said with a tired sigh. "But Miranda, the very future of immortals and humans is at stake if you kill Xander. I don't know how. But I know they are connected."

And I believed her. Or at least, I believed that she believed. Bianca was a caring, compassionate goddess. There were few people I trusted, and even fewer gods. But Bianca proved to be pure of heart, with the interest of mortals at the forefront. A rarity among the immortals, from what I'd learned.

However, that still didn't make her right, did it?

Wow Miranda, you are going to go with your gut over a god who can literally see the future? Don't you think highly of yourself?

No. Of course I recognized the Oracle was an authority to be taken seriously. Still, I didn't feel right about this. Not about leaving Xander in his prison, out of his mind with power and pain.

And if it was such a bad thing, why would the god of the dead himself direct me to kill him? I trusted Bianca, but I trusted Grim even more. Still, the math didn't add up.

Maybe I was the wrong person to be the caretaker of the blade? Maybe it required someone with cold calculation to sort through all this. Yet, my heart was getting in the way, telling me I couldn't just let Xander suffer like he had.

A migraine started at my temples, even as a dull sucking ache throbbed in my heart.

Bianca pulled my hand off my cup again to give my fingers a squeeze. "I know you are a good person. I know you want to do the right thing. Please, Miranda. Do the right thing."

Chapter Thirteen

THE BEAST

I'd been waiting for Miranda. It felt like an eternity between her visits, and our evenings had become my favorite part of the day. Before her, I didn't have a favorite part of the day. Before her, my life was knitted together by moments of excruciating pain.

I could try to tell myself her arrival, triggering my heart to gallop and throb with excitement, was only because I looked forward to dying. But it had become more than that.

Our verbal sparring woke up parts of my brain that had slumbered so long I'd thought they died before the rest of me could. When Miranda's cat-like eyes flashed as her body squared off, preparing for a fight, tendrils of warm blood snaked through my body. Scratching at the paint on her perfect veneer, trying to get underneath to the real her, had sparked an obsession.

Perhaps I'd get to peel away some of her armor before I died my final, true death.

I inhaled a shuddering breath of anticipation, my eyes fluttering close.

Death.

Every day I neared my true, perfect end. Freedom from flesh and bone. Oblivion.

"Well, Ms. Badass. Aren't you going to kill me today?" I asked, letting a grin curl my lips upward.

She stared at me for a long time as if trying to figure something out. The smile slid off my face. My gut churned with anticipation and foreboding, a sickly charged sensation.

Before she could respond, her phone rang with an ear-splitting shrillness that felt like a physical blow. Panic raced through me like a lightning bolt. The air shimmered like a place over hot coals and the blaring in my head felt like a river of water being pulled through a pinhole.

My fists balled into shaking fists. Teeth cracked when I clenched my jaw, in an attempt to gird myself. I couldn't afford to lose control. I couldn't afford to scare her off.

I wanted to die today. I *needed* to die today.

"Make it stop," I growled.

Miranda fumbled for the phone, but it slipped from her fingers.

Do dee do dee do.

The jarring melody continued to drill into my senses. The notes blasted through my ears, shattering my fragile mental defenses. My hands shook, my veins popping out as my skin twisted and morphed into a blackened shell of rage. Unholy fire ignited inside me, a raging inferno ready to scorch the world and anyone unfortunate enough to be standing nearby. It would be so satisfying to grab her and thrust her hard against the bars until the noise ceased. Technicolor violent fantasies drove my insanity to dangerous heights.

No, I absolutely would not fucking hurt her. No one hurts my dark angel, not even me. My fear of hurting her or scaring her surged faster, outrunning my crazy. Still, I didn't know how long my need to protect her would keep my senses intact. If I fell over the edge, she'd see, see me for what I really was. She'd never come back.

I gripped the bars so hard they shuddered. "Turn it off!" I roared.

Miranda winced. Her fingers wrapped around the phone, and she went to dismiss the call.

"Oh crap," she muttered as a face appeared on her screen. She whipped the phone away so whoever it was couldn't see me.

"Hi mom," a young voice chirped.

The bell clanging in my head fell blissfully silent, and I sagged against the bars. *Fuck, that had been close.*

"Hey kiddo, sorry, I actually can't—"

But the boy interrupted. "Mom, we had the best day ever. They let us assemble actual robots. It was the coolest. Have you ever done anything like that?"

I focused on the steady beat of Miranda's heart. On the voice of the kid. I slowly but surely reeled in the power that almost took me entirely.

"No Jamal, I haven't but I need to—"

Again, he interrupted her. "You need to have more fun. You don't have enough fun. Maybe you should ask Vivien and Aaron to play board games with you. We have a whole day for board games coming up. Oh dang, I got to go. They just brought out the pizza. Love you, bye!"

The call went dead.

"Love you too," she muttered. Then she blew out a heavy breath. "I'm so sorry. I didn't mean to answer."

Jamal. Knowing her kid's name, hearing his voice, somehow gave me another piece of the woman I saw every day. There was something I instantly liked about Jamal. In the brief moments he spoke to his mother, he exhibited a candidness and maturity that matched hers. More than that, he seemed somehow unruined by life. As if the heavy weights of living hadn't yet crushed any vital part of him yet. I wondered how much of that was his own indomitable spirit, and how much was Miranda's wisdom and guidance.

"It's alright," I assured her, though my voice was hoarse now. I was spent from holding back the surge of power. "Are you going to take his advice?"

"What?"

"Are you going to practice having more fun?"

"Don't fuck with me," she said in warning. She thought I was trying to mess with her about her kid.

"It's good advice, you know."

"Oh really?" she snorted in disbelief. "Are you down here playing ping-pong by yourself?"

"I knit," I said without pause.

"Har har."

"Your kid know you are a badass blade wielder?" I asked, my curiosity getting the best of me.

"Unfortunately, he knows more about the supernatural than anybody should have too. Grim saved his life once when some vampires used him as a pawn. I'm very grateful he is unusually mature, but he is still a sensitive soul."

The distress on her face kept me from asking any more questions about her son's knowledge of gods and monsters.

Then she walked over to the lone chair and opened her lunch sack. She pulled out a prepackaged bag of chips and ripped it. Her face rearranged into an unreadable mask.

Why wasn't she over here stabbing me through the heart? She seemed to be considering something, very intensely.

Something was wrong. Very wrong.

"What is it?" I asked, trying not to crawl out of my skin.

Why was she so distant?

Miranda waited until she finished chewing and swallowed a chip. My fingers twitched, desperate to rip the bars apart and shake her until she told me what happened.

"I'm not sure I can kill you," she said quietly, dispassionately. Her eyes drifted across the room.

Inside my skull, a storm of panic raged. Lightning bolts of fear struck at the core of my thoughts, threatening to shatter my fragile equilibrium all over again.

I began to pace back and forth, never taking my eyes off her. "What the fuck are you talking about?"

It would have been better if she yelled it, if she dug her heels in and faced off with me. But Miranda turned off like a switch, so cold and distant.

"Can you calm down first?" she asked in an even tone.

"No, I can't fucking calm down. You just said you aren't going to kill me."

"Please," she said, wincing.

The lights flickered. My power was going berserk and hurting her.

Before I could register the impact I had on her, I found myself up on the bars by the ceiling. I didn't remember climbing up here. Instead of reacting, she continued to stare at me impassively, as if waiting for me to get over my fit. Like I was some kind of child.

I leapt off and landed silently on my feet, reeling the excess in, though it pained me to bite back all the energy and pain I wanted to let explode out.

"Explain," I ground out.

Miranda lowered the chip bag. "Bianca came to me. She said if I kill you, something terrible is going to happen. End of the world terrible."

My teeth cracked under the pressure of my clenched jaw. They would heal later. And I would hate even that. I was broken and I wanted to feel every piece of my brokenness. Chop myself up into little pieces until I looked how I felt. Box my bits up, send them to Miranda with a red bow. The tag would read, "I go to pieces."

My crazy runaway train of thought jerked to a halt, bringing me back to clarity. I would never do that to Miranda.

I was struck by the miracle of that. When I started to spiral there was usually no bringing me back from the precipice. But I'd already recovered once today, saved by the need to protect the woman across from me.

Miranda must be some kind of enchantress.

Or I simply knew she was the key to my freedom, one death at a time.

"Miranda. Please don't do this."

"I can't be responsible for ending the world." Even as she said it, I saw regret and uncertainty in her eyes. The door hadn't fully closed on my salvation, not yet. And I planned on digging my claws in and ripping it back open.

I stepped up to the bars and encircled the cold metal with my hands. "Bianca's visions aren't always as they seem."

Miranda didn't say anything.

"Did she say how it would happen? How my death would lead to the end of the world?"

After a pause, Miranda shook her head.

I let out a sigh of relief. "How could my death possibly bring about the end of the world?"

Miranda dropped her lunch sack to the ground and pushed off from her chair. "I don't know. You tell me." Frustration edged her words. "I'm trying to do the right thing here."

And she was. I knew it. Miranda was like Grim in that she was trying to protect others. Yet she somehow missed how terribly delicate and fragile her own humanity was. I coveted her humanity, and the power she held in her delicate being.

"Killing me is the right thing, Miranda." The lights flickered and Miranda stepped back from my flux of power. Without thinking, I grabbed her hand and pulled her to the bars.

Her brown eyes widened. They were a couple shades lighter than her skin, making for an irresistible contrast of color. Like sparkling brown sugar irises set against rich walnut. And I wondered, not for the first time, if she tasted as sweet as she looked.

With my other hand, I reached through the bars and caught her face. My thumb stroked along her jawline, trying to ease the pain I caused her. She inhaled sharply but didn't move away. "Miranda, if I thought there was a chance my demise would end the world—would end your world—I wouldn't ask."

I sunk every bit of meaning, of feeling into those words. I needed her to believe me.

Maybe I'd been cut off from the world outside too long, but Miranda somehow connected me to it again. It hadn't taken much, but it was true all the same.

"How can I tru—believe you?"

I realized there was something more here for both of us. Something pulsating. Something alive. Something connecting us.

Her body pressed against the bars, meeting my hard chest with her soft curves. My fingers trailed across her cheek. Fucking hell her skin was so smooth, so soft, over a bone structure that would make any man hard to gaze upon.

But she was more than skin and bones. So much more. My little badass. Who was free to live her life, but I could see invisible chains around her. She held herself back, and I wanted to rip away the constraints so very badly.

My gaze dropped to her lips. Full, inviting lips made me forget how to breathe. "Miranda. Please," I rasped, caught in a whirl of desire and desperation. I wasn't sure what I was pleading for anymore.

Her breath hitched, shallow and fast, and I could almost hear the gears turning in her mind, could see the battle waging in her eyes.

"Wish granted," she murmured, her voice as sharp as the weapon she plunged into my chest, a cold, keen contrast to the heat brewing between us. The breath hitched in my throat, as my heart split under the blade.

The pain was immediate, intense, yet it wasn't enough to tear my eyes away from hers. There, in those beautiful depths, I saw conflict, uncertainty – a mirror of my own.

Her indecision stabbed me sharper than any blade. I'd placed this burden on her, forced her to bear the weight of my death. Guilt gnawed at my conscience, but it was too late to take it back. Instead, I reached through the bars, pulling her face to mine.

I kissed her right on those gorgeous fucking lips. I told myself it was gratitude, but as soon as my lips met hers, I knew it was so much more than that.

She froze under me like a deer in headlights, but she didn't move away.

I kissed her in slow, soft laps, the tip of my tongue flicking over her decadent mouth. Finally, her soft, wet lips slid against mine, her head tilting to press in, to kiss me back. I moaned at the sensation, her lips so soft and inviting, like they were made for me.

Lips parted and I swept my tongue in her mouth. *Fuck*. She was sweeter and more intoxicating than the wildest of fantasies that had haunted my solitude. My little badass was exquisite, erotic.

Something split wide inside me and reached for her with greedy phantom hands.

I needed more. More Miranda. More of her hardness, more of her softness. I'd drink every last drop of her, no matter how bitter or sweet. Heat and tingles whipped around inside me, stirring an insatiable hunger.

When my gaze met hers, I found the same intense passion mirrored there. Her hooded, lust-filled eyes, usually composed, were wide with an emotion that echoed my own – a raw, wild desire. An affirmation that she, too, was lost in this whirlpool of shared intensity. The sight of her, so unguarded, did unspeakable things to me. I knew then that our passions were intertwined.

Her shuddering breath puffed against my lips as her fingers burrowed into my hair. She kissed me like she had never kissed anyone before, like she was discovering a new world.

I tasted her fear, her pleasure, her deep dark passion.

She wasn't close enough. The hand cupping her chin moved to the base of her skull, while my other one grasped her sexy hip. I pulled her closer, which pushed the sword deeper into my heart. I grunted as I felt life bleed from me faster, but it was worth it to get closer to her warm skin.

Though I tried to ignore it, the darkness closed in around me, relentless, pulling me away from Miranda's sweetness. For the first time ever, I wanted to cling to life, just for a little longer.

The last thought I had before succumbing to oblivion was I hoped this was my last death rather than never taste her again.

Chapter Fourteen

THE BADASS

The next morning, I lay in bed, until almost seven AM. It was my day off, but I was still usually up and at 'em by five.

Maybe I was getting sick. That was the only explanation for what was happening in my body.

Unless your kakuchie can catch cold, this is not that, my brain informed me.

"Shut up."

Last night, Xander kissed me.

Since I'd stepped into that basement, Xander excited parts of me I long thought dead. He turned me into a puddle of liquid heat, but I never let it compromise me. Even though I'd traced the outline of his perfect lips with my eyes, I never expected him to lay them on me.

When he did, it changed everything. The moment his lips pressed against mine, I went from being a bystander in a muted life to the strongest yet most vulnerable version of myself. It was like coming back to life, as I served him death.

My finger pads ghosted over my lips, chasing the phantom pressure of his, trying to rekindle the sensation. Or maybe, just maybe, I was attempting to understand how one man's kiss could cause such a seismic shift in me.

Was the kiss so intense because he was a god, or because it had been so long?

Years, my judgmental brain whispered.

"Shut up. I've been busy raising a son and working," I said out loud again. Still, a gnawing sensation ate at my gut, demanding attention, or the very least, a name.

Loneliness, my brain whispered again.

"Arrgh," I cried out even as I paced the living room. "How dare you think that. You don't need anything else. You have friends. You have a son who is amazing, kind and smart."

But no matter what I said, I felt the effects of a need I'd tried so hard to shove away. And I fucking hated it.

I would have called a friend, but it was daylight and Vivien was likely already asleep, and Aaron was off rock climbing for the entire weekend. There was no one.

There's someone, my stupid brain said again.

"Nope, I'm not going to him." I laced up my tennis shoes, prepared to do the only rational thing here. Burn it all off at the gym.

My tablet rang and buzzed on my dresser table. Normally, I'd leap to answer it, knowing who it was. But I was moving slowly today. Still, I was no less happy to answer and see the smiling face of my kid.

Jamal grinned from ear to ear. "Hey mom."

"Hey my baby, how is camp going?" I settled in the small cream-colored sitting chair by the window. I bought the comfy seat with the hopes I'd read books and sit in peaceful silence, but I somehow never found the time to do either.

That was all it took for Jamal to launch into stories about the high ropes course they traversed the day before. His best friend, Jun Hie, who came all the way from Tokyo to take advantage of the program as well. They'd met last summer, and they'd picked up right where they left off, bonding over the latest in robotics and astronomy.

I lived for that toothy smile on his face. To say I was grateful for the program and scholarship, so he could attend, was an under-statement.

"You okay, mom?"

"Of course, baby. Why do you ask?"

"I don't know," he said, studying me as close as he could through a camera. "You seem. . .sad. Are you taking care of yourself?"

My kid. The eleven-year-old going on forty.

"Of course, I am," I said, a little too defensively.

"Are you taking time to have fun?" He spelled it out for me as if I didn't understand his original question.

I rubbed my forehead. "Baby, you know I gotta work." And these days, work was killer.

Ha! I could be funny when I wanted to be.

Jamal frowned. "You don't work all the time. And if I'm not there to make sure you have fun, you should go play with Vivien and Aaron."

"Who's the parent here?" I asked, failing to suppress a smile.

He shook his finger at the camera dramatically, before breaking out into laughter.

Then Jamal turned serious again. "Mom, are you lonely?"

A spike stabbed through my heart. "Of course not."

If we'd simply been talking over the phone, I would have missed the stink-eye he gave me. "You know you always tug on your hair when you are lying."

I released braids as if they were made of fire.

Jamal took a deep breath. "I need to go in a couple minutes here, but it's time we had the talk."

I straightened in my seat. Oh god, he's barely eleven. Why would he need to have the talk now? I wasn't ready. It was all happening too soon.

"I think it's time you started dating again."

I would have been less surprised if he slapped me across the face with a live fish.

"Baby, I—"

His tone was stern and far beyond his years. "I can't be there all the time, and someone else needs to treat you like the queen you are."

"Hey Jamal," a voice called from the background.

"Sorry mom, I gotta go. We are preparing to go on a backpacking trip where we can do some serious star gazing. It's gonna be the coolest."

I barely had a chance to say goodbye before he hung up.

There I continued to sit, in the stark silence, chewing on what my kid just said.

He wants me to date?

Well, dammit. I'd been using Jamal as a smoke screen to keep myself unavailable to relationships, and now my own kid ripped away the safety blanket I had, leaving me exposed. I could run from my own feelings, but it was a hell of a lot harder when he held up the mirror, showing me all the parts I'd been avoiding.

Just because he told me to do it didn't mean I had to.

If your own kid thinks you need to get laid, you need to get laid.

"That is *not* what he was saying."

He may not get the mechanics, but he gets the mood, and he knows you are too uptight.

I hadn't felt uptight yesterday with Xander.

Standing and stretching my legs, I didn't think the answer is fucking a half feral god before I kill him for the umpteenth time.

Stopping at my bathroom door, I scrubbed a hand over my face.

Oh fuckity ducks. I'm going to have to start dating again.

Before I could think about it too much, I grabbed my phone and downloaded three different dating apps. I didn't do anything halfway. Which meant I had a whole other mission to complete before Jamal came home. Go on at least one date with a perfectly normal guy.

But before I tackled that, a trip to the gym was still in order.

* * *

After lifting weights for thirty minutes, I wound my braids up into a bun and crossed to the boxing gym that was attached. I paid extra for the access, and ever since I started having to fight off gods and vampires, I found it a wise investment.

Finding myself an available bag in a corner, my fists slammed into it until sweat dripped into my eyes.

Loneliness.

Pow pow. My knuckles crashed into the bag over and over. I tried to beat away the feeling.

I'm not lonely. Loneliness wasn't a factor. It was just a feeling and feelings couldn't control me.

I'd learned that after Rashon passed.

Xander's words returned to me.

Pain means feeling and you work very hard not to feel, don't you?

Pow pow.

My breathing turned shallow as I tried to punch his words away. Tried to fight away how quick he cut to my core.

"Jeezus, Miranda, you pissed today or what?"

I pivoted to find myself face-to-face with Amos, the boxing gym owner. A massive wall of muscle with a shaved head that gleamed. His skin tone was rich as midnight, with bluish-red undertones. A crimson shirt stretched across his powerful barrel chest. Amos had the warmest smile, gave the best hugs, and punched like a beast. Not that he'd unleashed that power fully on me when we were sparring, being so far out of my weight class. But he was helping me level up little by little when I could fit in one-on-one sessions with him.

"I'm not pissed," I responded, winding a couple braids back up that had fallen out of my bun.

He held his hands up and chuckled. "Sure."

Okay, so I even said it like I was pissed.

"Just don't go breaking my bags. They are hella expensive." Then he seemed to think better of it. "On second thought, break the bag if you want. It will only make the others train harder, and they'll think I'm responsible for your badassery." He tossed a look over his shoulder to where a couple of guys were training. One of them pretended he hadn't been staring at me, while the other gave me a suggestive grin. I wouldn't be surprised if he approached me to ask if we could spar in an attempt to get my number.

Should I say yes if he did? I did just download dating apps to my phone.

The idea made my skin crawl and something at the pit of my stomach longed for the feel of someone else's lips. My already pumping blood ran hotter. The way he groaned echoed in my ears. My mouth hungered for his salty masculine tongue sliding against mine. How he pulled me closer even as it sunk the blade in further. Like I was worth all the pain in the world, if he could get me a little wild. A throbbing kicked up at my center like a heartbeat.

Nope. I'm choosing to ignore all pangs of desire for a completely off-limits immortal.

The pangs didn't fucking listen.

"Then if I break one of your bags, you owe me a month of one-on-ones," I said, trying to bargain.

Amos squinted at me. "Deal." Then he turned back to his clipboard and walked off, leaving me to it.

My clothes clung to my soaked body, and my muscles had turned into overcooked noodles. Not to mention the buzz of arousal still ran through me. It was time to throw in the towel. I checked the big clock hanging over the sparring ring.

Two fucking PM? Would this day ever end? Maybe I could just go into work?

No. I needed to try and relax. I promised Jamal before he left that I would try to have some fun. I'd humored him at the time, but now I realized how spot on my eleven-year-old son was.

Flipping open one of the dating apps, I easily set up a profile. Three pictures, one of me in a dress for church last Easter, one of me and Jamal at the beach, though I cropped out his face as it was thrown back in laughter, and the last an old one of me in my army fatigues. I found men were often bothered by my service, so it was best to weed those ones out right away. I quickly typed that I enjoyed working, working out, and hanging out with my son. In no time at all, I was swiping on the faces of men who lived in the area.

Thankfully, I was far away enough from the Strip to get actual residents of Vegas, but still, none of them really piqued my interest. None of them had burning sapphire eyes or a presence that jumped out of my phone. None of them had a smirk that both irritated and excited me.

Realizing I was being too picky, I swiped right on a couple I found mildly attractive. Almost instantly I got matched. I had no idea what came next. Messaging? Dates? I clicked off my screen. I'd figure it out later.

But first, I needed to swing by Sinopolis and take care of the business of the day. Killing a god. Releasing my braids so they could dry, I grabbed my bag and headed out. The Vegas sun-baked air immediately began drying the sweat on my body.

My eye caught on the back of someone slim in an orange hoodie near my car. Wait, they were trying to break *into* my car.

"Hey!" I called out.

Something clanged to the ground as the person bolted. I broke into a run after them but stopped at my car. One minute the hooded person had been there and next, they'd disappeared. On the asphalt lay a slim jim.

"Fucking car jackers." I picked up the flat piece of metal. "I never cussed this much before Jamal left. Guess that means I'm chilling out."

"What was that?"

I jerked my head up. A guy getting into his vehicle a couple cars away stood by his opened door. He thought I'd been talking to him.

"Uh, nothing. Just talking to myself." I hadn't done it this much since Rashon passed away. Another sign my stress was getting the best of me.

The guy gave me a strange look before getting into his car.

I sagged against my Jeep, feeling the weight of more than I could express into words. Glancing through the windows of my car, it occurred to me the attempted jacking might not have been about taking my vehicle.

Bob lay in their sheath, on the back seat.

Are you an idiot, Miranda? Leaving something that important out in the open?

I slid into the front seat, putting Bob up in the passenger side next to me. I managed to resist the urge to buckle them in. Now that would have been crazy.

I turned the engine on.

Side-eyeing the blade, I reached over and snapped the buckle in.

As I pulled out of my parking spot, I said, "I really am fucking losing my mind." Though something told me Bob was grateful to be extra secure.

Chapter Fifteen

THE BEAST

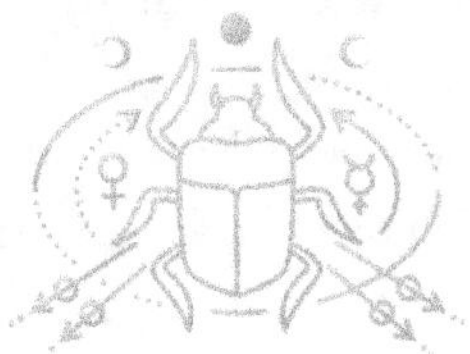

The ding of the elevator had me as excited as one of Pavlov's dogs. Whether it was the strike of her sword, or the slant of her mouth, the unrelenting pain that usually gripped me had become less potent. The searing agony that once clouded my thoughts and haunted my existence had dimmed. The debilitating bouts of madness, the blackout spells had been remarkably absent in the past few days.

It was as if the edges of my torment had blurred, faded at the seams, turning from vivid scarlet slashes of pain to muted hues of manageable discomfort.

Miranda, had begun to transform my endless torment into bearable stretches of anticipation.

Come kill me again, sweetheart. Kiss me again as you do.

Miranda emerged, her skin glistening more than usual. Tight fitting workout clothes clung to her muscular, tight body. I had to bite back a groan. Fucking hell, she was gorgeous. And fierce, and smart, and a hard-ass. I could *definitely* see what a hard-ass she was in those pants.

And I couldn't wait for her to kill me. She really was my personal angelic badass.

Before I could even open my mouth, she held up a hand. "You can't kiss me. Not ever again."

Some part deep inside me growled at my acquiescence, not wanting to promise any such thing. After all, hadn't her own spawn told her she needed to have fun last night? I could help. I could help her have *a lot* of fun.

Kissing her had been a hell of a lot more than just fun. It had been a revelation, a cataclysmic event that set my world ablaze. I'd been swept away in a torrent of raw emotion, of sensations I didn't know I was still capable of experiencing.

Her taste, her touch had seeped into the hollows of my existence, filling the spaces I hadn't realized were void. Her kiss was not just pleasure—it was a lifeline, an anchoring force that momentarily tethered me to the world of the living.

But I was, after all, a man on a direct course to death.

Though I selfishly didn't want to spend the rest of my life—short as it may be—knowing what she tasted like and not having her again.

Her eyebrows lifted expectantly. She was waiting for an answer.

I blinked. "Okay."

Her posture visibly relaxed.

"You're early," I pointed out in a gruff tone, trying to pretend I didn't care about what she just said. That it didn't rankle me, and that I instantly wanted to haul her up against the bars and kiss her until she lost it.

Calm down. You need her to kill you, not run off in a huff.

"It's my day off." She said it as if she'd been walking on a bed of nails and sucking on lemon juice the whole day.

The urge to laugh rose in me. Not a crazy explosive cackle, a genuine laugh. But I bit it back.

"And looks like you're enjoying every minute of it," I said.

Miranda pulled the blade from her coat and neared my cage. Every hair on my body rose with excitement. For my oblivion?

I inhaled deeply.

No. For Miranda. I was excited to be near my angel of death. Especially with the close call, I wanted to bury myself in her, lose myself in her and forget the monster I was.

She stopped inches away from me.

Sweet fucking reaper dogs, how does she smell even more delicious? If I didn't watch myself, my tongue would loll right out of my mouth, as I panted in lust like a cartoon character.

"Someone tried to get the blade," she confessed in a low tone.

All humor and attraction froze before cracking into a million pieces. I gripped the bars. "What happened, exactly?"

Miranda told me about the person in the orange hoodie. She couldn't even tell if it was a man or woman, or how old they were. They were slight of frame and fast as hell.

"They could have just wanted my car," she said, unconvincingly.

Panic gripped my chest in a vice before crawling up my throat like a gang of worms. "Miranda, you can't let anyone get their hands on that blade," I said.

She pushed some of her braids back in frustration. "You don't think I know that?"

"I'm serious. The consequences could be dire."

She got right in my face. "You seriously think I don't know? Of course, I know beast boy. I don't intend to let anyone take it from me."

My eyes trailed from the blazing fire in her eyes to the blade at her side. "Do you even know how to use that thing?"

Her lips quirked in displeasure as she cocked her hips in that way when she was annoyed or impatient. "I'm pretty sure I've proven that more to you than anyone."

I shook my head. "I mean, do you know how to wield a blade, sword fight?"

Uncertainty crept into her eyes.

So that's a no.

"See that panel over there?" I pointed to a box of electronics with buttons and levers. "You can open the door and come inside. I'll teach you how to use it so no one can ever take it from you."

"No fucking way."

My eyebrows shot up. "No fucking way?" I echoed. "Sweetheart. You need help, and I'm very invested in giving you that help."

"Oh yeah, Miranda," she mocked, "Why don't you walk into a cage and trap yourself with a feral, overly powerful god. Nothing could possibly go wrong."

I honestly couldn't tell if she was talking to herself or me.

"Miranda," I said sternly. "I won't hurt you. I promise." And I'd never been so certain of anything in my life. In fact, lately I calmed when she was near. Her mere presence drowned out the pain I experienced day in and day out. I couldn't account for it. It was more than my daily deaths. It was her.

Miranda eyed me. No one I'd ever known could pack so much suspicion or sass into one look. It devastated me in ways I hadn't expected.

"I can take lessons from someone else," she said finally.

I shook my head. "If a god is crazy enough to go for a snatch and grab of the blade, risking you'll stab them, you'll need to know how to fight them off using what you have. And you have the blade that can hurt them the most."

She shifted her weight onto the other foot. "I don't know if it was a god who tried to break into my car."

"It doesn't matter. If someone is trying, it will only encourage others to follow."

Miranda pursed her lips.

Wild, untamed energy rose in me. I wanted to rip the bars away. But not because I was losing control, it was because I wanted to get close to her. I wanted to get inside the clockwork gears of her mind to give myself a fighting chance.

Don't abandon me now. Let me in.

After what felt like an eternity, she raised the blade, pointing it at me. "If you step out of line, I'll kill you."

I let out a sigh of relief, my crazy levels dimming back down. "Perfect," I said in agreement.

"When should we start?" she asked.

I grinned. "What are you doing right now, sweetheart?"

* * *

WHEN SHE HIT THE BUTTON TO OPEN MY CAGE, AND THE BARS SLID to the side, I backed up, giving her ample room to assure her safety.

I jerked my head toward the controls. "You might want to turn the lights on too."

She did as I suggested, without taking her eyes off me. She didn't trust me. But I wouldn't be so callous with her safety.

Or maybe I was simply too desperate to get even close to the woman whose narrowed eyes could have sliced through me.

The kerchunk of the overhead lights was as abrasive as the sudden blinding light. "No wonder you prefer them off," she muttered, blinking against the assault. "And here I thought you were just playing at being Batman." Miranda froze, her eyes widening. "I'm sorry, you probably don't know who Batman is."

I frowned. "Of course, I know who Batman is."

Miranda waved a hand at my cage. "How? You don't even have a toilet in here."

Dammit, I had to suppress a smile again. "This is not the entirety of my quarters."

Her brows furrowed and her luscious lips deepened into a pout.

I pointed at the elevator. "I get notified when someone is coming down to my level and come out to this." I looked at the barren bars and sighed. "Greeting chamber."

"So where are your quarters?" she asked, coming closer to me. Then she looked over her shoulder.

"Worried, sweetheart?" She should be. With so many deaths, it was easier to control my power. But that didn't mean she was entirely safe. I was playing a dangerous game. But to protect the blade, it was worth it.

You won't hurt her, I assured myself.

Her head snapped back to me. "Don't call me that."

"Afraid everyone is going to figure out the badass has a sweet heart?"

Miranda rolled her eyes.

As she did so, I lunged forward and plucked the blade of bane from her hands.

"Hey," she cried out. "I wasn't ready."

Flipping the blade and offering the hilt back to her, I said, "That's the point, sweetheart. Now why don't you try to keep your hands on the most important weapon in the world and stab me if I come at you?"

"I don't want to hurt you," she said, taking the weapon back.

I blinked. "You kill me every day."

Miranda shrugged, clearly uncomfortable. "That's different."

I stepped closer to her, forcing her to look up several inches to meet my eye. We were so close. I could taste the kiss from yesterday and it sent a hot rush through me. "Maybe I deserve it."

Gods, was she really as painfully gorgeous as I believed, or had I just been away too long?

"I can be the judge of that, what did you do?" she said, her voice lowering. The moment somehow turned intimate.

Nothing separated us. I could sense her fear. But there was more than that. Excitement.

Was she thinking of that kiss yesterday as well?

My eyes lowered to those impossibly full lips. I regretted that I didn't get to explore them more yesterday. I didn't get to nibble on them. I didn't get to push my tongue past her teeth and taste the depths of her already intoxicating mouth. But then my imagination started to take things further. There were more places on this hot little human I'd like to probe and penetrate.

This close, I heard her heart rate speed up. My mouth quirked, trying to hold back a smile.

"Well? Are you going to tell me why you deserve to be punished?" she asked, before licking her lips. She asked one question, but her energy was nothing but excited, inviting.

I snatched the blade as easy as taking candy from a baby and backed away with a teasing grin.

The seductive energy about her evaporated instantly. I shoved her right back into frustration and mission-mode.

"I'm going to teach you how to use this thing, so you don't screw things up for both of us." The words were meant to be menacing, a dire warning, but I couldn't help my grin. I suddenly felt like I was a cat who'd been given a toy after eating a bunch of catnip.

* * *

I WRENCHED THE BLADE FROM HER HAND FOR THE THIRTEENTH TIME in ten minutes.

"You're still too slow." I spun the weapon in one hand. Vaguely, I wondered if she was impressed.

A growl of frustration rumbled from her throat. My scary little badass was getting worked up.

"Bob, you traitor," she muttered.

"I'm sorry. What was that?"

"Bob," she said, holding out her hand. "It's what I call the Blade of Bane."

My twirling stopped abruptly. "You named the most powerful weapon that can decimate immortals. . . Bob?"

Miranda pushed some braids back over her shoulder. "That's its name," she said impatiently. "Blade of Bane? B. O. B. Bob."

I observed the weapon in my hand, trying to swallow the moniker.

"Give it back," she said, her voice suddenly serious as a heart attack. Concern tightened her eyes, her shoulders squaring off.

I flipped the sword over, offering her the hilt again. Miranda took it and turned her back on me to walk to the other side of the cell.

"I don't even know if I should be doing this," she said, and I couldn't tell if it was for me or for herself. "The blade was given to me and only me. I was told I wasn't to allow it to fall into the hands of any immortal and here we are practically playing catch with the damn thing. I'm an idiot."

"You're not an idiot." The words came out harsh. Miranda's gaze flew up to meet mine. "And better me than someone who really wants it."

"How do I know you don't?" she accused.

"What?"

"How do I know this isn't some ploy to have Bob all to yourself?" She clutched the weapon tightly. "That you aren't luring me into a false sense of security so you can wield this weapon and slay gods and reap power?"

Extending my arms out, I said, "Miranda, the only one I want dead is me." That only made her frown deepen. "You're too serious," I observed.

"*I'm* too serious?" Miranda let out a scoff before crossing the distance back to me. "I have a duty. A duty to the blade to protect immortals and all of mankind. I have a duty to Bianca to take her seriously and not to destroy the world. And I have a duty to free you from your pain."

"Oh well then, I didn't realize you were so important."

She pointed Bob at me.

For fucks sake, was I really calling it Bob now too?

"That's not what I said."

I stalked around her slowly, in a circle. "Sure you did. You are the most important person on this earth, and you have zero time for pleasure or fun."

She twisted to keep her eyes on me. "And you are down here having a barrel of fun every day. Oh wait, that's just because you have zero responsibilities to anyone else but yourself."

My smirk fled faster than my good humor. "Don't compare us. We are not the same."

"No, no, go on. You can criticize me for trying to do the right thing, but I can't point out your hypocrisy. You don't have a pot to piss in, buddy. I may be struggling to figure out how to wield a power that could help or hurt the entire world, but you are only concerned about yourself. Would you even care if your death did trigger the end of the world? Or are you so selfish that you wouldn't give a damn? Maybe I should rethink this entire situation."

I stopped in front of her again. Power began to churn in me, responding to the bait. "Don't toy with me, Miranda."

"Why? Aren't you having fun? Isn't this the fun you are talking about? Don't you enjoy toying with me anymore, beast boy?"

A growl escaped my throat. "I'm helping you right now, protecting your precious little status of savior of the world."

"Excuse me?"

"You want to be a superhero, wielding Bob against the evils of this world? Well, I'm helping you right now. How is that selfish?"

"You are only doing it so the key to your freedom doesn't escape you," she shot back.

Okay, that was true, but the situation had become more complicated than that. I genuinely cared about Miranda's ability to protect herself. But she'd hit a hot button, and I wasn't up for admitting that.

Foolish little mortal scoffed at my attempt to help her? A million other people would beg for the chance to be favored by me. And she threw it back in my face.

"You're damn right. I don't want you fucking things up for me because you are too proud to get help. And that's what I'm doing, helping you." I said the words with as much condescension as I could muster. Fire flashed in her eyes. I'd pushed her too far.

"Please, you have nothing better to do. Is this really about making me spend time down here with you, so you don't feel so lonely?"

She might as well have cut me through the heart.

The instant look of regret told me she knew she went too far.

"You're right. I don't have anything better to do. Maybe I do just want you down here, trapped in this cage with me. I want you for entertainment, Miranda. Because I'm so bored and lonely." I laid the sarcasm as thick as a slab of butter on toast. Even so, I slunk toward her in lazy strides. Her back stiffened as she watched me approach.

"Although if I wanted you to help me pass the time, I could think of far more fun things to do than sparring." I looked her up and down, not bothering the hide the hunger I felt.

"Stop," she said, her tone stiff.

Even from a distance I could hear her heartbeat kick up. Fear? Or excitement?

"Maybe we could spend our time more pleasurably between deaths?"

What was I doing? Acting like a sexual predator, and I couldn't even blame my crazy on this one. Miranda had simply frustrated me into wanting to cross lines. I wanted to cross all her lines. It was only fair, wasn't it? A prisoner's compensation?

I studied her from top to bottom. From the absolute perfection of those long, tight braids, to her luscious lips, to the fullness of her breasts, the flare of her hips, and to the impossibly white sneakers.

This anal-retentive woman needed someone to shake things up for her. She was as brittle as a twig from all her pent-up emotions, and she had no idea. And fuck if I didn't want to be the one to break her.

Blood rushed south as I imagined what it would be like to get her to lose control. Could I get her to scream, to beg for more, as I pounded into her tight body?

Miranda's gaze bounced between my crotch and my face. The loose pants did nothing to hide my sudden arousal.

"Don't make me kill you," she warned, holding Bob up. Fear shone in her eyes. Was she scared of me? No, she was scared of what our argument had morphed into.

"You are going to have to, or Miranda," I said it slowly, licking my lips, "I'm going to kiss you so deep, I'll taste your soul. And then there will be no hiding from me."

Pain speared through my heart, taking my breath. We'd had quite a bit of time to recover from our sparring match, but Miranda was breathing as hard as if she'd run a mile.

Copper filled my mouth, and though I'm sure I looked gruesome, I couldn't help but smile. Because I learned something Miranda may not be fully aware of. She wanted me. She wanted me badly.

Chapter Sixteen

THE BADASS

What the fuck was I doing?

"A date, Miranda." I muttered to myself. "You are going on a date. Like a normal woman with a normal life."

My phone turned over and over in my hand. Last night I found one of my online matches was amenable to meet me for lunch.

The Mexican restaurant had brightly colored chairs and tables and mariachi music blared from the speakers. The place was relatively empty for a weekday at noon. It was my second day off and I'd found a totally new way to spend it.

After tossing and turning, dreaming of Xander, his hard body sliding against mine, in tandem with blood spurting out of his mouth from being stabbed, I got up extra early and hit the gym again. I'd gone until I'd exhausted myself, then cleaned up and showed up at the restaurant fifteen minutes early.

This is the right thing to do, I assured myself. You need to start dating and you absolutely cannot be thinking about a particular god who you killed to keep from kissing you.

I only killed him because I was terrified of how much I wanted him. If Xander kissed me, I don't think I'd let him stop.

When I saw him again tonight, I was determined to be on a totally new level. A new Miranda, in fact. The best, most exciting part of my day wouldn't be murdering the hottest, craziest god who clearly wanted to do bad, naughty things to me before I stabbed him to death.

New Miranda had a life outside that basement.

Maybe this guy I met would be so interesting I would think of nothing but this nice normal man after this date? Maybe I'd want to assault him with pillows and introduce him to my son?

My stomach lurched so I grabbed another handful of corn chips, hoping the food would help calm my nervous guts.

Catching sight of a tall man walking in, I paused my demolition on the bowl of chips. He was handsome, with neatly styled hair and warm brown eyes. His white linen shirt accentuated his tan features. He was attractive in a clean-cut way, just like in his pictures.

I smiled up at him as he held out his hand for a handshake. "Miranda, it's so nice to meet you in person. I'm Jim." He smiled brightly at me, and I could tell he was pleased with me in real life as well. No cat fishing here.

As we sat down, something similar to a bell, signaling the beginning of a wrestling match, dinged in my head. Let the date begin.

We ordered some tacos and shared about our families and our careers. He was a single dad, divorced, and worked in tech. He loved his two golden retrievers and golfed whenever he could. More than that, he was genuinely interested in me. He respected my time in the service without being intimidated or weird about it. He asked all the right questions about Jamal, relating my stories to that of his daughter, Abby.

Even though the conversation was nice enough, I couldn't help feel like something was missing; something intangible. Was this really a date? It had been so long since I'd been on one. I wondered if they were all just pleasant lunches with strangers until one lunch you suddenly wanted to bang their brains out.

Jim was nice. Perfectly nice. Uncomplicated, respectful, and...and, oh fuck I was bored. I was so bored I wanted to cry.

My thoughts slipped back to Xander's wicked grin and intense, ocean eyes; and that kiss he laid on me. Somehow, the ghost of our one kiss burned my lips as if reminding me of what I truly wanted.

Good luck, Miranda, I could almost hear him taunt in my head. *Think he can help you have fun?*

I shifted in my seat as hot liquid pooled in my lower belly.

"Are you alright?" Jim asked.

"Uh, yeah, sorry, I'm just a little distracted today."

Instead of getting offended, he leaned his elbows on the table and laced his fingers together. "Oh yeah? What's on your mind?"

It was a perfectly reasonable question. It was sincere and the right thing to say.

However, telling Jim I was counting down the minutes to when I could visit my crazy, feral god in the Grim Reaper's basement would not be an appropriate response.

"Work has been very intense lately," I supplied lamely. Jim didn't need to know I killed a guy to keep him from kissing me because I freaked out and worried I'd like it too much.

Or worse, that I was thinking I would have to do it again.

When the check came, I insisted on splitting, and Jim didn't protest.

His hand reached across the table, covering one of mine. "I really enjoyed this, Miranda. You are a beautiful, interesting woman, and I'd like to see you again."

The feel of his warm, dry palm on my hand should have been comforting. It should have felt good, like his words. But all I wanted to do was pull away. I somehow managed to keep it there on the table, stiff as a board under his.

"Thank you, Jim. That's very nice of you, but I don't think that would be a good idea. You are very nice yourself, but I don't feel that...spark. You know?"

It was like a switch flipped inside him. His warm brown eyes suddenly became cold and distant. His hand retreated.

Before I could take a breath of relief, he pushed away from the table and stood up abruptly. "Women," he muttered, shaking his head as he grabbed his coat off the back of his seat. "Never knowing a good thing when it's in front of them."

And with that, he turned and stormed out of the restaurant without another word.

I sat there for what felt like an eternity, stunned at what had just happened. Xander might be crazy and unpredictable, but at least I knew it.

This was beyond. For fuck's sake, was this what online dating was going to be like? Rubbing my forehead, I couldn't help but think this probably wasn't the *fun* Jamal had in mind for me.

Chapter Seventeen

THE BEAST

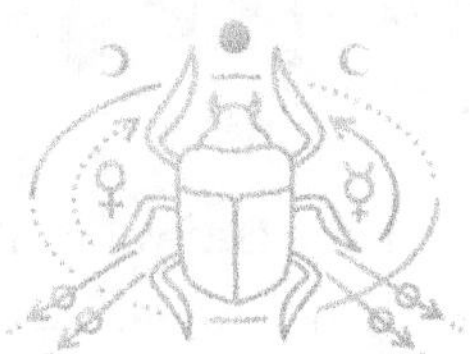

The next evening when Miranda came to see me, I had something new in mind.

"What is that?" she asked, blinking at my little setup. Her shoulders were stiff and her face was an unreadable mask. Miranda had turned stone cold again.

Because we'd broken a barrier and she came inside my cage? Because I kept taking Bob from her without much effort? Or because she was worried I would threaten to kiss her again, or worse, actually follow through with it.

Though I could see why she would find the setup in my cell strange today.

I looked at it again to make sure it wasn't. With my hallucinations, who knew what I'd pulled up from my chambers. It had required a special delivery from Timothy.

But no, I hadn't mistakenly laid out a banana and a pair of underwear, or something equally ludicrous from a delusion. It was a table with two chairs. On the table, a game was spread out.

"It's Monopoly," I said, stating the obvious.

"I know what it is. What's it doing here?"

"Why, sweetheart," A wicked grin slid onto my face. "You look as terrified as a lamb being led to slaughter. You aren't afraid of a little... fun, are you?"

"Don't be ridiculous." Her body stiffened further. If she tightened up anymore, the rod in her ass was in danger of breaking.

"I'm afraid I'm usually hysterical," I countered. "But I'm deadly serious about this, sweetheart. Taken on your son's advisement, you'd best start having fun. So we are going to fit a little game in before our sword training from now on."

Her gaze bounced between the board game and me with abject terror. "We don't need to do that."

"I suppose your tin heart couldn't handle a little game. You might be in danger of enjoying yourself, and we can't have that, can we? You are so very busy and important that there is no time for enjoyment."

Her lips thinned. I'd hit my mark, and my grin widened as I knew I had her now.

Miranda stomped over to the control panel and slammed her hand on the blue button, and the cage door unlocked with an audible crack.

* * *

ONE HOUR LATER AND NEITHER OF US WERE HAVING FUN. MIRANDA and I wore twin expressions of grim determination.

Not five, anything but a five. I can't get a five. My little ship can go anywhere else and I can survive if I just don't roll a five.

The dice fell from my palm, rolling across the board.

As soon as the cube settled, Miranda's eyes lit up with a vindictive fire. "Ha! Boardwalk baby." She pumped her fist before pointing at me. "You can't even afford it, honey," she said in an exaggerated tone that rankled all my chains.

A growl ripped out of my throat as I surged to my feet. The board went flying, sending her tiny hat and all the money into the air. The round table crashed on its side before rolling out of the way. Miranda jumped to her feet as well, facing off with me wearing a positively evil grin.

"How?" I yelled. "You must be cheating."

"Maybe I'm just that good," she countered.

Even though a part of me wanted to respond with a lascivious comment to that, I was far more aggravated about the loss. "How were you cheating? That is the only way you could have won!" I was shouting now.

"What? You can't believe a mortal can beat a god? Get used to it, beast boy."

"No," I said, tugging at my hair. "You can't have won because *I* was cheating."

Her victorious snarl evaporated as she stood there stunned. "*You* were cheating?"

"Yes." My fists clenched at my sides. "I was sneaking money from the bank the entire time. So you must have been doing so, as well. Or maybe you were cheating in some other devious way?"

Miranda's eyes narrowed. "You dirty little snake. Well guess what? I don't need to cheat to beat your ass."

Another growl of frustration emerged from me.

"Are we having fun yet?" she taunted, spreading her arms out. "Is this the fun you wanted to have? Because I'm having loads of it. I feel like a gleeful child again."

Tension flared between us, and the danger of the moment struck me.

Cold fear shot through me as I realized I was about to lose control and hurt her. Stressors far less than this had sent me into a raging blackout. Any second energy would plume and lash out in painful waves.

Yet it didn't come. A palpable current thrummed between us, but I wasn't teetering on the edge of sanity. The pain of my power had been reduced to a shockingly bearable dull roar.

Bob killed off even more of my power than I supposed. A wave of gleefulness mixed in with my combative, hot-blooded state. My emotions were always mixing swirling vortexes, but I was starting to enjoy this. Fighting with Miranda while staying in control.

Every movement of hers, every flash of her eyes, every sharp word that fell from her lips acted as a stimulant, heightening my awareness. This newfound sense of control didn't just keep my powers at bay, it fucking thrilled me. It actually thrilled me. Our combative tussles reminded me of two lions play grappling and it left my chest heaving and my dick hard.

As I pondered this new level of being, Miranda smashed her lips against mine.

Heat and arousal exploded in me. I met her kiss with my own ferocious energy. My tongue pushed its way past her lips and we both groaned as she opened up to me. My pants tightened. Her taste was still unreal, even more delicious than the enchanting scent of her skin. The softness of her mouth unhinged me in a way I'd never felt before. I hungered for her. Oh gods, I wanted, no needed to possess her. Everything else disappeared except for the woman and my white-hot need to devour her.

She slammed her hands into my chest, and we broke from each other.

"Get off!" she yelled, panting and flushed.

I ran my hand through my hair, reeling. Was I losing my mind? Had I kissed her and didn't realize it? I had only moments ago reveled in my control, but I must have imagined it.

Oh fuck, how out of control was I?

She was right. This was a terrible idea. Miranda needed to get out of here. We needed to put the bars between us. We could never do this again. Not while I was so out of mind to get to her. This uncontrollable level of passion would surely lead to me losing control in one way or another. While she hacked away at the beastly parts of me, another kind of beast had reared its head and wanted to take a bite out of her.

Miranda grabbed me by the back of the head and kissed me again.

Okaaay, maybe I'm not the crazy one here. She clawed at me like she couldn't get enough. I met her hungry kisses with my own desperation. I knew she had a deep vein of passion in her and apparently the levee had broken. My hands swept along the curve of her back as she clutched my shoulders. Oh fuck, it felt good. The feel of her body against mine after thousands of years of empty space around me, had something screaming from the center of my chest for more, more, more.

Her leg rose, and I caught it, wrapping it around my hips so my rising hardness could nestle at her center.

"Oh fuck," she whimpered as if the sensation caused her pain. I rocked into her softness and growled. Fuck, I wanted to be in her. I wanted to be in her so deep, she could taste me at the back of her throat. I shoved my tongue into her mouth, deeper. It was an assault, mimicking what I wanted to do to her. Fill her, finish her.

My fingers slipped under her shirt and ran along her warm, bare skin. I let out an even louder groan. I was so fucking aroused and caught between wanting to revel in the sensation of our touching and ripping her clothes off. It both satisfied me and drove my desire higher, hotter, until a sweat broke out over my body.

Miranda's hand slid over my chest and shoulders, gripped my hair as she rocked herself faster against me. She broke our kiss, gasping, her head falling backward. The little minx rode my hardness like a woman possessed. My raging need took a back seat as I watched her get off through our clothes. I placed a hand on her back and pulled her leg and hip forward, forcing her to arch further. I ground into her, feeling so hard I could pound nails with my dick. A wet heat spread between us with each rocking motion.

So close. We were so close.

The erotic vision she presented as she rubbed and groaned, face scrunched in concentration, nearly fucking undid me. If I hadn't already brought myself off by my hand twice today, I would have come right there. At some point, I'd picked her up by the hip, so she was writhing on me midair. My counter thrusts pushed her closer to the edge.

"Oh fuck," she gasped. "Right there, oh fuck, don't stop."

The world could explode around us, burn down, or freeze over and I wouldn't stop. I licked my lips, mouth dry from watching her, wanting her to finish. She had every iota of my rapt attention.

A long guttural moan left her throat before it hitched upward. Her eyes flew open, and her head snapped up as her body shuddered. I held her as she orgasmed, still rubbing against her sensitive cleft.

The sounds she made burned into me. Her scrunched up expression hit me like a sledgehammer. Her lips were parted even as she was locked into her orgasm, like the relief was so intense it was completely wringing her out. I stilled, suddenly afraid of moving. I didn't want this to end. I wanted this to be my eternity. Even with my own erection becoming painful, I didn't care. Not if I could experience this forbidden side of Miranda. My badass was an erotic visage and her clothes were still on.

The power she held over me was unprecedented.

Slowly I tilted Miranda into an upright position, sliding her down my body until her feet touched the floor. When those pretty brown eyes met mine, I realized there were flecks of emerald and gold surrounding her irises. Again, I wondered if she wasn't some kind of supernatural creature based on the hold she had over me.

Her glazed eyes all too quickly returned to their usual sharpness. They widened and her brows furrowed as I watched the uncertainty take hold of her. What I wouldn't give to keep her from where she was about to go.

Miranda pushed away from me gently, and I released her. I wanted to scream, but I swallowed it and fisted my hands to keep from grabbing her again.

I need you. I need you. I need you.

The demand throbbed in my mind, but I shoved it deep down.

It was only because of her and all she'd done for me that I was capable of grabbing hold of my madness with a tight grip.

Miranda's eyes held a strange wonder as if she were seeing me clearly for the first time. I studied her right back, drinking her in with my eyes, trying to brand the image in my mind. Her breasts rose like waves cresting the shore while sweat glistened on her face and skin like a river of diamonds. I fell into the fathomless black pools of her dilated pupils, while the heavenly scent of bergamot and sex wrapped around me.

Did she also notice the grasp I had on my sanity?

Fuck, not only that, where shards of electrified glass used to travel through my veins, I was now pumping hot with endorphins and desire. Is this what living felt like?

The only pain I felt emanated from hard-on so intense it pinched as well as throbbed. But witnessing Miranda succumb to release was far more gratifying. This might be the best day of my entire existence.

The best day since I met her lips for the first time.

It almost scared me to think of what tomorrow could bring. I'd never expected this. I had never expected *her*.

Her eyes bounced back and forth from each of mine, as if rapidly processing something. Then Miranda dove for her sword, grabbing it before plunging it into my chest.

Shock didn't even register, it happened so fast.

Regret instantly filled her eyes, along with the glassiness of unshed tears. Her hand shook on the hilt of the blade.

I understood. My little badass had let herself be vulnerable, and I'd seen it. She had to kill the witness.

I was always out of control and vulnerable, and it still pained me. It's why I didn't mind my condemnation to solitude. I didn't want anyone to see me like this. It only made me feel crazy.

She looked so scared. Scared of herself? Of what we just did? Of what she felt?

Life leeched out of me, but I reached out and covered her hand on the blade with my own. I tried to give her a reassuring smile.

It's okay. I'd die for you.

It was the best death I'd ever tasted. Knowing it would ease her pain.

And then I was gone.

Chapter Eighteen

THE BADASS

I ran out of there so fast I forgot my jacket. I merely clenched Bob as I dashed for the car. My brain raced. I couldn't get hold of a single thought until I was in my house with the door shut behind me.

Back against the door, I slid down. Strange mewling sounds escaped me. I didn't know what they were until I touched my face. I was crying.

"What the hell is wrong with me?" I asked out loud.

"It's likely all that killing. It can't be good for you," a voice answered.

I froze, fear slicing through my shame. "Who's there?" I jumped to my feet. Bob was poised out in a threatening manner to any intruder. The red of Xander's blood stained the tip and another wave of pain and shame smashed into me. Still, I remained vigilant.

"I'm right here." The voice said again. It was male with a French accent.

I swept my arm to the left and then the right, still seeing no one, though it sounded like it came from right next to me.

"Oh dear, I figured you might overreact."

My heart pounded out of my chest. Where was this guy? Had the thief trying to get in my car returned?

"You see, I've been quiet for many, many years. But it seems this has been damaging both of us."

"What is damaging?" I asked, still not understanding. I backed toward the center of the room, spinning slowly with the blade. The voice moved no further away yet no closer.

"All the killing. Normally I detest it, but Miranda this is really becoming unbearable."

What the fuck? The panic rose faster in my throat. "How do you know my name?"

"Well we have spent months on end together, though really it's only been the last several weeks that we've really gotten intense about this whole killing a god business."

No. No, I must be going out of my mind. Still, my eyes slowly fell to the glint of my blade.

"I've been killing gods, immortals, and fae for millennia but does anyone ask me how I feel about it?"

I dropped the sword and backed up fast as lightning, flattening against the door. "No. Way."

"*Ouch*. No need to be so dramatic."

"You," I said in a shaking voice. "You've been affecting my aim, trying to keep me from stabbing him."

"Well, yes. But can you imagine how it is for me? I may be an enchanted blade that kills immortals, but does anyone ask how *I* feel about it? Does anyone ask how *I* feel about all the blood and icky gore? No. Nobody cares that I'm squeamish or that I'm a pacifist."

My hands clutched my head. In the same day I have now flubbed a date, played monopoly against a god, dry humped him into a mind melting orgasm before I killed him, and now I was having a conversation with a talking sword.

"Bob?" I asked, hoping against hope I only had a mild hallucination and that it wouldn't speak again.

"I can't say I entirely appreciate the moniker, but I do feel it has brought us closer together. And while we are on the subject, I'd prefer you stop referring to me as 'they' or 'it.' I am quite a masculine weapon, and am a 'he.'"

"Oh my gosh, I can't handle this right now."

"Well unfortunately, you are the only one who can handle me, so you are going to have to get it together, Miranda."

"I—I've got to make a call," I said, then shook my head. Why the hell am I qualifying what I'm doing to a sword?

I left Bob there, in the middle of the living room and walked into the bedroom, shutting the door behind me.

I called Vivien. Thankfully, night had fallen, so I knew she would be up. Otherwise, she was dead to the world during daylight.

She didn't pick up. I called twice more before she picked up.

"What's wrong?" she asked immediately. I never called so insistently, so she knew it was urgent.

"Bob is talking to me."

Silence.

Well that's a first, my friend being at a loss for words, but not helpful right now. "The sword, it's talking to me," I reiterated.

"What is the sword saying?" she asked in a tone that suggested she didn't want to set off the crazy person any more than possible.

"He says he's squeamish about blood, that he's a pacifist, and oh also, he has a French accent." Okay. Maybe I did snap. Maybe this was all some fever dream brought on by Jamal's absence.

Or what I just did in the basement with Xander. Fuck, it scared me beyond anything. I'd gladly run back into a warzone than face the feelings that rushed to the surface after what we did. I felt completely wrung out, like something deep inside me had exploded and left nothing of me behind. And then I'd opened my eyes and found Xander watching me, looking at me like. . .like I don't know what. But I felt completely naked and the fear rushed at me a million miles an hour and I had to get away, I had to get him to stop looking at me like that, he had to stop seeing me. The me no one got to see.

So I stabbed him.

A *totally* proportionate reaction to the situation.

And now the sword took issue with my actions.

What the actual fuck?

I rubbed my face, my breath coming in short, panicked bursts.

"So we were wrong about Bob being nonbinary?" Vivien mused.

"Yes, but that's not the point. The sword is literally talking to me or I'm having a nervous breakdown."

"Have you been nervous?" she asked. I could hear she was taken aback.

"No," I answered automatically. "Yes. Maybe. I don't know." I covered my mouth, contemplating how much to say. Would I tell Vivien? She was my best friend. If anyone taught me it was safe to divulge about sexual encounters, it was her. But that was different. It was her and it didn't seem to make her vulnerable. Something about what I'd just done felt so completely shameful, I didn't know if I could even tell her.

For a brief moment, I was grateful for the talking sword to divert my attention from my issues with Xander.

Maybe it was time to invest in a therapist.

"Okay, okay, okay," she chanted as if trying to pull it all together. "Here's what we're going to do. I'm gonna wrap up my bullshit with the baby vamps and you are going to meet me at Sinopolis and we are going to get some answers."

"Okay," I agreed weakly. I felt lost. I never felt lost. I always had direction, duty, and my shit together. I had it so together, I had it together for everyone else. But in this moment, I could only follow my friend's orders and try not to think about anything.

Thirty minutes later, I strode into the grand lobby of Sinopolis. I tried to ignore the rioting feelings inside me at knowing what lay far below my feet.

Vivien was already there waiting for me, decked out in a red mini dress and knee-high boots.

"So what's the plan?" I asked.

"We are going to take a little visit to someone who would know all about Bob." Then she said in a hushed whisper. "Is he still talking to you?"

Maybe I had overreacted. Maybe it was a little mini mental break after what happened with Xander, and I just needed a chill night at home to restore my sanity. This was all unnecessary and I was being silly.

"Oh, she could put her hands around my hilt anytime," Bob said.

My face scrunched. Apparently, Bob was a bit pervy too. "Please tell me you heard that."

Vivien's green eyes narrowed in confusion. "No."

Dammit.

"Bob is definitely still running his non-existent mouth."

She twisted her lips and nodded solemnly. "I see invisible reaper dogs no one else can see, so I totally get you." Then her expression turned thoughtful as she tapped her lower lip. "Maybe that's why we're friends? Bonded by the crazy."

I was about to respond when a dark shadow advanced from behind her. With a quick look around, I noticed how suddenly empty the lobby was. A spike of cold fear shot through my stomach.

Then the dark mass came into focus, and I recognized Grim in his black suit. He held a finger to his lips, motioning for me to keep silent.

But Vivien already noticed I'd become distracted. Her eyes widened as she whipped around, arm swinging to land a punch.

Grim easily caught it. She threw out the other fist and he twisted her by the first arm until her back was to him. She tried to kick him, but he dodged out of the way. Their movements were concise and supernaturally fast as they fought.

Grim locked down both of her wrists in one hand behind her back, forcing her to face me again. The whites of Vivien's eyes nearly swallowed her irises as if she knew what terrible fate was about to befall her.

A fluffy white pillow poofed against her face with a gentle pat. When it dropped away, Vivien still wore the same stunned expression.

"That makes six to four," Grim said in a low rumbling voice before dropping a kiss on her cheek. He released her arms and turned to me. "Hello Miranda. I'd stay to chat, but my staying would only put me in danger."

And then he was gone, pillow and all.

"That sonofabitch," Vivien railed, throwing her hands up.

"So you're losing the war huh?" I was grateful for a distraction from my talking sword problem. Which was an even greater distraction from getting off on Xander's magnificent boner.

It was a Russian nesting doll of distractions.

"I ain't losing nothing," she said, holding out a finger. Vivien was incensed. "It isn't over until it's over."

As amused as I was by their hijinks, my mind travelled back to the disastrous Monopoly game between me and Xander. Had it been fun?

I enjoyed winning, and it brought out both of our competitive streaks, but I wouldn't necessarily call it fun. It was exciting though.

Then I thought of what happened right after the game. That had been fun. Until I realized what I'd done and it wasn't anymore. Shame washed over me again, but I swallowed it down.

Talking sword first.

Vivien led me to the garage and her cherry red Range Rover with the special tinted windows in case she got caught out in daylight. In no time, she drove us far off the strip to a warehouse. I knew this place. She'd brought me here once before.

We headed to the very back of a dusty factory to a freight elevator. Vivien pulled the cage aside and smashed the button. The cage jerked then descended at a painfully slow rate.

"I didn't bring any Doritos or bananas," I said casually. This wasn't my first visit, but that didn't put me anymore at ease. Vivien had been down here plenty of times before me, but that didn't mean either of us enjoyed what was to come.

"I didn't have time to grab them either." Vivien was silent for a beat. "I'm thinking we won't need a bribe though. Not this time."

She was likely right. If anyone knew about the blade it was the person we were about to see. And based on our past interaction, this person may have a vested interest in Bob.

When the elevator finished its descent, Vivien yanked the cage open. Overhead fluorescents turned on with heavy ker-chunks, lighting a darkened hallway.

A camera dropped from the ceiling, along with an automatic gun. It honed in on us, ready to strike if we made a wrong move.

"What do you want?" A familiar yet irate, tinny voice demanded from the microphone.

Vivien nodded at me.

I stepped forward though my hackles rose under the sights of a weapon. "I want to know more about the blade of bane."

Silence.

I looked over my shoulder at Vivien. She nodded again, encouraging me to go on.

I sucked in a deep breath before saying, "It speaks to me."

Another beat, and then the camera and gun zipped back up into the ceiling. I let out a breath.

We continued to the big double doors Vivien wasted no time sliding open. On one side there was a thirty-foot wall of fifty monitors. Some of them played anime, others played the news, but the majority appeared to be live footage of streets, shopping malls, or other public places.

The other half of the room looked as if someone had plucked a cozy grandmother's room and popped it in here. A girl lounged amidst the floral couches and chairs surrounding an antique coffee table. A large decorative rug cushioned the setup from the cold concrete floor.

A mixture of must and potpourri hung heavy in the air.

The high-backed chair in front of a long table of electronics and keyboards swiveled around.

A heavy-set woman in her late fifties squinted at us suspiciously. She spoke with a thick Filipino accent that was clipped with her impatience. "So, the blade speaks to you, does it?" Echo. We'd met before.

"Oh no, not her," Bob cried, clearly unhappy.

"Oh, quiet you," Echo shot back.

"Hi Echo," Vivien waved cheerfully at Echo, then at Echo's daughter, splayed on the couch. "Hi Aoiki."

Eighteen or so, Aoiki wore a school uniform decorated with chains and goth jewelry. Her wide nose and almond skin tone resembled Echo's, while her narrow yet mischievous, mono-lid eyes matched her Japanese father's.

The young girl waved back with a bright smile. "Hi Vivien."

Aoiki's head rested on the lap of another girl wearing a matching uniform, with serious eyes and a sleek, black bob. She was Asian as well with square features and even thinner eyes. Chinese, if I had to guess. She wore a matching school uniform to Aoiki's and from the way she stroked Aoiki's hair, I got the sense they were more than friends.

I didn't respond to Echo's acknowledgement of Bob's voice at first, unsure of Aoiki's companion.

"She's cool." Aoiki reassured me, as if reading my mind. "This is my girlfriend, Sunny."

"Hiya Sunny," Vivien said with another enthusiastic grin.

Sunny returned a small smile.

"Don't let that mad woman touch me," Bob carried on in a wail. "She's a brute. She tried to sharpen me by grinding me down, and she did it dry no less! Don't let her touch me, Miranda, I beg of you. I'm serious Miranda, take me out of here right now," Bob demanded.

"You are the whiniest weapon in all history," Echo groused. She didn't seem self-conscious in front of Sunny, so I guessed that was good enough.

"You can hear him?" I asked Echo, needing to hear the confirmation I wasn't alone in my crazy.

"Of course, I can," Echo said, getting to her feet and shaking out her brightly colored mumu. She grabbed the cane resting against the table and wobbled toward us.

Vivien and I came here when we'd been looking for the god killer, and Echo used her skills to help us locate it. But she'd made an addendum. She'd only help us find it if Vivien promised not to wield the blade. Not just that, Echo specifically told me I was the only one who could be its keeper, and we'd agreed.

"Don't listen to her, she's a brute," Bob sputtered.

"Okay, one of you needs to explain what the hell is going on, right now," I demanded.

Vivien's eyebrows shot up in confusion before her gaze settled on the blade and she realized she was missing part of the conversation. So she slipped away and crashed on the couch next to Aoiki. It was then a little white wiggling nose poked out from under the couch. A small white rabbit with black circles around his eyes, army crawled out from under the couch and immediately jumped up into Vivien's lap.

"What's up Darth Vader?" she cooed affectionately. He sniffed her in earnest. Then a fawn-colored rabbit the size of a small dog lumbered out from behind the couch. Her big ears stood out tall from her long face and flopped gently as she made her way to over to Vivien as well. "Hi Lulu," Vivien added, reaching over to scratch between the long ears.

The genetically engineered rabbits had been crucial in our mission to retrieve the blade, serving as the perfect distraction.

And though they were adorable, and my hands itched to go pet their soft fur, I needed answers.

"Why can you hear the blade? Why did you pick me to wield it? What aren't you telling me?"

Echo's face tightened. She was a volatile, explosive woman and I expected she was preparing to lash out at me. But then she let out a big breath as if all the fight left her. "I suppose if we must do this, we might as well do it over tea. Ryuki," she bellowed loudly enough to make me flinch.

A sweet smiling man popped out from a door on the far side. His build was sparse, his head almost bald and he wore an apron as he carried a tea tray. There was something about him that reminded me of an imp who lived in an ancient wood from one of Jamal's story books. "Yes, my beloved," Ryuki answered his wife.

"We'll need more cups," she said.

Soon we were all settled in the makeshift living room, everyone holding a cup of tea. Lulu lumbered over to my side and I was happy to reach over and pet her head. She leaned in gratefully.

"Why do you know about Bob?"

Echo's permanent scowl only deepened. "Bob?"

"The Blade of Bane. Bob," I explained.

"Ha!" Aoiki laughed as she put an arm around the very quiet Sunny. "That's awesome, I love that."

Even Echo's lips twitched at that.

"It's not funny," Bob announced with a sniff of offense. I don't know how he managed that without a nose.

Looking at Ryuki and Aoiki, I asked, "Can you hear it too?"

They both studiously averted their gazes. Even Sunny became far too interested in her cuticles.

"What the hell?" Vivien flopped her hands on the couch. "Am I the only one out of the club? I want in on it too."

"Why?" I asked again.

Echo sipped her tea then set it down with a heavy sigh. "I've been alive a little longer than you."

Aoiki snorted and Echo shot her a stern glare. Still, her daughter said, "try a couple thousand years older."

Wait, what?

"Aoiki," Echo snapped in reprimand.

"What?" Aoiki shrugged. "You are beating around the bush which totally isn't like you."

While I was still reeling from the new information, Ryuki reached over and squeezed his wife's shoulder. "My love, she deserves to know."

"Fine, fine," Echo waved a hand, before it settled on her husband's hand.

"Are you gods?" Vivien asked, her jaw having gone slack.

"No, but we have been here almost as long. We are what some would refer to as fae."

"Fae as in fairy?" I asked in disbelief. I knew the term from some of the books I read to Jamal in kindergarten.

Echo nodded slowly while Ryuki smiled at me. Aoiki watched me as if my top might blow. Sunny averted her eyes as she sipped her cup of tea. *Her too?*

My brain hit a brick wall and went splat. I put my tea down and stood up, paced away then came back again.

That's it. Too much for Miranda to handle in one day.

"Oh my god, you have to show me your wings," Vivien said with a squeal.

Chapter Nineteen

THE BADASS

"Fairies. You are telling me you are fairies?" A bit of hysteria had crept up into my voice. I fought it back down.

Ryuki grinned and blushed in a way that was far too adorable for an old man, while Aoiki watched me with a mischievous sparkle in her eye, as if waiting for me to blow a gasket so she could pull out the popcorn. Sunny seemed more apprehensive about me blowing my top. Echo simply studied me with her usual scowl, waiting for me to accept the truth.

"First vampires exist, then Egyptian gods, and now fairies." Vivien clapped her hands. "There have to be werewolves, ooooh maybe mermaids?"

One of Echo's eyes bulged grotesquely while the other narrowed in displeasure. "We prefer the term fae. And the supernatural has a way of hiding in plain sight, only the keenest can find them."

The hungry look on Vivien's face intensified. "That wasn't a no," she said in a sing-song voice.

I also couldn't help but notice that it wasn't a no.

"Are you going to pop?" a hesitant Bob asked me.

After becoming a vampire, Vivien had embraced the supernatural lifestyle and most of its eccentricities. I'd been on the outskirts of a lot of the immortal battles and in a couple myself. While I learned to be highly adaptable in the Army, I still found this new world pushed my limits.

Focus on what's important, Miranda.

"So the fae are immortal, like gods?" I pulled my shit together and throwing any would-be hysteria in a box and filing it away for either later, or never.

"No," Echo shook her head while rewrapping her fingers around her cane. "But we do live an awfully long time." She rapped the walking stick against the ground with an explosive clack that bounced off the warehouse walls. "And we don't forget easily."

"How old are you? I always thought you were twenty-five." Vivien flattered Ryuki.

The old man blushed at her flirtatious question. He spoke with a heavy Japanese accent. "Oh, you are close. But more like two thousand and twenty-five."

Vivien sat back. "Whoa." Then she turned to Aoiki.

Aoiki still maintained that mischievous glimmer. "I'm the baby of the family. I'm only five hundred and sixty-two. And a couple years younger than this hottie," she said, jerking her head toward Sunny. Their fingers twined and released repeatedly, playing with each other's hands.

Vivien turned to get Echo's age, but the old woman snapped. "It's not polite to ask a lady her age."

Ryuki reached over and grabbed one of her hands. "You age like a fine wine, my beloved." Then he dropped a kiss across her knuckles. Her expression softened and her cheeks reddened like little apples.

Vivien and I exchanged a look, and I knew we were thinking the same thing. The woman acted more like curdled milk, but we would never voice that.

"Bob is a fae blade?" I needed this all spelled out for me. It was too much to comprehend as a grown woman with her feet firmly on the ground.

Who was I kidding? I was spiraling further into a world that seemed to get deeper and darker with every step.

"That is correct," Echo said matter-of-factly, returning her hands to rest on the top of her cane.

"So why me? Why not have a fae wield the blade?"

The weight of something pulled at Echo's features, aging her almost instantly. "Because you are mortal. You know the value of life. Because you are a warrior. You have had to balance the choice before in war. Because you are a just person, Miranda."

My eyes narrowed. "How much do you know about me, exactly?" I didn't like the idea of someone checking up on me. Privacy mattered to me, especially with a young son.

Echo raised an eyebrow in challenge and swept an arm toward the monitors. "I see, and I calculate. It's part of my magic."

"And also, your talent," Ryuki added, beaming at his wife.

Echo jabbed a blocky index finger in the air. "If not for your involvement, I would not have helped unearth the blade of bane."

Vivien stilled, her expression suddenly serious.

Echo went on. "In ancient times, the gods became tyrannical, unruly. They were cruel and callous with the rest of the creatures of this earth. Soon, the fae found themselves in danger of being extinct, as the gods had become greedy and coveted their magic. The fae needed a way to fight back. So the oldest and strongest of us harnessed their powers to create a powerful weapon able to cut down the gods. It cost our fae elders their lives, but the blade of bane was born."

"Next thing you know, she'll pull out my baby pictures," the blade whined.

"Shh," I hushed at him, so she could go on.

"The fae finally leveled the playing field and through an example of force and power, were able to cut down the most greedy and dangerous of gods. It was then that balance was restored."

Ryuki's eyes dropped to the ground, shaking his head. "But the fae warrior grew too powerful with the blade and began to kill indiscriminately, both fae and gods alike. And we had to turn on the fae warrior to take the blade back. It was then decided that the blade was too powerful, and we hid it, even from ourselves. Once in a great many years, the blade will surface at the time it is needed most. And then when it completes its mission it is lost to us all for a time again."

"What is your mission, Bob?" I asked.

"As you may have noticed, I cannot control my comings and goings. But I must concur that I've noticed I am found at pivotal times. I believe that is part of my magic. Though I must say that this is the first time I have been wielded by a mortal. Inevitably when a fae gets their hands on me, oh it all starts out roses and sunshine. Well except for the murdering bit. But then they grow hungry for power, and they all eventually turn corrupt with time."

"But I can't be corrupted by time because I'm mortal," I added.

"That is what I am hoping," Echo said with a sigh.

Vivien raised her hand. "Question. Does this mean that these little dudes aren't genetically engineered?" She pointed down at Darth Vader who had settled on the couch next to her.

Aoiki laughed. "They are familiars. They are their own kind of magic. We are engaged in a magically symbiotic relationship. They help us and we help them. Not very differently from how the gods and sekhors join to their mutual benefit."

I reached down to scratch Lulu's head. The oversized rabbit pushed her head up, directing me to stroke her nose.

"There aren't many familiars, just like there aren't many fae. Our numbers are few," Aoiki clarified.

"And we like to keep to ourselves." Echo announced.

"Speak for yourself," Aoiki muttered while sharing a look with Sunny, making me think her girlfriend had similar feelings. Her mother sent her a sharp look. Echo barked words in a language I couldn't even begin to identify.

Aoiki's eyes dropped to the ground, but I doubted she'd stay quiet on whatever disagreement they were in for long.

"What makes you think my judgement is so great?" What with Bianca urging me to stop killing Xander as it will bring about the end of the world, and my feelings for Xander, I felt more unsure than ever. "I don't know what I'm doing," I confessed.

Echo squinted one eye at me, studying me closely. Or perhaps trying to see into the secrets of my heart. Who knows all that she is capable of.

"Before you even set foot in here, I knew everything about you there is to know, on paper that is."

By the glint in Echo's eye, I suspected she knew *much* more than just paper judging by the monitors on the wall.

"I calculate, I see patterns, behavior, and trends. I know you, Miranda. You will make the right decision."

I finally gave into my instinct, sliding down to the floor to pet Lulu who happily crawled right into my lap for more affection. For some reason that made me want to cry. "Is this the part where you tell me to trust my gut?" My voice was hoarse.

"No," Echo snapped. "You do not make decisions from the gut. You make your decisions like this one does," she jerked her head toward Vivien. My vampire friend froze petting Darth Vader to pay attention, as if she were an escaping convict caught in a spotlight.

The tight muscles in Echo's generous jaw line relaxed as she leaned in. "With your heart."

The soft long ears slid between my fingers as Lulu set her head on my thigh, leaning into my touch. "You want me to follow my heart? Like this whole thing is a Disney movie?"

Bob snorted. I wasn't even going to begin to ask how the hell he got my reference. When did French-accented swords get a chance to binge Disney movies?

No, I was too caught up on the hard reality of my situation. Extracting myself from the sweet rabbit, I rose to my feet. "You want me to follow my heart? When my whole job is literally to kill others? How in the ever loving fuck weasels am I supposed to do that? Killing and love have nothing to do with each other." My voice had reached a frenzied peak.

"Love?" Vivien echoed. Her eyes were fastened to my face, as if stunned to find something there she hadn't noticed before.

My stomach dropped out from my body with a hundred-mile whoosh. What the fuck did I just let slip out? Did I really say that? "Heart. I mean heart," I corrected far too adamantly and far too late.

Then Vivien and the others averted their gaze as if trying to give me a private moment, which only served to further wash me in my shame.

Love? Was I serious? That was ridiculous. I didn't love him.

I was just lonely, and desperate for some physical connection. Yeah, that's it. I went on one bad date, and it made Xander more attractive. But only temporarily.

The amount of deep, soul moving connection, and excitement I felt when it came to fighting and flirting with Xander had nothing to do with anything. That was a childish notion, and I left childish things behind me when I gave birth to one.

But why the hell would I say *that*? The 'L' word? Is it because I felt I met my match?

Wow, Miranda, we think highly of ourselves, don't we? Our only equal could be a god?

But something in my gut pulsated with an undeniable knowing.

I couldn't shake how Xander listened to my child from a scant few minutes of conversation and then went to the lengths to set up a ridiculous board game, to help me have *fun*. Even if it had been an abysmal failure, the thought he put into it had rocked me. And then he unearthed something far more vital. The sexy, unrestrained woman I wanted to be.

Every time I visited him, he cracked me open a little more. He was fearless in the face of my strength, something that had intimidated others. Rashon, my first husband, had always tiptoed around me whenever I was 'on edge', but not Xander. He leaned into my intensity, eagerly craving more.

But it wasn't just about what he did for me. Whenever his god-like facade cracked, Xander's vulnerability peeked through, humanizing him in ways I never expected. The dry humor that laced his words, even in the midst of his darkest moments, struck a chord in me, revealing a wit and resilience that I found irresistibly compelling. I craved those glimpses of his genuine self.

Despite his pain, or maybe because of it, Xander's character shone brightly, raw and unabashed. He was a raging storm, yet he had an inexplicable calming effect on me, like the eye of the storm - still and serene amidst the chaos. The raw honesty of his struggle resonated within me, a poignant melody to my own inner battles.

He was a whirlwind of chaos and pain, yet in those moments, I found myself drawn even closer to him. I felt an inexplicable desire to soothe his torment, to stand by him in his battle, to become his rock.

It had grown beyond mere attraction; it was a connection that penetrated deeper, into the very core of my being.

It was fucking exhilarating. It was life altering.

I was the biggest idiot of all time.

While I struggled with my insane emotions, Aoiki was the only one who didn't shy away. She nailed me dead in the eye. "Sometimes it happens like that. Sometimes love smashes into you like a Mack truck, and rationale has no ground to stand on. You can either go with it or dig your heels into the ground and miss the opportunity to fly." Her hand tightened on Sunny's, and the other girl met Aoiki's gaze with a mirror of loving devotion.

The serious admission from a girl who seemed so young—excuse me, a five hundred something year old fae—only unsettled me more.

We had gotten so far afield of why I'd come. I came to learn more about Bob, about why I'd been chosen to carry him. Putting my professional voice back on like one dons a jacket, I said, "Thank you for the information and the tea. I may be in touch in the future regarding the talking sword. I appreciate your time."

Then I shot a hard look at Vivien. She picked up on her cue and extracted herself from Darth Vader and followed me out without another word. Thankfully Bob also remained mercifully silent.

Only when we stood in the freight elevator side by side, did she speak.

"Do you want to talk about it?" she asked, her voice softer and more careful than I'd ever known her to be. It would have been far more normal if she came at me like a battering ram, demanding to know more. It only heightened my awareness of how wrong and screwed up I was.

I said I loved the god I killed every night. Maybe I was as mad as he was.

"Nope," I said, popping my 'p.'

I could feel her disappointment fill the space around us. Great, now I felt guilt on top of everything else.

Vivien was an absolute open book. Everything she thought or felt came out, and I supported that. Her free, open expression was part of her.

But it must look like I didn't trust her, but it was really because I couldn't face my own feelings much less put them all out in the open air. They would solidify, become real, and I couldn't afford that. It was better to keep all my rioting emotions inside under lock and key.

Vivien opened her mouth and then closed it several times as if debating what to say. Finally, she landed on, "You don't have to kill him."

My body nearly sagged with the weight of her words. Because it was something I so desperately wanted to believe, but at the very center of my heart I knew it was the right thing to do. I had to release Xander from his torment. Even if that meant carving off a piece of myself in the process.

So all I said was. "Yes, I do."

Chapter Twenty

THE BADASS

My heart pounded as I ran through the darkness, my lungs burning with each breath. I stumbled, catching myself just in time before I fell face first onto the ground. The scenery swirled around me. The bright lights of the Vegas Strip, the polished black marble of Sinopolis, and then the vast desert stretched out before me in a barren, deathly wasteland.

Fear had taken hold of me. Something was stalking me, something malevolent, and larger than life.

Running faster, I pushed myself to flee, until I couldn't breathe, my eyes watered and stung.

The sands pulsed and a wave of black rushed over them, turning the hard granules into soft silt, making it even harder to move.

BOOM. The earth shook.

"Miranda." A voice called out my name. I couldn't tell if it was male, or female. All I knew was it hungered to take me. Claim me? Kill me? I didn't know.

Sweat covering me, my legs started to give out, but I pushed on.

BOOM.

Something massive was right behind me. It was too big, too powerful and I wouldn't survive it.

Then I felt it. A pin prick of burning on my back. I instantly felt scorched as it spread. I was an ant under a magnifying glass.

"Miranda." The voice called again, just as my body finally gave up. My knees buckled and I crashed to the ground. I was covered in sweat, every bit of muscle trembled and shook from the exertion. A strangled sob escaped my lungs. I couldn't catch a breath.

As the entity drew closer, the heat from my back spread until it was suffocating, and I felt like I was going to burn up from the inside out. I wanted to scream, to fight back, but I was paralyzed with fear and pain.

My gaze lifted enough to see Xander in the distance. He paced back and forth on the silt, behind his bars. His sapphire eyes burned, wild with fear. He was the only one who could protect me, but he couldn't escape his prison. Xander shook the bars, but they were immovable.

The heat grew stronger, burning me alive. God, it hurt so fucking much.

"Miranda," Xander reached out to me through the bars. "You have to kill me. It's the only way to stop him."

I shook my head, tears streaming down my face. I couldn't do it. I couldn't kill him, even if it meant saving the world.

In my last moments, I turned to face the presence more powerful than the sun. A scream caught in my throat before frying away, my flesh sizzling and turning to ash.

My eyes flew opened. Still covered in sweat and violently shaking, the world came into focus as I woke from my nightmare.

I found myself on my knees, the cold, coarse texture of concrete biting into me. I trembled, disoriented and vulnerable, like a newborn calf dropped into an alien world.

Where the fuck was I?

Harsh, flickering fluorescent lights punctuated the dimly lit cavernous space. The sharp, metallic smell of oil and stale air invaded my nostrils.

A parking garage?

Someone bellowed my name. "Miranda," Bob yelled. I gripped him fast, but he was so heavy my shoulders tilted to one side. His metal shook, as if he were trying to wake me up.

"I'm awake," I said, my words hoarse. Barely able to maintain my balance, I tried to rise, my shaky limbs protesting against the effort. I had to figure out how I ended up here. But first, I needed to stop trembling.

"Oh, sweet Afterlife," Bob breathed. "I couldn't wake you up."

"H-how did I get here, Bob?"

His tone was darkly serious. "You got in your car and drove here. Your eyes were open, but you were unresponsive."

Looking over my shoulder, I saw my car perfectly backed into a spot. Straightening slowly, I noticed it was the parking garage of Sinopolis. On unsteady legs, I made my way back to my vehicle, collapsing in the driver's side. I set Bob down on the passenger side.

"How are you feeling?" Bob asked gently.

My lips twitched at the corner. Yesterday I'd been beyond freaked out by my talking blade, but today I was grateful for his presence.

"Not good, Bob. Not good at all." Somehow being honest with him was easy.

"There there," he soothed. "We need to get you home, with a nice cup of tea. Perhaps. . .perhaps we should find someone to drive us home?"

My knuckles flexed on the steering wheel as I turned the car on with my other hand. I'd left my keys in the ignition. It was just after four am. Cold air blew from the vents and it felt good against my overheated body.

"No," I breathed. "I got this. It was just a nightmare." Still, I didn't put the car into drive. I just sat there, trying to find my footing.

"I've never done any sleep walking before, Bob," I said, voicing my concern.

"I'm not so sure you were sleep-walking, Miranda." he said, still using that gentle tone.

I sighed, resting my forehead against the steering wheel. "I was dreaming. Dreaming of something terrifying, something that was coming for me. It was going to burn me up, burn the whole world up. Like a vindictive sun."

"Sounds frightful."

"Xander can't do that can he?" I was scared to ask the question. It was more for myself anyway. Was my subconscious detecting a danger in him that Bianca had foretold?

"No," Bob said with certainty. "I've tasted his blood many times now, unfortunately," he said with evident disgust. If he had a nose, it would be severely wrinkled. "The god's dominion is water and the seas. While Nun, or Xander, possesses an unsteady current of electromagnetic field of power, it can't do what you describe."

I let out a breath. Since when did I take stock in dreams?

Since you sleep-walked from your house across the strip to work, my brain answered.

"Hey Bob?" I turned the AC off, my sweat having turned ice cold on my body.

"Yes, Miranda?"

"Do you know who tried to break in the car that day I was in the gym?"

"I didn't see their face, whoever it was wore glasses and a bandana."

I pulled the car out of the garage and headed back home to catch a couple more hours of sleep. It didn't make any sense, but I couldn't help feel the strange occurrences were related.

Things had gotten too complicated, and it was far past time that I simplified them.

Chapter Twenty-One

THE BEAST

Would she come again? Or would she leave me here? For once the pain of my existence didn't hinge on the influx of my power.

It stemmed for my insatiable hunger to rest my eyes on Miranda, hear her voice, eek some bit of personal information about her.

What else did she label other than her lunchbox?

What did she do at work all day?

What did her bedroom look like?

Did she like flowers? And if so, what kind?

I'd gotten a glimpse at the real, unguarded woman and she was even more powerful and ravishing than I first supposed. Nothing else mattered but getting another little piece of her into my damned existence.

I spent most of my day pacing the cage, unable to be anywhere else. I'd lived for millennia but this, *this* felt like eternity.

Come to me, come to me, I chanted even as my eyes remained fastened on that elevator, willing it to ding and announce her arrival.

If it took years to will her back, I would do it. I would pace here day and night until I manifested her return.

The high-pitched chime of the elevator nearly sent me to my

knees. My heart threatened to burst out of my chest in the few seconds before the doors opened.

Oh gods, oh fuck, why did I feel giddy and anxious and possessed all at once? I paced back and forth along the bars even faster.

When she stepped out of the elevator, I stopped cold. Miranda had donned casual attire again. Tight fitting athletic pants that rose to her mid waist, leaving a few inches of bared flesh between that and her sports bra. She wore her signature leather duster and a pair of boots. Her deep bronze skin gleamed as if she'd been exerting herself physically, and suddenly I was as parched as a dying man. Whatever activity or workout she'd clearly been partaking in only intensified her scent. I inhaled a shuddering breath as I gripped the bars, my cock hardening. Suddenly, I knew with absolute certainty I could rip these metal barriers out of my way to get to her if I needed.

Despite the energized gleam in her eyes, lines of either worry or exhaustion lined them. Normally she seemed serious and duty driven, but today there was some air of sadness surrounding her.

Was this because of yesterday? What about our interchange could have made her...sad?

"What is this?" she asked, looking past me to the round table I had set up again.

I couldn't tear my eyes away from her even as I answered. "It's a game. It's called Candy Land. I thought we could try again."

"We can't play games anymore, Xander." Her voice was flat and empty.

I instantly hated it. I needed to stoke the fire I knew burned bright inside her.

Sass me, fight me, fuck me, just don't detach.

I smirked, running my hands up and down the bars. "Of course, we can. What else are you going to do with your time off? Not to mention your kid said—"

"Don't talk about my kid," she snapped.

Miranda was strung even tighter than before.

"Is this about yesterday?"

Instead of answering, those luscious, perfectly kissable lips pursed.

It was. I didn't know if she was embarrassed, ashamed, or disgusted of what happened, or because it happened with me.

A better man would tell her what she wanted to hear.

It won't happen again.

We can keep it professional.

But I wasn't a man at all. I was a half-feral god who scented a woman more powerful, more resilient than any immortal I'd encountered. So I wouldn't lie to her.

I *didn't* want to respect her boundaries. I wanted to cross these bars and plow straight through her emotional barriers and get to her the way she got to me. I wanted her obsessed, smitten, and hungry as fuck for more of me.

So I did something else. I pushed one of her big bright red buttons.

"Are you telling me you are afraid to play Candy Land, a child's game with me?" I scoffed, arranging my face in the most condescending smirk, as if I'd known she was a lowly human without a backbone all along.

It couldn't be further than the truth, but Miranda couldn't know that I was a god ready to worship at her mortal feet. For one more kiss, one more death.

The trepidation hardened in her eyes. I'd hit my mark, but I needed another strike or two.

"You're afraid you can't control yourself around me because you are falling in love with me, sweetheart? Because if you can't manage this simple task, we might as well forget about blade training." I let my lip curl in disgust.

Her posture stiffened.

Just one more little push.

I raised my hands as I let my expression smooth with indifference. "But my mistake, I didn't know you'd be so emotional about boardgames. I'll put it away."

Something defiant flashed in her eyes as her nostrils flared.

My heart stuttered at seeing her riled up. It beat out an excited message of anticipation.

Miranda stalked over to the control panel and hit the button opening my cage. "Let's get this over with so I can kick your ass, *after* I finish kicking your ass." She dropped into the chair across from me.

As the doors to my cage opened, I knew I had her right where I wanted her. I grinned, savoring the thrill of the chase, knowing that every move I made was a calculated risk, and every breath I took brought me closer to my ultimate goal.

Time. I just earned myself more time with Ms. Badass herself.

Miranda sat across from me, eyes flashing with defiance as she glared at me over the game board.

I leaned forward, locking eyes with her. "You know I'm going to beat you this time, right?" I said, trying to goad her into a response.

She rolled her eyes, shaking her head. "In your dreams, beast boy. You cheated last time, but it didn't help you then. What makes you think it will help you now?"

I darkly chuckled, picked up and shuffled the cards with colored squares on them. "Oh, you think you're so clever, don't you?" My voice dripped with sarcasm. "I have a few tricks up my sleeve this time. And don't worry, I'll play fair."

"Oh that's reassuring," she said dryly, then sniffed. "Even if you cheat, I'll still kick your ass. Just like last time."

Her competitive mode had been activated and she wasn't even thinking about what had happened after the game yesterday. I liked her in here, in these bars with me, comfortable and unafraid.

But *I* couldn't forget a single sensation about the softness of her full lips or the inferno she made explode to life inside me yesterday.

Miranda pulled a card first, the colored blocks determining how far her little gingerbread man could go. Her face was a tight mask of fierce intensity. We went on for a couple rounds, our cards keeping us neck in neck on the board.

And as the game progressed, I found myself becoming more and more invested in the outcome, driven by a fierce desire to come out on top.

Then I lost my edge, she advanced several spots in front of me.

"Ha!" she exclaimed, giving me a smirk. "Looks like I'm in the lead."

I narrowed my eyes at her. "Don't get too confident, sweetheart. You haven't even gotten to the Peppermint Forest yet."

She raised an eyebrow. "You realize we are taking this game far too seriously, don't you?"

I shrugged, pretending to be nonchalant. "I just don't like to lose."

I was focused on the dark angel across from me rather than the board in front of me. I learned yesterday that playing games with Miranda was more than just a way to pass the time. It was a way for me to push her boundaries without scaring her.

I gave into my long-standing curiosity and asked, "Do you miss him?"

Without even looking up, Miranda responded. "Always. He's the light of my life and while he's away at camp, the house feels colder, emptier. But Jamal loves camp, and he'll be back. I'd do anything just to see him smile."

Something in my chest swelled uncomfortably at hearing her devotion to her son, and how he gave her life. It made me want insane things. Like to meet this kid who she thought hung the moon, or even be like him in making her life fuller, more complete. I wanted to be that reason for the secret smile at the corner of her lips, or the sparkle in her eyes. I was a selfish sonofabitch.

"I actually meant your husband," I corrected.

Miranda's eyes slowly raised up to meet mine, their light brown sugar hue captivating me. Against the smooth, silky texture of her skin, they shone like precious gems, drawing me in closer. "Oh. You mean Rashon." Her voice, soft, flowed over me, sending shivers down my spine.

Jealousy warred with my need to know how she felt about a dead man. I'd no doubt he was worthy, not just because he died a hero's death, but because he'd earned the respect and love of the woman across from me.

Her gaze fell back to the board game though I know she wasn't actually seeing the brightly colored illustrations. She was looking inward for the answer to my question. How deep did she bury her feelings for him? I knew she'd covered them up and pushed them down like she did all her emotions, but the question was how far? Was she so in love that the pain required a deep grave in her mind so she could function?

That idea created a sour taste in my mouth.

She started slowly. "Rashon and I were very young when we got married. He was a good man." Her expression softened, the corners of her lips curving up as she dove into her nostalgia. "He had the greatest smile."

My fists balled into fists at my sides. How often had I smiled at Miranda? Was it pleasing? Or did it only communicate my bitterness and pain?

Why was I being childish and comparing myself?

Miranda slightly shook her head. "He loved Jamal more than anything." Then her smile disappeared. "But we didn't get enough time to really get to know each other. We both hoped we'd have more time." Her words came slower as she seemed to deliberate each one. "I think a lot of the time I more miss the idea of him. I grieved the future we were going to build together. But we weren't around each other enough for me to miss how he made coffee in the morning or kiss me good-night. Sometimes I wonder if that makes me a bad person, not missing my own husband. Forgetting about him entirely at times."

Then she jerked, as if realizing I was sitting right there hanging on her every word. She pushed her braids back on one side. I tracked the motion, her elegant fingers moving in slow-motion as they curled around the delicate shell of her ear.

Invisible bolts tightened in my chest. I was half grateful the ghost of her lover didn't haunt her, and half wished she could have had that future. Conflicting thoughts often warred in me, but this was a particularly hard juxtaposition of ideas that I swallowed down like razor blades and cotton balls.

"I've never said that out loud before," she confessed, abject terror entering her eyes making her pupils shrink to pinpricks.

Before she could freak out too much, I said, "You aren't a bad person, Miranda. I think you know that. And from what I can guess, your— Rashon wouldn't have wanted you to love his ghost more than your present." I took a gamble on imagining him to be a practical man, that's who I envisioned Miranda with. Someone steady, who could support her and others, a beacon of strength.

Something in my chest caved in as I thought of how opposite I was to that.

Miranda visibly swallowed before she held out the deck of cards. "Your turn."

I allowed my fingers to stroke hers as I took the stack. For such a small surface area of connected skin, a massive spark leapt to life and travelled through my entire body, warming me.

Our eyes locked, forcing us both to face the vulnerability she exposed. I tried to silently communicate to her that it was safe. I was safe.

Our touch broke and so with it, went my lie.

Who the fuck did I think I was? Trying to convince her I was safe? I wasn't. But thankfully, even in the moments I deluded myself, I doubted she'd forget. Miranda was far too sharp to fall for the bullshit I even fed myself.

We continued to play, both of us getting more and more competitive as we advanced through the different colored spaces of the board. When she landed on the Molasses Pit, Miranda groaned in frustration as she was forced to miss a turn.

"I can't believe I'm falling behind," she groused, crossing her arms over her chest.

I couldn't help but feel a surge of satisfaction as I danced my gingerbread man past hers. "Looks like the tides have turned," I said with a smirk.

Miranda shot me a glare, but I could see the glint of amusement in her eyes. "Don't get too cocky," she warned.

Was she actually having...fun?

As we approached the finish line, our movements became more frantic, each of us desperate to be the first to reach kastle. When Miranda drew the last card that would determine her fate, she held her breath as she flipped it over.

"It's a red one," she exclaimed in excitement with a fist pump. "I win."

Miranda victoriously marched her little gingerbread man to kastle, beating me fair and square.

I groaned in defeat. For a moment, I felt a twinge of disappointment, a sense of frustration at having come so close and yet fallen short once again.

But then I looked up, meeting her gaze across the table, and something inside me shifted. My ego slid to the side, I saw Miranda not as a rival or an opponent, but as a partner, a kindred spirit who spent all their time feeling this life was about burden. Her burden was duty and responsibility, mine was surviving and managing pain.

Miranda grinned, her eyes sparkling with mirth. "While you are shit at playing games, we've definitely confirmed you are a sore loser."

"Well, you sweetheart, are a poor winner. Do you rub it in your kid's face when you beat him at a game?" I didn't even bother asking if she let him win. Miranda was too upright to pander to anyone, even a child.

She rolled her shoulders back. "I treat him like an equal."

I scoffed. "I hope your kid doesn't cry easy."

"He is very mature for his age," she said, a little bit of pride sneaking into her expression, a slight smile curving her lips.

Her kid was right. She did need fun. And in that moment, I realized how badly I needed it too. But I also wanted more.

My hunger for her returned with a vengeance. I leaned forward, my eyes locked onto hers. I grinned, feeling a sense of anticipation building within me. Our game may be over, but the real competition had only just begun.

"Let's make a bet this time," I said, a sly grin spreading across my face. "If I win the next game, you have to kiss me."

Miranda's eyes gleamed with ferocity, like a shark smelling blood in the water. A hint of a smile tugging at the corner of her lips. "And if I win?"

My little badass couldn't resist a bet. I wondered how many people knew that?

I leaned even closer, the heat of her breath mingling with mine. "You get to decide."

Her eyes widened in surprise, but I could see the spark of desire igniting within them.

"You're on," she said, her voice low and husky.

Then her expression smoothed as she returned to business mode. "If I win, we skip the sword fighting lesson and we skip straight to me killing you. I'd like to enjoy what time I have left of my day off."

My heart pounded in my chest, heat crawling up my neck with panic. This was more than just about a bet. Miranda was drawing a line. If she won, things would return to a more professional interchange of death between us. If I won, I got to continue to push a boundary I desperately wanted to break.

If she'd really regretted yesterday, she would have run for the hills. But she was still here, and it was game on.

And I intended to win this time.

Chapter Twenty-Two

THE BADASS

I couldn't believe I'd agreed to this ridiculous bet over a game of freaking Candy Land. I knew it was a bad idea, and I absolutely knew better. I eyed the colorful board. The truth was skill had little to do with this game. I was really leaving this up to chance, and that wasn't like me.

But down here, in this isolated cell, it was easier to take risks, to throw caution to the wind and just live in the moment.

But Xander still wasn't going to get that kiss.

Then again, I hadn't planned on getting off on his hard body yesterday or talking about Rashon today.

The way I acted around Xander both terrified and exhilarated me. It was like coming to life while realizing at the same time that I could die just as quickly.

Maybe it was all spilling out because I knew my secrets would remain in the walls of this prison, and die with him, or the way his piercing sapphire gaze seemed to drag out all the most important innermost desires like the ocean's undertow. Whatever it was, I found myself wanting Xander more and more with each passing moment.

I partially blamed Jim. What a douche. It's his fault Xander suddenly looked a million times more appealing. It was his fault that I suddenly found this game the most entrancing, captivating activity. It's his fault I was pushed into taking on this bet.

As we set up the board for the second time, I tried to focus on the game. But my body grew hotter, the aching hunger in my chest spread. Xander's scent filled my nostrils, a tantalizing blend of salty ocean air and warm, masculine musk. His eyes bored into mine without reserve, pinning me in the gut.

My lips tingled, wanting, waiting.

Nope nope nope.

The sooner I win, the sooner things can go back to how they were, I insisted to myself.

I ignored the part of crying out that it wanted more. More of Xander, more of the woman I was around him. Around him I felt equal parts sex goddess, clever wit, and absolute badass.

Topside, back in reality, I felt like a workhorse who ground herself to the bone so she wouldn't have to think about her own life.

And in this makeshift dungeon, reality was far far away as I played with my tiny, plastic, red gingerbread man.

The idea of the world ending, or killing Xander also slipped away as we continued to play.

The game progressed quickly, with both of us determined to win.

Our little tokens wound up the board, and headed toward the sweet ending. I was ahead, but he was always right behind me. As the game wore on, I could feel the tension mounting, the stakes growing higher with each turn.

About to move my little gingerbread man, there was something about the way Xander scrutinized me from under his long dark lashes that made me hesitate. His gaze was intense, almost predatory, and it made me feel hot and flustered.

The memory of his lips on mine assaulted my mind in high definition, making my stomach flutter and my heart speed up.

I moved my gingerbread man only one space forward. It was a weak move, but I didn't want to make it too obvious. Xander raised an eyebrow, but he didn't say anything.

His plastic player moved ahead of mine.

I drew another card and played it, deliberately foregoing the yellow square that would have slid me up Licorice Lane and put me in the lead. Xander's gaze was now riveted on the board, while I licked my suddenly dry lips. My nerves twisted into a tight cord at what I was doing.

What *was* I doing?

If he said anything, if he so much as met my eye I would either stop what I was doing, or just get up and leave. Get right back in the elevator and return to reality where life was orderly, if not a little dull.

Xander passed Duchess Gumdrops, while I landed on the Molasses Mudslide and slid back down the board by a considerable distance.

I could feel the tension mounting, both of us silently daring the other to voice what was happening. I didn't have to land on the Mudslide, and could I really say I didn't know better while playing an easy child's game?

I'm not losing on purpose. I'm doing the best I can, I blatantly lied to myself.

Xander drew another card. With only a twitch of his lips did he slide his gingerbread man into the Candy Land.

My stomach dropped out of my body, and I swallowed hard.

"Game over," he murmured.

I tried to keep my expression neutral, but my heart pounded in my chest and I was sure Xander could hear it.

I couldn't meet his eye, knowing what I'd done was so blatant, so foolhardy, so desperate and completely unlike me. Xander slid his chair back with an audible screech before rounding the small table. He held out a hand to me.

Still avoiding his gaze, I slipped my fingers into his, allowing him to pull me to my feet. His strong grip found my hips then tightened, sending jolts of heat straight to my sex. I kept my focus steady on his broad, muscular pecs, marveling at how insanely good he smelled. I don't think I could even imagine him wearing a shirt at this point. My fingers itched to trace the numerous scar lines branded in his flesh.

Xander guided me backward, forcing my feet to shuffle in compliance until my back hit the bars of his cage.

"What are you doing?" I asked, my words coming out breathy. I still couldn't look him in the eye.

Then he encircled my wrists, pulling them up and over my head, guiding me to hold onto the bars. The move caused my chest to push out, my full breasts meeting the warmth of his hard body

His hands slithered down my arms, as his lips evened up to my ear. "I'm going to kiss you, Miranda."

"O-okay." I stuttered. I actually fucking stuttered. Every nerve ending was screaming for him to do it.

Touch me. Make me lose my mind. Kiss me until I can't think. I don't want to think anymore. I don't want to be responsible anymore.

My eyes fluttered closed as his mouth hovered over mine. Fuck, why did he smell so delicious? The heat of his breath against my overly sensitive lips sent my anticipation through the roof and I couldn't even try to suppress the full body shiver.

Though I didn't open my eyes I felt him smile at that.

Lips brushed against mine. The pressure was so delicate, so teasing, causing the flutters in my stomach to morph into a hoard of butterflies on speed.

How was he so in control? The one time I wanted him to lose control and push my limits, he doesn't even open his mouth to slip me tongue. I'm frustrated and suddenly insulted.

I started to drop my hands but his shot back up, forcing me to hold the bars again.

"No, no," he chided in a low voice. "This is *my* kiss. I'm going to take it how I want it, sweetheart."

The sharp command in his voice belied the tenderness in which he continued to kiss me. Anytime I tried to open my mouth or press in deeper, he pulled back. At last, a frustrated growl escaped my throat.

He chuckled darkly. "I may be a beast Miranda, but look how in control I am right now? It's all because of you. Any other time I would be out of my mind, half feral, trying to rip your clothes off and bury myself into your sweet heat. Fucking you within an inch of your life until you beg me to give you a break to recover."

My breath caught and my lower lips were instantly soaked. I hate that he voiced what I wanted. It's what I'd secretly been hoping for, and I was trying to keep it a secret even from myself.

Shame burned up the heat of my arousal and I moved to push past him. Fuck swordplay today. I'm going to kill him and go.

I'm pushed back, my ass and back slam against the bars but not so hard that it really hurts.

"What did I say?" Xander warned. "I get my kiss the way *I* want it, and I'm not done collecting on my winnings."

I opened my mouth to say something scathing, but before the words could even form in my mind, he grabbed under my thighs and hauled me up so hard and fast, I was shocked to find I'd blinked and my legs rest on his shoulders, my hands now gripping the bars behind me for balance.

For the first time since starting the second round of our stupid game, I meet his eye. Xander's hands gripped my thighs as he gazes up at me with his devastating sapphire eyes.

"W-what are you doing?" I stuttered again, feeling completely off balance emotionally and physically perched on Xander.

"I'm still claiming my kiss." He smirked wickedly up at me, never breaking eye contact as he leaned in and laid a kiss right on my center.

I sucked in a breath so fast my head spun. The intimate touch nearly fucking sent me.

Self-consciousness was a brief thought as I knew he must realize my wetness already gathered where he could feel it, taste it. But then even more moisture shot down to soak through the center of my leggings.

Xander's hands tightened on my thighs.

His words came out careful and low. "I won that one, sweetheart. But I think..." he licked his lips, reminding me of a hungry jungle cat. "I think you want me to kiss you a second time."

He was sin. The literal incarnation of sin and temptation. Yet my pride fought for dominance over it. It muscled and punched at what he was offering, wanting to order him to put me down so I could march out of here, indignant and independent of his affect.

"Yes," I whispered, even as terror warred with my desire.

Xander's smile turned dark with satisfaction. "Wish granted." Then he pushed his lips to my center again. The pressure was more insistent as he opened his mouth and let his tongue swipe up my cleft through my thin leggings.

My hips jerked forward. A strangled sound escaped my throat as my fingers tightened on the cold metal bars. He continued to open mouth kiss my lower lips, his tongue probing, seeking entrance despite the barrier of the fabric.

"Xander," I gasped as the pressure of his tongue found my clit. All my thoughts scattered like a flock of birds. "*Ungh*."

His hands moved, digging into the globes of my ass. "Fuck sweetheart, when you moan my name, it makes me hard as steel." Then he went back kissing me deeply, thoroughly until my hips were bucking and I was halfway to sobbing for relief.

"You threw that game, baby," he said in between kisses. "You wanted this. You want me. You want the beast to fuck you."

I was out of my mind with desire, the sounds coming out of my mouth were unrecognizable. Even on the rare occasion I pleasured myself, I stayed quiet, holding it all in.

My feet hit the ground and I was shocked by the literal sensation of coming back to earth.

Xander's face had changed, it was now a feral mask of need and determination. He pushed my coat off and it hit the ground with a thud. I was grateful Bob was in his sheath. I hoped it acted like a blindfold so he couldn't "see" what was happening.

My tight sports bra ripped up and off my body.

"How fucking dare you bind these gorgeous breasts up," he snarled, before attacking them with his hands and mouth. My left breast generously filled his palm as he licked and sucked on the other one. Tingles and heat spiraled out from where he touched me.

It was true. I had shapely breasts but I kept them bound up in sports bras, never going for the lacy, shape-flattering pieces Vivien used on her much smaller ones.

But now that they were out, being feasted on and worshipped, I never wanted to wear one again. Even as I let him run the show, I felt sexy and empowered.

Xander's hand snaked down, fingers skimming under my workout leggings instantly finding the split of my sex without the barrier of panties. I didn't wear them with these pants.

His fingers toyed with my heat. I choked. The foreign and shocking sensation of someone other than myself touching me there completely threw me.

When a long digit slipped up inside my tightness, penetrating me, I stopped breathing all together. My hands clutched at the corded muscle of his shoulders, hanging on for dear life.

He began to make the come hither motion, hitting a spot I didn't even know I had, while his palm ground into my clit. I cried out, my torso trying to curve against the onslaught of sensation.

"That's it, my sweetheart," he breathed into my ear, his hot breath washing across my neck causing goosebumps to pebble the skin of my entire body. "You are going to come for me, aren't you?"

It was all too much, too fast. I hadn't been touched like this, treated like this in so long my brain couldn't digest it.

"No," I ground out. And it was true. My body clenched down and fought it. It didn't want to let go of control. My brain was rebelling, still trying to bring reason to the table.

"Wanna bet?" he dared me, his tone dangerous. The lights flickered around us and I felt his power crowd into the room, pressing against the exposed flesh of my half naked body. Xander was losing control and I didn't even fucking care.

Then his mouth covered mine and I was lost again. Lost to his passion, his need, and the most delicious taste of a man I'd ever known.

No, he wasn't a man. He was a god. A dangerous immortal of power who could destroy me. Those bars were there to separate us for a reason.

We needed to stop. We were nearing something truly dangerous.

Still my body bucked against his hand as I hyperventilated. My body clenched, working hard to tamp down my rising orgasm.

More than ever I wanted him to wreck me. This beast had clawed his way through walls I'd never intended to let him bypass. He inspired a part of me to emerge that I thought long dead, and now, I was addicted to being that woman.

The lights flickered more violently.

"Fuck," he muttered against my lips before removing his hand.

I cried out at the loss, tears gathering in my eyes, as pressure nearly exploded in my chest. No! I needed him to touch me. I felt starved. I forgot how good it could feel. I needed more. I needed him or I would die.

Xander backed up, sucking his middle finger into his mouth before slowly pulling it out. He still looked at me like he was preparing to devour the rest of me.

A hot shudder tore through me.

"Tell me what you want." Xander's voice was hoarse, either from desire or trying to stay in control. "Whatever you want, and I'll give it to you."

"Take those off and sit down," I ordered, words bypassing my brain, coming straight out of my mouth.

The fabric of his pants pooled at his feet as he stepped out of them. The rod that emerged was massive, his hand already fisted at the base. My mouth watered, and I instantly wanted to find out how much I could shove down my throat before his toes curled and he groaned. The other part of me wondered if I could fit all of *that* in me.

It had been so long since a man had been inside me, much less a god. I was usually fully in my confidence to handle anything, but he might damn well break me in two.

So why was I so quick to kick off my boots and shove my pants down? Wasting no time, I strode over to him in three steps before settling in his lap. His hands found my hips again, making me feel secure and powerful. My wet center pressed against the length of his hardness, nestling him against me without letting him inside. A thrill swept through me like a wave. Was this really happening?

"Miranda." He gasped my name like it was a prayer as those brilliant blue eyes searched mine, looking for I don't know what. Mercy? Release? Connection?

Reaching down, I encircled the velvet hardness of his cock and lifted my hips. Slowly, I settled onto the tip of his dick. Oh. My. God. Even that small amount had me throwing my head back and groaning at the sensation of being stretched.

So long. It had been so long. And had it ever felt like this?

My name fell off his lips like a never-ending waterfall. Both of us were falling to pieces and he was barely inside me.

I lowered a little more. Fuck, I was already so full. My entire body broke out in a sweat. "Gah," I hissed. Despite my work outs, none of that had prepared my body for this.

"Fucking hell," he said, and dropped his head forward so he could suck on one of my breasts, moaning into me. It sent vibrations straight down into my already sensitized center.

Another few inches and I feared I would die.

When I finally had him fully inside me, my nails broke the skin on his shoulder, my thighs and entire body shook. It was too much. He was too big. And whatever spot he just hit inside me must also be my emotional center because an unprecedented wave crashed over me. I wanted to cry, shout, and scream at the same time. As if all the emotions I'd pushed down, shoved into little boxes so I wouldn't have to deal with them had exploded open at once.

"It's okay, sweetheart," I heard Xander say before he found my lips with his. "I've got you. I've got you," he chanted in between deep, searching kisses. His hands slid up my bare back, soothing me as a couple tears escaped the corners of my eyes.

Fully inside me, Xander didn't move though I knew he must have been desperate to do so. Slowly I adjusted to his size and the wave of emotion calmed a fraction. When I took my first shallow breath after I don't know how long, I rocked my hips.

"Oh fuck," I cried out, pleasure ripping through me in a totally new way.

Xander's teeth pressed into my breast as he panted heavily.

I continued to rock my hips, my head falling back as I surrendered to the feeling of being intimately impaled again and again.

His power still pressed in around us. It pulsed with the rhythm of our bodies. I started out moving gently up and down before his hands gripped my hips, easily lifting and lowering me in longer strokes.

"I could die like this," he rasped. "So very wet. So very tight."

My eyes squeezed shut as thoughts of reality tried to bombard the moment.

I *would* have to kill him. After this I'd have to pull out my talking, pacifist-sword and run him through.

The absurdity of it all made tears crowd in my throat again.

I didn't want to kill him. The petulant child in my banged her fists on the ground in protest.

"Baby, I need you to come for me," Xander crooned, resting his forehead against mine, still rocking my hips up and down. "I need to see you come again. It's all I want." His words ended between gritted teeth. As if it would kill him if I refused his wish.

My body tightened up, fighting against his words.

My teeth gritted. No. I didn't want to let go. My brain couldn't decide if it's because that would end this moment, or because I couldn't let myself let go.

"Don't fight it," he growled, glaring at me, somehow knowing exactly what I was doing.

"Don't tell me what to do, beast boy," I said, sounding more in control than I felt.

"Oh no sweetheart, now you've done it," he taunted. In a moment we were up and against the room, my back pressed against a cold concrete wall this time. The contrast of his hot body on one side and the freezing hardness behind me only heightened my awareness of how much he filled me. My legs wrapped around his hips.

Xander rocked his hips into me, faster than the slow steady pace we'd been keeping while seated.

"No," I ground out, pulling on the hair at the back of his hair.

"You want me to stop?" he asked, his pace slowed.

"No," I practically yelled.

His pace picked up again, the friction faster and hotter than before. My brain went fuzzy as I screamed incoherently, still fighting the building pressure every step of the way.

I chanted curses, pulling at the hair at the base of his skull.

"You are fucking driving me crazy," he growled.

"You were already crazy," I shot back, barely able to keep my eyes open as he slammed his rock-hard monster cock into me over and over again.

"Give in, sweetheart. Give it to me."

"No," I insisted again. We were fucking and still fighting. He wanted me to give him all of me, unrestrained, but it was too scary. I'd given enough ground. I refused to give any more.

"You want to, I know you do," he gritted through his teeth. My ass bounced off the wall as he pistoned in me. Sweat covered both of us. Pressure built in me, pushing me to heights I'd never known.

And I did. Part of me desperately did, but it wasn't my nature anymore. My nature was to hold things in. It kept me safe. And alone. Alone was safe.

I could stay safe if I kept everything inside.

Suddenly he stopped. I blinked, aware my thoughts had manifested in my facial expression. I must look fucking pitiful.

I couldn't allow myself to let go or give in, even though I balanced on the edge of the most tremendous orgasm of my life. How many times in one night could I want to cry? I never felt like crying. Not at cute commercials or touching movies. But a damn had cracked inside me.

His fingers cupped my jawline, his thumb brushing against my cheek.

"No one has to know."

Whatever reaction happened on my face, he gave a curt nod too. Like he knew what I was feeling, even when I didn't.

Then he slammed back into me over and over, licking up my neck, fondling my breast and whispering in my ear. "No one has to know."

A wire tripped in my brain as the fight I'd been waging for so long turned on me. Fuck. I realized I'd only made my release ten times more intense, as it built up relative to the fight I gave it. I was suddenly at the top of the highest rollercoaster, locked in, and the clicking to the top had stopped. There was no way to go but down.

I broke into bone wrenching shudders, screaming bloody murder as I bucked and keened on Xander's hard dick. Everything came down to the chaos of pleasure exploding in my body.

I don't know when he moved us, but I blinked and found myself lying flat on the ground, still coming uncontrollably. He drove into me, somehow pushing my release even higher. My legs wrapped around his waist, trying to find purchase, as my mind shot out of my body like a cannon. I was still screaming even as he pumped into me with a roar that shook the bars. The lights flickered and then exploded in a wash of sparks.

His warmth flooded my insides. A flash of panic about protection flashed across my mind before I remembered I was on the pill to manage my period better. And supposedly he hadn't gotten action in thousands of years.

The gentle rocking of his hips on my mind wiped away the worries as aftershock shivers rushed through me again and again until my body was spent and boneless under his.

Leaning over me, his hair hung in his eyes but there was something soft at the center of his ferocity now. "You are the most gorgeous, *impossible* creature I have ever beheld."

The tenderness was too much. It struck me under my ribs and I had to turn my head away.

Out of my periphery, I watched his lips tighten, brows furrowing as if he were in pain. Then he smoothed his expression, his demeanor turning impassive. Xander got up, helping me back to my feet. As soon as he left my body, I felt clearer about things. I could think again. For better or worse.

Cold reality closed in around me. My entire body was numb as I walked over to my discarded jacket and pulled out Bob.

"No, please no Miranda," the sword begged me. "You don't have to do this. We don't have to. Not with the blood and the death. You like him. It's okay not to kill him. We can both be happy."

The lump in my throat was immovable as was my mind. Whereas last night I'd struck Xander in a knee-jerk reaction to my shame, this was cold and calculated.

Xander looked at me in disbelief from under the hair that had fallen in his eyes. "What? No pillow talk?" He let out a dark laugh but there was no humor in it.

"This is why I'm here," I said plainly. "You asked me to do this."

His jaw tightened and his expression flattened, becoming unread-able. "You're right. I did."

I crossed the distance between us, the blade raised. Bob cried out.

"Miranda, you can't do this to him. Not after what you just did together."

"Shut up," I said in a harsh whisper.

Xander's brows bunched together, but he didn't say anything.

Bob continued to adamantly plead with me. "Miranda, I know about death. Doing this, now, it will kill a piece of you too. I know. I know death."

I stopped a foot away from Xander. He stood there, hands balled into tight fists, accepting the fate I was about to deliver while still looking pissed.

Sword in my hand, poised at Xander's heart, Bob became impossibly heavy. My wrist strained to keep the blade straight as it vibrated. Bob was trying to thwart my aim.

The lump in my throat grew. It crowded out my vocal cords. My heart suddenly felt as weighty as my blade, as heavy as a stone. As if it was also trying to drag me down, keep me from doing what I was about to do.

My arm dropped.

Then without a word, I turned, put on my leather duster over my naked body, grabbed my clothes, shut the cage behind me then got onto the elevator. I didn't look back to see Xander's face as I left him there. The doors closed behind me, and I didn't turn around. Clutching my clothes and boots to my bare chest, the elevator automatically started its ascent. I'd need to dress fast before it arrived on the lobby level.

But I wanted it to stop. I needed a minute. A minute or two of safety.

A red button appeared before me. Before I could think, I pressed it. The elevator halted. I should probably freak out about the magic/intuitive elevator, but I was already past full capacity of mental and emotional overload.

Dropping my boots and clothes to the floor, I sat down right there. My arms encircled my knees, pulling them to my chest as I rocked back and forth.

What was I doing? Who was I anymore?

How could I kill him when I lov–

"Don't you dare finish that sentence, Miranda West," I said out loud, my voice hoarse.

"Oh Miranda," Bob said from where he lay on the elevator floor next to me. "It's going to be okay."

I don't know how long I sat there, rocking back and forth while a talking blade comforted me over my fucked up life and the feelings I had for a beastly god who resided in the Grim Reaper's basement.

Chapter Twenty-Three

THE BADASS

The next night at Xander's cage again, I dropped my duster to the ground on the chair. I tried to put what happened between us behind me.

"What the holy hell are you wearing?" Xander blurted out.

My head snapped up. "What?"

"You have a line with bunches around your backside."

I twisted around forgetting what I'd even worn today. "Oh, my booty shorts? I got them from a site online."

"They should be illegal."

My eyebrow raised, letting him know he was sidling up to danger. "You got a problem with how I dress? Because I'm a grown-ass woman and I can wear whatever I want."

"Sure, you can, but if you want a bunch of people glued to the ass you're flaunting..."

"Maybe I do. Is that a problem?" I asked stepping closer. My body felt lighter than usual. Almost unreal as I challenged him. I stalked over to his open cage, ready to take this fight to the next level. He met me in the middle, only inches separating us. Heat and intensity vibrated between us.

"Enchanting the masses with your perfect rear can cut into your services for me," he said, voice husky and low. It sent hot shivers through me, which heated into pure desire.

I couldn't tell if we were fighting anymore. Is this how Vivien felt when Grim first realized how provocatively she liked to dress? Granted my friend had the taste of a high-class hooker, but she rocked that shit.

And now that I was getting blowback over a measly pair of shorts, I suddenly wanted one of her skimpy dresses to parade around Xander and give him a coronary.

"The shit you're saying is some masochistic bullshit, you realize." I'd never let my son Jamal talk to a girl about her clothes like this. And I sure as hell wouldn't stand for it. I don't give a damn if he is a big scary, feral god. I deserved respect for my choices.

"The shit I'm saying is that I can't focus if you're going to wear those. It makes me. . ." His eyes glazed over at the same time a supernatural spark ignited in them. "Miranda," he growled. "The things you do to me when you're on the other side of those bars... you could be wearing a paper sack and still drive me right into madness. Have you no mercy for a poor god like me?"

I was stunned. All thoughts of my kid flew right out of my head as I realized what Xander was saying. He advanced on me, and I didn't retreat. Standing mere inches from me, the heat of his chest radiated into mine. My nipples tightened, but his eyes were trained on my lips.

"Miranda," he rasped. Then he reached his hands around me and grabbed my ass cheeks, dragging me to him. His eyes fluttered shut. "Fuck," he muttered. Then he picked me up and my legs naturally wrapped around his toned waist.

I groaned loudly when his hardness ground into me. His body felt mind-meltingly good. Logic threatened to crowd its way in and ruin the moment, but I managed to keep it at bay. All I could focus on was how his hands massaged my ass, pressing me against the hard length in his sweatpants.

Again, my body took on a weightless feel as if I weren't really here.

He didn't kiss me. Instead, he ran his nose up along the column of my neck. Then his lips skimmed my sensitive flesh until I was ready to beg him to latch onto me anywhere. Suck, lick, bite me anywhere, anyway he could.

A wave of power rippled through the air, beating into my body.

"Xander," I said in warning.

My bones creaked and groaned as another wave of intensity seemed to clamp down on them, making them strain under the weight.

Pleasure was swept away by pain. His name escaped my throat in a breathless gasp.

The heat of desire turned into something else. My skin burned. It burned painfully and I was reminded of the dream I had before. The one where I was running and couldn't get away from an entity far more powerful than anything I'd know.

Forcing my eyes open, I looked down at Xander, but it wasn't him anymore. He'd changed, morphed into the monster that had stalked me before. It wasn't his signature blue flowing energy that wafted off him. Xander was bright and scalding like the sun. Beams shot from his open eyes into my chest until I screamed from the searing agony.

He set me on fire, my skin bubbling and melting. He refused to release me from his arms. I had to kill him, or I would die. Thankfully my sword was in my hand. I raised my arm before plunging the killing blow into his chest.

"Miranda!" a familiar voice screamed.

The world swirled around me, but the blinding light only grew brighter accompanied by a blaring horn as I realized I was seconds from my end. I dove and rolled away, my skin scraping along the asphalt as I tumbled into the grass. The car sped by, not even slowing.

"Oh thank fae," Bob breathed a sigh. "I thought we were goners for sure."

I blinked hard several times, my fingers digging into the grass and dirt underneath me.

I'd been sleepwalking again. And this time, I found myself on a highway near my house. I clutched Bob but I was still in the oversized shirt I wore to bed.

"What the fuck?" I breathed.

"What the fuck, indeed," Bob agreed. "I think it's time we start discussing the prospect of putting chains on your bed to keep you from taking these little midnight jaunts."

Rolling over until I lay on my back, I let out a heavy sigh. "Bob, I can't believe I'm saying this, but I'm thinking you might be right."

Chapter Twenty-Four

THE BADASS

Today it was back to work, but I could already tell my heart wouldn't be in it. I was exhausted. The nightmares and sleep walking were really wearing on me.

How did one treat those things? Therapy?

Pretty sure that wasn't an option for me. Unless the gods had a psychiatrist who specialized in immortal problems.

As I drew closer to Perkatory, I saw Vivien was conversing with someone else at our usual table. The perfectly styled hair and burgundy suit gave him away. Timothy.

I connected eyes with Aaron who was still behind the café counter, making someone's latte. He was likely too far away to hear what they were talking about, but his mouth was turned down. His eyes were serious as they bounced from me the two talking.

Something about his expression told me I was better to skip the Perkatory line, and head straight over there. As I approached, Vivien caught sight of me. Her lips tightened as she leaned back in her chair. A signal to Timothy to stop talking. Something was definitely up.

I stopped between them. "What are we talking about?" I asked in a falsely casual tone.

Vivien pouted off into the plants, while Timothy stared at her with a hard look.

Timothy was a god who knew how to keep things locked down like a steel trap. So I moved my focus onto Vivien and crossed my arms, waiting.

She still stared at a green frond but shifted in her seat.

I could almost feel Timothy willing her not to break.

I simply waited.

Vivien straightened in her seat, still avoiding my gaze. "Nothing," she mumbled, looking down at her barely touched blended sugar coffee.

The tension in Timothy didn't let up. It was a battle of pressures on her, but Timothy didn't know he'd already lost.

"I don't think you should kill Xander," The words burst out of her as her hands flailed in defeat.

"I agree!" Bob practically shouted, though no one else could hear him.

"Vivien," Timothy cried out in exasperation while rubbing the spot between his eyes.

A smile barely twitched onto my lips at winning the battle of wills before it disappeared again. I slipped into the seat, after a quick glance around to make sure no one around paid attention to the vampire casually bringing up the fact I murdered someone every night.

"What is going on here?" I pressed, interlacing my fingers and setting my forearms on the table. And why the hell were they talking about my situation when I wasn't present?

"Vivien asked to speak with me," Timothy said, still shooting daggers at her with his eyes. She was suddenly preoccupied with sucking noisily from her straw.

"She thinks I should let you out of the 'deal,'" he said using air quotes.

I turned to my friend, who avoided my eye like a kid caught with their hand in the proverbial cookie jar. "Okay, first off, why aren't you talking to Grim instead of Timothy? And second, I'm not on the hook to Grim or Timothy about this."

Vivien's auburn mane swayed as she shook her head. "I try to keep personal matters and business separate with Grim. It's better for our relationship." She practically rolled her eyes saying it, which told me it was his rule, not hers. I could only imagine the damage my well-meaning friend could cause when he was trying to judge souls for the Afterlife or obliteration.

"And you are doing it for them. They are the ones who asked you to do this. But you don't have too, Miranda."

"That's what I was telling *you*," Timothy waved a frustrated hand at her. "This is her choice. Hers and Xander's."

"It's a terrible choice," Bob muttered, though no one else could hear. "All that sticky blood. *Gew*." I felt him shudder in my coat. To appease him, I'd spent considerable time cleaning him in the evenings. But my blade acted like a prissy pony.

Not so hard. You missed a spot. We need more oil, don't rub me dry!

Vivien shot a glare at Grim's aide. "Timmy, this isn't so simple anymore."

He visibly cringed at her nickname for him. The two bickered like a couple of siblings.

"They have feelings for each other," Vivien went on in earnest.

"Vivien," I cried out at the betrayal, my palms slapping the table. How could I freaking forget that if the vamp couldn't hold her load for anyone else's secrets, how could I expect her to keep her trap shut about mine?

A serious mask replaced Timothy's ire as he turned to me. "Is this true, Miranda?"

My cheeks heated up and suddenly I wanted to be anywhere else. Thank god, I hadn't yet told Vivien about how physical things had gotten. But it was all a game, and she wouldn't understand that.

"W-w-would that be so bad?" Aaron interrupted. The line for coffee had dwindled, and the other barista was handling it.

Aaron stood by Timothy, and again, a palpable tension of sex, want, and frustration vibrated between the two them. Aaron's brilliant aquamarine eyes pinned Timothy down with a silent accusation.

It made me want to push my chair back a couple inches.

Timothy's tongue poked at the inside of his cheek as if he were trying to compose himself. "Yes. It would be. She is a human, and he is an immortal. Mixing the two worlds is a bad idea."

"Vivien and Grim seemed to have m-managed just fine," Aaron countered.

Timothy was back to pushing at that spot between his brows. "We are not having this argument again."

Though they were clearly having their own not-so-subtextual conversation, I felt chastised by Timothy. It was *my* hand in the cookie jar now. I was making things complicated with Xander, and if I hadn't told big-fang-Macgee over here, no one would have known.

Before they could get into it further, I turned to Vivien. "Xander asked me himself. He's in pain. He needs to be released from that."

Though recently he seemed to be less. He wasn't losing control; he wasn't radiating the small hairs off my body like when we'd first met.

She released her drink to cover my hands with her icy cold ones. "But you are easing his pain just by showing up. He's been an immortal, alone all these years. Do you know every baby vamp fears is? Being alone. They'll watch everyone they care about die. For the first time, you are giving him companionship and maybe. . .more." she threw me a sheepish grin, having guessed what had been going on.

Timothy stiffened at that, as did Aaron for, I'm sure, an entirely different reason.

"He still has to die," I said to her quietly.

Her face twisted up in anguish. "Does he? Even Bianca said killing him could have a catastrophic outcome."

"Bianca?" Timothy asked, his body turning stiffly toward me in alarm.

I quickly explained what she'd told me about killing Xander leading to a terrible, end of the world event.

"But Xander said her visions aren't always cut and dried. That it's too vague. He swore there was no way his death could cause such a thing." I rubbed my palms on my thighs, they were suddenly sweating. Had I been compartmentalizing too much?

I'd told myself she was wrong and I was doing the right thing, but bringing the prediction of doom back up made me question it all over again.

Not to mention a tiny spark inside me came to life, hoping Timothy would agree it was too dangerous. That I needed to stop.

Then what? Xander would remain caged in the Grim Reaper's basement, and I'd occasionally go down to bang the gong with him in between his monstrously painful episodes? A bunch of worms squirmed in my stomach. That didn't feel right either.

Timothy's expression turned to stone, and I could tell he was going inward, debating something. Aaron watched him with rapt attention. The fingers on his right hand twitched, as if he was dying to reach out to Timothy. But the god would keep Aaron at arm's length as long as Aaron was a mortal. Or maybe as long as Aaron was a loose cannon, adrenaline junkie. Timothy liked things orderly, predictable, and under his control.

Aaron wasn't any of those things.

When those dark eyes finally blinked, Timothy said slowly, "Xander is correct. Bianca's visions don't always mean what you think they do on the surface."

"She said my bringing back Grim would have dire consequences."

"Don't you mean pillowy consequences?" I asked, unable to keep myself from the dig to lighten the mood.

Vivien lips parted in surprise even as she glared at me in disbelief that I'd gone there. I half expected Grim to materialize and swat her with another pillow. Or maybe I was just hoping for it to get out of this conversation. I felt pinned and it was hard to breathe.

Then her teeth clicked shut before she went on to prove her point. "Vivien argued, her fingers digging into the table. "What if the end of the world is barreling toward us because of what I did? What if this is another link in the chain to a catastrophic event?"

"Is Vivien right about you and Xander?" Timothy asked, training all his attention on me again, making my skin prickle with an uncomfortable, shameful heat.

"We have spent a lot of time together." I licked my lips trying to buy myself time to find the right words other than, *yeah, we fucked and it was earth shattering and I don't think I can stop it from happening again.*

I was learning the harder I fought him, the faster I fell into him.

"I wish I didn't have too. . ." I quickly redirected my sentence when

I heard the affection and sadness mingle in my own voice. Tightening it up, I said, "But I understand my duty, not only to Xander and Grim, but to the blade."

"The *talking* blade," Vivien corrected.

Aaron and Timothy's faces held twin confusion. I slowly turned to stare at Vivien, feeling betrayed for a second time.

"What?" she challenged, indignantly throwing her arms out again before crossing them across her chest and pouting. "You know what I am."

I did, dammit.

"I must have a chat with Bianca," Timothy said, pushing his chair away to stand. Except when he got to his feet, it brought him to eye height with Aaron, their faces inches away.

The smolder in Aaron's eyes was only matched by the intensity of Timothy's. It was like some kind of sexy face off, that Vivien I sat back and watched like a couple of voyeurs with popcorn. Who said women didn't have a thing for watching two impossibly sexy men together?

Aaron's gaze dropped to Timothy's lips, caressing them with a look before meeting Timothy's eye again. The god's jaw tensed and twitched as his hands balled into fists.

Vivien and I had been waiting to see if one or both of them would break for months. And if they did, we weren't sure if they would fuck or fight. Maybe both?

I sure as hell understood the fucked up dynamic now. Xander riled me past my sensibilities. It was intoxicating to be pushed out of control like that.

Get it together, Miranda. You have to stop this. You are going to kill him like he asked, end of story.

As if hearing my internal pep talk, Timothy turned stiffly on his heel and walked away. Aaron closed his eyes, inhaling deeply before his shoulders sagged.

I released a breath I didn't know I had been holding. Even Vivien gave a low whistle.

"He's so f-fucking stubborn," Aaron finally let out between clenched teeth.

"Yeah, but isn't that kind of what you love about him?" Vivien pointed out.

A grim smile curved at the edge of his lips. "Maybe."

Then he left us to go work the line that was forming up again at Perkatory.

Once we were alone, I said, "I love you Vivien, but stay out of my business."

"I can't do that, Miranda," she said, giving me an unusually grave look. "You're my friend. Honestly, the first real friend I've ever had. And I love you too damned much to let you get in your own damned way."

Deciding to skip the line at Perkatory and settle for the subpar coffeepot in the surveillance office, I stood up. "It's already done Vivien. There's nothing to do about it."

She grabbed one of my arms. "He's bringing something out in you. I've seen you smile in a way I've never seen before. I'm also watching you fight it. And I need you to think whether fighting what's happening between you and him has to be this way, or because you are scared of what happens if he lives?"

I gently pushed her grip off me and walked away without responding. I tried to keep from thinking about her words, but they haunted me the rest of the day. A swirling echo in my head.

What would happen if he lived?

Chapter Twenty-Five

THE BEAST

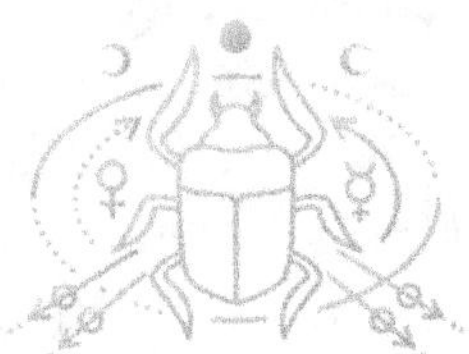

B*ing.* I looked up from the spring where I relaxed. My heart jumped into my throat. It was too soon for Miranda to show up, but despite my best efforts, my hope soared that she'd arrived early.

She'd walked away without killing me for the first time in over two weeks. I'd expected to have a bad night. Not long ago, my powers would arc, shutter, and burn in and out of me until I shifted and went crazy and blind with the pain. But whether she'd carved away enough of my power, or because of the salvation I found in her kiss, in her body, I felt more steady than I had in a long time.

Yesterday had been a mess of competition and passion. I needed Miranda to come back to me so I could soothe it away. And frankly, so we could do it all again. I'd researched another game to play, and I even learned to shuffle the deck of playing cards I procured.

I hadn't decided on our challenge or our game for today. Poker? War? Go Fish? If nothing else, I needed the activity to serve as a distraction to keep me from tackling her the second those bars slid open. All night and morning I'd rolled around in the memory of her scent, her taste, the sinful fucking sounds that escaped her as she slid up and down my rock-hard shaft, finding her pleasure.

The screen up at the top corner of my quarters showed a different person travelling down the elevator to my lair. My good humor and growing erection were instantly shot down.

Still, I surged out of the water and wrapped a towel around my bare waist, not bothering to dry off. I padded my way across the stone path up to the cage. The door opened with a heavy metal groan as I pushed my way through.

There I found Timothy standing on the other side of the bars. Hair perfectly gelled in a pseudo-messy coif, today he wore a silken burgundy suit with his usual tie clip. The uptight ass always looked perfectly put together. Not that I despised him, but his perfectionism gave me annoying pin-prickles in my forehead.

"How may I assist you?" I taunted with a grin, knowing that was usually his line.

Except today, instead of the usual matter of fact, down to business attitude, Timothy's mouth with a thin slash of displeasure.

"I need you to back off," he said without preamble.

I opened my arms to the bars separating us, wordlessly stating the obvious.

"You know what I mean," he countered.

He hadn't come right out and said it, no, but I was beginning to suspect. . .

"Miranda," he clarified, raising his chin. "You need to back off."

Timothy and I rarely got along, and part of that had to do with him thinking he could tell me what to do to fit into his tidy little boxes. I didn't fit in boxes, I tore them to shreds until there wasn't one left. And him getting involved in my business, intensified my dislike.

"Our arrangement isn't your business."

"Maybe not, but Miranda is my business."

My hackles rose faster than a rabid dog's. "Go on," I dared him, my tone dangerous. My sanity suddenly slipped and slid across the thinnest of ice that separated me from violence. If there was something between these two. . .no, I couldn't even imagine that or I'd lose all control.

"Not like that, you idiot," he chided, instantly seeing through me. "My proclivities don't lie there." His dark eyes darted away as if he were thinking of someone else in particular where his proclivities did lie. But I didn't care about that.

"Well then Thoth," I said dryly, using his ancient name, "why don't you spell it out for me, on account of the fact that I'm fucking crazy, and beating around the bush only compels me to want to beat you. . .with a bush."

He gave me a curt nod. "I understand you need Miranda."

The way he said it struck a chord deep inside me. But it wasn't just about her killing me. Miranda was more than that. She tasted like life and hope, and looked at me like I couldn't get away with shit. I was addicted.

Thoth went on. "But keeping her down here for extended periods of time isn't good for either of you. Getting involved with you in any other way, isn't good for either of you."

I had to suppress the snarl. "And what makes you think you know what's best for her or me, Thoth?" I demanded in open challenge.

He sniffed. "I know you are a fiery train wreck barreling toward the edge of a cliff. Miranda is my friend. I don't want to see her trapped on your ride and plummet over with you."

A sick feeling filled me. The imagery of what he described was far too accurate. I didn't want to do that to her.

I had no words. No snarky comment. No hateful things to spew at him. Because he was right, and I wasn't sure which I hated more. The fact that Timothy had a point, or that I'd not given any consideration to hurting Miranda in lieu of chasing the short-term pleasure I felt with her.

I melted back into the shadows.

Timothy took his cue and pressed the elevator button with a ping. Then he looked over his shoulder. "And if you do hurt her. I'll make you really wish you were dead."

I knew he meant it. And what more, the scrap of respect I had for the uptight priss rose considerably. Fuck.

Chapter Twenty-Six

THE BEAST

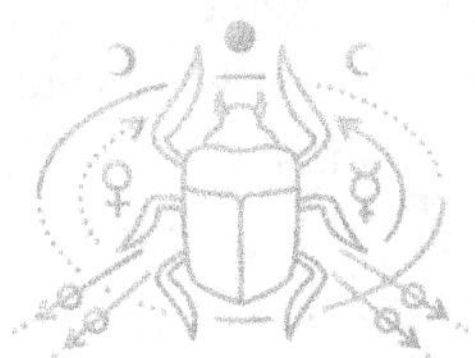

Even before Miranda breached my territory, I was already against the bars, bracing for the final blow. Today, she wouldn't step inside my cage. The playing cards, diminutive table and chairs had been tucked away. There would be no idle conversation or games. Just business, then she could return to her normal life, while I confronted the remainder of my death.

Miranda stood immobile. She didn't reach for Bob.

Avoiding the allure of her breathtaking visage, I fixed my gaze just beyond her left shoulder and waited.

"No game today?" Uncertainty tinged her voice.

"No games."

"Why not?" Indignation underpinned her query.

A crushing wave of realization, triggered by Timothy's words, made my heart implode. I had wanted her to long for me, even depend on me. And now it was clear, I had succeeded.

But my need for death surpassed my desire for her. I was betraying her by drawing her in, knowing I was on the precipice of my exit from this life.

I was truly detestable. A harsh, manic laugh erupted from my throat, uncontrolled and uncontained.

Miranda's eyes narrowed. "What's going on, Xander?"

"What's going on?" I parroted, my focus still off her face to avoid falling under her enchantment, "is I'm waiting for you to fulfill our agreement and end my life."

"No games, no sword lessons, no. . ." Her voice trailed off, unable to encapsulate our shared past.

The knowledge that she wanted to spend time with me, that she wanted me, was as heart-wrenching as it was exhilarating.

"You're lonely," I declared, my voice as icy as I could manage.

"I'm not lonely," she replied, her words automatic.

"Sure, you are." I shot her a condescending smirk, no longer able to keep my gaze from meeting hers. A surge of desire and resentment swelled within me like a tidal wave, ready to decimate a city of reason. If I couldn't have her, I'd burn everything down.

"See this cage?" I gestured to my surroundings. "It keeps me separate from everyone. It ensures their safety from me, but it also keeps me alone. And there?" I pointed directly at her. "That space in front of you? You've enclosed it with bars. You've created a cage for yourself, and you carry it everywhere you go."

"Don't be ridiculous. I haven't done any such thing," she retorted, even as her pupils contracted in fear. My words had hit the mark so accurately, she couldn't even accept it.

Cocking my head to the side, I persisted, "You've grown so accustomed to loneliness, you don't even notice your cage anymore. But you can't come play in mine anymore. Because soon, it's going to be vacant here, and I won't have a single thought or memory of you." I pointed upwards. "You need to venture out there and free yourself. Because there won't even be a ghost of me to comfort you."

"I don't need your ghost. I need—" she stopped herself.

I decided to take a different angle. "I don't need you, Miranda. Even if I live, what happens after you are gone? Do you have any idea what it's like to watch everything you love die?"

"I have some idea," she said quietly.

Her husband. A mortal who couldn't survive the passage of time. It was a wound that would never fully heal.

She licked her lips and spoke. "When I was a child, I begged my parents for a puppy. For a full year I worked to convince them that I could handle the responsibility. I did double the chores. I saved up my money. I even treated one of my stuffed animals like it was a real dog and carried it around with me. Still, they always said no. But that didn't matter to me, I kept pretending that little stuffed dog was real. And then my ninth birthday came. They set down a big box on the kitchen table after I'd blown out my candles. I still remember the light blue wrapping paper with balloons on it, and the way my heart leapt when I saw the big airholes on the lid."

I had no idea where she was going with this. I should stop her, but I couldn't.

"And damned if it wasn't the cutest puppy with the biggest doe eyes."

"Why do I get the feeling this story doesn't have a happy ending?" I said dryly, even as my heart strings pulled.

"Because it doesn't," she said, her face clearing of all expression, a mask she painted over her emotions. I had come to recognize it well.

"I weirdly grew too used to the stuffed animal. The puppy was so full of energy, he was always stepping on me, never giving me a moment alone. I'd been alone a lot before then and I didn't know how to handle him constantly being in my face. One day I was in the back-yard, and I just wanted to play with my dolls without him biting off their heads or running off with them. I got so frustrated I sent him away. I wasn't watching him," she whispered, and I could feel her pain in the air as sharp as a knife. "The puppy walked out into the road and got hit by a truck."

Fuck. That was terrible.

I frowned. "That wasn't your fault, Miranda. You were a kid."

It's not like she wanted something bad to happen to the dog. She just needed some space. I understood that. Not just because I required an inordinate amount of alone time, but from what I'd learned of Miranda there was a quiet stillness at her center that needed to be respected.

Then again, I spent most of my time riling her up. But I was playing with the parts of her that were long neglected, that clearly wanted to come out and play.

"Of course, it was my fault. I didn't protect the puppy, I was too busy playing instead of taking care of it. And the dog died because of me."

"And you've been trying to make up for it ever since."

A wan smile spread across her face. "I suppose I have." The smile disappeared. "But I've learned from that not to let things in that will hurt me in case I lose them. That if I relax or have fun, everything will fall apart. Fun is for my child, not for me. And while I loved Rashon, he never really got inside me, not to the parts he could potentially destroy. But you've somehow gotten inside me," her fingers pressed to the center of her chest.

Despair wailed up from my depths. This is what Timothy warned me of. I was doomed to hurt her.

She was handing over her most private, vulnerable parts on a silver platter to me. I might as well be a butcher, ready to hack it all into pieces.

The reality of what a disaster this was, fully hit me. I might as well be one of the gods of chaos. And it sickened me.

Miranda closed the distance between us until her hands wrapped around the bars beside my face. Her light brown eyes searched mine as she whispered, "Sometimes I forget what these bars are for. Because when I part them, I know you won't hurt me. You won't hurt anyone, Xander. Not anymore."

I stepped away, though every nerve in my body screamed in protest at the increasing distance. My voice was flat, emotionless. "Miranda, I don't want to live."

"But you're getting better. You don't have to die. Don't you see? You can control your power, you aren't out of control anymore."

My hands slammed on the bars so hard they shuddered, and lights flickered all around us. "I am not in control," I bellowed.

And I wasn't. Perhaps I'd gained a modicum of control over the pain of my overflowing power, but when it came to her, I was entirely out of control. I wanted her more than reason. Maybe even more than death, but I wouldn't hurt her. I absolutely refused to do that. I'd much rather die.

"Yes, you are," she stubbornly countered, sticking out that

tempting lower lip. She stalked over to the control panel and hit the button, opening my cage.

Damn it.

"You won't hurt me," she declared. "Come with me." She extended a hand. "Let's go aboveground. If you step out of line, I'll kill you, and we'll try again tomorrow."

How dare she?

How dare she tempt me with a dream long dead and buried? After so long, I'd have no idea how to return to the world. I was meant for shadows and solitude, or death.

Spinning on my heel, I retreated back into the shadows of my cage.

My spirited little badass had lost all sense and reason. This was evidence that Timothy was right; things had gone much farther than they should have.

If I have to hurt her, to sever this bond that I've foolishly entangled her in, then so be it. I pivot once more and strode toward her, falling back on my bitterness, my resentment, all the pain that had turned parts of me dark with cruelty.

"Miranda, I am not safe. You are not safe with me."

"Yes, I am." She fully believed it, her hand still extended with unwavering confidence in me. She walked further into my cage, ready and willing to trust me. It repulsed me.

I let out a harsh laugh. "You think you want this? That makes me wonder then. Did you ever even love your husband?"

The change in direction was so sudden, her hand dropped. "How can you say that?" Pain saturated her words.

I shrugged. "I'm just saying, it sounds like you chose him because he was safe and self-sufficient. You thought he could take care of himself, and you wouldn't have to. But then he died."

Miranda shook her head. "Shut up. You don't know anything about me or Rashon. He was a good man, and he shouldn't have died."

I had my foothold now. I advanced on her, sneering. "That's the thing, Miranda. Of course, he should have. It's what mortals do. No one makes it out alive. Or rather, no one should."

"I know what you are doing." She tried to act like my words didn't affect her, but the quiver in her voice told me her subconscious was shaky at best on the topic.

I circled her with slow, predatory strides. "If you loved him, you could never want me, Miranda. I am the opposite. You want to take me out into the world? He saved people, I would hurt them. Sometimes it would be an accident, and sometimes. . .not." That at least was a truth I was certain of. Captivity and pain had stripped away the remnants of humanity I possessed as a god. "Rashon took care of himself, but you would always have to watch me. Make sure I didn't hurt someone. Hurt you." When I circled behind her, I whispered in her ear, "hurt your son."

Miranda shook her head hard, as if trying to dislodge my words. But I knew the fear I was planting in her would grow. She could put herself in danger, but not her child.

The idea of harming a child revolted me, but I had to lean into the idea to convince her.

"It's best for everyone, Miranda," I said, reaching into her jacket. I reveled in the warmth of her body and her scent far too much as my hand withdrew her blade. She took it from me, and I backed away, adopting a combative stance.

"Kill me," I commanded. "And this time, you are going to chop off my head. Perhaps that will do the trick."

Miranda's brows were furrowed in a mix of anger and pain.

"Do it," I growled when she didn't respond.

"No," she shot back, even as her grip tightened around Bob.

"Do it," I yelled, taking a few menacing steps toward her. My movements were jerky and unpredictable. I would never hurt her, but I needed to provoke her.

"I don't want to," she said, something sparking through her anger. Fear?

Yes, fear. It's what I needed. I could break her bond to me with that.

I retreated to the far side of the room, melting into the shadows.

"Fucking do it," I roared, letting my body partially shift into the monster I truly was. Then I rushed straight at her. The whites of her eyes were all I saw before her blade slashed through the air. Suddenly, I found myself flying until my head slammed into the ground. I felt both heavy and light at the same time.

My brain took another second to register that she'd done exactly what I asked before everything went black. I hoped this would be the last time, so I wouldn't have to live with the terrible things I said to her.

* * *

I blinked. I blinked again. The concrete wall of my cell came into focus.

Godsdammit.

I was hoping decapitation would do the trick.

Apparently not. My head throbbed, and my throat was sore. Still, another piece of the all-consuming magic has been chipped away.

A sniffle caught my attention. Pushing myself up off the ground, I found I wasn't alone. Miranda sat, curled up in a ball on the far end of the room, her arms wrapped around her knees. Tears streamed from her red rimmed eyes as her body shook.

I'm next to her in an instant. Without thinking, I wrapped my arms around her.

I hushed her in soothing tones, trying to generate some kind of heat in my body so I could envelope her in warmth. The wretchedness I felt was nothing compared to any death she had bestowed upon me.

I'd meant to hurt her, and I had. I truly was a fucking beast.

Miranda worked to gain control of her hiccuping sobs but failed. Still, I understood her words. "Please don't make me do that again."

I'd been so focused on getting her to kill me, I didn't think of the horror she might witness at taking off my head. She was supposed to separate my head from my body and separate herself from me at the same time. But she'd stayed. That hadn't been the plan.

"Why didn't you leave?" I asked in frustration, rubbing her arm. She felt cold, too cold.

She shook her head. "I couldn't leave you like that. I was too scared to leave. And then when you started to. . ."

She stayed. Miranda stayed and watched my decapitated body slither towards my head until I knitted myself back together.

Her head shook more vigorously. "I couldn't leave you like that." She wiped her nose on her arm. "Please don't make me do that again," she repeated, her voice so hoarse it threatened to shatter my heart.

Oh gods. I pulled her until she was forced to unravel from her ball and plaster against my chest. My arms wrapped tightly around her, as tears soaked my chest. "I won't. I won't make you do it again. I'm so sorry, sweetheart." Then I pulled her into my lap so I could hold her more completely. To my surprise, she let me.

We stayed that way for a long time. Me rocking her and holding her tightly. My senses filled with the salt of her tears, and bergamot oil. Eventually, Miranda stopped crying, but I didn't even think of letting go. She continued to tremble for a long time after. Even when that stopped, I continued to hold her against me.

I broke my badass. I couldn't forgive myself for that.

Only when her breath evened out, did I realize she fell asleep. I didn't want to wake her. So I stood up, with her still in my arms and walked to the back of the cage. I opened the door and left the cell behind us.

THE BADASS

Even in Xander's arms, the stress didn't leave my body. I stayed partially aware, afraid I'd forget he was really alive. I needed to keep a part of my consciousness on to cling to that fact.

If we had left off like that. . .if he hadn't healed and woken up. It would have been like being stuck inside a nightmare. My heart thudded dully, grief still welling inside me though he was fine.

I suddenly understood Vivien better when she lost her shit over Grim getting hurt. He was a god, he couldn't die. Or not in the conventional ways. But while immortals were used to the occasional stab wound or car explosion, my human brain wasn't conditioned to be 'okay' with it. Everything in me had twisted up in sickening knots.

Xander was awake and whole, but my brain and body wouldn't calm down.

At one point, I felt Xander pick me up and move us onto something soft and comfortable. Exhausted and tense, I couldn't force myself awake for what felt like a long time. I only cracked open a lid when I no longer felt the warmth of his embrace.

"Xander," I cried out in a panic, jerking up, my eyes flew wide. I couldn't comprehend what I was seeing, or figure out where I was, at first. Then everything slowly came into focus.

I sat up on a massive bed in a huge rocky cavernous grotto. Several pools of water reflected against the stone walls with a magical shimmer of light. The room was lit by soft, warm torches that cast dancing shadows across the walls, somehow creating a cozy, intimate feel in the cavernous space.

I breathed in the scent of the warm, humid air, and my eyes drank in the beauty of the many pools, each one unique in its shape and size. Some were small and circular, while others were long and winding, stretching off into the distance like a river. The pools were filled with crystal-clear water.

I slipped out of the bed, covered in supremely soft white sheets. My bare feet met rocky ground, but it was smooth and somehow warm. I only wore my camisole and panties. My clothes were neatly folded in a pile by the bed.

The walls of the grotto were rough-hewn and uneven, giving the space an ancient, timeless feel. And yet, despite the ruggedness of the stone, the entire space was infused with a sense of tranquility and peace.

As I walked around, I could hear the sound of water trickling from a nearby waterfall. The sound was soothing, and it drew me closer until I was standing in front of it, watching as the water cascaded down over the rocks and into the pool below.

An inexplicable warmth crept over my shoulders, the distinct signature of Xander's presence. I swiveled around. His gaze was a penetrating mix of shadow and fire, casting sparks that caused the very air to bristle with energy. Yet, in this tranquil space, he seemed strangely soft, his strength manifesting as a protective veil rather than a threatening force.

"How are you feeling?" he asked. Apology was etched deeply in his eyes as his fists closed and relaxed repeatedly, like he needed to let off nervous energy.

The need to throw myself into his arms was overwhelming, but I was so thrown by my surroundings that I crossed my arms over my body. "A little cold, but I'm okay."

I hadn't been cold when he'd been in bed with me. And some part of me recognized the temperature of my body was directly related to the stress I'd been undergoing lately. If I didn't watch it, I was going to get sick. When I was younger and I got too stressed out, I'd get colds. But I'd learned to manage my emotions so well, I hadn't been sick in many years.

Xander took my wrist, unfurling my arms. "Come here," he said.

And like a little idiot, I went with him, following the beast to wherever he led.

I was guided up to one of the medium sized pools. With a push from his thumbs, his pants slid off his hips and puddled on the ground at his feet. Then he stepped into the water and it instantly began to bubble as if jets had been turned on.

God, he was fucking beautiful. My scarred, broken god. Regret and pain radiated from his eyes, as his face shone with hope that I would follow him in.

I shouldn't forgive him. I should stick Bob right in his heart and stomp away. But I'd been broken down into little pieces when I'd—Jesus, I could barely say it in my mind—chopped his head off.

It really put the horror in horrible.

His hand stretched out toward me, inviting me to join without pressing the issue. It was my choice.

I slipped mine into his before stepping into the water, not bothering to take off my garments.

A smile flickered at the corner of his lips. Gorgeous bastard. I shouldn't give him relief after what he put me through, but it was more like I couldn't deny myself comfort. And the hot water lapping against my legs instantly made me feel better. I followed him further in until I could crouch down and the water line stopped at my neck. It was like some giant, ancient hot spring and I instantly felt soothed by the heat working its way through my muscles.

Xander watched me carefully, slowly approaching, neck deep as well. His hands wrapped around my waist, and he floated me until my back was pressed against the pool wall.

His gaze dropped to my lips, leaning in but giving me plenty of time to protest. Plenty of time to shove him back, call him a monster, and storm out of here. I didn't though. I told myself again, I needed, no, I *deserved* the comfort.

Xander kissed me so tenderly, my toes curled, and my heart swelled. His mouth opened and slanted against mine, filling unexpected parts of me with his depths. He kissed me like. . .like he loved me.

But I knew it was just an apology. An immortal couldn't love a mortal, I told myself. Just like Candy Land, I was a game. I may be his favorite game, but a game none the less. I melted, letting his kiss wash over me, feeling my heart ache with the longing I'd been trying so hard to suppress. I knew it was wrong to let him touch me, wrong to let myself be vulnerable to him again, but I couldn't help it. The warmth of his lips, the heat of his body, all of it was too much to resist. I wanted him, needed him, despite everything that had happened.

Xander deepened the kiss, exploring my mouth with his tongue, his hands roaming over my body as if he couldn't get enough of me. I moaned, my body responding to his touch, despite the doubts that lingered in my mind.

For a moment, I let myself forget about everything else, lost in the sensation of his touch, the feel of his lips on mine. The way his fingers grazed and massaged my neck so he could gain better purchase on me, molding me to him. But reality soon came crashing down, and I pulled away from him, breaking the kiss.

"Don't you ever make me do that again," I barked at him in my sternest tone.

He shook his head. "Wish granted," he confirmed.

Then I grabbed him by the back of the neck and hauled him down for a deeper, searching kiss. I wanted to disappear in him.

The water bubbled more emphatically around us. Xander took my arms and splayed them on the edges of the pool. I was impatient and wanted to fight him, but something about his expression stopped me. He swam back a few feet then raised his hands. His palms glowed blue before they lowered into the water.

Shoots of water connected with my body. Swirling vortexes caressed my breasts, varying in temperature from cool to hot, making my brain turn fuzzy with arousal.

A shoot of water licked up and down my cleft through my sodden panties that suddenly felt heavy and cloying. I let out a gasp, as my center became molten.

"Did I mention," he said casually, "That I'm god of the seas?"

"You might have," I said breathlessly. My panties were slowly pushed to the side to make way. Then another tiny vortex found its way around my clit while there was still the sweeping motion up and down my pussy. My jaw parted as all my muscles turned liquid.

There was a parting of the seas joke tumbling around my sex-addled brain, but I couldn't catch it and pin it down.

My head fell back as the magic jets held me captive, playing me like an instrument.

"Fuck, Miranda," Xander growled. "You don't know how fucking incredible you are."

"Sure I do," I shot back, then let out a high-pitched moan as what felt like a column of water penetrated me.

"WH—," I asked.

The column of water was moving inside me. I was panting now. I put my hand against the side of the pool and tried to hold myself up.

The heat of the pool had made me pliable, and the pressure was as soothing as it was insistent in pushing my arousal higher.

Xander directed the column of water deeper and faster. It curled up and hit a sensitive spot in me that had my rocking my hips riding the sensation that coiled tighter and tighter in my lower stomach.

"I've thought of you in a bubble bath, more than once," he confessed, his irises blown out as he watched me with blatant hunger. "I've thought long and hard of how I could top your lavender scented froth to get you to relax.

The vortex quickened around my clit, and I gasped again. Xander finally drew near, kissing me, filling my senses with his power and masculinity.

I came for him then. I came hard and long. And I just kept coming. He didn't stop. The water continued to invade me, hitting a specific spot I didn't know I had, again and again.

The climax was beyond anything I'd ever experienced. I couldn't have imagined it. I was floating and was slowly drifting in and out of consciousness.

When I'd finished, the pool stilled around us. Xander pulled me close. My body was limp as he swam me to the edge. My arms reached for him. He scooped me up but kept me in the water, floating to and fro.

"Is that your version of an apology?" I asked, trying to sound coherent and alert.

"Gods don't apologize," he explained, even as a smile tipped up one side of his mouth.

"Well as nice as your apology was, it's not a substitute."

Deep blue eyes met mine as his grip tightened around me. "I'm sorry," he whispered in a ragged tone that begged forgiveness. "I'm so very sorry, sweetheart."

"I meant it's not a substitute for this," I said, pushing away so I broke from his hold. Then I reached down and encircled his long hard cock with my hand. Even the feel of him made my mouth turn dry as the anticipation built around how I was going to fit all that in me, again.

"Miranda," his tone was still a plea, begging for me to stop, or for me to continue. I wasn't sure.

The words crowded in my throat again, wanting to work at convincing him that he didn't have to die. I kept them stuck there, not wanting to ruin the moment.

"While your power is epic, I just want... I just want you." When did my voice get so raspy? Xander's eyes lit up with surprise.

And then we were out of the pool and he was carrying me back to the bed at the center of the grotto.

Chapter Twenty-Eight

THE BEAST

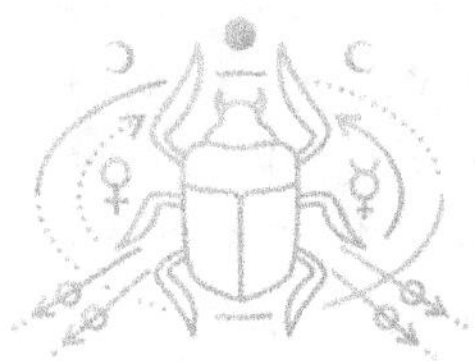

She wanted me. *Me.*

Even when I freely roamed the earth, the humans would prostrate themselves before my almighty power, but not before *me.*

I lay her dripping body down on my bed, my chest squeezing so tight with the prospect of having another being here. I'd resigned myself to the doom of remaining in my prison alone. But suddenly, my cave didn't feel so oppressive.

Leaning over Miranda, I captured those full, sensual lips in a kiss.

I thought I'd found salvation in the death Miranda would serve me, but this was so much more than I could have ever dreamed. My hands slid up her bent legs, starting at those perfect ankles, smoothing up her muscular calves and gliding back down her sinful thighs.

Miranda shivered, her long dark lashes fluttering. She must be cold, still wet from the spring. I needed to heat her up, but I didn't plan on using a towel, and she was going to be wetter than when we started.

The pads of my fingers played along the slit of her mound until her hips bucked.

This wasn't a game though. Right now, we were just two beings who wanted each other. Nothing else mattered.

I'd show her. Show her that while I was the god here, she was the one deserving of worship. I'd slay her with pleasure and draw her blood out with a kiss.

I kneeled and spread her legs wide. I brought my lips to her pussy, and with my tongue, I licked away the water. The saltiness of it tingled my taste buds and whetted my appetite.

Her hips shot off the bed as she cried out. The sounds made my cock rock hard. I found the sensitive bundle of nerves between her folds and swirled my tongue around it. I was obsessed, addicted, and ready to drown in her pussy. Without preamble, I stuck three fingers up into her slick channel. She squealed and squirmed at the sudden invasion, but they were instantly coated with her desire. So I brought them up to her hot mouth, sticking them down her throat, forcing her to taste herself. Her body undulated as she sucked my fingers while I continued to devour her sex.

Her sultry groans vibrated through me. I savored every moment of her enjoyment, something I hadn't experienced within the chaos and darkness my life was consumed by.

I licked and sucked and teased her until she was a quivering, slippery mess. Until she gripped my hair in her fists. Then I plunged my tongue into her, fucking her in earnest. The sound Miranda made made me feral. I drove into her even harder, faster, penetrating her delicious, sinful center.

Nails scraped along my scalp, urging me on. And yet, she was fighting it. I could feel her body brace against me, struggling to maintain control, trying not to fall over the edge I desperately wanted to push her over.

Why were we always fighting?

And why did I love it so much. Reaching out and gathering my power, I pulled it to me until I moved it all into my mouth, wrapping it around my tongue. I unleashed the power to follow the rhythm of my tongue, sending shockwaves and pressure into her, bombarding her.

"No, no," was all she got out before her knees jerked up, her upper body curling forward as she screamed. Her muscles rippled with release around my tongue, her hips and thighs jerking and shaking, completely overtaken by pleasure.

I backed off as she rode out the end of her orgasm, delighting in the mess she made on my face. I licked my lips, feeling way too fucking satisfied with myself despite my hungry, hard cock still demanding attention.

Miranda tugged me up for a kiss. Her mouth opened for my tongue and I happily swept inside, letting her taste herself — sex, the sea, and citrus.

My hands gripped her hips and I brought her to the edge of the bed. My cock pulsed at the entrance to her sex. Her glassy eyes widened, her ragged breath hitched. We were far from done.

Her head fell back and her hands roamed over her breasts, plucking and pinching her nipples. I watched her for a moment as she pleasured herself for me. She was magnificent. Her full, pouty lips pursed as I eased into her willing body. Her inner muscles clamped around my cock and I groaned at the sensation.

"Oh no. Please," she begged, still not wholly giving in to what she wanted.

"A god could get confused with how many times you say no opposite to the all the other ways you tell me yes."

Her eyes opened to glaring slits.

So now was *not* a good time to go over her psychology. Right.

My hands grabbed her hips and I slammed into her, over and over. I was going to bury myself so deep inside her I could never leave again.

She cried out and grasped the sheets, clutching them tightly.

Even as she said it, her body tensed against me. I knew. I knew though she wanted every bit of me, she would yet again fight her desire every step of the way. But I also knew if I didn't let up, that her resistance would turn against her and drown her in pleasure. I intended to do just that.

I let go of her hips and she wrapped her legs around me so I could better drive into her.

"Miranda," I whispered into her ear again. "No one has to know. Just give it to me baby." My cock slid through her wetness as she clenched and contracted around me. So close. . .

A seemingly endless moment passed as our bodies melded together, sweat sticking us together. Her breasts pressed against my chest. I didn't want to stop, but I'd been holding back my release so long, it was going to rip right through me. I stilled and felt her tense.

My angel of death groaned, turning her head to side. She was fighting her release.

I'd have to take it from her. The more she fought, that harder, the faster I pounded into her. She was close. I could feel it. I could tell by the way she held her breath, poised on the edge.

I bent my head and sucked on her elegant column of neck. Her head turned away, eyes clenched shut. She was on the edge, fighting tooth and nail to maintain control.

"Xander. . ." she gritted between her teeth.

"Give it up, sweetheart. Come for me." I wanted to swallow her scream. I wanted to drink it down and die happy.

I reached out and rubbed her clit, my thumb pressing into it just so. I felt her shudder and watched her as her body gave over to what I'd made her feel.

I kissed her, drinking in her scream of pleasure. Her body shook for me and I felt so alive.

Driving into her once, twice, and my own head snapped back as my release shot from me so powerfully, I couldn't see straight.

Somewhere at the back of my mind, I feared hurting her with my power, turning into a monster. But no, I would never fucking hurt my goddess of death. My enchantress. My badass with a sweet heart.

When I came too, we were both panting, my dick softening in her. The feel of her fingers gently stroking my hair relaxed me so completely, I never wanted this moment to end. Not for life, not for death. Just this, forever more.

"So that's how you know about Batman?" She asked after a while.

What?

I pulled back to look into her face. I twisted to follow her gaze. A cluster of monitors showed the empty elevator, the entryway of my cell, and the third one played a 1960s episode of Batman on mute.

Looking down at her again, my lips morphed into a crooked grin. "You thought I was down here for millennia with no means of connection to the outside world? You should see my library. You'd be impressed."

With a glazed, satisfied look in her eye, Miranda nodded. "I bet I would." She sighed a little. "I have an ever-growing stack of books on my bedside table. When I was younger, in high school, I loved to read. But since Jamal. . . I keep buying books that I swear to myself I will make time to read, but the pile continues to grow as I never make time to actually read them."

I pushed back several glistening braids behind her ear, absorbing everything she said.

We drifted into awkward silence. Not about what we'd just done, but because we hadn't resolved anything. Not really.

I'd never make her behead me again, but I didn't believe in me like she did. I'd lost sight of what I was doing and Timothy pointed that out.

Did I want to die anymore? Could I be allowed to live?

To change my mind after wanting death for thousands of years was too severe and violent a turn for my mind to take.

Slipping my soft member from her hot body with a dual groan of protest, I pulled her body against mine, drifting into a light sleep.

I could live, for tonight anyway. Tomorrow I'd deal with Timothy's threats, the madness of my broken brain, and the woman who was making me question everything.

Chapter Twenty-Nine

THE BADASS

There were no dreams, no nightmares, in Xander's arms that night. For the first time in what seemed like forever, I felt rested to the marrow of my bones. It was comforting to fall asleep in one spot and wake up in the same place. I was already stirring from slumber, cocooned against a firm chest, arms wrapped around me like a protective barrier, when the intrusive ding of an elevator forced my eyes open.

My gaze snapped to the flurry of movement on one of Xander's security screens. A parade of all too familiar faces had me springing upright.

"Oh, fuck," I blurted.

Xander made a half-hearted attempt to pull me back into our shared warmth, but I swiveled and swatted him away. "Xander, get up. We've got company."

His brows knitted together, a crease of confusion forming between them before his sapphire eyes flickered open. "What?" he rumbled, his voice laced with suspicion and displeasure.

As I fumbled into my pants with frantic haste, Xander took in the animated scene on the screens.

"Fucking hell," he echoed, a growl rumbling in his throat as he raked a hand through his tousled hair

Fully dressed, I snatched up my duster with Bob safely nestled inside. I pivoted around, searching for an exit. Strangely, until that moment, the thought of wanting to leave hadn't crossed my mind.

Xander was up, his pants slung low around his chiseled hips, a sight that kindled a familiar warmth coursing through my lower body, stirring memories of our shared intimacy. But I pushed all arousal and emotions aside. A storm was about to hit, and I needed to stay focused.

"This way," Xander said, leading me to a stone staircase that curved around and up a wall. With each step, I slipped more into battle mode. By the time we stood in front of the large steel door, I was ready.

As it swung open, a tumult of yelling and arguing assailed us, hitting like a sucker punch

Silence dropped like a curtain as I stepped into the room, Xander right on my heels, his hand a comforting weight against my lower back. Yet, no amount of preparation could brace me for the confrontation ahead.

Bianca, Grim, Timothy, and Vivien were scattered around the room. Confusion creased Grim's brow at our arrival, while Bianca's eyes ballooned in shock. Vivien, however, couldn't mask her triumphant smirk, her eyes dancing with delight. As if she had been in on my secret all along.

She was my friend; I shouldn't have felt embarrassed. But so many people charging into my private, intimate moment made my skin crawl and my heart pound. My stomach knotted up, then knotted again.

"What is this?" Grim asked, looking back and forth between me, Timothy, Xander, and Vivien. It seemed my friend had kept some secrets after all.

"See?" Vivien said, pumping her fist in the air. "No one has to die."

Bianca watched me closely, and I tried to avoid her gaze.

Xander stepped forward. "What brings you all here?" he asked, sounding unimpressed. "I haven't had this many visitors since we moved from Egypt."

Timothy's mouth tightened, and I suddenly felt like a teenager caught sneaking a boyfriend into my bedroom. Except his disapproving look was aimed at Xander.

Grim gestured at the goddess in the soft pink dress. "Bianca came to me insisting that I put a stop to our arrangement."

"Hear, hear," Bob chimed in.

I bit my lower lip to keep from shushing the blade, as no one else could hear him. At least he'd remained silent during my other, more intimate moments. Who knew I'd appreciate a blade's discretion so much?

Bianca's light blue eyes darted between me and Xander. "Then you can't do it? You can't go through with it?" The conflict in her eyes told me she didn't necessarily approve of our relationship, but I think she was willing to accept it if it got her what she wanted.

"Miranda will follow through as planned," Timothy interjected.

Vivien's impish smile transformed into a displeased frown. "Hey, just because you aren't getting any, Timmy, doesn't mean you have to dampen other people's happiness."

I tensed. Was this happiness? Was that what I'd experienced in Xander's strong arms, in his bed, in his cave? Or was it merely a fleeting moment of peace?

Timothy whirled to face Vivien. "Quit stoking the fire, Vivien. Can't you see this is a recipe for disaster?"

"That's exactly my point," Bianca interjected, her voice tense. "If she ends Xander's life, catastrophe will follow."

"That's as vague as saying if you toss a coin, you might hit a leprechaun or just get a heads or tails," Vivien shot back.

Bianca's nose wrinkled as her brows knit.

It was a weird saying, but I completely understood her meaning. That's part of why we were friends.

Grim's voice, steady and low, cut through the escalating tension. Acting every bit the judge he was, he commented, "Bianca, your prediction could use more specificity and clarity if it is to hold any weight.

"I'm telling you," Bianca urged, "if he dies," she pointed at Xander, "we are going to face a world-ending threat."

"You also said that would happen if I revived Grim," Vivien countered, stepping protectively in front of Grim. She wouldn't change anything about what she did and dared Bianca to say otherwise. Vivien seemed to have forgotten they were on the same side.

Bianca brushed her hair back from her face. "That's what I'm telling you, Vivien. This is all connected. Bringing Grim back has tipped a line of dominoes into motion that are falling faster and faster, bringing us all here. And it very well may take us to the end of days."

"Bianca," Timothy snapped, his voice tinged with frustration. "Xander deserves death. It is his right. He has been denied all these years, and the world has only suffered from his presence."

Xander's spine curved as if he'd been physically hit.

Timothy kept going though. "He is the reason we left our home and came here, to get far from the ocean. He causes brownouts with his overflow of power and is one step away from being a nuclear bomb."

"But he's better," Vivien said, her tone pleading. "Miranda has been cutting a lot of his power away, and he is better. They can have a happy ending."

"Xander has been too far removed from the world," Timothy chided, his eyes narrowing at her. "He cannot reintegrate, not after so long. It would be a danger to everyone. It's not just his power that makes him dangerous."

I nervously licked my lips, watching the battle unfold, feeling excluded. I had been prepared to be thrust into the melee, but it felt worse being left out of it.

All this time, Grim had been silent, his gaze heavy upon me. He was studying me, like he could see all the mistakes, all the strange games, and the bizarre dance I'd engaged in with Xander. I'd started out as a professional, but now I'd fallen into another mode altogether.

"Love," my brain whispered. "You've fallen in love."

Or was it Bob that whispered that?

But Grim had also forsaken all the rules because he loved Vivien. I was ready for him to take the work out of this, tell Timothy that it was clear I couldn't go forward with this. Not with Bianca's vision. I was going to be released here and now from my duties by the Grim Reaper himself, and then we'd go from there.

"You are such a baby," Vivien said, wheeling on Timothy, her stance defensive. "This feels way more about your piss-poor excuses to keep Aaron at an arm's distance than it is about Xander and Miranda's situation. Do you just not want anyone to be happy if it can't fit into your little boxes?"

Timothy's face flushed fully red. I'd never seen him so out of sorts. A crackling power filled the room, different from Xander's. It was more lightweight and nipped at the skin like little sparklers that almost, but didn't, hurt.

"That's enough," Grim bellowed, his face flickering into a skull of deep, sucking darkness. It made the pit of my stomach drop out, as if my body anticipated instant death. But Grim's face cleared back into the whiskey-colored human eyes, gaze still trained on me and Xander.

"Bianca, I give your visions great credence, but if there was one thing I know, it was that death was necessary for the health and well-being of this entire realm. Xander's anomaly threw even the elements into chaos. And as the protector of humanity, I could not condone his existence to continue in such a way. Miranda swore she would uphold the duty of her blade and made the judgement that it would be so. I trusted she would abide by her judgement without emotions clouding the matter."

The breath was sucked straight out from my lungs. Instead of grabbing and clinging to Xander's arm protectively, I curled my hands into fists. My boss's eyes were a mix of disappointment and regret. Disappointment in me, regret for having to be the enforcer in the situation.

"Grim," Bianca breathed sharply as if he'd slapped her. The god of the dead held dominion over all other gods, and what he said, went. She'd been shut down, and there was nothing she could do about it.

Vivien's expression was crestfallen, her shoulders curved in disappointment. Her eyes welled with tears, and I knew my best friend well enough to sense she was taking his judgement personally. While she was a vampire, she still had an overabundance of humanity and did her best to influence him with it, but it was clear he would not be swayed on this matter further.

Timothy adjusted his cufflinks, avoiding my gaze. He'd gotten what he wanted. But a bitter seed of resentment in me agreed with Vivien.

Timothy had made my situation with Xander some strange avatar of his own issues with Aaron. He wanted to ruin our chance because he didn't have one of his own.

No, that wasn't fair. Timothy was my friend.

It was me. Me who wanted Grim to change his mind. But there was someone else's will I answered to over Grim's. My shoulders straightened. I told Grim I wouldn't do it for him. I would judge based off the plea of the god himself.

"I agree," Xander said. "Thank you for making this simple, Grim. I've always appreciated your sound judgement."

I pivoted to Xander, incredulity contorting my features. My eyes, usually guarded, laid bare the sting of betrayal. I expected him to be defensive and cold like he usually was when he was trying to push me away. But instead, I saw sound logic and agreement with Grim.

I could fight him on being stubborn, but I couldn't fight this.

"Xander, I—" I couldn't. I couldn't do it. I couldn't kill him because I loved him.

My throat closed around itself, strangling the words out. I could barely admit it to myself, much less in front of so many others.

Xander gave me a half-smile and grabbed my shoulders, kissing my forehead. "This was always the plan," he said, reaching for my duster and pulling out Bob.

Bob cried out in protest, "No, no, no! Tell him, Miranda! Tell him you can't kill him because you love him. That every time you end his life, you kill a little bit of yourself. And tell him I don't want to taste his blood anymore. It's. . .it's icky."

Despite Bob's childlike whines, his words struck me in the heart, but I couldn't bring myself to say it. So, I took Bob's hilt from Xander while the god urged me on silently, and everyone stood there waiting for me. My throat tightened, and my chest felt heavy.

Xander tried to comfort me, saying, "It's okay, sweetheart," with a crooked smile that held both swagger and resignation.

I knew Xander would wake up again, and I would have to kill him again. Each time, he would be closer to his final death until it was the last time.

Vivien was right. He was less powerful than before. The city hadn't been plagued by brownouts. He didn't mutilate himself or lose control. But I was only one piece of this decision, and I was judging it with my heart.

In a raspy voice, I replied, "Wish granted," and then stabbed him in the heart, in front of the other immortals. Every part of me iced over as I made myself cold to his death, to his fate, and my hand in it.

My job had gone from helping an immortal find relief from an eternity of pain to killing someone I loved. And right now, it was me who was dying inside.

THE BEAST

It has been two days. Two near eternal days since Miranda killed me, or even fucking showed up.

I hadn't slept, hadn't eaten, I hadn't even gone back down to my chambers. I simply stalked the bars of my cage back and forth, minute after minute, hour after hour, waiting for her. My angel of death.

Without an explanation of her absence, I wracked my brain for a suitable substitute. Is this because she didn't forgive me for forcing her to decapitate me? Is this because she saw another side of me, and she couldn't stand me now?

I thought turning into my godlikeness and losing control in front of her was a vulnerability I couldn't bear. But taking her into my inner sanctum and experiencing bliss with her in my bed, in my personal springs where no other being visited, had been a whole new level of vulnerability for me.

Or was this a rebellion against Grim's judgement and my desires? Was she flat out going to defy the death order?

Was she right? The blade had killed off so much of my excess power, I felt almost...normal.

Whatever that was.

It was a time where I was a powerful god, in control of my faculties.

It felt far away now, but I knew the times I'd sparred with Miranda, the times we'd played our games, I'd exhibited a control I couldn't remember having. She truly was safe with me. The need to protect and be with her magnetized my shattered pieces, bringing me into a new kind of wholeness. They didn't fit together like pieces of a puzzle; it was a clump of shards. Was that enough? Was that enough for an existence?

But an existence without Miranda—I was falling apart at the very idea.

I thought living in pain and power was hell, but it was nothing compared to this new prospect. Living an eternity, being denied death, and never seeing Miranda again.

I'd be trapped down here, thinking of her sweet taste, her seductive eyes, her strength and softness. I'd be haunted by her, yet never getting to see her again.

My hands trembled violently as emotion surged in me. I'd been teetering on a thin edge, but my control snapped like a brittle twig. A roar exploded from my chest and throat as the lights blew in a tremendous display of sparks.

Images of Miranda taunting me from outside the bars, continually walking away to the elevator to leave played on repeat. My skin thickened with rage and blue energies surrounded me as I was stuck in the loop of pain and rejection.

I needed her. I fucking needed her now.

If I could just get to the other side of the bars, I'd grab her, shake sense into her. Tell her she can never leave again. Not until I was dead.

She could dance on my bones. She could carve out my face.

Thoughts jumbled and jammed together as my vision filled with flickering hallucinations of black sands, harsh sunlight, and all-consuming darkness.

Something let out a roar exactly like mine from nearby. Or was that me?

Bars bent under my strength, freeing me from my confines. I exploded forward like a cannon ball.

The hot black sands of Egypt, my homeland, scorched the soles of my feet. Bright lights and screaming sirens and horns assaulted my senses.

Words tumbled out of my mouth, but they were other words from the other people, the power of other gods. They were all here, crowding me out, threatening to explode my brains.

"They want her blade. They want her hands. They are in her brain and her mind and her brain. They toy with her, wind wind wind, chatter chatter chatter."

My heart pounded so hard and fast, I feared it would break through my chest. Rage and need collided; two powerful tidal waves smashing into each other, rocking the entire ocean.

Miranda came into view, throwing a terror-stricken glance over her shoulder. She was being chased. A bright blazing heat followed her. She was going to burn. Like I did. My throat turned dry.

Then she blipped out of existence. She'd been taken. I cried out in rage. I had to get her. Had to get her back.

An oak door appeared before me.

She was through the door. I had to break it to get her. I'd break everything and everyone to get to her.

My foot kicked into the wood, and it crashed open.

"Miranda," I roared, slamming the door open. I had to find her. I had to find who took her. If they so much as frayed one of her braids, I would rip their eyeballs out and eat them.

A voice broke through my insanity. "Xander?"

All my broken pieces slammed together, yanking me into the present, grounding me in reality. And I found myself inside a house I didn't recognize, facing a completely shocked Miranda.

Chapter Thirty-One

THE BADASS

I blinked.

This wasn't my cage.

This was a house. I was outside in the real world. The air was different. There was so much of it, and it blew all over the world before ruffling my hair up off my forehead.

Miranda's house emanated a comforting blend of practicality and warmth, its earthy tones and inviting furnishings creating an inviting atmosphere. Framed photographs of her son, Jamal, adorned the walls, capturing his radiant smile that radiated joy and innocence. While his eyes and mouth mirrored Miranda's, the distinct features of a wide nose bridge and darker skin tone clearly bore resemblance to the man depicted in the well-framed, official army photo—his father.

I blinked.

What the fuck had I done?

Miranda stood halfway between the kitchen and the living room of her house. She wore purple sweat pants and a black tank top. The coffee table was littered with used tissues, and it looked like she'd made a cocoon of blankets around her on the couch earlier and could return to the same spot later. Half empty mugs also covered the table, while the television flickered colorful light into the room. The sound of rushing water from a faucet filtered in from another room.

Miranda stared at me wide-eyed.

"You're okay," was all I could manage to say.

Her brows furrowed, as if she couldn't understand how I stood inside her house.

I didn't understand either. But I was here.

"You didn't come to kill me," I explained lamely.

She started to say something but was overtaken by a sneeze. Grabbing first one, then two tissues, she blew her nose. When she got hold of her sneezing, she answered in a nasal, congested voice. "I have a cold, so I called into work."

For fucks sake.

"No one told me." My tone was defensive. Suddenly I felt foolish standing there at her threshold.

"You left your cage?" she asked, jaw still hanging in disbelief.

"Yes, well. I thought something had happened to you."

She shot a look over my shoulder. It was then I realized I left the door open. It barely hung from one of its hinges. I closed it as best I could, not entirely sure I was on the right side of it.

"How did you know where I live?" she asked.

How did I know? I searched my addled mind. Had I found her by pure instinct? Or was it something more tangible?

"You have it neatly labeled inside your lunchbox." And I remembered it. I remembered everything about her.

She spoke again, slowly as if trying to make sense of things. "You broke out of your cage because I didn't come to kill you, and you thought you needed to come rescue me?"

Okay well now I felt absolutely stupid. My overreaction was of epic proportions.

"I didn't know where you were," I said with vehemence. Was I defending my intrusion to her, or my out-of-control reaction to myself?

Yet, her expression softened. As if she was touched by what I'd done. Then her eyes shut as she swayed a little on her feet. In a flash, I was at her side, easing her back onto the couch. I laid my hand on her forehead. Heat radiated into my palm even as she shivered. "You are burning up."

She was ill. I shouldn't take such great pleasure in touching her but hell if it wasn't the most soul-satisfying thing in the world right now to hold her.

"I'll be better by tomorrow. But I guess I can kill you now since you are here," she said even as her teeth chattered, trying to get up.

I gently guided her back down.

"No, that's not why I came." It pained me to think she believed I may have come here just to make sure she performed her duty to me. Who knew how many more blows it would take to kill me? It could be a hundred, it could take only one more? Either way, it was more important she take care of herself first. If I'd known what was preventing her to come to me, I would have waited.

...probably.

"You need to rest," I assured her.

Miranda let out a loud sniffle, momentarily giving the impression that she wanted to speak. However, she shook her head ever so slightly, as if rejecting the notion. "You should go. I don't want to get you sick," she said.

Without thinking, I replied, "I can't get sick."

But then it dawned on me, her unspoken consideration. I asked the question tentatively, my heart swelled with hope, almost fearing her response. "Would you like me to stay by your side?"

"No." She said it so fast, I knew that was exactly what had been rolling around her brain.

Game over, sweetheart.

I stood abruptly, with purpose. "Too bad because I'm not leaving." Walking to the kitchen, I picked up the steel tea kettle and filled it with water from the sink."

"Even if you can't get sick, I can't...entertain you," she said.

I raised an eyebrow at her. "What do you mean, entertain me?"

"I'm not up for, you know." She coupled her incoherence with waving a hand back and forth between us.

"For fucks sake," I said, horror dawning on me. "I didn't come here for sex, either."

I followed the sound of running water to her bathroom. She'd been preparing to run a bath. Noting the water was hot, I stopped up the drain. A variety of bubble bath serums sat around the edge. I instantly grabbed the lavender one and dumped half the bottle in. Fuck, I loved this scent on her skin.

Miranda stood in the doorway; a large blanket wrapped around her shoulders. She frowned at me as if I were a misbehaving child. "What are you doing?"

"You may have a fever, but you are also chilled. We need to get you warmed up."

"I can take care of my—of my—*Achoo*."

"Has anyone told you that you sneeze like a mouse?" The woman suppressed all of her instincts, even her sneezes. It was unexpectedly adorable.

The brows over her eyes furrowed deeper. Her pallor was ashen even as she defied me. "I do not."

She didn't shy away when I drew near, but she clung to the blanket even as I tried to remove it from her shoulders.

"Let me help you," I said, softly.

Miranda's full lips parted a moment before closing. Knowing her, she was caught between saying no or she didn't need help from anyone. Playing dirty, I yanked the blanket off her. Then moving in a most unthreatening manner, my fingers went to the hem of her shirt.

I waited, silently asking for permission. Though she still remained pensive, she lifted her arms as I pulled the shirt off.

Fucking hell, her nipples tightened in response to the cold air. I wanted to taste them again. But I wasn't a beast in that respect. I would never maul her when she was in such a state. Not until she was just as hot and willing as the last time.

As Miranda pushed off her pajama pants, she swayed again. I grabbed her, keeping her upright. It also brought her naked body flush against mine. The heat of her chest on mine felt so fucking good.

Her eyes turned up to meet mine. They were bleary and bloodshot, but I could see a heat behind them. "I can take care of myself."

"Of course you can," I assured her. Still, I walked backward, drawing her with me until we were next to the sudsy water.

She licked her lips, slowly, and I expected her to kick me out any second. "Let me help you in."

"Okay." The word was so soft, I needed to rely on my supernatural hearing to catch it.

I held her hand, guiding her into the half-filled tub. Bubbles built at an incredible speed. She sank into it with a groan, and her shivers intensified. With her knees up she leaned her head on them as if trying to warm herself.

"C-can y-you hand me that wr-wrap?" She asked through chattering teeth, pointing to the counter.

I grabbed the purple silk cloth. Miranda had already begun to twirl her braids up into a bun. Before she could stop me, I put the cloth over the back of the bun and tied it in the front.

"Is the water too cold?" I asked, watching her continue to shake.

"I'll warm up soon. You can go." Her voice was strained. But I didn't want to go. Instead, I grabbed a hand cloth and dipped it in the water. I smoothed it over her back, trying to help warm her. Her lids fluttered shut as I continued the ministrations.

"This is really weird," she said, cheek resting on her knees, eyes still closed.

"I'll say," I muttered in agreement, watching the water rivulets trickle down her perfect smooth skin. Then I set the rag aside and raised my fingertips over the water. I drew it up in a sheet over her back, like a cloak. To keep the water from cooling, I directed it into a continuous running fountain so hot water was always covering her skin. I became mesmerized by its motion over her strong, elegant back.

Cracking one eye open, she said, "I'm still convinced this is some kind of fever dream."

"Do you often dream of men bathing you?"

"That is none of dream Xander's business," she slurred.

I failed to suppress a smile. Miranda was in a bit of a delirious state. I liked it far too much.

Over and over, I wet the rag in the bubbles before running it over her back in tandem with the water I commanded to surround and caress her. Steam curled up from water and around her body, obscuring the mirror. It wasn't long before she stopped shivering and her breath evened out.

Something in my chest squeezed so tight I almost wondered if Bob hadn't run me through. Being alone all these years, I'd been denied companionship, physical touch, and the ability to care for another. My fingers dipped through the layer of water to stroke down the bare flesh along the ridges of her spine. Having the opportunity to indulge all three, it made me feel…important, connected, and mortal.

Or how I imagined a mortal might feel.

Truthfully, I was bitterly jealous of humans. Their lives were so much more precious than immortals simply because they were finite. They were a song with a beginning, a middle, crescendos, and refrains before they ended on a furious dramatic timbre, or on a soft fading note. An immortal's life was continuous, monotonous, and unchanging. We didn't age, we didn't die, and we didn't have the opportunity to experience that same level of meaning.

This was beyond dangerous, but I was so far away from that basement, that cage, and the version of me that knew my place.

Something stung behind my eyes, causing my lip to curl. Each time Miranda had buried her blade inside me, she'd left a piece of her in there as well.

I lifted the dozing woman out of the water, waving all the moisture away from her body with my power, sending it back into the tub so she was instantly dry. I carried her to the bedroom. She didn't rouse from slumber, even as her arms curled around my neck. The tightness in my chest twisted tighter. Laying her down in her bed, I pulled the sheets up and around her. Then I slid in next to her.

She moaned and turned to wrap her arms around me. Her body molded into mine, a perfect fit.

"Miranda," I said just above a whisper. I half expected her not to hear me.

"Mmm?" she didn't open her eyes.

I swept my hand down her bare arm, enjoying the silky feel of her skin.

Something pressed up against my rib cage. The words I'd been denying. The thing I'd been most afraid of. I was more afraid of the sentiment lodged in my throat than I ever was of not getting a chance to die.

I thought that had been my worse fear, never dying.

But this, this, I was one thousand times more afraid of. It was only into Miranda's ear that I could whisper it.

The words came out shaky. "Miranda. I want to live."

She didn't respond or open her eyes, but I could feel her thinking, hard.

"You're right. For a while now, I've been in control. That is, until tonight. I want to live, but I need you. Without you, my demons will still eat me up from the inside. Say you'll stay with me as long as I live, and I can do it."

Her eyes opened at that. She sniffled, clearing her stuffy nose. "Are you proposing?"

I pulled her against me tighter. "Maybe I am."

She frowned and tried to move away, but I wouldn't let her.

"Xander, this is crazy. You are outside your cage. You aren't thinking right. You've had a taste of freedom and now you have lost it."

"You're right about one thing. I'm crazy. I've been crazy for as long as I can remember. But even all the voices in my head love you and would never hurt you."

"They love me?" she said in a strained voice.

"*I* love you, sweetheart," I clarified with vehemence. "I know all that came out jumbled and backward, but like you said, I'm crazy." Then I flashed her a grin meant to devastate her resistance.

"You've made me so different," she confessed in a whisper filled with fear and awe.

"Any version of you is the right version," I said, my arms tightening around her. Suddenly I was afraid. Scared she didn't like what she'd turned into around me. Maybe she'd rather be something else with someone else. I honestly couldn't blame her. Shackling her to a crazy, feral god was likely a punishment.

Then after a pause, she said, "I love you too." Her words tripped on emotion. Or congestion. I didn't mind either.

I kissed her softly, sweetly, with all the aching tenderness threatening to crack in me. I kissed her with a promise that I would reward her love her and trust.

"As soon as you are feeling better, I'm going to show you exactly how much I fucking love you, sweetheart."

"Promise me one thing," she said, her fingers curling into my chest.

"Anything." And I meant anything. I'd fucking rake down the moon from the sky if she wanted it. I knew a guy.

"No more board games," she said, closing her eyes and snuggling into me.

A laugh rumbled through my chest. "Deal."

Chapter Thirty-Two

THE BADASS

"Something bright flashed through the window. The heat of the light was scalding, and I shied away from it. The room was bathed in an eerie, fiery glow. It seemed almost alive, pulsating with an insidious intent. This wasn't the gentle caress of dawn's first light; it was a harsh, consuming blaze.

Beside me, Xander was a comforting presence, lost in the serenity of his godly dreams. The way his chest rose and fell, the soft, almost purr-like snore he gave every third breath, it was all so normal. It was at odds with the lurking threat I felt seeping into the room.

"Bob," I whispered, reaching for the sword I kept by my bedside.

"What is it now, Miranda?" it muttered, the sarcasm in its voice almost tangible. I wasn't even going to try to figure out how or why a sword would sleep.

"I think we have a problem," I replied, clutching the hilt of the blade. The metal was comforting and cool, the familiar grooves fitting perfectly into my palm. "Something bright."

Bob let out a sound akin to a snort as I hastily pulled on a pair of panties and oversized tee-shirt. "You woke me for a lightbulb? Really, Miranda?"

This wasn't just any bright light. It was malevolent. The room seemed to shrink around it, as if it were absorbing the life force of everything around. I slipped out of bed, careful not to wake Xander, and moved stealthily towards the window. The light outside was blinding, but I forced my eyes to adjust.

Suddenly, the light morphed into a fuzzy, glowing entity, its brightness a cruel mockery of the sun. It was all consuming, eating up the darkness, consuming the night. I gripped Bob tighter, my knuckles white with the intensity. The Blade of Bane hummed, as if sensing the impending danger.

"All right, I see your point," Bob finally conceded, the tone of its voice changing from its usual dry wit to something more serious. "That doesn't look like any lightbulb I've ever seen."

Summoning all my courage, I crept out of the bedroom to the living room. Scalding brightness shone in through the front windows and cut in from around the edges of my front door, trying to get in, trying to hurt me.

There was a presence on the other side of that door. And I held the only weapon that could destroy anything and anyone.

A certainty settled into my gut. If I didn't cut this thing down now, everything was going to burn up. Me, Xander, and everyone I cared about.

I could feel Bob's energy coursing through me, a tingling sensation that spread from my fingertips to the soles of my feet. I could kill it. I knew it in the marrow of my bones that this was the moment to do it.

I threw the door open and leapt out of my house. Bob and I flew through the air with a true strike that would kill the enemy.

A high-pitched scream reverberated, jolting me from my brave attack. My eyes snapped open, the glow of the fuzzy entity fading as I blinked in the face of Xander. Surprise widened his eyes, a flicker of astonishment dancing within them. I wasn't outside at all. I was still in the living room of my house.

I looked down at the sword in my hand. Bob was buried deep in Xander's chest. The menacing, world-ending entity was just another dream. And I had been sleep walking again.

But more than that, behind Xander cowered a small figure. My son, Jamal.

My son. Home from camp?

Confusion and panic grappled for control of my brain.

What was happening? Nothing made sense. "What. . .what are you doing here, Jamal?" My voice was rough from sleep and confusion.

My words hung in the air, unanswered. Jamal was frozen in place, his eyes wide with terror. His gaze flitted between me and the stranger I'd run through in our living room.

Oh my god.

The realization hit me like a ton of bricks. I'd been about to hurt Jamal. I'd almost killed my own son. But Xander jumped in the way.

Glyphs lit up along Bob's blade. That hadn't happened since the first time I used the sword to kill Xander.

Xander crumpled to the ground, and I fell to my knees with him, trying to hold him up as best I could.

I pulled the blade out of Xander's heart, and a blue glow of energy shot out, winding around the blade, traveling upward and winding around my arm. It was the same hue as Xander's power.

What the hell?

A strange buzzing thrummed through my bones, spreading out to my entire body. I'd only felt this one other time. When the goddess Bast threw herself on my blade, and died.

"Oh Miranda," Bob said in a way that made my stomach drop out of my body.

No. No. It couldn't be. This wasn't it. This wasn't the one that did it.

Xander's eyes met mine, an inexplicable sadness mixing with his pain.

"Miranda," he rasped, his voice a mere whisper. "I. . . I couldn't let him get hurt."

"Xander," I choked out, tears blurring my vision. His life force was ebbing away, his divinity dimming with each passing second. "What. . .what have I done?" Panic rose in my throat like a pile of bugs growing higher until it was in my mouth. I had to push back the urge to throw up.

Xander's pained gaze flickered to Jamal. My son didn't know him, didn't know anything about him. And yet Xander had sacrificed himself for him.

"You made me want...to live, sweetheart," Xander admitted, his voice barely audible.

"I know," I replied, my voice a broken whisper. "We get more time now. We get to have more time. You changed your mind. This can't count."

Wetness covered my cheeks as my tears spilled uncontrollably. This couldn't be it. This was a nightmare too. It was a mistake. I needed to take it back. Oh god, why couldn't I take it back? It was only a short while ago Why couldn't I reach back just a little and take it back? A sob wracked my body as I clutched at Xander.

"But you. . .you'll still live . . ." His hand weakly reached out, brushing against my cheek.

His hand fell away, his eyes losing their spark. His chest heaved one last time before falling still. The unkillable god who had once been too powerful, too vibrant, lay lifeless in my arms.

A deafening silence filled the room. I clutched Xander's form to me, a raw, deep pain tearing through my heart. I had killed him, night after night, chipping away at his power, at his life force. And now, in a cruel twist of fate, I had delivered the final blow once he'd decided to live.

The sound of Jamal's quiet sobs filtered through to my ears. He didn't understand. He couldn't. I still didn't know what he was doing here, but he knew his mother had been about to kill him before a stranger jumped in and sacrificed himself. I held Xander closer.

Two words kept circling my brain, taunting me, shredding any remaining pieces of my heart.

Game over.

Chapter Thirty-Three

THE BADASS

The next couple days were a blur. Half clouded by grief, half from the cold medicine I was taking.

It turned out someone had contacted Jamal's camp, posing as me, insisting Jamal needed to return home because of a family emergency. Whoever had called had even sent a plane ticket and instructions for Jamal's trek home.

My kid's plane landed late, but I'd supposedly even arranged for a rideshare. When Jamal let himself in the house with his key, he found his mother charging at him with a sword. Xander had awoken and had gotten up to look for me just as Jamal arrived. Seeing what I was about to do, he jumped in between us, taking the killing blow.

I'd numbly managed to call Timothy who said he'd be right over and not to move.

Jamal apologized over and over again, his backpack still on and luggage by the door. My heart broke further. None of this was his fault. He didn't know who Xander was but that didn't matter. He still thought it was his fault Xander died.

I took Jamal into his bedroom and tried to explain as best I could who Xander was. An immortal I had tried to help, who I cared about very much. Then I had the even tougher job of explaining my nightmares and the sleepwalking. I was adamant that I would never know-ingly hurt him.

"I'm sorry I came home early," Jamal sniffed as he cried. I heard the front door open and the sounds of many feet and shuffling. Timothy had arrived with help, to clean up. The thought made me sick.

I pulled Jamal tightly into my arms, my head lightheaded from the cold medicine, and fighting back tears. "Oh baby, never apologize for coming home. You should always feel safe to come home. I—I don't know what happened."

And I didn't. But I was going to find the fuck out.

Uncle Javier was over a lot after that. He'd been one of the ones to show up at my house that night along with Timothy to clean up. He came to me and asked me *the* question, once Jamal was out of earshot.

"You steady?"

The lump in my throat almost kept me from answering. "No. I'm not steady."

He nodded and squeezed my hand. Then just like the last time, he showed up at my house the next morning to make coffee, eggs, and bacon. He played video games with Jamal while I rested in bed, still sick and grief stricken. I was so very grateful for Javier. He wasn't just a friend. He was family and he acted like it. I'd die for him back in the day and I still would today.

I still kept Bob nearby out of habit though I half hated him. He did his best to cheer me up and reiterate it wasn't my fault. And that at least we don't have to kill anyone. I didn't have a lot to say to him.

It took days longer than I planned, but when I was well enough I set up a meeting. Six am sharp, I arrived at Perkatory, to get my to-go mug filled with a strong americano.

I hadn't brought Aaron up to speed, but based on his soft, pitying expression and saying my coffee was on the house was all I needed to know Vivien spilled everything.

She'd forgone baby vamp duty as much as she could to come be with me. It wasn't that long ago our roles were reversed.

But she wasn't the one I asked to meet with this morning.

Timothy slipped into the seat across from me. He wore a dark purple suit today. Stress and responsibility pulled at the lines around his eyes.

"I'm so sorry Miranda. I never wanted it to happen like that," he started.

I held up my hand, stopping him. I wasn't here for that.

"I've been having nightmares for a couple weeks. They've caused me to sleepwalk."

"Yes, I heard," he murmured.

"They started after someone tried to break into my car. I think they were trying to get the blade. And Jamal was sent home because someone posed as me. I don't have many vulnerabilities other than my child. Do you see where I'm going with this?"

His dark eyes studied me closely. "I think I'm beginning to."

"Someone orchestrated this. Someone wanted Xander dead too." The pain under my chest was sharp and unforgiving for days. It flared at my words, but I muscled past the feeling.

Timothy pressed at the spot between his brows as if trying to dig for some information. He already knew what I was going to ask.

"Who? Who would care if Xander lived or died? Or who would want the blade?" I still didn't fully understand what this entity wanted. Maybe they wanted to break my spirit so I'd never use the blade again and they could take it? Or maybe it was about Xander the whole time. It was all muddled, but a single thread of connection was clear.

Timothy shook his head after a while, dropping his hand. "I couldn't say. Xander has not had any enemies since Aten. And the sun god was slain by the blade you wield."

"Maybe someone who cared about the sun god then?" I asked, pressing him for more.

Timothy bit the inside of his cheek, his eyes glowing a light green for a moment. It was if he was accessing some information from an internal database. It was why I chose him.

Then coming back to himself, he frowned. "No one I can think of. You must understand, Aten changed everything."

"Xander said he thought Aten was getting too powerful, but no one paid attention until it was too late." I added.

Timothy nodded solemnly. "Before Aten, we were a polytheistic society. Everyone prayed to many gods. Aten thought he deserved more than that and influenced the Egyptian pharaoh and all their followers there was only one true god. Him." A dark shadow passed over his face. "When Aten killed Xander, he went too far. We all descended upon him, but the damage had been done. It was then that Osiris forbad any god from taking on worshippers ever again. We couldn't recruit, we could use the old names anymore. It is why our identities have morphed amongst the Greeks, the Romans, and into the present-day celebrities. We were to be stripped of power equally so that humanity could rise to power."

"Who was angry about that? Did anyone blame Xander? Was anyone on Aten's side?"

Timothy shook his head. "We were all guilty of Xander's demise having let him face Aten alone. None of the gods supported Aten's lunacy, and he was hated in death for the price he all cost us. There is no one would help him to this day and age."

The gung-ho parts inside me wilted. None of this was helpful. It was a history lesson without any clues to who tried to steal the blade from me. Who had been fucking with my head. Who made me kill the crazy god I loved.

Seeing my despair, Timothy reached a hand across to pat my arm.

"There are many gods who possess the power to design dreams and hallucinations like the ones that caused you to sleepwalk. I'll make a list and we'll start investigating them."

I swallowed hard and nodded. Timothy understood I needed to do something, anything, or I'd fall apart. But I could already tell by his demeanor, it wasn't likely we'd find anything pertinent among the gods.

Clutching my cup, I started toward the security office.

Timothy was at least trying, and I felt his sincerity. While I didn't agree with the stance he took, I knew he'd only wanted to protect me. I was still pissed at him, but I'd get over it.

The person I wasn't a fan of was Bianca. Resentment stewed in me. She promised the world would end if Xander died. And while I didn't want that to happen, I found her baseless ravings to grate on my nerves even though she didn't show up to press upon the matter.

My booted steps angrily echoed across the lobby of Sinopolis as my duster swept out behind me. Judging by the looks of others, I was a dangerous, moving thunderstorm.

It wasn't enough that I lost a future with one man I loved, but now, twice. It was cruel. It was almost too purposeful not to be fate. It reminded me of what Xander said about being punished. Was I being punished? By Osiris or some larger consciousness that thought this was what I deserved?

"Miranda," a voice called out, stopping me.

I turned to find Aoiki running up to me. She wore her school uniform per usual, hair up in pigtails with big pink fluff balls decorating each dark waterfall of hair. Her hands clutched the straps of her cute kitty backpack as she hurried over. Without preamble she threw her arms around me in a tight hug. "I'm so sorry. I'm so so so sorry."

My arms remained at my side as I violently fought back the tears she forced to the surface. I didn't want to do this right now. Not here, not like this.

Finally, she let me go. I'd be cold and put her off, if it weren't for the compassionate look on her face. "You loved him, didn't you?" she asked.

I could only bring myself to nod stiffly. Aoiki was a lot like Vivien. Not really aware of boundaries or conscientious to tip toe around painful subjects.

Aoiki grabbed my free hand with both hers and shot a look around as if to make sure no one was listening. "There's a way to bring him back," she said in a hushed voice.

All my attention perked up at that. Suddenly, I was squeezing her hands back. "What?"

"The blade, Bob, has a way to call back the entities it kills. You can bring Xander back."

"I can what now?" Bob asked in a muffled voice from where he was tucked in my coat.

Excitement and hope welled inside me, nearly bursting through my chest.

I tried to tamp it down. "That's not true. The blade of bane is the only weapon able to permanently kill any immortal."

A sly smile crept up her face. "Miranda. I take the same high school physics class year after year. Some of the shit they teach is totally off the mark, but they are right about one thing. Matter can ever truly be created or destroyed. Things merely change. There is a way to change him back into a god again."

I deliberately tried to numb myself against the hope Aoiki was dumping on me. It was too much, and I wasn't thinking straight, "Why are you helping me?"

She shot me a look like the answer was positively obvious. "Because I know what it's like to be in love. If I were to lose that love, it would break me."

Sunny. She was talking about the quiet fae girl with a bobbed haircut. How long had they been together out of her five hundred sum years?

If I had five hundred years with Xander I doubted it would be enough. I missed him so hard it made my bones brittle. I missed his touch, his eyes, his wry sense of humor. Hell, I missed his crazy. I knew I could help him control it, and I felt robbed at not getting more of a chance.

Then Aoiki whispered while looking around to make sure no one heard. "Can I meet you tonight? Where he died?"

I immediately made plans to have Jamal stay with Uncle Javier. "Yes," I nodded.

"Good," she said, with a nod. "I'll see you at nine PM."

Then she ran off, mentioning she couldn't be late for school *again* and risk detention.

The idea that I could get Xander back made the minutes of the rest of my day crawl by. What if we were going to be reunited in a matter of hours?

That would change everything.

It wasn't over until it was over.

And when I got him back, I was sure Xander would help me figure out who set me up to kill him and why.

Chapter Thirty-Four

THE BADASS

Aoiki was an hour late, but when she arrived she had Sunny in tow.

"Sorry about your loss," Sunny murmured avoiding eye contact with me as if she was painfully shy.

I only nodded, unable to respond to yet another person's sympathies. I hated it. And if tonight went well, they would be unnecessary.

The girls set down their backpacks in the corner of my living room. "Sorry it took us a while longer, we had to sneak out."

"Your parents don't know you are here?" The mom alarm went off in my head.

"I tried to feel them out on it, but I didn't get the sense they'd exactly approve."

"Why not?" I asked, feeling suddenly uneasy. They had helped me find the Blade of Bane, they had ultimately helped Vivien resurrect Grim.

Aoiki rolled her eyes as she tightened a pigtail. "Who knows. My mom was in one of her moods today. You know how she is."

It was true, Echo was temperamental to say the least. And she was the one who told me to follow my heart. Everything in my chest screamed at me that bringing him back was the right thing to do.

So even though she wasn't here, I might as well have had her blessing.

"So what now?" I asked, suddenly feeling nervous.

Aoiki smiled at Sunny. "She knows what to do. Sunny can call Xander back."

"Do we need his body or something?" I said, still unable to shake the nerves in my stomach.

Sunny shook her head. "That's not necessary. Matter will regroup when I call it. I just need the sword."

Something flip flopped in my guts. I wasn't supposed to give the sword to anyone.

"What do you need the sword for?" I'd let Xander hold it when we'd sparred, but he truly had no desire to wield it. It felt safe. This...didn't. I didn't really know this fae girl. I would have felt more comfortable if Aoiki asked to hold, but still, even then the idea squirmed in my guts.

"My ancestor was one of the fae that wielded the sword before me," Sunny explained with a small smile of pride. "I know what to do with it. I know that it is capable of more than people think."

"She's very smart," Aoiki nodded with beaming pride.

I slowly drew Bob out from my duster jacket.

"Are you sure this is wise?" he asked quietly.

"You don't think it is?" I asked in turn.

"I honestly couldn't say. Like any being, even I lack the full perception of my full potential."

"You wouldn't be killing anyone," I said, feeling the need to soothe him for some reason.

"I suppose so. And if it will make you happy, I can try."

Something pinched in my heart. How strange was it to bond with a sentient weapon. To have it care for your wellbeing.

"Thank you," I said. I laid Bob out across my hands before passing him over to Sunny.

Her eyes gleamed with intensity and reverence as she took the sword.

Sunny dropped down her knees and continued to hold the sword as it laid across her palms. She closed her eyes and began to chant in another language.

Aoiki grabbed my arm and pulled me off to the side but didn't let go of me. She held me fast while Sunny continued to speak.

After a few minutes, a low pressure built in the air and the smell of ozone rose. Aoiki's grip only tightened on my arm with excitement.

Then sparks shot off Bob's blade. He yelped in surprise a couple times but settled after a while.

This is the right thing to do, I repeated to myself. *The world of immortals doesn't abide by the same rules as mortals. Xander shouldn't be gone for all time. He was ready to live. He deserves a chance.*

Still, something I couldn't name wriggled in my belly. So I focused on what it would be like to be in Xander's arms again. Hell, I'd even break the promise and play a board game with him if he wanted. As long as he came back to me.

The pressure built and built, the ozone smell growing so strong it stung my nose. Sunny continued chanting, her voice growing louder and louder.

A rushing wind picked up in the room despite there being no windows open. It swept at my face and tossed Aoiki's pig tails around.

Soon it felt like being in the middle of a tornado. The wind roared in my ears so I could barely hear Sunny scream over it.

I wouldn't be surprised if the neighbors called the cops. Not that law enforcement would know what to do about this.

Then another shooting spark lept off the blade, bigger than the first mini ones. Then another, and another. They shot out of Bob like shooting stars.

Another sound pierced through the howling wind. Bob. Bob was crying out. "No. No no no!"

I started forward but Aoiki pulled me back. "She's not done yet," she screamed in my ear.

"Something's wrong," I yelled back.

Aoiki's brows furrowed in confusion before she regarded Sunny again.

The girl was lost in concentration, as if she were searching internally for something even as words spilled out of her mouth.

More shooting stars exploded from Bob as he cried out in protest. Aoiki's certainty seemed to falter as her lips twisted. She could also hear his screams.

She released my arm and took a couple steps forward. "Sunny," she yelled to her girlfriend.

Sunny either didn't notice or pretended not too. She chanted faster and bigger, brighter shooting stars escaped Bob's blade.

"Sunny, stop," Aoiki cried out, also realizing something wasn't right.

Bob screamed out, "Miranda, help. Help me."

Okay, that was enough. I started forward, ready to wrench Bob out of Sunny's grip when an explosion of light went off.

I threw my arms up to protect my face even as I was thrown back against the wall. I hit it hard before sliding to the ground. I instinctively curled into a protective ball. It wasn't just any light. I'd felt this before. It was powerful, malevolent and gleefully destructive. It was the entity from my dreams. Except this wasn't a dream. It exploded to life in my living room, searing my skin, my mind.

I felt phantom fingers sear my arms, my legs, as if it was exploring me, studying me. I trembled, unable to move, unable to fight.

After I don't know how long, it receded. I blinked hard against the fading brightness. I sucked in deep breaths, trying to calm the panic that had overtaken me.

Wha the fuck had that been?

"Sunny," Aoiki cried. I barely caught her running out the front door of my house. It slammed shut behind her.

Despite her exit, I wasn't alone.

A naked, muscular figure lay on the ground next to Bob who had fallen silent. Despite lacking all the scars that had marred it before, I recognized the body instantly.

I scrambled to my feet and ran over to the man on my carpet. He pushed himself up onto his elbows, those intense sapphire eyes met mine with a burning intensity. Xander's expression radiated cold hatred and it was directed right at me. It stopped me in my tracks, several feet separating us. My stomach dropped out of my body as heat and panic prickled the skin on my forehead.

"Miranda." My name came out a raspy accusation. "What have you done?"

The gravity of his words told me everything was not alright.

Not by a long shot. And it was all my fault.

EPILOGUE

Bianca

"**I**s this what you saw?" a low, masculine voice asked.

I didn't pause brushing my hair from where I sat in front of my vanity mirror. The piece was from the baroque period, one of my favorites. So much champagne, cake, and opulence. The bright lights and hedonism of Vegas was not so different from such a time.

Fallon, formerly known as the god Horus, hadn't knocked, even though it was my bedroom. Presumptuous as always. I met his gaze in the mirror of my vanity. His one blue eye gleamed brilliantly against his rich black skin. His other brown eye did not hold the same magic, but held a different kind of power. Hands tucked in the pockets of his slacks, suit coat open, his white shirt was unbuttoned at the top, revealing a swath of muscular skin that made my skin heat up. Though I'd never let on that he had such an effect on me.

Fallon was beautiful like the other gods, yet so different in his fierce power. To most I was considered the darling of the immortals, but to Fallon I was frivolous and naïve. He never passed on a chance to make me feel less than. I hated him for it.

I went on brushing my hair where I sat at my vanity. "I suppose so." In my vision, I'd seen bright white death. It hadn't made sense then, but hindsight brought all of this into terrifying focus.

"You should have come to me. You know I've always seen the future more clearly than you." There was a harshness in his tone I didn't appreciate.

My hairbrush slammed down on the vanity. "And why couldn't you have seen this for yourself? Why couldn't you have gone to Grim and told him to stop her." I'd believed Xander's death would trigger the end of days, but I didn't realize it would actually be his resurrection that would release fresh hell upon all of us.

Fallon remained silent, leaning against the doorway.

In that silence, I reflected on my hatred for him. I hated how my heart beat faster when he was near. I hated how he always disapproved of me. I hated how he'd come here just to censure me.

"You're scared," he said finally.

I swiveled around on my ottoman. "Of course, I'm scared." I couldn't keep the tremor out of my voice. "Every entity ever slain by the god killer has been released back into the world. Monsters we long thought we'd never have to contend with are out on the streets doing Osiris knows what. And *he's* back." Fear gripped my chest and I forced myself to say his name. "Aten is back. He won't be satisfied until he's killed us all. He wants to be the one true god."

"That will never happen, Bianca," Fallon said in a surprisingly soothing voice.

I got stiffly to my feet. "How helpful you are now, with your empty assurance based on what? Nothing."

I tried to walk past him, but Fallon's hand shot out, grabbing my wrist and pulling me to him. "Bianca," he said, his gaze dropping to my lips for a long beat that made me forget how to breathe. Heat tingled at the back of my head. When he met my eye again there was determination in his expression.

"He won't hurt you," he promised in a low voice.

I jerked my arm out from his grasp. "You're right. Aten won't. The glimpses I've seen, incoherent and unhelpful as they are," I said, taunting his assessment of my power, "I get to witness it all. I'll watch everyone burn." Tears crowded into my throat. My heart squeezed so hard I feared it would pop. "Even you." The last part came out a ragged whisper.

With that, I fled my own bedroom. Fallon didn't need to go on. It was because of my own inability to see, to articulate, that we would all suffer.

Especially Miranda.

And for that, I could never forgive myself.

The Badass

Vivien, Aaron and I sat at our usual Perkatory table. Aaron wasn't working today but came in when he'd heard what happened.

"So Xander really refuses to see you?" Vivien asked, her tone disgusted. I nodded curtly; my hands wrapped tight around my to-go cup.

"T-that's unfair," Aaron said with a scowl.

I shrugged one shoulder. "Is it? I unleashed who knows how many evils by letting Sunny get her hands on Bob." My voice was matter-of-fact while my insides were leaden.

"Is Bob talking yet?" Vivien asked softly.

I shook my head. I felt so brittle, I feared any large movement would shatter me. Since the ritual Sunny performed, Bob was silent as the grave. I hated it. I missed his complaints, his companionship. I'd hurt him and let him down.

"I've done every wrong thing," I announced, already knowing it's what my friends thought as well.

"That's not fair," Vivien argued.

If my friends truly favored the world being fair and just, they would realize I deserved every bit of punishment I was receiving, and more.

"It's true," I shot back. "I was told not to let anyone else wield the blade."

"You were trying to save someone you loved." Vivien dug her heels in harder.

I sighed. "I know you are saying this because you love me, but I'm not worthy of that right now. I made a mistake that goes against everything I ever stood for. I've always sacrificed so much to help others, and at the first opportunity of selfishness I took it with little thought and now the entire world will suffer."

Vivien sucked in a big breath of air as if preparing to tell me all that was wrong with what I said, but Aaron grabbed her arm to stop her and said to me. "W-what now?"

I was grateful for him pausing her tirade. There was nothing she could say that could convince me otherwise right now.

While his question was practical. That's what I needed to be. On the ground with both feet, and a level head. Listening to my heart got us into this mess.

"I have been relieved of my duties at Sinopolis," I informed my friends. Vivan gasped and Aaron's eyes flew wide.

"My one and only task now is to track down every immortal that has escaped the blade and kill them again. Grim assures me he will do everything he can to equip and support me in this endeavor."

At first I'd been terrified I'd lost my livelihood. Grim assured me my duties were more important than any others. That I would be compensated handsomely as I was now employed by all the immortals to hunt down what they call the dark ones.

Ironic, considering the biggest bad was made of light, but I didn't mention to Grim when he debriefed me.

"Javier is taking my place as head of security and I am to start hunting," I finished.

"Jesus," Aaron said, running a hand through his thick blonde waves.

Vivien slouched in her seat, crossing her arms with a scowl. "If you ask me, Xander is a massive stupid head for staying mad at you. You did it to save him. Because you love him."

I winced at her voicing all my stupidities and vulnerabilities. "Vivien, I just released the massively bad entity that is responsible for killing Xander in the first place. I basically breathed life into his nemesis. He doesn't want to see me. Ever."

"It's also k-kind of l-like you broke his DNR. D-do not resuscitate," Aaron pointed out. "That's a very personal thing to people."

Vivien's jaw dropped as she stared at him in accusation. "Wow Aaron, real helpful, way to make her feel better."

"He's not wrong," I muttered, even as I felt his words spear through my heart. When Vivien revived Grim it had all been roses and save-the-day vibes. But I was the bad guy in this version. Life wasn't fair, but I could take my consequences. I deserved them.

"D-do we know how Sunny is involved or w-where she is yet?" Aaron asked, trying to change the subject.

I shook my head, crossing my own arms, needing to bring some warmth to my core. "No. Aoiki is shattered. They'd been together for two hundred years, but it looks like Sunny had cozied up to Aoiki all this time, for this very chance. I'm guessing Sunny was the one who got Jamal out of camp and sent him home," I snarled. I would rip out the fae girl's throat the next time I saw her. I didn't care if she looked like a minor. "She must be some kind of follower of Aten's."

"Echo is furious with Aoiki," Vivien said quietly.

Aaron and I exchanged a look. The older fae woman's ire was scary enough. Her full-blown wrath was terrifying.

We all fell into silence for some time, each thinking about all that had gone wrong and all that was yet to come.

"F-fuck Xander," Aaron said finally, breaking the silence. Vivien and I looked up at him in surprise.

"Y-you are alive Miranda. D don't let these immortals rob you of your life. You need to love again, you deserve it. J-Jamal deserves to see you live. Not sh-shrivel away." He looked at me with earnest aquamarine- colored eyes.

I swallowed hard. Goddammit. He used the trump card. My kid. The ultimate leverage anyone can use when you just want to check out or go on a self-destructive path. But you know if you do, you are going to cause some familial trauma the kid will pick up. And then he'll grow up to have shit like self-loathing or an inability to commit as an adult.

Crap.

"He's got a good point," Vivien gently added. They already knew they had me.

I blew out a breath of frustration before reaching in my duster pocket and pulling out my phone. I unlocked it then slammed it on the table. In

front of both of my friends, because I knew I wouldn't be accountable otherwise, I opened the dating app I installed.

The first face to appear was a handsome black man with light brown skin, happy green eyes and a brilliant smile. He was amicably divorced, like fitness, was man enough to admit he loved India Arie, and hoped to be a father one day.

Aaron and Vivien silently read the description as I browsed through his photos. My friends shared a look with raised eyebrows. They didn't need to say anything for me to hear what they were thinking.

It was like he was fucking made for me.

With a sigh, I swiped right. Instantly, an explosion of hearts and flowers appeared on the screen as the app announced we'd matched together.

Xander was right about what he said when he died. I would go on living. Even if that meant without him. And I was going to make it a fucking good life. No matter what my aching heart said right now.

I didn't need a crazy god to make me the sensual, powerful woman I was.

I did that on my own.

My heart screamed in pain and protest at that.

Tough nuggets though. I'd show that stupid organ in my chest that life was best led by the head.

My heart only quieted up when I promised it a bubble bath later with a good book and a glass of wine. Because between hunting immortals, I was going to need all the recovery time I could get.

CLAIMING THE BEAST

Chapter One

THE BADASS

"Here kitty, kitty." I psst psspt'd into the dark.

It was three in the morning, and I prowled through the back alleys behind the Vegas hotels that served the best breakfast buffets. The pungent odor of rotting shellfish, meats, and sweets grew so intense, my eyes watered and I had to hold my breath.

Why was I here?

Because I was hunting a god spawn.

A dangerous divine being that chose to stay in his primordial animal form. And the last thing Vegas needed was for humans to run into an otherworldly creature with fangs and realize gods and monsters walked among them.

Grim, my former boss and god of the dead, shared that my target's name was Sheshem, a lion-like spawn of the goddess Sekhmet. Unlike Sheshem's distant, vampiric ancestor, this fanged creature had a sweet tooth for syrup and an appetite for shrimp—raw, fried, you name it.

Back in the ancient days, the big scary cat god spawn had inadvertently released a plague of darkness on the earth so he could extend his hunting grounds, and the only way to stop him had been to kill him and his connection to the dark plague.

But in the present day and age, he seemed quite happy with his hunting forays in the city of Las Vegas. He mainly left a trail of ravaged dumpsters, metal peeled back in strips.

While Sheshem's return to this world hadn't caused anything so dramatic like a plague, he was a dangerous entity that couldn't be allowed to roam free.

And Sheshem only set his paws on this earth again because of me. Guilt sliced through me as I paced up and down the stinking alleyway. I deliberately opened a dumpster to attract Sheshem's delicate and discerning senses. The longer I waited in the dark, the more antsy I got.

"Oh Bob, I wish you'd give me a few words of encouragement," I whispered to the blade I held erect, ready to slay or defend myself. The sword remained stubbornly silent, causing a pang of guilt to spear through my gut.

It's my fault the Blade of Bane didn't speak anymore.

At first, I was freaked out to have a psychic connection to a weapon with a French accent and a strong aversion to blood, but I'd grown accustomed to having him in my head.

His silence was only another damning side effect of my massive mistake. One that stole Bob's voice and released Sheshem into the world.

A low rumble vibrated through the air, resonating from the deep, shadow-clad recesses of the alley. My pulse quickened, a tumult of adrenaline and foreboding surging through my veins. I tightened my hold on the blade as I retreated several steps, my gaze piercing the darkness in anticipation.

The moment stretched, taut with expectation, until the shadows themselves seemed to shift and coalesce. From their depths, Sheshem emerged into the scant light of the moon.

My breath hitched, caught between awe and fear. Its fur, if one could call it that, shimmered with a spectral quality, translucent and flowing like liquid obsidian, edged with a luminescence that hinted at otherworldly origins. Its eyes, twin orbs of chaotic energy, burned with a fierce intensity, a swirling maelstrom of colors that defied the natural order.

I felt small, vulnerable—every inch the mortal I was.

But I wielded the most powerful weapon in the world, the Blade of Bane, aka Bob, the only sword that could kill a god. My duty was to make penance for my mistake as well as protect this world, and I'd fulfill those responsibilities no matter what.

As I reoriented myself, blade in hand, all I could think was: *Bring it on, Sheshem.*

Fangs bared, the god spawn roared—a sound that was a grotesque cross between a lion's roar and impossibly, a rattlesnake. It lunged, and my blade swung up, narrowly blocking its claw from my face. I staggered, almost tripping over some errant trash.

Dodging another claw swipe, I managed to thrust my blade toward its face. But Sheshem dodged with such speed, it was like trying to spear a shadow. It leapt at me, and I jumped back. My head smacked against brick with a sickening crack. My vision turned black for a second as dizzying pain exploded in my brain.

I was cornered against a graffiti-covered wall. Sheshem readied to pounce, its claws fully extended, eyes locked on me like the final piece of shrimp on a brunch platter. This was it. I was going to die at the paws of a pancake-loving, kitty-cat god.

A blur of motion swept through my peripheral vision, landing between me and my would-be killer.

It wasn't an illusion. A figure landed in front of me, a barely contained tempest of power and agility. For a moment, the world fell away, and there was only the silhouette bathed in moonlight, standing like a sentinel ready to protect me from certain death—Xander.

The man—the god—I lost everything for.

Chapter Two

THE BADASS

Xander didn't bother wearing shoes or a shirt, making him look almost as feral and out of place as the god spawn. The neon lights from the Strip filtered through the alley, casting a contrast on the contours of his muscled body.

Scars once riddled the entirety of Xander's body—a body that I'd touched every inch of—but they'd all disappeared. He was flawless now, courtesy of his rebirth from the Blade of Bane. Whereas I was now damned by the same action.

Xander spared me a glance, and for a split second, our eyes met. A myriad of emotions passed through those turquoise depths—worry, relief, anger? Whatever they were, I severed them from my mind, like hacking off a gangrenous limb. He was the last thing I should be thinking about.

Xander clenched his fists and let out a challenging roar, meeting Sheshem's intensity. What happened next was nothing short of incredible. He lunged forward, fist meeting claw in a blur of motion and raw power. They clashed, Xander ducking and dodging the deadly swipes with the grace of a dancer, landing punches that actually made the hulking god spawn stagger.

Finally, with a growl that shook the alley, Xander landed a punch square on Sheshem's snout. The creature reeled backward, let out a ferocious snarl, and then bolted, vanishing into the labyrinthine maze of darkened alleyways.

"What were you thinking, Miranda?" Xander turned back to me, panting, his eyes ablaze. "If Sheshem hadn't been in a playful mood, you could've been killed. Your military training didn't cover sword fighting and gods. You are way out of your depth."

Playful mood?

Emotions welled up in me, all mixed and tangled so I couldn't pull any one of them apart.

How long had it been since I heard his raspy voice?

A month.

So why did it feel like an eternity? I'd been starved of hearing words spill from those frowning lips. It'd been forever since I'd been captivated by the way his hair hung loosely over those striking azure eyes. They held a permanent disdain, as if he didn't care about one single goddamn thing in this world.

An ache yawned inside of my chest so fiercely, my breath caught.

Xander once cared about me. A gaping hole formed in his ruthless indifference, and that's where he held me. A literal god looked at me like I was the only woman in the world. The only one worth his attention.

I swallowed past the large lump that lodged itself in my throat.

Calm the fuck down, Miranda. Of course, he looked like heaven and hell, saran wrapped in sex. He's a literal god. The Egyptian god of primordial waters, once called Nun. Any and every person would be gripped by the desire to fall at his feet and beg to worship him.

The image of him between my legs, worshipping me with his tongue zapped me with a white-hot electricity I tried to shake off even as my skin turned feverish.

But I fucked up.

And when I last saw him, his gaze burned into me with such rage and resentment, it burned away every last bit of what we had together.

I tried to ignore how frustratingly captivating his face is even when he's irritated. *Especially* when he's irritated. Like he can't decide if he wants to fight or fuck me.

We usually settled on a combination of both.

I gritted my teeth. "No, the army didn't teach me how to fight gods with a sword. But I'll adapt. I always do." With that, I turned on my heel and made my way down the alleyway.

Energy crackled along my spine, letting me know he was following me. "Adaptation won't keep you alive against gods," he shot back, his voice tinged with concern that did nothing but fan the flames of my already complicated feelings for him.

He was right. But admitting that would hurt more than Sheshem's claws ever could.

Xander had tried to train me to wield the blade. Yet too often, our sessions morphed into something else—something sexual and forbidden.

My heart hammered in my chest, heat building in my veins, forcing feelings to the surface.

Lop.

There, I cut them off again. Another gangrenous limb gone.

I felt nothing for him.

"Thanks for the save," I said flatly, even as adrenaline pumped through me. "Now, if you don't mind, I have a kitty-cat god to hunt."

"Kitty-cat god? Are you crazy? It's not a house pet. You could have been killed." Xander's expression changed; no longer a dangerous, feral scowl but something else. He looked regal, as if he'd changed from the beast I first met in the Grim Reaper's basement, and into his godly persona.

Ignoring his protest, I picked up Bob and turned on my heel. "You can't do this, Miranda," Xander insisted.

"That's where you're wrong," I replied, not slowing my stride.

Two strong hands gripped my shoulders, forcing me to face him. Instantly, he was too close. My skin tingled, my head went fuzzy, and I involuntarily wet my lips. Xander's pupils dilated, as if he too sensed the undercurrent of desire throbbing between us, between all the places we'd been and lost.

"Why are you here?" I asked, shrugging off his grip and stepping away. "I thought you hated me."

His brows furrowed. "Hated you?" he echoed in confusion. His eyes cleared as he looked away. "I was upset."

"Upset," I scoffed, throwing my braids over one shoulder. "For four weeks, you've been *upset*." I hated the way the pitch of my voice rose at the end of that sentence.

"I didn't ask you to bring me back, Miranda," he murmured, a soft growl imbuing his voice.

With Xander's dying act, he saved me from stabbing my own child in a supernaturally-induced hallucination.

When the dream cleared from my eyes and I found Xander pierced through the heart by my own hand, I thought he would regenerate like he did every night I killed him. But whether fate is a cruel bitch or his sudden desire to live triggered it, Xander's power had ebbed enough that I was able to kill him for good.

Right there, right then, he died a true death at the end of my blade.

I couldn't leave it at that.

"I know you didn't ask me to save you," I said stiffly. "Believe me, I realize my mistake now." I threw away my life the day I revived him.

I regretted ever asking for outside help, allowing myself to be manipulated by Sunny—the fae who performed the spell—who clearly had ulterior motives.

Not only was Xander released from the prison of the blade's steel, so was everything the blade ever killed. It was a massive jailbreak of all the destructive gods and monsters that had been destroyed and trapped into the steel of my blade. All thanks to my feeling-clouded idiocy.

Now the most primeval deities this world had seen since the beginning of time walked this earth again. And it was my fault because I had a crush on a beast in a cage with a death wish.

The purge had also robbed Bob, my talking blade, of his voice. We'd known each other a short time, but I felt bonded to him, and now that my sword was silent, I felt more alone than ever.

My hands clenched against the stupidity of my own actions.

"What do you think you are doing then?" he asked even softer now.

That's when I spun on my heel and backed Xander up against a wall, the sharp end of my sword pricking at his throat. His eyes remained impassive even as he lifted his chin. As if he didn't believe I'd do it.

He should. I killed him every night for weeks.

But if I did it now, he would die instantly, his soul trapped in the blade I held.

"I am dealing with the consequences of my actions," I said, only growing angrier when I heard the tremor in my own voice. "I have to kill every one of those monsters I let out. Perhaps I should start with you, since you are here."

But this wasn't about Xander. He wasn't slain because he was a threat to this world. He was only a threat to my good sense.

"They can't expect you to do this." His eyes bore into me, until I felt his penetrating gaze travel all the way to my toes. "It's suicide, Miranda. You can't fight immortals as a human."

My arm dropped, the blade going with it. "It is my duty, my penance." I paused. "Put on a shirt and some shoes. You look like some damn homeless maniac." My irritation was way too apparent. Hopefully he'd think I said it because I think he's indecent, not because it's distracting as all hell.

I hated the way his stupid carved abs flexed at my comment.

"You didn't know what you were doing. It wasn't your fault," Xander argued on, ignoring my commentary on his dress—or rather the lack of it.

I narrowed my eyes. "Didn't seem to stop you from blaming me either."

The moment the searing light of the purging spell lifted, Xander appeared there in my living room with a look in his eye so full of hatred it was a live wire electrocuting me.

Then he took off, and I hadn't seen him since.

Until now.

Xander's jaw went slack with surprise before he recovered a moment later. "Miranda. I was upset. Angry. Not at you, but at the situation. To exist in a world with *him* again..." Xander's blue eyes spiraled off into a place I couldn't reach him. The feral edges of him returned as I watched him enter the personal hell of his past.

The stately god receded, once more becoming the beast I met in the basement—a god driven insane by an overabundance of power that kept him alive and in pain for thousands of years. But he'd apparently preferred that hellish existence over living in the same world as his nemesis again.

Aten, the sun god, was roaming around somewhere, and it would only be a matter of time before he made his move. To him, there could only be one God, and he'd do anything to wipe out the other immortals. And judging by the magnitude of their fear, he might have the power to do it.

The other gods whispered and fretted. They wanted my head before Grim stepped in. They blamed me for releasing Aten. They should.

A vise clamped around my heart and squeezed so hard I expected my ventricles to pop like balloons.

When Xander's eyes refocused on me, I looked away.

He whispered, "You can't go after him."

I repeated the little poem-like order given to me by Grim. "I am to kill every god who'd been slain by the blade before."

Before I could turn and walk away, Xander stepped in front of me again. "He'll kill you, Miranda."

"Maybe," I said, staring at a spot on his chest, breathing in the intoxicating scent of the salty sea and sandalwood. "But this is my duty, my penance. No one but me can pay it."

I risked touching him so I could push by him, but Xander grabbed my shoulders again, dragging me close. "Miranda, I can't let you do this. I can't let anything happen to you. I..." The oceans in his eyes roiled as he fought to get the words out. "I *love* you."

All the cells in my body stilled, petrified by his impossible words. My throat thickened until I couldn't swallow. I pursed my lips to keep from drowning in the tormented depths of his cerulean eyes.

Gone was his indifference. All his intensity, his desire, was trained on me, and it drilled through me like a power tool, gutting me.

How fucking dare he?

How dare he try to play on my emotions after being absent for a month? I thought my heart broke the night I killed him, but I'd barely tasted heartache until he stared at me with such accusation, such open hatred before disappearing into the night.

Sure, I'd made my bed and I had to lie in it, drowning in my own mistakes. But if someone loved you, they either tried to pull you out or lie down with you.

He did neither. I sacrificed so much for the god in front of me, and he'd rejected me.

It had been a miracle he'd pried himself into my heart in the first place. There was absolutely no way he would get in again. I'd sealed all the cracks, and no one would breach that barrier. Ever.

Envisioning ice swirling out of my eyes to freeze him in place, I said, "I thought I loved you, but I was an idiot. It was only because you'd awoken feelings I thought I'd never feel again. But I don't need those feelings, and I don't need you." I enunciated those last words with extreme prejudice.

He didn't back down. Instead, he stepped in closer.

"You want me," Xander insisted, his face lowering until his mouth was mere millimeters from mine, causing my lips to tingle in anticipation and my belly to flip-flop wildly.

Chemistry, nothing more, I insisted firmly to myself. There was nothing sexy about vinegar and baking soda, and that's the sum of what we were to each other. Chemicals.

"I want to kill gods and be left alone." I struggled against his grip, but Xander held me fast.

His lips pressed against mine in a fierce possessive kiss that bent my body backward, even as he held me to him.

Sharp pricks scratched at the back of my eyes as his mouth molded to mine. My chest felt like it was going to blow apart until my heart was scattered in gruesome red ribbons at his feet.

The same time Xander broke the kiss, I wanted—*needed*—him to keep kissing me even as I hated him more than I ever hated anything or anyone in my life. Even more than reckless drivers, more than the last remake of *Pride and Prejudice*, more than people who chewed with their mouths open.

I shoved him away.

"Don't come near me again," I warned, even as I stalked away, never looking over my shoulder.

No matter how every fiber of my being begged me to.

Chapter Three

THE BEAST

When Miranda entered Grim's penthouse, she stopped in her tracks as soon as she saw me. Eyes narrowing, she looked back and forth between me and the god of the dead with accusation and wariness.

Fuck, the taste and feel of her mouth against mine still burned me like a ghost. I craved her so badly my fingertips itched.

Instead of the Blade of Banee being sheathed on her back this morning, it resided inside her duster. In skintight pants that rose up past her belly button and a crop top, both in army print—a nod to her past—she looked every bit the delicious little badass I remembered and more.

Gone were the suit jackets and façade of professional courtesy of a woman who worked for others. Her shit-kicker boots and leather duster only added to the visage of her fully embracing what she was. A warrior.

The god of the dead stood next to me in his pressed black suit, hands laced behind his back. "Hello Miranda," he greeted formally.

The old boy was nervous.

Who knew even the Grim Reaper could be intimidated by a five-foot-four mortal with glowing brown skin and cat-like eyes that flashed with live fire? Maybe it's because her tensed jaw promised death?

His, specifically. But I had no doubt I'd be next.

After spending thousands of years in my underground prison and grotto, Grim's modern and luxurious penthouse atop the Sinopolis hotel was a sight to behold. The decor featured sleek eggplant-colored couches, black marble, and state-of-the-art appliances—all of which showcased his wealth and moodiness.

Had I been amongst my brethren all these years, I supposed this might be how I would be living now too.

After years of living in a dark, damp place both physically and mentally, I had reached my limit. If I lived here, I'd ditch the gloomy hues and decorate with more bright pops of color.

But the only luxury, the only home I recognized or desired, stood twenty feet away from me, and was looking progressively stabbier.

Gods, the sight of Miranda made my body riot with desire, pride, and raw need. I wanted to wrap my hand in those long, thin velvet braids and toy with her until she punched me or fell apart in my hands. But mostly, my body vibrated with agitation, knowing I couldn't have her.

Not yet anyway.

"What is this?" Miranda asked, her suspiciously slit eyes bouncing between Grim and me.

"Miranda," Grim started, but paused when her scrutiny drilled into him. "I've decided you could use some assistance with your endeavors."

Miranda arched an eyebrow. She wasn't buying this. I didn't expect her to, my clever girl.

Her shoulders rolled back as she regarded him coolly. "No."

"No? No, what?" he asked, hands falling to his side.

"No, I will not be working with Xander."

I couldn't help the grin that spread across my face. Nothing got by her.

"Sure you will, sweetheart," I mocked. Those molten brown eyes turned to me, openly incensed.

That's it my little badass, put all the energy here. The more you give me the anger, the more you'll fall into my gravity until I've captured you entirely. The same way you've ensnared me.

"Xander," Grim warned in a low voice before addressing Miranda again. "I know things have changed considerably—"

"Are you talking about the part where I lost my job working here at Sinopolis?" she asked drolly. "Or the part where the entire immortal community holds me personally responsible for the biggest disaster since the bloodthirsty goddess Sekhmet went on a rampage turning mortals into vampires?"

"Miranda," Grim sighed, taking a seat on one of the black leather chairs while pinching the bridge of his nose. "You answer to a higher calling," Grim explained. "You were chosen by the fae to wield the Blade of Bane. This was always to be your fate. I simply helped elongate the normalcy of your life for as long as I could."

Neither Miranda nor I moved to sit, standing across from each other at either end of an invisible tether.

"I'm not a child. You don't need to coddle me." Her hand curved tightly around the blade's hilt.

Bob. She called the Blade of Bane Bob.

Grim opened his hands. "Of course you aren't, but Miranda, you were the one who insisted on clinging to mortal responsibilities, and we allowed it. But in lieu of what's happened—" He stood up again, as if remembering he is the boss. "—you must kill all of the gods who escaped the blade. They were slain for a reason, because they were a threat to our world and left unchecked—"

Miranda cocked a hip and tilted her head toward me. "So you're saying I should kill him again? For the safety of the world?"

The only one in danger is you, sweetheart. I'm coming for you.

"He's not exactly the threat I'm referring to," Grim said dryly. "And as Xander is not only adept in swordsmanship, but also has a familiarity with a number of the most dangerous gods you are now in pursuit of and lacks an occupation at the moment, he can help you hunt."

"Listen, I know what I've done." Miranda's composure broke as real panic entered her eyes. "And I'm paying for it. But I don't think I deserve this punishment."

Grim crossed to Miranda, standing between us even though she and I never broke eye contact.

"This isn't punishment, Miranda. The other gods raise their voice in outrage, but it is because they are scared. Scared of what's out in the world now." He took her hands in his.

Instantly my hackles rose, but I worked to keep my possessiveness in check.

I'd convinced Grim to arrange our partnership and I wasn't about to screw over my chance at being near my dark angel again.

Grim's word was final, so I followed Miranda to the elevator where we stood side by side, her eyes trained on the changing floor numbers. I opted to bite the inside of my cheek to keep from saying anything smug that might compel her to stab me.

"Don't you know the rules of civilized society?" she mocked. "No shirt," her eyes scanned my chest, leaving a trail of heat in their wake, before lowering, "No shoes, no service."

"I'm more interested in providing service," I leered at her.

Miranda's eyes flashed with anger as she turned to fully face me. "Keep your service to yourself, Xander." Her hand tightened around the hilt of her blade even as her cheeks turned a beautiful rosy shade. "I don't need you tagging along, and I certainly don't need to be distracted."

I simply chuckled, taking a step closer to her. "Oh, but you do need my help," I replied, my voice low and dangerous. "And as for distractions," I leaned in, my breath hot against her ear, "you know you can't resist me."

Miranda's face twisted with anger as she shoved me away from her. "You're disgusting," she hissed, and the elevator doors opened. We stepped out into the lobby of the hotel, and I could feel her eyes burning holes into me as we walked towards the exit.

Outside, the sun beat down on the city, and the unfamiliar rumbling, bleating sounds of traffic filled the air.

My ears began ringing and my throat tightened as the caustic stench of exhaust filled my senses. The urge to escape to a dark and quiet place intensified as the chaotic surroundings threatened to overwhelm me.

But there was something I wanted more than peace.

Now that I was in Miranda's orbit, I didn't want to break away.

The tension between us was thick and palpable as we made our way down the street. I didn't know where she was going, but I'd follow her to the ends of the earth if she let me.

"You know," I said after a moment, breaking the silence between us, "you're even more beautiful when you're angry."

She growled. Actually growled.

"You may be the chosen one, but you'll need my expertise if you want to survive in the world of the gods," I replied, my voice low and menacing.

Miranda stopped at a parked, sensible silver car, and turned to face me, her jaw clenched. "I can handle this on my own."

"You can't possibly believe that," I retorted. "You may be strong, but you're not invincible. The gods are dangerous, and you'll need all the help you can get."

Miranda's eyes narrowed, and the tension rose between us once again. I knew she didn't trust me, but I also knew that she had no choice but to work with me.

I'd made sure of that.

Setting both hands on the scalding metal of the vehicle, I boxed her in. "Trust me, Miranda." My head tilted down toward her as my voice softened. "I won't let anything happen to you."

Miranda stiffened at my nearness. Oh fuck, I was close enough to inhale the heady mixture of bergamot and her skin.

Miranda hesitated for a moment, her eyes searching mine as if looking for something. A reason to believe me?

"Never," she said, her voice cold. "I suppose I *have* to tolerate your presence for the sake of completing my mission, but nothing more."

I couldn't help but grin at her stubbornness. It only made me want her more.

"Don't worry, sweetheart." I reached up to smooth my thumb over her tense jawline. Her skin was like warm silk. "I can handle a little hostility."

I knew that I was getting under her skin, but I wanted to get deeper. I wanted to dig into her heart and nest there for all eternity.

The way she now lived inside of me.

Miranda pushed my hand away so violently, I knew I was in danger of losing the appendage. "Touch me again, and I'll show you hostility." The way her teeth were bared promised violence.

That's fine my little badass, as long as I get to be close to you. For now...

I nodded and shoved my hands in my pockets to keep from reaching out and doing it again. Rocking back on my heels, I asked with all the innocence in the world, "So when do we go hunting?"

Chapter Four

THE BEAST

"What in the hell are you wearing?" The whites of Miranda's eyes nearly swallowed her dark irises as she stared at me, slack-jawed.

We agreed to meet in the Sinopolis lobby at dusk to go god hunting.

Looking down, I pulled out the edge of my shirt, checking to see if I got anything on my new purchase.

"What?" I asked, not seeing whatever horrified her. "You said to get a shirt and shoes."

Miranda's head slowly shook, the horror on her face fixed in place. "And *that* is what you chose?"

I frowned. "The shopkeeper said red was my color." Plus, I liked the big white tropical flowers on the Hawaiian shirt.

It still felt strange to cover up. My clothes never lasted long when I was locked in my cell. My madness would drive me to claw at my own chest until I pulled out my own heart, deranged with the need for a death I could never reach. After a while, I stopped fighting my near constant state of undress. But Miranda had a point about regular people looking at me like I was crazy or dangerous.

I was, but they didn't need to know that at first glance.

"He lied," she said drolly, her face going flat, still scanning me from head to toe with open judgement in her eyes and twisted lips. "And anyone wearing socks with sandals should be shot on sight."

My frown deepened. On that point I couldn't entirely disagree. I'd modeled my look after the street vendor, and while I loved the bright cheerful colors and floral shirt design, the socks and sandals immediately proved to be impractical.

Miranda chewed on the inside of her cheek, irritation flashing in her dark eyes. "And could you at least button that thing the rest of the way up?"

Again, I glanced down. I'd only done half the buttons to offset the claustrophobia I felt at being covered so entirely. I settled on telling her a half-truth. "It's hot."

That wasn't a lie. While summer was coming to a close, the days were only heating up carrying over into sweltering nights.

And I didn't have to guess at why. The sun god's presence was all around me, even if I didn't know exactly where yet.

Miranda rolled her eyes at my reluctance to button up, shrugging her shoulders as if she suddenly felt uncomfortable. If I didn't know any better, I'd swear I saw a spark of lust in her eye before irritation drowned it out.

I followed her as we made our way through the bustling lobby and out onto the city streets. The sun had dipped below the buildings, casting a golden glow over the strange garish buildings on the Strip. I'd seen them in pictures and on video through the years, but I'd only been on the streets for a short time and the adjustment was... intense.

My teeth automatically gritted as my senses endured the onslaught of color, sound, and smells. A bachelorette group screamed in excitement as they passed by in an overwhelming cloud of different perfumes. An overweight, sweat-soaked family of tourists who stank of irritation and hunger trudged by, one of them clipping my shoulder with theirs without any follow up acknowledgement. Several poorly dressed men lining the street forced little slips of paper depicting barely censored naked women into my hands without so much as a smile. The irrational urge to retreat back to my cell yanked at my guts.

"You good?" Miranda asked. It took a second to pull my fractured senses together so I could focus on her. Eyebrow raised, Miranda looked genuinely concerned.

Keep it together Xander. Stay calm, stay cool, let her see how you've changed.

"The best you ever had, baby," I quipped back. My lips slid into a lascivious smile though the sheen of sweat now covering my body had nothing to do with the pressing Vegas heat.

I'd expected Miranda to roll her eyes so hard they'd threaten to fall out of her head. Instead, she kept that unerring gaze trained on me, as if she could see right through me. It both thrilled and terrified me to capture her complete attention.

To further the picture of ease I was trying to sell, I slipped my hands into the pockets of my shorts. It was also so she couldn't see them shake.

Keep it together, you crazy fuck.

I couldn't let her see the loose threads that I feared would continue to unravel.

Finally, she nodded and turned her attention back to our walking path.

I removed my hands from my pockets, clenching and releasing my fingers to try and shake off the tremors.

Miranda's eyes continually scanned the crowd, always on high alert.

"So, exactly how have you been choosing which god to target?" I asked, needing to focus on what we were doing rather than the busy Vegas Strip.

"They usually leave behind a general trail of chaos, and the longer they've been left to run wild, the more reckless they become."

"How so?" I asked, if nothing else, to keep her talking to me. I was addicted to every word that fell from her lips.

Godsdamn, those perfect lips.

She sighed. "The Obelisk hotel disappeared for several hours before reappearing, all the casinos in the Martini went off with jackpots at the same time, it rained *inside* of the Menaggio, and of course, strange animal sightings are showing up on the internet from people recording with their phones. Usually, the activity picks up once the sun goes down."

I nodded. "Sounds like my asshole brethren. So are we going after any one of them in particular?"

And how can I keep you as far away from them as possible?

I knew I didn't stand a chance in hell of keeping Miranda out of danger when she was determined to run headlong into it, but that didn't mean I couldn't do anything about it.

Miranda's jaw tensed. "I still plan to go after Sheshem, since he has an easily discernible pattern. Even though you stepped in and ruined my chances last night." She grumbled her last words.

I stopped at that. "I *saved* you."

There was Miranda's classic eye roll I knew so well. She didn't bother replying to that. We both knew it was true, but it must gall the shit out of her that I saved her perfect, shapely ass. I had to jog a few steps to catch up to her again. I followed until we were cruising the back alleys of restaurants. Miranda deliberately unlocked or opened certain dumpsters as if to draw a path directly to us.

With my heightened senses, the stink of garbage was enough to make me toss my last meal, but I muscled my gorge back down.

"This is disgusting," I finally said after our long stretch of silence.

Miranda shrugged. "Consider it all one big cat trap. There isn't a night when a hotel brunch restaurant doesn't complain of the garbage being splattered across the alleyway and the dumpster ripped into shreds. So, this is our best bet."

Even though we turned off the Strip a while ago, there were still too many odors. Too many lights. Too many sounds.

Everything pounded into the side of my brain like so many nails. My fists clenched tight in my pockets.

Don't let her see. Don't let her know. She can't know how fucking broken your brain is.

A bowl of broken spaghetti.

A rotting meat pile.

You're shit. You're nothing. You don't belong. This world isn't yours. You have no world. Worlds won't swallow you—

A blessed breeze swept by, and Miranda's scent engulfed me, clearing away the incoherent jumble of stabbing thoughts.

I almost shuddered in relief as I breathed in the singular scent of her skin and bergamot. That sweet, refreshing citrus scent wafted from her skin that was also somehow deeply complex and round.

Sweet fucking hell, I wanted to bury my face in her throat, lick her from ankle to chin, until she had completely saved me.

I wanted to save her too. Save her from the hardness that was turning her brittle.

"Do you really think this is the best idea?" I asked. "A stakeout at the dumpsters, waiting for Sheshem to show up like a rabid raccoon? Maybe we could go patrol the Strip, check out a show, search the wax museum for evil," I teased, trying to inject some levity into our tense mission.

Miranda shot me an irritated glance. "We stick to the plan. It's not about what's fun, Xander. It's about what works."

I raised an eyebrow, a challenging smirk playing on my lips. "But what if I have better ideas? Something less... dumpster-divey?"

Her response was firm, unwavering. "We're not improvising. I've mapped this out. We follow the plan, Xander. No deviations."

I probed further, testing the boundaries of her resolve. "Ever think your plans are a bit... rigid? There's a whole spectrum between dumpster diving and going off-script, you know."

Miranda's tone turned defensive, her words laced with an icy chill. "Rigid keeps us alive. And I don't recall your improvisations ending well last time."

Softening my approach, I said, "Hey, I get it. Control feels safe. But sometimes, a little chaos can be our ally. Trust me."

"It's not about trust." Realizing she'd raised her voice, Miranda closed her eyes and took a calming breath before continuing. "It's about minimizing risks, now shut up and be patient."

So that was a no on getting her to relax around me. But we were stuck together for the foreseeable future, so I had time. For once, time was an element in my favor.

Miranda may be a no-nonsense badass, but I knew her vulnerabilities, her fragile humanity even if she wanted to deny she possessed any weakness.

Whenever she spoke of killing a god, a frenetic kind of desperation entered her eyes. She'd hadn't achieved her goal yet and it was killing her.

The more she reinforced her walls of protection, the more she tried to expunge her vulnerabilities, the more delicate she became.

I'd be fucking damned if I let her crack. Or if she does crumble, I'll either be the one to put her pieces back together, or better yet, I'll be the one to make her fall to pieces, my tongue between her thighs, pushing her over an edge so pleasurable she forgets anything and anyone other than me.

Fuck. If I didn't get myself together, I'd end up sporting an obvious hard on. And she might get the idea I get randy over trash.

As if sensing my shift in focus, Miranda turned toward me.

She licked her lips slowly, maybe even nervously. "Don't look at me like that."

"Like what?" My voice was husky even to my own ears.

"Like you want to devour me." Her brows were pinched in a frown, but her breath hitched. My little badass *liked* the idea of me eating her up.

"Would that be so bad?" I asked, taking a step closer. Miranda started to step back but stood her ground at the last second, letting me invade her personal space.

A ray of streetlamp light sliced across her eyes, turning the deep, fathomless dark of them into the color of honey. The pressing dry heat also had her covered in perspiration, making her warm brown skin glow and sing like a siren. The song beckoned me to slide my hands over her muscled, toned arms, into the dip of her tank top to find the generous swell of her breasts.

Instead of answering, her lips tightened. I groaned. It only made me want to cover her mouth with my own and coax that beautifully full mouth apart.

Something about my thoughts must have broadcasted on my face because Miranda's eyes widened, and her hands pushed against my chest as if to keep me at bay. But the beast in me was taking over, and I wasn't sure if anything could stop me now.

Right then, I knew nothing could stop me. I was going to kiss her so deep, so thoroughly, I wouldn't stop until she was dripping between those thighs.

Chapter Five

THE BEAST

Dipping in, I tasted her sweet breath. She didn't move away. Tingles swept across my lips and pressure built in my cock. I was millimeters from heaven again.

A crash boomed from nearby, and both of us jumped back. Before I registered what happened, Miranda charged off in the direction of the sound.

My instincts kicked in and I followed her, pushing through the narrow alleyway. The smell of garbage intensified with the sickening stench as we neared the source of the commotion.

Ahead, a massive shadow loomed, its outline unmistakable even in the dim light. Sheshem rummaged through a dumpster with a voracious appetite. The sight of the deity, feasting on leftover pancakes and shrimp from the trash, was both surreal and pitiful.

We were once gods that ruled the lands and all humans. Now, Sheshem was a dumpster cat, and I couldn't seduce the only woman in the world that mattered. Pathetic.

Miranda moved with stealth, drawing her blade with silent precision. She was a warrior in her element, every muscle tensed for the strike. I readied myself, preparing to flank the creature. I had no intention of letting Sheshem's claws get anywhere close to her.

We crept closer to the hulking cat god, carefully coordinating our steps to avoid any noise. Miranda's blade gleamed in the dim light, a silent promise of a swift end.

Suddenly I was heartened by the idea this could all be over rather quickly.

Maybe we'd have time for a midnight swim in a pool after this?

Just as we were about to pounce, a large, clumsily set cage, draped with a net and various shiny objects, crashed down from above. It landed with a loud clang a few feet away from Sheshem, missing its mark entirely.

The cat god, startled by the sudden intrusion, let out a roar that reverberated off the walls. In an instant, it bounded away with supernatural speed, disappearing into the darkness.

Two figures stumbled into view, both dressed in cheap glittery magician costumes, complete with capes and top hats. One wielded a net, while the other brandished what looked like a toy wand.

"Hey! You ruined our trap and scared off our star attraction!" the taller of the two magicians exclaimed, frustration evident in his voice. He was a young, lanky fellow with a greasy ponytail and acne scars, and his outfit looked like it had seen better days.

The other, shorter and rounder with a fast-receding hairline for his age, chimed in, "Yeah, we've been planning this for weeks! That cat was going to be the centerpiece of our new act at The Mystical Mirage."

Miranda's eyes narrowed as she sheathed her blade, her posture radiating annoyance. "You two were trying to catch *that creature* for a magic show? Are you out of your minds?"

"I know I've been out of circulation for a while," I said to Miranda, eyeing the two morons, "but exactly how dumb have humans gotten over the years?"

"Excuse me, we are professional magicians," the taller magician retorted. "We are Marvelous Max," he gestured to himself then his friend, "and the Amazing Alfonso, and we're going to revolutionize Vegas entertainment with a real-life mystical beast." He wiggled his fingers at us in a way that made me want to rip them off his hands.

His companion, "Amazing Alfonso", piped up, "Yeah, and we

would've caught it too, if it weren't for you guys charging in like a bull in a china shop!"

The situation was absurd; the two wannabe magicians in their shabby costumes and their botched trap were like something out of a low-budget fantasy film.

They must have dumped cologne on this morning and it made my stomach turn until it was difficult to think.

Miranda stepped forward, her body language all business. "Look, this isn't some game. That *beast* is a dangerous animal. You're lucky it ran off instead of turning you into its next meal."

I'd like to think Sheshem would have better taste, but he was already rummaging in dumpsters. These two looked like they crawled out of a glittery trash can themselves.

Max's frown was downright petulant, reminding me of a five-year-old child about to throw a tantrum. "We... we have a system. We're setting traps all over the city. High-tech stuff."

Alfonso nodded eagerly. "Yeah, high-tech. With nets... and, uh, shiny things cats like."

Miranda turned to me, a mix of frustration and resignation in her eyes as if to say, "Can you believe these two idiots?"

In a dry, matter-of-fact tone I said to them, "You are both going to get eaten."

Over my limit with irritation, not only because we lost Sheshem but because I almost had a perfectly delicious moment with the goddess to my left. "Here's some free advice: Leave hunting to the professionals. Go play with your card tricks and leave the real dangers to us."

Max bristled at my words, his pride wounded. "We are *not* giving up. This is our big break!"

Alfonso, however, seemed less convinced, his eyes darting nervously around the alley. "Maybe we should rethink our strategy, Max..."

Closing the distance until I stood right in front of the two morons, I bared my teeth and said, "This is our hunt, and if you two don't back off you will both end up either in that cage or in the big cat's stomach. Get it?"

"Yeah, right." Alfonso curled his lip as he looked me up and down. "Like we are going to let a low-rent Magnum PI intimidate us."

I stuck a finger in both of their faces, packing all the menace I could muster into my words, "I'll take the compliment of even resembling a handsome beast like Tom Selleck, but that's not going to save you from an ass kicking if you don't back down."

While my bouts of pain locked in a cage usually had me senseless for most of my days, my body had given up just as often, too tired to shift or think, and the invention of television had been one of the few blessings I'd appreciated. That and the age of books on tape helped keep me from tearing the pages out of paperbacks or splitting hardback spines in half during a sudden fit, or accidentally ruining the books in either of the pools of water I recovered in.

I knew better than anyone that Tom Selleck was a gift. And while I was pissed as hell at these two idiots, I was seriously considering how I'd look with a mustache.

"We don't have time for this," Miranda said behind me, clearly done with these two idiots. I couldn't agree more.

"Last warning," I growled. "Stay out of our way."

"This is YOUR last warning. Stay out of *our* way," Max threatened.

I turned on my heel, shaking my head, walking with Miranda before I cracked their stupid skulls against each other.

Miranda kept pace with me as we strode out the long alley and toward the Strip. "Have all humans become so idiotic over the years?"

"Were we really all that smart in your day and age?" Miranda asked with genuine curiosity in her voice.

"Good point. You, my little badass, have made the exception seem like the rule."

Her lips twitched as if she were trying to hide a satisfied smile. She didn't even balk at my nickname for her.

There. Miranda had relaxed just a little, and I reveled in the victory.

"Magicians trying to catch a god spawn for a Vegas act," Miranda muttered, her voice tinged with disbelief. "What's next? A circus ringmaster trying to tame a sphinx?"

I chuckled, despite the irritation still simmering inside me. "In this city? I wouldn't be surprised."

Miranda glanced at me, a wry smile briefly flashing on her face. "You know, for a second there, I thought you were going to lose it with those two."

I shrugged. "The thought crossed my mind. But then I remembered I'm trying to be a civilized god now."

"Civilized? You?"

"Hey, I'm wearing a shirt, aren't I?" I gestured to my Hawaiian shirt. "And it's... mostly buttoned up."

Miranda laughed, a genuine, unguarded sound that filled the night air. It was a rare moment of levity in our usually tense interactions. For a fleeting moment, I saw the woman behind the warrior, the vulnerability behind the strength.

But as quickly as it came, the moment passed, and Miranda's expression hardened once more. "We can't let those two interfere again. Sheshem is dangerous, and they're clueless."

I nodded in agreement, my gaze fixed on the bustling crowd ahead. "We'll keep an eye on them. But right now, we need to focus on our own hunt. They are a distraction."

Miranda sighed, running a hand through her braids. "Yeah. Let's keep going and maybe, just maybe, find you a shirt that doesn't scream 'tourist', or Magnum PI." She paused. "Though you might look dashing with a thick mustache."

I knew it!

Chapter Six

THE BADASS

My hands closed around my red-eye, a blissfully large cup of coffee topped with two shots of espresso. After the oppressive heat of the night, I was grateful to be back in the air-conditioned bliss of Sinopolis, sitting at Perkatory, the cafe in the lobby.

I told Xander I was going home after our night of fruitless hunting to make sure he wouldn't try to tag along for my morning routine.

Where he headed off to, I didn't know, and I tried not to care. I really tried, but questions like where was he living, and what had he been doing the last several weeks hammered into me with relentless force.

I certainly wouldn't admit to him or myself that when he walked in silence next to me I felt less alone, and intrinsically understood. That he'd reached inside of me and nestled in right next to my heart, making me feel at home in his presence.

I'd never admit those things.

I toyed with the cup sleeve. On it was a printed skull in a coffee cup logo with the slogan—*good to the last drop*. This little coffee stand had become a regular part of my routine. Perkatory was an oasis smack dab in the middle of the gleaming black marble and gold filigreed lobby of Sinopolis.

Lush greenery created a canopy of tranquility and isolated the coffee stand. The gentle rustle of leaves in the air-conditioning forced the subtle floral scents to mingle with the aroma of freshly ground coffee beans. This little spot always felt like my own personal sanctuary.

Vivien slid into the chair across from me, also finished with her nocturnal duties. Though my vampire best friend had a better night than me, judging by the fact her fishnet stockings were still intact and her auburn hair maintained volume and style as if she'd just done it. While I felt like a limp, exhausted noodle. Stains from the trash bins and nasty alleyways marked up my dark tank top. I felt disgusting, but I needed a moment to decompress before I went home and woke up Jamal to get him ready for school.

"How'd it go?" Vivien asked.

"Y-yeah, how'd it go?" a second voice chimed in as Aaron sat down. He adjusted his black apron with the Perkatory logo as he sat in the last chair. The coffee line was low enough that he could let the other barista handle it and join us, completing our little trio of friends.

"Fine," I said, sipping the dark brew.

Aaron and Vivien exchanged a glance.

"Did you f-fuck him?"

"...in a dumpster?" Vivien added, her nose wrinkling.

My jaw dropped as I turned to face Aaron. "Okay, I'd expect that from her," I pointed at Vivien, "but from you? Et tu Aaron?"

He shrugged his muscular shoulders up into the tips of his wavy, sun-bleached hair. "I-it's a v-valid question." Aaron's stutter had been getting slightly better from speech therapy, but ever since his surfing accident years ago, the stammer was his constant companion.

"No," I said icily, my shoulders stiffening. "He has absolutely no effect on me anymore. And I have zero intention of ever letting him touch me again."

Except for that moment when he almost kissed me... again.

A growl of frustration escaped me.

Aaron and Vivien leaned back from me a couple of inches.

"Yeah, no effect whatsoever," Vivien said airily, giving Aaron a look.

I gave them a rundown of the hack magicians who ruined my chances of slaying Sheshem. "After that, I couldn't get a bead on any gods or monsters the rest of the night."

"So... it was just you and Xander hanging out until dawn?" Vivien poked and prodded like a nosy little kid. It was hilarious when she did it to others. Not so much when she did it to me.

"Yes. It was... fine."

"Y-you said that," Aaron pointed out.

Usually, my friends gave me a sense of peace and pleasure. Staring into my coffee, I considered chucking the rest of it at both of them.

"What happened to getting back in the dating game?" Vivien asked. "When Xander disappeared a month ago, after the... incident, you said you were going to."

I did say that, didn't I?

I'd said I was never really in love with Xander after all, that it was only infatuation. We'd been in an intense, stressful situation that was sexually charged, but after some reflection (unfortunately only after I brought him back and released havoc on the world) I had come to the conclusion I was only in lust with the god.

Determined to fall in lust with someone else—anyone else—to prove my point, I'd gone on a couple dates. Every time my stomach would lurch with nausea almost as soon as the meeting began, and it wouldn't let up until I parted ways with whatever perfectly nice man I'd met. It was like I was repulsed by any man who wasn't Xander.

God damn it.

And now that he was back, invading my space, teasing me, protecting me, my body hummed with that same intense satisfaction and need rolled into one big ball that lodged itself under my ribcage.

I'm not in love with him. I never was, I insisted to myself. That would be crazy.

"Have you heard anything about rogue gods or monsters wreaking havoc?" I asked Vivien, changing the subject. "I lost the trail of the one I was tracking last night and nothing else came up." Which meant a full night of stalking the streets with a god who looked at me like he wanted to throw me against the nearest wall and ravish me until I died.

The kind of stress that inspired must have originated from the fourth or fifth level of hell. I'm usually adept at keeping my emotions under wrap, but Xander made it so damn hard, digging his hooks into me until I wanted to explode... one way or another.

The intensity in Vivien's green eyes let me know she was aware of my evasive tactics, but she let it slide. "Nothing concrete, but the gods are restless. Nervous."

"Because of Aten," I finished for her.

Vivien drummed her fingers on the table. "Apparently, he's one scary motherfucker."

Aaron shook his head. "I can't imagine what k-kind of god would scare the shit out of the other immortals." Then with a look at Vivien, "Other than Grim of course."

Vivien grinned at the mention of her hot husband and god of the dead. "He's just a pussycat underneath all that dark, gloomy death stuff."

"Yeah, sure." Aaron drew out the words with evident disbelief.

Vivien's impish smile faded, her fingers playing with the edge of the table. "They are all freaking out though. Grim is afraid that gods will start to turn on each other in fear."

"Why?" Aaron asked. "Are they worried some of their own are working for Aten like that little fae girl did?"

My hand tightened around my cup. The memory of trusting the wrong person still sliced through my chest with a triple helping of shame and regret.

Vivien shook her head. "None of the gods support Aten's monotheistic agenda— aka murdering the shit out of all the gods until he's the only one left. But when gods get upset, they get unpredictable and temperamental."

"Turn bitchy and childlike?" I offered.

Vivien pointed a finger at me like a gun. "Bingo. So Grim and Timothy are cooking up a way to pull them all back together. Like a big *rah rah* morale boost."

The downturn at the corner of her lips showed she was less than thrilled.

"How does that work?" I asked.

Vivien shook her head and gave me a wry smile. "They are still working on a plan, so I'll let you know when I do."

By the way she avoided my gaze and fidgeted, I had a suspicion she knew exactly what they were planning.

I had to leave her explanation at that as I had to get home before Jamal woke up. Parking my car in the driveway, I was surprised to find a man I didn't recognize pulling my garbage can to the edge of the street. As I stepped out, the man turned and unleashed a powerfully beautiful smile. It hit me like a tractor beam.

Well over six feet tall with light brown skin and shocking green eyes, the black man's head was shaved clean and he was as handsome as all get out. This may well be the finest man I had ever seen in my life. He belonged on the silver screen next to some leading lady he effortlessly wooed. Yet all his attention was directed at me, warming me from the inside out.

"Hi there," he said, striding forward to close the distance and shake my hand. "I'm your new neighbor. I hope you don't mind. I was worried you'd miss the trash pick up, so I thought I'd pull yours down."

The gears in my brain that came to a grinding halt began again with slow ker-chunks. "Oh, uh, thank you. I appreciate that." The knowledge I was still wearing dumpster-stained clothes suddenly made me self-conscious.

"My name is Michael." My neighbor still didn't let go of my hand, and I suddenly found myself not minding so much as I got caught up in his gaze. The light olive hue of his eyes made a striking contrast to his skin which was damned near mesmerizing.

"My name is Miranda," I said, suddenly remembering myself.

The curve of his lips somehow made me feel like he was bestowing a special smile patented just for me. "Miranda." The sound of my name from his mouth sent heat spiraling through my stomach.

My reaction surprised me, but then again, I supposed it was rare I was the object of such a handsome man's attention.

Turquoise eyes made of crashing oceans flashed in my mind.

Okay, maybe not so rare these days.

The front door opened, and a face etched with lines of age and frizzy white hair stared out at us with curiosity. "Miranda?"

I dropped Michael's hand. "Hey Mama Jean." Then I nodded to Michael. "Sorry, I've got to—" I gestured to my house, words failing me, but still indicating I needed to get inside.

"Of course," he said, holding up his hands with another dazzling smile. "It was enchanting to meet you, Miranda."

Again, the way my name rolled off his lips did a number on my spine, so I had to suppress the need to shiver under his gaze. I hurried inside, shutting the door behind me.

"So you met the new neighbor," Mama Jean said, pointing out the obvious.

My mother-in-law's brown, near black irises melted into the whites surrounding. While her back was starting to bend, her brain was sharp as steel. She'd had Rashon much later in life, which put her closer to the age of my own grandmother.

I feared Mama Jean noticed my reaction. Rashon passed away many years ago, when Jamal was practically a baby, but it felt disrespectful to ogle someone in front of her. Though she'd said many times life was for the living, and I couldn't let the memory of Jamal's father hold me back.

"Yeah, he seems nice," I said, hating how breathy I sounded. The attraction I felt also unsettled me.

Maybe because I wasn't used to all this male attention, and after a night with Xander, I was starting to crack. But I had to put all that away in a box and switch on mom mode.

"Is Jamal awake?" I asked, heading toward my room to change my shirt real quick. I'd shower later.

A genuine smile broke out on her face, making her look so much like her son. The pang of pain I used to get no longer reared its ugly head when I saw the likeness. I only felt an appreciative fondness and comforting nostalgia in my brief time with Rashon.

"Yes," she said. "He's showering now."

My shoulders fell, releasing tension I didn't realize I'd been holding there. "I don't know how to thank you, Mama Jean. You've been a godsend since I started this night shift." I rubbed my forehead. *And before that.*

Rashon gave me a child and a parent.

Mama Jean waved a dismissive hand at me. "Honey child, you don't need to thank me. We are family. It's what we do." She stood in the doorway to my bedroom as I stripped the disgusting tank top off.

Mama Jean had always been adamant about staying in my and Jamal's life. While my parents retired to Florida years ago, Mama Jean moved out here from Georgia to be close to us. She took care of Jamal when I was still on active duty.

After I got out of the army I did my best to stay independent, but her constant presence somewhat accustomed me to counting on her, and after my massive cosmic mistake I had to lean on her more heavily than ever. Thankfully, she didn't mind.

I pulled on a soft T-shirt. Instantly, my battery filled fifteen percent. Soft, clean clothes was one way to my heart.

Not that I'd ever tell Xander that little tip. I needed to keep that god far away from my fleshy blood-filled organ.

I finished changing and stepped back into the living room, where Mama Jean was setting the table for breakfast.

Jamal came bounding out of the bathroom, his toothbrush still in his mouth. His bright eyes landed on me, and he gave a muffled, "Mmng!"

I chuckled, ruffling his short crop of hair. "Good morning, kiddo. Ready for that math test?"

Jamal nodded vigorously, foam from the toothpaste dribbling down his chin. "Mm-hmm!" he mumbled, before dashing off to spit and rinse.

Mama Jean shook her head affectionately. "That boy. He's growing up too fast." Mama Jean's gentle hands moved with practiced ease as she buttered pieces of toast. The rich aroma of the coffee enveloped the room, mixing with the gardenia scent of her favorite hand cream.

"Yeah, he is," I agreed, watching Jamal with a combination of pride and wistfulness. I loved being his mother almost more than anything.

Jamal returned, his face clean, and sat at the table after dropping a kiss on his G-Ma's cheek. He glanced at me, his young face suddenly serious. "Did you catch the bad guys last night, Mom?"

"Bad guys?" Mama Jean said, halting her pour of coffee abruptly.

I gave Jamal a meaningful look to lock down his comments around his G-Ma.

He turned away and gritted his teeth. While Jamal knew far too much about the immortal underbelly of Vegas, Mama Jean was blissfully unaware, and I planned to keep it that way.

"You know, people who want to scam the casinos. Bad guys," I supplied to Mama Jean. She thought I still ran security at Sinopolis. I didn't love lying to her, but I'd learned long ago that there were necessary lies to keep loved ones and civilians safe as well as at ease.

"Well Lord have mercy, because you came in smelling like a garbage truck honey. Are you sure they are paying you enough?" She held out a steaming mug of coffee to me. I really should pass on more caffeine if I wanted to sleep, but truthfully, I didn't want to.

I'd only dream of *him*.

"Uh." My thoughts raced as I looked down into the dark elixir of life as I took it. "A high-profile patron lost their jewelry in the trash, and we helped dig it out for her."

"Oh well, that was awful good of you." Mama Jean nodded.

As Jamal chattered about his upcoming test, I smiled and listened, treasuring these mundane yet precious moments. They were my anchor in a life filled with chaos and danger.

Tonight, I'd face the supernatural again. But for now, I was just a mom, sharing breakfast with her family.

THE BEAST

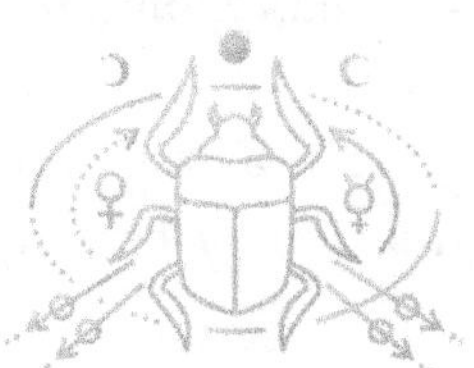

The daytime passed in a torturous crawl, every second a burning needle piercing my sanity. I was practically vibrating with anxious energy as I paced the opulent lobby of Sinopolis for two hours before Miranda even showed up.

The clack of polished shoes against the smooth marble floor grated against my eardrums, a constant reminder of the passing time. More than once, someone bumped into me, not bothering to look up from the little glowing phone in their hands. People were more like zombies now.

The bright lights overhead seemed to buzz loudly in my ears, creating a sense of disorientation and unease. Desperate for some relief, I had resorted to wearing sunglasses even indoors, hoping they would offer some reprieve from the harsh lighting.

Growing more agitated with each minute that ticked by, I started to fear I'd neared a snapping point.

Which is why it was absolutely the fucking worst when a primly dressed Timothy clipped his way directly toward me in expensive shoes and a lush verdant green suit. Per usual there wasn't a hair out of place framing his Asian features that were arranged into a cool mask of control. Grim's second-in-command had a strong distaste for me, always barely tolerating my existence. I didn't care for his neat freak routine either.

"To what do I owe the pleasure Thothy-pie." I bared my teeth at my fellow immortal, belying the levity of my words. I bastardized his ancient name, Thoth, just to see his jaw tick.

His back stiffened. "I heard Grim has aligned you with Miranda in her pursuits. No doubt a situation you manipulated to get close to her again."

I rolled my eyes and sneered. "Come to warn me away from her again?"

Because now that I'd gotten a taste of her, I couldn't let go. I *wouldn't* let go. I'd spend the rest of eternity trying to claw my way back into her heart.

Timothy regarded me with a gaze that cooled the temperature around us by several degrees. "I suppose my wisdom would be lost on you then?"

"It's called an opinion, and they are like assholes. Everyone has one and they all stink."

Timothy visibly recoiled at my crudeness. I deliberately laid it on thick to offend his sensibilities. I knew I wasn't good enough for Miranda, but I didn't need Timothy rubbing that in my face.

"Fine." He held up a hand. "You don't need my opinion, but how about a few facts?" Before I could stop him, he barreled forward. "Miranda is mortal and you are not. How do you think this ends, Xander?"

Despite all the hot tension pulsating in my body, I coolly observed my nails and replied, "With us living happily ever after."

"You'll stay with her until she grows old and gray and crosses over to the afterlife?"

My stomach churned.

"If need be," I said, though truthfully I hadn't considered the future..

Timothy sighed, his shoulders dropping several inches. "I know you think I am your adversary, but we aren't so different." We mutually sized each other up, him in his perfect suit and controlled lifestyle and me in my loud Hawaiian shirt, messy hair overdue for a cut, and raging mental instability.

Still, he went on, his voice lowering. "You don't know the pain of loving someone so hard you'd turn yourself inside out, only to blink and find they are gone with an eternity stretched out before you, absent of their lifeforce."

The scowl remained on my face even as I swallowed hard. I didn't want to give Timothy any space in my brain, but I could already feel his words burrowing into my neurons like tiny mites that would eat away at me.

Even the thought of an existence without Miranda's lifeforce in it made my skin crawl and acid rise up my throat. It would be unbearable.

"Why do you hate me so fucking much?" I rasped, my fists tightening into balls.

Timothy's expression softened, surprise flickering in his eyes. "Don't you see, Nun?" he asked, using my old name, causing a spark to ignite in me. A hand fell to my shoulder, imprinting a level of sincerity I'd never experienced from him before. "I don't hate you at all. I am still trying to protect my friend and you from yourselves before it's too late." Timothy's eyes flickered over my shoulder.

I knew without looking that he'd spared a glance at the man who worked at the coffee stand. The mortal with the beach boy looks and the damaged voice box.

The one Timothy yearned to be with.

The sincerity in his voice made me all the angrier. Though whether I was angry because he kept trying to interfere or because he had a point was unclear.

I shrugged his hand off and stalked away from him, wanting to put as much distance between me and Timothy's words as possible.

Yet they clung to me, like a sticky patina. Even long after the god had left, the words sunk into my pores infecting me with ideas that combated the feelings I had for Miranda.

She was mine, and I had to make her see that.

But the future looked bleak even if she was the briefest shining light of my existence. Not to mention, I wasn't sure what she would think of our coupling. Mortals were sensitive about aging in contrast to the immovable nature of gods.

Maybe there was a solution. An eternity with Miranda, one where we were bound together for all time. Like Grim and Vivien. A god and his sekhor.

My palm slammed into my temple several times with rapid blows.

No. I could not think of asking her to become a vampire when she didn't even believe we belonged together. Still, my thoughts jumbled into muddled spirals, causing anxiety to rise in every strand of muscle until I was sure I'd explode. I had to get out of here. I had to collect myself or things would get messy.

Just when I'd been about to turn and head back to where I'd been retreating during most of my days, she strode through the door.

Miranda stole the breath from my lungs before ripping my beating heart out. Maybe it was my madness, but I swear I could feel my brain drip out of my ears as my eyes devoured her lithe figure dressed in dark, form fitting combat clothes.

The sleek material clung to every curve and muscle of her body, accentuating her toned arms and legs. Her tank top revealed the defined lines of her shoulders and the dips between her biceps and triceps. Even as her dark eyes bore into me with hard scrutiny, they were the most mesmerizing feature I had ever seen.

Not to mention they were a perfect juxtaposition to the soft near over-fullness of her mouth.

Fuck. That mouth.

Every aspect of her being exuded a raw violence and sexuality that left me reeling. Her expression always broadcasted that she'd suffer no fools and not even the strongest god or man could tame her.

In that moment, I wanted to beg her to kick my ass because it would give me a sick kind of satisfaction to have her unleash all of that strength on me.

Apparently, the long torturous years of seclusion had turned me into a masochist.

Walking right up to me, Miranda had no clue I was crumbling before her.

"Ready?" she asked.

I shoved my hands in my pockets and gave her a mute nod.

With a cool glance down at my feet, she gave another sharp nod. "Better."

I followed her gaze to the heavy boots I now wore that were far more practical than the sandals. Miranda scanned back up to my chest where my bright turquoise Hawaiian shirt was only fastened by one button, since I still felt claustrophobic wearing shirts.

Miranda whirled around and I had to take several long strides to catch up to her quick pace as we walked out into the evening, the sun quickly setting with fiery oranges shooting into the sky as the day died before us. Instantly, we were both shining with sweat from the baking heat.

"That color looks good on you. Brings out your eyes," Miranda said, keeping her focus forward.

The lump in my throat doubled in size.

A normal person would say something like, "Thank you," but all my brain could pound out beat after beat was, *I'll make you mine, I'll make you mine, I'll make you mine.*

So I kept my mouth shut and matched her pace. Perhaps a little hunting would clear my mind. And if I was very lucky, a little violence would work off this extra energy before I took it out on Miranda.

* * *

THE HEAT WAS A TANGIBLE WEIGHT, PRESSING DOWN ON US AS WE moved through the streets. It felt like the city was holding its breath, waiting for something to happen. We were on the hunt for Sheshem, but the massive cat god remained elusive, slipping through our fingers like smoke.

We'd hear rummaging in dumpsters around the corner, but once we got there, the devastation had been done, leaving rotting food exposed and used napkins rolling around free.

Miranda coiled like a spring, pulling in tighter with each missed encounter. She moved with a predator's grace, her eyes constantly scanning the alleys and shadows. Despite the odds stacked against her, her determination only grew.

While I only became crankier, unhappy I couldn't work out the extra energy thrumming through me.

I should be grateful. Not that long ago, this level of agitation would have power ripping me apart, turning me into my monstrous god-like-ness, out of my mind with violence and pain.

I wouldn't do it again though. I'd managed to keep myself from turning into the beast for weeks now. I had to make sure it was safe before I approached Miranda.

While my power had normalized, I was anything but balanced. It had taken brutal hours, days, weeks of pushing the jumbled parts of my mind into a working lump of control.

But right now, I was beginning to think control was overrated.

"We're chasing shadows," I grumbled, scanning the rooftops. Sheshem could be anywhere, watching us with those big, feline eyes and mocking our efforts. "Maybe you should go home."

Miranda shot me a look. "This is my responsibility, Xander. I can't turn away from this."

I scoffed. "That's only because the other gods are putting pressure on you, letting a mortal do their dirty work."

She stopped, turning to face me. "*I'm* the one who made this mess. I take full responsibility and will deal with the consequences."

I turned on her, fury filling me up like a kettle beginning to boil. "You shouldn't have to deal with the consequences. You're a human."

Even as I said it, Timothy's words reared up and slapped me in the face. I did my best to squash his reservations back down into the dark recesses of my mind. The details of our future could be figured out later. Right now I was trying to win her back.

Though right now she was looking at me like she wouldn't deign to spit on me even if I was the last being on earth and fully on fire.

"Stop underestimating me."

I could practically hear her grinding her teeth.

"Fine." I stepped closer, my nostrils flaring as I breathed in her heady scent. "You think you can take on the gods. Let's see what you got."

I lunged at her. Miranda reacted instantly, her blade flashing. But I was faster, a blur of motion, godly speed at my disposal. I dodged her strike, my hand closing around her wrist, pulling her close.

Our eyes locked, inches apart, and the heat radiating off her body drilled into mine. Her heart raced, her breath quick and shallow. The air was charged with something more than just the tension of the hunt—something deeper, primal.

I released her hand, stepping back. "You're too slow. You need to anticipate, react faster."

Miranda's eyes flashed with frustration, and she attacked again, her movements fluid and calculated. But again, I was faster, evading her strikes with ease.

We danced around each other, a deadly ballet in the empty alleyway. Every touch, every near miss, sent a jolt of electricity through me. I could see it in Miranda's eyes too, that fire, that undeniable spark.

"You're holding back," she accused, panting.

I grinned, adrenaline pumping through my veins. The irritation had given way to excitement as we sparred. "Wouldn't want to hurt you, sweetheart."

Something flashed in her eyes at the pet name I gave her when she'd visited my cell nightly to kill me. It rolled off my tongue like sugar, and I could almost taste her even now.

She growled, lunging again, and this time I let her get close, close enough that our bodies almost touched. Our gazes met, and for a heartbeat, the world stood still.

"You can't win this, Miranda," I said in a low husky tone, even as my focus drifted down to her lips. For a minute, even I wasn't sure if I was talking about her suicidal hunt for the gods, or this thing between us.

She shook her head. "This isn't one of your games, Xander. It's not about winning, it's about doing what's right."

"Is it right if you get killed trying to track down immortals? What happens if you come face to face with... him?" My guts wrenched up into a tight ball, heat gathering in my forehead as flashes of her burning up under his powers slammed into my temple.

I watched Miranda's throat swallow hard as if something thick was stuck in there. "Then I'll deal with that too."

"Over my dead body," I snarled, before lunging at her again. She quickened her pace.

Aten was as vicious as he was cruel. He would take her apart piece by piece with zero remorse. It's what he did to me. Aten flayed me alive, sending me back to the cradle of life. I emerged from the cradle thousands of years too soon, corrupted with too much uncontrolled power where I remained in a living hell until my mistress of death came along.

Aten had wreaked havoc on me for the past five millennia, and I was a god. Miranda was mortal. I wouldn't let him anywhere near her.

"That's how we got here, isn't it?" she threw at me.

A wry smile pulled at my lips. At least she could joke about what happened. After all, she'd been around my dead body quite a bit.

With that, I gained a couple inches closer to her inner defenses without being shot down.

It took everything in me not to try to claw off her armor, but I knew it would get me nowhere. Miranda's defenses had become a second skin, and she hated being naked. But fucking hell and godsdammit, I wanted her naked in every way. Bare and vulnerable, just so I could show her I'd be the only armor she ever needed from the world.

We circled each other, the tension palpable in the dimly lit alley. Each of Miranda's attacks was faster, more precise, pushing me to dodge with a grace I reserved for battles of a higher stake.

"You are mortal. You can't depend on speed to save you," I coached.

When she lunged with a particularly aggressive thrust, I side-stepped, using her forward momentum to spin her towards me. The move was calculated, intended to disorient, but she was quick to recover, launching a high kick aimed directly at my chest. I caught her leg, the contact a spark in the charged air between us.

Our eyes locked in a heated gaze, her chest heaving in quick bursts.

"You're going to need to be smarter. Monsters only answer to their base instincts. Gods are arrogant. They will underestimate you, which you can use to your advantage to exploit their weaknesses."

Her response was not verbal but physical—a twist and a pull that should have sent her stumbling away from me. Instead, the momentum crashed her into me, pushing us both off balance.

My arms shot out and instinctively wrapped around her to prevent us both from falling. Our faces were inches apart, her breath warm against my skin, stirring something within me that had nothing to do with our combat.

For a long moment, we just stared at each other, the air thick with unspoken words and suppressed desires that shimmered before us like heat waves. I could feel her heart beating against my chest, fast and hard.

Then, slowly, almost hesitantly, Miranda tilted her head up, her mouth parting slightly. My gaze dropped to her lips as she licked them slowly before whispering, "You said to exploit their weakness against them." Her voice was soft, her breath tickling my face, pulling me deeper into the moment, into her.

Her words didn't penetrate my brain as it went fuzzy from her closing the distance between us, my lips parting in anticipation of tasting her.

In a swift movement, Miranda slipped from my hold, her leg sweeping out under mine, sending me crashing to the ground. I blinked, finding myself on my back, the hard ground pressing against my shoulders and my breath jettisoned from my lungs with a tight, painful squeeze.

Miranda, quick to capitalize on her advantage, straddled me with a grace that belied the deadly intent of the blade she now held to my throat. The metal was a chilling touch against my skin.

"You mean like that?" she asked, tilting her head with haughty triumph.

Despite the blade at my neck, despite the precarious position I found myself in, I couldn't help the surge of admiration that went through me. I grinned at her.

That's my girl.

Pinned beneath her, I was acutely aware of every point of contact between us. The pressure of her thighs around my torso threatened my sanity.

The desire to close that distance was overwhelming. I saw the same longing mirrored in her eyes. I leaned up onto my elbows and surprisingly, she allowed me to brush the blade aside before reaching up to push her braids back behind the perfect shell of an ear I wanted to nibble on until she gasped and shivered.

Her breath was warm against my face, a tantalizing hint of closeness that drew me in, the world narrowing down to the space between us.

As I leaned up for a kiss that promised to shatter the walls between us, our moment teetered on the edge of becoming something more.

Just as our lips were about to meet, an exasperated, nasal voice shattered the moment.

"Oh no, not you two jerks again!"

The voice snapped us back to reality like an icy splash of water.

We were on our feet in seconds as Max and Alfonso emerged from the shadows of the alley, annoyance etched on their faces.

They didn't know the *meaning* of annoyance. The urge to rip off their faces and throw them away like bits of trash overwhelmed me. My brain thundered with violent images as my emotions roiled with disappointment.

"What are you doing here?" Miranda snapped, her hand instinctively readjusting around her weapon.

Max, in his glittery magician costume that seemed even more out of place in the stark reality of the alley, rolled his eyes dramatically. "We were on the trail of our star act again, but it looks like we've stumbled upon a different kind of show," he said, eyeing us with a mix of disdain and lewd suggestion.

Alfonso, fumbling with his toy wand, chimed in with evident frustration. "Yeah, and we probably would've caught him if it weren't for you two always popping up and ruining everything! You are chasing off the star of our show."

Miranda's expression turned thunderous with irritation. "What did I tell you two idiots? You should not be tracking the massive murder cat." She enunciated the words as if explaining to a couple of slow minded children.

"You should stop getting in our way," Max shot back, before giving Alfonso a slight nod.

The moment Alfonso waved that cheap plastic wand, muttering some half-cooked incantation, I was hit by the urge to laugh.

"You are bound by the chains of the Houdini's heir, unable to break free until the moon kisses the sea."

It sounded like something out of a bad fantasy novel.

I scoffed. "Really? That's your big—"

A wave of dizziness hit me like a punch from a drunken boxer. My legs buckled, and the world spun. Miranda's concerned face blurred into a kaleidoscope of colors before darkness swallowed me whole.

When I came to, it felt like only seconds had passed, but I was laying down next to something warm. My right arm was cut short of movement with the rattle of something metal.

A pair of sparkling brown sugar eyes blinked back at me. Miranda.

We were chained to a bed that seemed to have been stolen from a medieval torture chamber placed on an otherwise empty stage.

Chapter Eight

THE BEAST

"Xander," Miranda's voice brought me back to the present, her tone clipped with irritation. "Tell me you can break these."

We were trapped together, handcuffed to a bed in an empty theater. I wish I could say I'd woken up in a stranger situation, but this kind of took the cake.

I shot her a smug grin and a flirty wink. "Of course I can, sweetheart."

My hubris got the best of me. I instantly realized I should have lied because I had my mistress of death exactly where I wanted her. Miranda lying next to me, her warm curves pressed into mine where she couldn't run away.

Also, I got a strange reassurance from being restrained. It likely had something to do with being locked up for most of my days. The sensation was akin to how someone else would feel with their grandmother's handknit blanket wrapped around them. Downright cozy.

But there was no taking advantage of this situation now, not that I let my mouth run before my brain caught up.

I tugged at the cuffs, expecting them to snap like twigs. Nothing.

My brows knitted in a frown. That can't be right. I pulled again, but something was holding some of my strength at bay.

"Hold on," I grunted, rolling over, pressing more firmly into Miranda's prone body. She turned her head, the only part she could move away from me.

Another jerk of my wrists. Nothing.

"Problem?" Miranda asked, her voice tight with impatience.

"No," I huffed. "No problem... Just..."

I twisted and rolled until I straddled Miranda's hips, covering her completely with my own body. The heat of her body scalded me even as she inhaled sharply.

Caught between my need to capture that sigh in my mouth and my pride, my pride won out as I refocused on getting us the fuck out of here.

I pulled at the handcuffs again and again. The chains rattled a mocking tune to my attempts to break the weak mortal metal. My agitation ratcheted upward as my efforts to break the chains grew near violent.

"Okay, okay, okay," Miranda practically yelled over the cacophony of my frustrated grunts and rattling metal. Her hands steadied my elbows even as I panted.

She took a deep breath. "What's going on? Is it some kind of god-proofed set of handcuffs?"

I searched my muddled thoughts.

Alfonso's ludicrous incantation echoed in my head, and I realized, with annoyance and disbelief, that it had worked. My godly strength, seemingly nullified by the power of bad acting and worse magic tricks.

"He's a hypnotist," I growled.

Miranda's brow rose in a skeptical arch. "And that works on gods?"

My lips twisted and a low growl vibrated from my throat.

"Oookay then," she drawled out. "Guess that's a yes."

It works when the god in question is weak of mind. I didn't want to admit that to her though. She didn't know. She couldn't know. It's why I stayed away for so many long weeks until I was strong enough to get back to her. I wanted to be normal, reliable, for her.

"Seems like we're stuck," I admitted, trying to ignore how close

Miranda was. Her warmth, the scent of her, it was all a bit too much for a god who was supposed to be focusing on escape, not the way her velvet braids brushed against my skin.

Our faces were inches apart, our bodies aligned in a way that was both uncomfortable and electrifying. I could feel every breath she took, each little movement sending a new wave of awareness through me.

"Do you have your phone? Mine isn't in my pocket," she asked.

"I believe they are over there," I said, pointing off to an edge of the stage where keys, phones, and even Miranda's blade sat on a chair, well out of reach.

"This is ridiculous," Miranda said. "We're supposed to be hunting a god, not playing out some magician's twisted fantasy."

"I know, I know," I replied. "But you have to admit, there's something poetic about us being chained together. Like fate is telling us we belong together." I waggled my eyebrows at her.

She scowled. "Don't get any ideas, Xander. As soon as we're out of this, it's back to the mission."

"Of course, the mission." Then I repeated the magician's dopey words, "You can't break free until the moon kisses the sea. So that means until dawn?"

"Great, just great," Miranda muttered, shifting slightly. The movement sent a ripple of awareness through me, every sense heightened by our proximity. "It's a ridiculous thing to say about a landlocked state."

"I estimate we have a couple more hours trapped here together."

At that, pure panic flittered across Miranda's face, widening her eyes and quickening her breath, causing her chest to heave. "That's unacceptable."

With that, she rolled us until she was on top. Miranda plucked a hairpin from her braids as if performing a magic trick herself. She directed the makeshift lock pick to the keyhole on the cuffs, but her hand stopped abruptly an inch away. Miranda's hand shook as she gritted her teeth, trying to push the hairpin into the hole. It was as if some invisible force was keeping her from getting any closer, the same force that held my strength back when I tried to snap the chains.

We were both under that doofus's spell.

Miranda growled and threw the hairpin aside, resorting to pulling and rattling the chains like I had. Her motions grew jerkier and more desperate as her panic mounted.

The urge to calm her down was overridden by a more powerful problem of my own.

Though it wasn't her intention, Miranda was riding and rubbing the part of me that had already grown to attention. The ache to thrust inside her gripped me like a massive fist.

My hands fell to her hips as I stopped breathing all together.

"You're gonna have to stop that, sweetheart, or we are both going to be in for more than you bargained for," I choked out.

Miranda's head tilted down at me, her braids falling to brush over my chest with alluring caresses. Annoyance gleamed brightly in her features, but realization dawned on them as she took in how I gripped her hips and the hardness that pressed into her inner thigh.

"Or," I licked my lips, daring to press my luck. "We could make the next few hours at least interesting and see how many times I can get you to scream my name." My voice was hoarse to my own ears.

I waited for the slap to ring out across my face and for the consequent sting of her rejection.

"Oh really?" Miranda said. Her voice and face were tense, as if she rode on the edge of something sharp. Something she would likely stab me with. "How many times do you think you could make me scream?"

My head snapped up so fast, it nearly flew off. Am I still caught in that ridiculous magician's thrall and in a full blown hallucination?

She asked the question as seriously as if she were asking about a cancer diagnosis. Miranda took everything too seriously.

I lifted my hips, hitting the soft warmth of her sex with my hardness. The contact dragged a groan from both of us. Miranda threw her head back as her hands curled around the bed's iron frame, the heat intensifying between us. "I'm betting at least five," I said roughly.

My hands found their way to her hips again, pulling her closer. The heat of our bodies pressed together was incredible, and my desire for her grew to near maddening hardness. We were both breathing hard, our hearts pounding in sync.

"You want to bet me?" Miranda dared me, her eyes challenging me to make good on my words.

We'd tried playing games in the past, but both of us were too competitive to relax into the frivolity normal people get from play. But I did discover she couldn't resist a wager, and I found that far more delicious a concept to play with than a board of Candy Land. Though that game really ended in my favor too...

My hips rocked gently up into her scalding soft heat. "What do I get if I win?"

Her dark orbs narrowed, even as her free hand fell onto the exposed chest of my unbuttoned shirt. It scalded me, my nipples wrenching up with tight anticipation.

"Wouldn't winning be satisfaction enough?" she asked.

A feral grin kicked up at the corner of my mouth. I was far more hungry than she could have guessed. If she knew how I wanted to possess her utterly and completely, she'd drop the bet all together. She'd likely break her own wrist to slip it from the chains and get far away from me.

As my straining cock rocked right into the dip of her cleft again, lust fogged my senses.

"If I make you scream my name five times, I get to take you on a date. You'll dress up, we'll have dinner, the whole real deal."

Miranda's glistening full lips parted in surprise before her face contorted as I rocked into her again. That hand clutched and clawed at my chest, leaving scratch marks.

Fuck. Hell. That felt so good, I almost forgot to stay focused on closing the bargain.

"And if I win?" she rasped, her fathomless pupils nearly swallowing her irises up.

"What do you want?" I asked. My fingers dug into her hips so I could roll up into her harder, faster. Miranda's head fell back with a gasp and her sweet, honeyed arousal filled the air until my mouth watered.

Sweet afterlife, it was going to take all my strength to focus on driving her to madness instead of burying myself in her and fucking her like a savage. It felt like it had been an eternity. But I had too much on the line.

"You throw away the hideous Hawaiian shirts," she finally got out.

"Deal," I barked, as soon as she stated her terms. Our lips crashed into each other, and the world around us faded away. All that existed was the heat of our bodies and the ravenous desire that drove us.

And if she truly thought she was winning this bet, she was the crazy one.

Chapter Nine

THE BADASS

I *t's just a bet. It doesn't mean anything,* I tried to tell myself. But I couldn't hold onto my own reasoning as hot tingles rushed throughout my body, bringing me to life in a way only Xander could evoke.

The god met my mouth with hot open mouth kisses of fierce intensity. His tongue explored my mouth, tasting and savoring as his hand gripped the back of my neck, drawing me even closer. I kissed him harder, trying to reassert the dominance I somehow lost even though I was on top of him.

Through our clothes, I could feel his desire for me. His need was just as powerful as mine in the hardness rocking against my aching wetness. The pure, raw sexuality between us sent shivers down my spine.

The hand holding the back of my neck released and scooped under my ass, pulling me up until I sat on his upper chest. "Get these fucking things off right now," Xander growled as he leaned forward and used his teeth to tug at the hem of my leggings, before he dipped lower and ran his tongue along the seam of my sex.

Blood shot to my head like a gun blast, leaving me dizzy.

Holy shit.

Urgency smashed into me. With our wrists still handcuffed to the bedframe, I un-straddled him, and we both pushed my pants off awkwardly and painstakingly. The skin-tight fabric stole my delicate yet soaked panties with them and I was no sooner free of them when Xander hauled me back up to his face, my legs splayed on either side of his ears.

He swiped his tongue up my wet slit, and the sound that escaped me was unrecognizable to my own ears.

Both my hands gripped the metal bed frame as Xander devoured me from below until I found a rhythm, riding his face.

The intensity built within me, like a wildfire raging out of control. My hips began to move in perfect sync with his mouth, riding him with a ferocity that matched his own.

"Oh god," I cried out as he brought me closer and closer to the edge.

"Fuck, Miranda," he rasped, his voice gruff and full of need. "You're so wet, so ready for me. Do you know how much I want you? I always fucking want you. You're in my blood now and I'll never get you out."

A fire ignited within me, fueled by his words and the heated intensity of his touch. The rasp of his stubble on my soft wet parts only drove me crazier.

A strong, unstoppable need built within me, like a wildfire raging out of control.

"Oh fuck," I cried out as he brought me closer and closer to the edge.

He was a mess. Xander, a god who didn't bother shaving regularly, desperately needed a haircut, and wore ridiculous Hawaiian shirts with combat boots. Any woman could see the neon sign above him flashing 'man child.'

Although, I was also above him now, my hips bucking wildly against his face. I chased that upward slope of intensity with wild abandon.

My abs wrenched up tightly as I grew more tense, more wound up. The irrational thought that I might die if I didn't find release soon took hold of my mind.

Xander's fingers and tongue worked in perfect harmony to elicit the most delicious sensations from me.

Every movement, every flick of his tongue was calculated and precise, driving me closer and closer to the edge. As I neared my peak, my mind became consumed with the fear that only he knew how to make me feel this way, that without him I would never reach this level of euphoria again.

Then his tongue turned rigid and his touch quickened, pushing me over the edge so fast I didn't know where the ground was.

"Xander, oh god, yes!" I screamed, throwing my head back as the waves of pleasure crashed over and through me. My body shuddered violently, writhing in the throes of an agonizingly sweet release, each contraction pulling me deeper into the abyss of pleasure.

My body still buzzed with need even as my knees relaxed from around his head. Xander looked up at me, licking his wet lips like the cat who got the cream. The devilish spark in his eyes radiated satisfaction that bordered on smugness. "That's one, sweetheart."

My competitive side reared up for attention. "That was your freebie. I didn't want you to think you didn't have a chance... even if you don't."

His thumb brushed against the sensitive skin where my inner hip and thigh met, as he stared at me like he could see straight through my bluff. Like he knew he was going to win.

And we both knew he wanted to win more than my body. I couldn't allow that though. Not when he hurt me so badly already.

No one hurt me twice. I was smarter than that.

Is that why you let him lick you to a bone shaking orgasm? my senses asked.

Before I could get into the debate with myself, I was on my back.

Xander's free hand pushed up my tank top.

The way we were chained, neither of us could divest ourselves of our tops, but I unbuttoned his shirt the rest of the way. My fingers trailed down the washboard of his cut muscles, making my chained-up hand jealous.

The fabric bound tight above my freed breasts, perking them up for him to drop and wrap his lips around my nipple. Electricity jolted from behind my bud of flesh, striking down between my legs, causing another rush of desire to coat my thighs. Fuck, why did I feel like I was even more desperate to come a second time?

Xander shoved his shorts down. Sure enough he wasn't wearing underwear, who could be surprised? The man clearly had a grudge against clothing.

I hated how I found that detail of him going commando so fucking sexy. I knew it would burn me up whenever I saw him in the future.

My mouth went dry as his thick cock sprung free, the tip glistening with his desire.

A smirk pulled his mouth in that sinful manner that made me want to either kiss or punch it off. Maybe both.

"You know what's going to make this easy, sweetheart?"

I scowled at him, openly communicating I wasn't interested in chit chat right now.

He dropped his hips, nudging at my lower lips with his cock, causing me to gasp and dig my hand into the sheets.

Xander kept nudging at my wet entrance even as he kissed his way over to my other nipple then up the sensitive column of my neck until his hot breath washed over my ear.

"Because I know you think of me when you touch yourself. I know when you grow wet, my name is already bouncing around your mind. And because it's already balanced on the tip of your tongue, I can push it out whenever I want."

As he said that last part, he thrust his rigid cock into me, filling and stretching me in ways I'd forgotten were possible.

"Oh god," I hissed between my teeth, my chained-up hand gripping the bed frame so tight my knuckles shook as he filled me.

"That's right sweetheart, I'm your god now and I'm going to fuck you into oblivion." His hand covered mine, even as he pumped in shallow, teasing motions. "Say it, Miranda. Say my fucking name." His words came out in a pained hiss.

My brain turned into a white fuzzy haze as all my senses were engulfed by pleasure. His words echoed around me even as I lost track of where I was. I was floating, flying higher and higher but not fast enough. I wanted more, I needed more.

"Do you want more, sweetheart? Say. My. Name." The words were thick hot honey, pouring into my brain and turning my blood molten. My hips bucked, trying to get more.

"Say it," his command came rougher this time as he pinched one of my nipples, giving me a white hot zap of pain and pleasure.

"Xander," I keened and moaned. "Please, I need more."

He immediately obeyed, his hips slamming into mine, shooting my breath up into my throat.

As we kissed, our bodies moved in a frenzy of passion, our lips and tongues exploring, our hands roaming, our bodies colliding again and again. He was my drug, and I couldn't get enough.

Something inside me cracked, and it was like meeting a part of myself I'd tried to forget. I tensed around him, on the verge of breaking.

He stopped fucking me so abruptly, my head spun.

Hovering over me, still, and dripping with sweat, he smelled liked soap, fresh sea air, and sex. He was unreal. "Fucking say my name, Miranda. Say it and I'll let you come, sweetheart."

I closed my eyes and whimpered. "Xander."

His next words came out through gritted teeth. "Beg me."

I shook my head, keeping my eyes wrenched shut tight. No. I'd already moaned his name a third time, but I wouldn't beg anyone.

"So we are back to that, are we?" he asked in a cold voice. "Fighting me while we fuck?"

He wasn't wrong. I suddenly didn't want to give him any more of me. It was all too much. I halted my orgasm, freezing it in place, trying to control myself.

"Fine," he snarled. "I'll fucking take it from you then." With that, he resumed a punishing pace into me. "You're my girl, and you know I'm completely and utterly yours. You feel that, sweetheart? That's my name pushing its way back into your mouth."

There was no sense or reality, just Xander's words and cock filling me up until I felt it... his name. It tasted salty and delicious as it landed on my tongue. The harder he fucked me, the closer it moved toward my lips.

"Say it, Miranda. Say it, like you know you're mine."

My body seized as I fractured on Xander's cock, his name wailing out of my mouth like a prayer.

I forced my heavy lids to lift and met his eyes which were stormy waves of cerulean blue. Sweat coated his skin, highlighting his ferocious intensity. Xander didn't just fuck me, he claimed me from every cell inside and out.

His pace didn't relent, overstimulating my over-sensitized body, rocking me into an acute spike of pain before I swung like a pendulum back into pleasure.

"It's been too fucking long," he rasped, face contorted in ecstasy so intense he seemed to be in agony. "Too fucking long. I can't—not without—I need you, Miranda. You are fucking air. Fucking water. I want to drown in you."

My responsibilities slipped away, my guarded nature dropped, and I met his thrusts as moans with senseless primal instincts. I was free, soaring, and surging with more power than I knew possible. Xander not only set me free, but he could handle all of me unleashed, just as I could handle him.

Then his powerful hands flipped me, pulling me up and onto my knees. The handcuffs tightened on both of us, drawing him even closer as he slid into me from behind. I cried out as he penetrated deeper than should have been possible. He covered both of my hands on the bed frame as it creaked wildly, threatening to collapse under us. He covered my back with his flexing torso. There was no one in the world but us.

"Xander." His name came out in a half-choked sob this time. I felt complete, alive, in a way no one else could make me feel—not even myself. Even though he was here, as close as he could get, I missed him so fiercely my insides threatened to blow apart. Whether the feeling of missing him was from before or in anticipation of him leaving my body, I couldn't tell.

His lips kissed gently along my spine even as his cock speared me deeper. My pleasure dripped down my thighs, and over his balls that smacked into me, causing a secondary jolt of pleasure.

"That's four, sweetheart," came his husky whisper in my ear. "Give me one more."

I shook my head, not even sure what I was trying to deny any more when he made my body sing and break so completely, but it was my nature to fight. It's who I was.

His hand slipped down, and two fingers pushed onto my clit with a firm grinding motion as if it were my own hand that knew exactly where to touch.

"Please," he begged, voice hoarse. "Say it, sweetheart. Say it so I can fill you up. I can't unless you let me." Xander's breath hitched, his pants becoming ragged and shallow.

A literal god was begging me to let him come by simply saying his name. A girl's brain could explode from that thought alone.

"You want it, don't you, baby? You want my cock to fill you up?" He pleaded, almost desperate. He was the hypnotist now and suddenly I wanted that more than anything.

"Yes," I gasped, my voice hoarse and strained. "Fuck me, Xander. Please, just—"

And then he was coming, his hips jerking wildly as he filled me with his seed with a long, wretched roar that echoed throughout the empty theater.

I couldn't help the rush of pleasure as he spilled inside me. Xander was nothing short of a wild animal, driven and untamed, and I wanted to take in every ounce of that energy. His warmth coursed into me, warm and thick, satisfying some part of my brain I rarely used.

The peaks of my breasts screwed up and electrified into tight buds, my stomach clenching and releasing. My body buckled beneath him, quaking in yet another release as he claimed me in the most intense way possible.

"Fuck, Miranda," he groaned, his body shuddering as he collapsed onto his side, pulling me with him. His arms wrapped around me tightly.

The sheets were soaked from either our sweat or desire, and we lay there, panting until the air cooled our overheated bodies.

"Sushi or Mexican for our date?" Xander asked, breaking the moment.

Chapter Ten

THE BADASS

The reality of what I'd done hit me like a bucket of ice cubes over the head. I'd been determined to keep him at arm's length. I had control of myself and the situation... until I didn't.

My self-respect, or was it my self-preservation, scattered like a flock of birds.

How much time had passed? I jumped off the bed, wrenching Xander along with me as I seized the hair pin again. Unlike last time, it landed in the pinhole, and I quickly unlocked the cuffs.

I snatched up my clothes and had them on before Xander even got up from the bed.

"Miranda," he said, his voice concerned but weak.

"We shouldn't have done that." All the self-hate poured in with more intensity than that last orgasm.

Okay, maybe not *that* intense, but close.

"Miranda, slow down," Xander ordered, but I was back in control of myself.

He stepped in front of me, completely nude and sexily disheveled, that stupid Hawaiian shirt still open, barely hanging on his shoulders, brows set low over his piercing, concerned eyes.

"I can't. I have to go. Jamal will be up soon." I swept by him, grabbing my effects off the chair and quickly finding my way out a door and into the morning heat that already promised to be another scalding day.

My brain raced at a mile a minute as my legs carried me in a half walk, half run, obeying my every instinct that told me to get as far away from the god in that theater as possible. We'd ended up in a place a mile off from the Strip, but I recognized this part of town. Only when I'd put a good distance between me and the sex god, did I order a ride to pick me up.

Thankfully the driver wasn't chatty, and I was dropped off at home just as Mama Jean and Jamal's morning alarms went off. I jumped into the shower, trying to erase what happened before they got up.

"You okay, honey child?" Mama Jean later asked with a furrowed brow over her coffee.

"What?" My head snapped up.

She reached out a buttery soft, yet weathered hand and set it on mine at the breakfast table. "You've been jumpy all morning. Like the devil himself might be chasing you."

I blinked.

My cool demeanor had been shattered after a couple hours in bed with Xander. I could actually feel the guilt and heat eat at my cheeks.

With a quick glance at Jamal, I saw he was absorbed with the game on his tablet while he ate his cereal. Normally, I'd force him to put it away and focus on his food, but I left him alone. I pulled my hand away from Mama Jean's.

"Too much caffeine I guess," I offered with a smile that felt shaky on my lips.

My phone buzzed in my pocket and I jumped several inches. Jamal even looked up.

"Whoa Mom, you okay?"

Now two people were giving me way too much attention. I shot up to my feet. "Gotta take this." I pointed to the phone before hastily beating a retreat to my bedroom.

"Hello?" I answered, not even bothering to screen who called.

"Miranda," Grim's low, steady voice filled my ear as dread landed with a thud in my stomach. There was something about the way he said my name, as if he was about to tell me something I wouldn't like.

"Could you come to Sinopolis? I need to have a word with both you and Xander."

I couldn't speak past the lump in my throat.

"I understand you've been up all night hunting, but there is something we must discuss and I'm afraid it can't wait until tonight."

"Uh yeah, sure."

Even as I gave my distracted consent, Jamal cracked the door to give me a smile and wave to let me know he was off to school. I blew a kiss at him before he disappeared.

"I can come now," I said, not hearing Grim's farewell before the phone hung up.

I threw the phone on my bed and covered my face.

Oh my god, did Grim know what happened? Was he going to talk to us about what happened?

About your failure to kill Sheshem or because Xander banged your brains out?

So far, I was painfully aware of what a failure I was. Unable to kill a single god and trap it back inside of the Blade of Bane, and unable to hold my ground on not fucking the feral god who got under my skin and hurt me.

"Oh Bob," I said to the silent blade that also lay on my bed. "I wish you were here."

Despite Bob's squeamishness about blood and death, he'd been dealing with all of this supernatural immortal nonsense longer than I had.

* * *

A REFRESHING AIR-CONDITIONED BREEZE BLEW OVER ME AS I entered Sinopolis, stepping on to the ocean of gleaming black marble. I'd spent so much time here, it truly felt like my second home.

That feeling did little to ease the knots of nervousness in my gut. Maybe one day I'd get over the feeling that meeting Grim wasn't the same as being sent to the principal's office, but apparently that wouldn't be today.

Grim strode out from the elevator, making his way directly toward me. The god of death was always a big, imposing dark mass in black suits, and though I worked for him before I knew what he was, I always felt that distinct undercurrent of danger around him.

My skin prickled and heated as someone stepped up next to me. Xander. The jackass still wore the same rumpled blue Hawaiian shirt and pants from last night. A memory of him curled over me, the shirt undone and flowing around his hard body as he fucked me senseless, slammed into my head like a baseball.

Knowing he was likely keyed into my every small motion, I focused all my attention on steadying my breathing so he wouldn't know he affected me.

I screamed his name five times as I splintered under his tongue, hands, and cock, and that was mere hours ago.

He probably knows he's affecting me right now.

Goddammit.

Grim got halfway to us before a child ran out into the lobby. She couldn't have been older than ten years old and she stopped directly behind Grim, giggling.

Grim turned around slowly before leaning down to her level. "And what are you doing here, little one?" he asked.

It was, in fact, a school day, so she should by all rights be in a classroom somewhere.

"My mom works at Wolf Town Club, and we are going to the dentist this morning." Even as she gave her explanation, her giggles only intensified.

"What do you have behind your back?" he asked, his brows furrowing.

Oh no.

Not again.

The little girl's arm whipped around, holding a child-sized pillow and smashed it into his foreboding face.

Then with a delighted scream, she tore off, leaving the pillow behind. "Vivien made me do it!"

I thought we might be beyond this, but the great pillow war raged on between Vivien and Grim. I believe the fight started as a way for her to unwind and focus on something other than the crushing duties of being Master Vampire and dealing with the tragedies and trauma of all the humans who were turned against their will and now learning to navigate a life with fangs.

But neither Vivien nor Grim did anything halfway, and their creative, sometimes almost lethal pillow attacks would come at the most unexpected times.

"That was... weird," Xander said, his brow deeply furrowed as he stuck his hands in his pockets.

I was going to explain the great pillow war, but standing next to him, after the things we did, robbed me of my voice.

Grim scooped the pillow off the ground and handed it off to one of his employees who walked by. His face now seemed to be made of stone, but his eyes gleamed with a fire that made me very, very concerned.

Chapter Eleven

THE BEAST

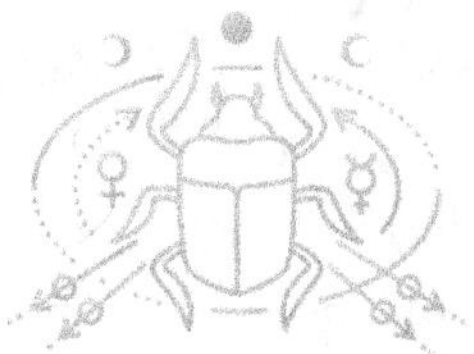

Because Miranda didn't reply, I couldn't be sure if what just happened was actually weird, or if I'd been kept below so long I didn't observe the normal social practice of swatting each other with pillows.

Would Miranda like that?

Getting used to living above ground among humans was more disconcerting than I ever wanted to admit. I chanced a sideways glance at Miranda. She'd showered off the sweat and sex I was still coated in. It intensified her clean bergamot scent which made my dick twitch even as a warmth spread from the center of my chest.

Instead of her combat clothes, she now wore high-waisted jean shorts, and a black, long-sleeved crop top that displayed a thin band of her taut, glistening stomach. I wanted to drag my tongue along that strip of flesh, but there was no chance of that between Grim's cock blocking presence, and Miranda being locked down tighter than a bank vault.

She didn't let a single expression or tell escape her stony expression, and I knew she was doing it on purpose. Miranda's poker face was top notch, but I was learning to read the small twitches underneath that gave her away.

"Apologies for the interruption," Grim said through gritted teeth as he stopped before us. "Let us go somewhere where we won't be interrupted by my wife's insanity."

"Good luck with that," Miranda breathed.

Okay, someone would have to explain the pillow thing to me at some point, but everyone was acting as serious as a heart attack so it would have to wait for now.

Grim led us toward Wolf Town Club, the most exclusive club on the Strip. This early, it was deserted.

I could see why this place was so popular. The centerpiece was a massive 360 degree bar, surrounded by a dance floor that I could feel the ghosts of writhing bodies on. Levels of balconies arose on all sides for those who wished to drink and look down at the fray.

Grim rounded the bar and pulled out a bottle of brown liquor and set it on the bar top.

"Can I offer either of you a nightcap? Seeing as all three of us just got off our duties?" The deep timbre of his voice echoed through the massive empty room.

Grim spent his nights judging souls for the Afterlife. But despite performing his duties, he looked as put together and slick as if he'd just arisen for the day.

I held up a hand. "None for me." There was no fucking way I could keep my sanity together if I dripped even a drop of booze on my broken brain. Miranda needed to see I'd changed, that I could be whole. No matter what. She needed that stability.

Though we'd fucked like mindless, out of control animals, so we backtracked just a little.

It was hard to be sorry.

Miranda shook her head, declining a drink as well.

Grim shrugged and poured himself a small glass of the stuff, though he didn't take a sip.

He stared at the amber liquid as he spoke. "I have decided it is in all of the immortals' best interests to conduct a convocation."

The barest arch of Miranda's eyebrow told me she didn't know what that meant either.

"You sound like Timothy," I joked. "Why don't you just tell us what is going on?"

I didn't care for flourish or bullshit. It's one of the reasons why I worshiped the no-nonsense woman next to me so much.

Grim gave a sharp nod before tossing back the small bit of liquid. "In plain terms, we are going to hold a ball."

"And this involves us... how?" Not to say I didn't appreciate Grim getting me in proximity of Miranda again, but this felt like he was wasting our time.

Since I'd been released from the basement, I'd stayed as far away from immortal affairs as I could, that is until I joined Miranda on her mission. Even then, I had no desire to socialize with my brethren.

Grim leveled a gaze at me. "Word has finally spread of Nun's revival, and the immortals have grown anxious to welcome you back into the fold."

My hands slipped out of my cargo shorts at that. *Oh, fuck me off a waterfall.*

My tone turned stiff and cold. "Thanks, but no thanks. I'm not interested."

"Xander," Grim said, using his best 'be reasonable' voice. "Things have been tense with the release of Aten and any number of chaotic gods."

I didn't bother pointing out I was one of the original chaotic gods.

He went on. "A soiree to unite our kind in celebration of the return of one of our strongest will both assure and invigorate morale. You know as well as I do, we are best when we are united."

I took a step back, cognizant that Miranda was studying me closely. "Forget it. I am not some showpiece you are going to use to rally those spineless narcissists." The last words came out in a snarl.

"As much as you dislike it, you are one of us." Grim sighed. "I know the last time you gathered with the immortals it didn't end well—"

"Forget it," I spat out, cutting him off. My vision swam and blackness crept in on all sides, but I fought it back.

The very thought of being near those assholes, much less the center of scrutiny, threatened my senses I'd been working so hard to keep under control.

Grim's proposal echoed in my mind in a hundred taunting voices. My jaw twitched uncontrollably and a deafening roar filled my ears.

Pain.

Time.

Isolation.

They beat at me with so many bludgeoning rocks.

They were afraid, all of them. Afraid of Aten and what he was capable of. And they wanted to see me, the one who dared challenge him, the one who saw through his manipulations.

The anger swelled and raged inside me, consuming my thoughts and clouding my judgment. My body was coiled like a spring, ready to snap at any moment.

Grim's voice lowered, snaking under my rioting senses. "The days have grown hotter, a blaze that will only continue to grow as Aten runs loose. They are afraid, Xander. With Aten no doubt plotting somewhere, they want to see you. The one who dared challenge him, the one who saw his machinations for what they were."

A wave of hot fury rushed through me, threatening to boil over and consume everything in its path. Tendons and muscles swelled, attempting to lengthen and change. My primal instincts wanted to turn me into something else. Something unhinged and uncontrollable.

"They can all fuck each other right off a cliff!" Only after the words escaped me, did I realize I screamed them. In my periphery, Miranda recoiled. Self-hatred added its white-hot lancing pain to the mix.

Grim continued to meet my gaze with unflinching resolve. I dropped my voice to a low, gravelly tone, that still dripped with venom. "Or better yet, they can burn by Aten's hand. It's what he did to me."

The threads on my string of sanity were fast-fraying, so I turned and stalked out of the club before I lost control.

Each step felt like I was walking through fire, my mind ablaze with memories of Aten and his cruel actions.

The abandonment of my brethren pierced me deeply underneath that.

If they had helped me, if they had listened...

I died to save us all and now I was some kind of idol in their eyes.

Grim and Timothy had been trying to talk me into rejoining our kind, encouraging me to take my rightful place the last few months. Where my body had healed, the wounds in my mind and essence were still raw, still festering with betrayal and pain.

Grim believed unity among immortals was our greatest strength against the encroaching darkness, but the scars of the past ran too deep for me to easily set aside.

The only being I cared to be around nearly just saw me lose it over gods who weren't worth even a minute of consideration.

I'd thought being near Miranda so soon after what we did chained to that bed would be good for her. She could see it was safe to be around me, no matter what happened.

Instead, Grim tried to hurl me over the edge of my sanity in front of her. Fuck him. Fuck them all.

Once alone, my hands gripped at my head as voices and thoughts bombarded me so hard, I had to grit my teeth.

I needed a mission. Something to distance myself from the aggravation Grim caused.

In the long empty corridor leading to Wolf Town Club, a tiny black puppy appeared, jauntily stepping its way in the direction I'd come. It was rare to see a reaper puppy. It was even stranger to see one wearing a blinged out pink collar, as it would have required Grim to create one from the ether.

My mind suddenly flew in another direction, the only safe direction—toward Miranda.

In a moment of vulnerability, she'd once told me a tragic story from her childhood. One where she felt responsible for the death of the little dog she'd begged her parents for. When she'd been playing on her own, it had wandered out into the road and been hit by a car. The way she relayed the story, I knew it laid down an important pillar in her soul, one that taught her to never lose vigilance, to never play, and to be careful with who and what she loved.

A plan formed in my broken brain even as I made my way toward Grim's private elevator. Stepping in, I hit the black button that led to his judgment chambers.

What could help take my mind off his revolting proposition more than an ill-advised mission into the afterlife to retrieve the soul of Miranda's long lost pet?

I already knew I wouldn't be sleeping, even after spending my every ounce of attention and energy on Miranda in that theater. Thankfully I knew a ferryman who owed me a favor.

THE BADASS

After Xander left, I turned to Grim. "I take it there was a reason you called me here too."

Grim's unerring focus remained on where Xander disappeared, deep in thought for a moment before he pulled his attention back to me. "Yes, I'm afraid you will not be exempt from this gathering."

I gritted my teeth. "Goodie." Suddenly I wished I had sprung for the drink. "I doubt they want me there to share a cup of tea and tell me what a good job I'm doing."

Grim shook his head even as his fingers flexed on the countertop. "I'm afraid they don't think they can trust a human, and I've come to the conclusion it would be best for them to meet you and understand what a considerable force you are."

I swallowed hard. That felt like a joke right now. I hadn't killed a single chaotic god in the preceding weeks. The pressure just doubled over on me.

"Vivien told me about the last ball," I said hesitantly, not wanting to set Grim off.

Vivien made a point to share what snooty meanie heads the gods, especially the demi-gods, were. My friend had a way with words.

One of the gods, Seth, had publicly presented Vivien with a collar inscribed with the words "Grim's Bitch," causing chaos and bloodshed that brought the party to a screeching halt. Vivien described Seth like an old George Clooney with an addiction to tanning, white suits, and gold chains who belonged on a yacht, throwing hundred-dollar bills at a bunch of young hoochies in bikinis.

Seth eventually lost his head to the Blade of Bane, but he was no doubt out on the streets again, thanks to me. Which also put him on my hit list.

I rose my chin to keep from letting my fear show. "Do you believe that this may be a setup to make an example of me?"

"I won't let anything happen to you, Miranda," Grim assured me. "Neither will Timothy or Vivien who will both be present."

Somehow that didn't feel nearly as reassuring as it should have.

Grim forced a smile that didn't reach his eyes. "Preparations are being made, and I've already entrusted Timothy and Vivien to see that you are properly dressed for the occasion."

I forced a smile. If the god of the dead thought playing dress up would mitigate my fears about mingling with the literal gods I had crossed, he'd gotten the wrong memo.

I started to head out but paused and looked back. "You really don't think he'll show?"

Xander's reaction was explosive and violent, a storm of emotion that tore through the air around him. At Grim's suggestion, his newly calm demeanor shattered into fragments, leaving behind a raw, unbridled rage that seared my skin. I didn't fully understand the reason for his outburst.

Grim leaned his arms on the bar in a surprisingly human posture.

"The last time Xander was among our kind, he was attempting to rally us against Aten who was making moves to become the one true god. We didn't believe him. And it's what led to his death."

My heart suddenly seemed too big for my chest. Xander died some several thousand years ago when he went against Aten alone. I'd learned that the spirit or soul or whatever you want to call it—of the gods returned to a place called the cradle of life where they arise again centuries later. However, Xander almost immediately returned to physical form. Having not laid in the cradle long enough, his powers were volatile and overcharged, causing power surges that would continually fry his own brain and body.

He'd suffered more than anyone, all because he tried to do something about the danger when no one else would.

His sacrifice saved everyone else, but no one saved him. Not until I came along with the Blade of Bane, where he demanded I keep killing him until he's put to rest for good.

And then I brought back the god responsible for his death.

"How did…" I trailed off, thinking better of my question.

"Burned him to death I'm afraid," Grim said, his own expression contorted with pained lines.

Oofta. Not that I imagined being murdered in any way was pleasant, but imagining Xander burning to death made me positively sick.

Leaving Grim, I walked straight to Perkatory to order myself a quad shot red-eye from Aaron. There would be no sleep today. Because I'd be damned if I went to face the immortals without putting back at least one monster in the box.

Which meant I had to take a different tack.

* * *

THIRTY MINUTES LATER, I PARKED OUTSIDE ECHO'S WAREHOUSE. I traipsed by unused machinery to the back elevator, down past the cameras and automated guns that dropped from the ceiling as a security measure and into the secret lair.

Echo's massive space was half tech heaven with several dozen screens showing different anime shows, news programs, and surveillance cameras. The other half of the space resembled an old grandmother's living room. Antique floral couches spread out over a generous, patterned rug, protecting the living quarters from the cold concrete floor.

It looked like Batman's grandma had decided to move into the Batcave.

"What took you so long?" Echo asked in her usual clipped tone, and thick Filipino accent. Echo's face reminded me of a scowling bullfrog with her wide features and narrowed bulbous eyes. The short, stout woman's walking cane was set off to the side of her computer command chair. Short, pudgy fingers flew across the keyboard.

"You should have come sooner," she scolded again, without looking up. "We'll find them. We'll find them all," she promised.

The idea that I could use my fae contacts to help track down potential god targets only just hit me.

Apparently, Echo had been waiting for me to come to the realization on my own. My molars rubbed against each other in a punishing grind, as I accepted the extent of my own ignorance. It wasn't like me to overlook resources.

"Why didn't you call *me?*" I asked. That call could have gone two ways.

Echo's fingers paused for the briefest of moments. Then she went on typing, forgoing a real answer.

But then again, there was another reason I'd stayed away. Someone I'd been avoiding.

With a quick glance around, I found only Echo's two rabbit familiars, one the size of a medium dog, and a small white one with a dark circle around its eye. Lulu and Darth Vader. They were snuggled together on the couch resembling two different sized loaves of bread.

The door swung open to what I presumed to be the rest of their underground home. My heart jumped in my throat.

Echo's husband, Ryuki, tottered in with a tray of tea. The sparse Japanese man gave me an impish grin I couldn't help but return.

"She's not here," Echo said, still not facing me though her gruff tone softened.

"Oh," was all I said. I wasn't going to pretend I didn't know who Echo was talking about.

Echo's daughter had been the one to convince me to bring back Xander, with the help of her girlfriend, Sunny. They claimed to want to help in the name of love. But Aoiki didn't realize her girlfriend had ulterior motives in performing that spell on the blade.

Aoiki had been betrayed, like me, but I didn't know how I felt about her.

Even thinking of the girl, and that night brought waves of shame crashing over me.

"Come, come," Ryuki said, ushering me over. His English needed a lot of work, but his hospitality was off the charts, balancing out his brusque wife. Most surprising was how he doted on her like she was the queen of Sheba.

While Echo did her thing, Ryuki and I sipped tea in companionable silence while occasionally petting the soft rabbits I'd settled down next to.

Echo's hands smacked with a tremendous crack as she let out a victorious cry. I jumped in my seat.

"Aha! Gotcha sucker."

Echo waved me over then swiveled her chair to face a different screen. "Here, on the Strip." I stood next to her, and she pointed to a live feed showing the bustling heart of Las Vegas. The neon lights flickered in the background, casting colorful glows on the faces of oblivious tourists and locals alike. In the midst of the crowd, a small figure darted between people, causing mischief.

"That's Bes," Echo clarified, her eyes narrowing. "According to Egyptian mythology, he's a protector, but now the little shit is just stirring up trouble. To mortals, he'll look like a particularly unruly child."

On the screen, the figure identified as Bes was no taller than a six-year-old, but with an unusual appearance—a wide, grinning face and hair that seemed to stand on end.

Every person he reached out and touched suddenly seemed overcome by some kind of emotion. Two people fell into a fist fight. A trio of strangers all disrobed and began to grope and fondle each other. Several people curled into balls on the ground, sobbing their faces off.

"He's in the pedestrian area near the Menaggio fountains," Ryuki added, his voice tinged with concern.

I grabbed my gear, feeling a mix of adrenaline and resolve. Bes needed to be stopped, immediately. "I'm on it," I said, heading for the door.

"Be careful, Miranda," Echo called after me. "Bes is tricky and unpredictable."

The city's pulse beat like a drum in my ears as I navigated through the traffic, the neon lights painting the night in surreal colors.

As I approached the bustling area near the Menaggio fountains, the chaotic energy grew palpable. A couple of people recorded on their phones from a still-safe distance, confused expressions marring their faces.

Amidst the chaotic crowd, I caught sight of my target—Bes, the small, mischievous Egyptian god. His devilish grin sent shivers down my spine as I pressed forward, determined to stop his malicious games. Fists collided with faces and bodies crashed to the ground all around me, but I remained focused on my goal.

I weaved to avoid a man smashing his fist into someone's eye. I stopped up short when a woman fell to her knees before me, sobbing to the heavens. Hands clawed at my clothes, along with pleas to come fuck them. I shook them off.

Bes clapped his hands together, delighted by the outbursts, as if it were a special show being put on just for him.

As I closed in, the tension in the air thickened like a volatile bomb ready to detonate. Once I got within twenty feet, Bes finally took notice of my presence and his smile widened into a sinister smirk.

He raised his chubby hand and summoned a searing orange energy that crackled and sizzled with ancient power.

Laughter turned to hysterical shrieks as people started lashing out, their faces twisted with wild expressions.

The mass of bodies and emotions surged around me. If I didn't do something, I was going to be taken down by the riot.

"Hey Bes, you want to mess with someone?" I called out, drawing the Blade of Bane and elbowing people out of the way. "Come play with me."

The crowd's mood shifted to confusion and fear at the sight of the weapon, their emotions still being toyed with by the god. Many of them ran screaming from me, crying out that I'd killed them.

Bes laughed, a high-pitched sound that grated my nerves. He leaped towards me, surprisingly agile. I dodged, but not quickly enough—his sharp, diminutive claws raked across my arm, leaving a burning sensation that told me his touch was more than just physical.

Gritting my teeth against the pain, I swung the Blade of Bane in a wide arc, but Bes dodged effortlessly, his laughter echoing mockingly around us.

His touch burrowed into me like a venomous snake, injecting its poison into my veins and unleashing all of my repressed emotions. My skin seared with a primal yearning, every fiber of my being consumed with the need to find Xander. Memories flooded my mind, of being chained to that bed with him, our inhibitions stripped away in fits of laughter and desperate clinging.

But then, anger boiled within me, threatening to erupt like a volcanic eruption.

My fingers twitched around the handle of the Blade of Bane, its cool metal offering a small sense of grounding in this chaotic moment. My skin prickled with the heat of my own anger and the icy chill of fear, a physical manifestation of the emotions raging within me.

This wasn't right—Xander had brought out these wild and dangerous parts of me, but he had earned that privilege.

As Bes appeared before me, I struggled to keep control of myself, fighting against the explosive emotions threatening to consume me entirely. I took a deep breath and tried to push back the memories and emotions that Xander's touch had unleashed. I needed to focus on the present.

The taste of copper filled my mouth as I bit down on my bottom lip, trying to physically restrain the emotions bubbling inside of me. My tongue tingled with the metallic tang, a reminder of the sharp edges of the Blade of Bane.

Bes appeared before me as I struggled to control myself. His tiny grubby hands wrapped around mine, trying to wrench Bob away from me.

No.

Bes shot back, his ass smashing into the ground with a yowl.

I didn't have the bandwidth to make sense of what just happened, I was still fighting against the swirling tornados of emotions. But unlike everyone else around me, I'd gone as still as a statue, slowly but surely reigning it all in.

Bes wouldn't get the satisfaction of getting any of those parts of me.

Hell, even I didn't give *myself* permission to feel like that, not without a pair of stormy cerulean eyes to be swept away on.

The surge of energy that had me nearly clawing my way out of my skin traveled through my veins to where I held Bob until it ebbed.

Just when Bes was in front of me a second time, taking another more careful chance at stealing my weapon, I came to myself.

"Don't toy with my feelings," I snarled at him.

Bes' impish grin fell.

With a swift movement, I feigned a strike to the left and then quickly reversed, catching Bes off-guard. The blade connected, and a look of surprise crossed his tiny face.

He disintegrated into a cloud of golden dust, the Blade of Bane absorbing his essence. The crowd around me had thinned, leaving a few stunned onlookers who were trying to make sense of what they'd just witnessed.

A couple of them clapped, unsure if they just witnessed a streetside attraction.

Vegas was so bizarre, people didn't question much. They usually just stood back and admired the spectacle.

The people released from Bes' power either blushed hotly, pulled their clothes on, or helped each other up before joining in the clapping. It was as if they believed they were part of some mass Vegas hypnosis trick meant for entertainment.

Pulling out my phone, I called Fallon. In ancient times, he was known as Horus. He was my contact to help clean up any matters that spilled on the street as he had a hypnotic way with people to make them forget any supernatural occurrences. He'd finish up here.

Clutching my wounded arm, I blended into the less crowded streets of Vegas as I waited for Fallon to arrive. The cut was deep and needed to be disinfected and bandaged, but victory thrummed through my blood. I did it. I really did it. I killed a god, trapped him back in the Blade of Bane.

"Miranda?" A familiar French voice reached into my mind.

I stopped short.

"Bob?" Emotion hit me like a tidal wave, as relief and surprise nearly swept me off my feet.

The adrenaline of victory still coursed through my veins, but the sudden return of Bob's voice brought a different kind of rush, one of poignant relief mixed with the unexpected sting of tears threatening to breach my defenses.

"How long have I been asleep? Uck, and what is that taste? Whose blood did I just eat? Blech."

"It's good to hear your voice." My own words, betraying the depth of my concern for the pacifist blade who had been my constant, albeit reluctant, companion.

"Oh, please, don't get all sentimental on me now. You know I abhor melodrama almost as much as I do bloodshed. And speaking of, could we perhaps avoid any more... gory encounters in the future? My constitution is simply not built for such... barbarity." Bob's attempt at maintaining his usual demeanor of complaint couldn't fully mask the warmth underlying his words.

The corners of my mouth lifted in a wistful smile. "I missed you too, Bob. More than I thought possible."

"Missed me? I was merely dormant, not on a holiday in the French Riviera. And now, look at the state I'm in. I feel like I've been used as a... a... kebab skewer at a rather bloody banquet." Despite his grumbling, there was a lightness to Bob's tone that I hadn't realized I'd been missing until now. "And do clean this nastiness off me, if you please. Maybe you could rub Tic-Tacs on me."

"Tic-Tacs?" That threw me.

Bob scoffed. "Of course I am kidding. I am a sword. I deserve proper care. It was a joke."

I laughed softly, the sound mingling with the lingering chaos of the Vegas night around me.

I wanted to ask him where he'd been, why Bes hadn't been able to take hold of Bob, and probably a dozen more questions, but they could wait.

"Alright, you over-dramatic cutlery, we'll get you cleaned up."

THE BEAST

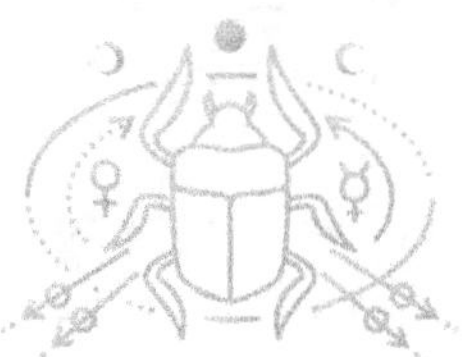

We planned to meet Sinopolis later tonight to go god hunting. That is, if Miranda even deigned to show up. But after what happened with us in that theater, I couldn't take the chance that she'd try to wiggle out to shy away from the discomfort. It was still only afternoon when I knocked on her front door.

The modest house sat on a patch of what used to be a perfectly curated lawn, though it was now scorched to dry brown blades from the heat. The autumn drought prohibited people from using water for the grass.

This street felt a million miles away from the busy, blinking neon streets of the Strip and something inside my chest unclenched, as if I could breathe easier. I wasn't sure if it was this part of town, a little slice of suburban bliss, or it was because I knew Miranda was on the other side of these walls.

As the door swung open, I was met with an elderly Black woman with white hair and smile lines at the corners of her eyes. She wore a floral shirt and stretch pants that were being put to the test by her expansive waist.

"Hello ma'am," I snapped out on reflex.

Had I gotten the wrong house?

No. I knew this was Miranda's house. I'd traveled here even when I'd been out of my mind. Looking beyond the older woman, I reassured myself that I recognized the furniture.

The older woman cleared her throat expectantly.

"Is Miranda here?" I finally followed with.

Shit, did I have the wrong house? The fear of not knowing my surroundings or my own mind began to cave in on me.

"Xander," a familiar young voice piped up.

Jamal pushed his way past the older woman to stand on the front stoop.

Relief swept through me. I was in the right place.

Jamal gave me a half toothy, half toothless smile, since he'd recently lost a couple baby teeth.

"Mom's not here," Jamal supplied.

"Oh." The need to slink away overwhelmed me as I suddenly felt I should not be here. Not without Miranda.

"Young man," the older woman snapped. "Where are your manners?"

Jamal's spine stiffened, and he bared his teeth in a silent 'uh oh.'

"Sorry G-Ma. Xander, this is my grandmother, Mama Jean. Mama Jean this is Mom's... uh, friend—"

"—from work," I smoothly supplied, readjusting the box I held to one arm, extending a hand to her.

She slipped a soft weathered hand into mine and I brought it to my lips, giving it a chaste kiss and smelling gardenias.

"Oh," she said in surprise, covering her chest with the hand I just kissed.

Fuck, was that wrong too?

"Sorry, I can be a little old fashioned." I gave her a wry smile.

"I suppose the world could use more of that," Mama Jean said in a more evident Southern drawl. The woman's posture and tense face told me she was sizing me up, and I wasn't sure what she was going to see. I sure as hell didn't have a good idea on how to cultivate a certain appearance for her. All I could hope was she didn't come to the conclusion I was an immortal with no social graces and severe mental health issues.

"What's in the box?" Jamal asked, pushing up onto his tiptoes to see inside. The flaps were mostly closed, but not all the way.

"Uh, a gift for your mom." Again, I got that extreme discomfort of knowing I wasn't supposed to be here. Somehow, interacting with Miranda's family felt entirely too intimate and private, and I knew she wouldn't like it.

"Well, come in and set it down." Mama Jean pulled Jamal back from the door, clearing the way for me. I stepped through, breathing in the homey bouquet of sunshine, gardenias wafting off Mama Jean, and the pervasive scent of Miranda's skin. The scent moved to my stomach and spread in a comforting warmth.

"My daughter-in-law should be back soon," Mama Jean supplied. "Take a seat and I'll make you something to eat."

"Oh you don't have to—"

"Sit, young man." She pointed to the worn wooden chair at their table.

She was definitely used to being obeyed, and I didn't want to be disrespectful.

"What's the gift?" Jamal asked again even as I followed the older woman's orders.

Putting the medium sized box on the floor by my feet, I met Jamal's eager look. "Well, if I stay, I better open it so he can stretch his legs."

Jamal's eyes turned as round as two eggs. "*He?*"

The box shuffled even as I fully opened the box flaps.

The squeal of delight from Jamal was ear piercing. "A dog! Oh my gosh, G-Ma, it's a dog."

Indeed, inside the box was a mixed mutt of every varying shade of color and breed, making for a medium small animal, who looked up at Jamal with mismatched blue and brown eyes, tongue hanging out the side of his mouth. His one ear stood erect while the other flopped endearingly to the side. One look at his bright, mischievous eyes, and you knew he wasn't an ordinary dog.

The mutt didn't appear to be a puppy, or particularly old either.

Though I suppose age wouldn't really apply to this creature anymore, considering where I stole him— err—got him from.

"You think it's appropriate to show up at someone's house with a pet as a present?" Mama Jean said from where she stood by the sink even as the dog leapt out of the box and earnestly licked at Jamal's face.

"I wouldn't know what's appropriate," I said honestly.

She crossed her arms and shook her head, even as her eyes softened when they landed on the dog who now had Jamal on his back to get a better angle to lick the boy's giggling face.

"I don't think my daughter-in-law will appreciate being given another chore."

"I'll take care of him," Jamal rushed to say even as he got back to his knees to pet and hug the dog.

"I haven't given her a chore," I said, defensively, setting my hand on the table. "The dog is well trained." She had no idea. The supernatural pup wouldn't cause Miranda any problems.

Mama Jean's eyes narrowed. "Are you giving me attitude, young man?"

"Miranda needs to have more fun, and I thought a dog would... help with that." I wasn't about to reveal Miranda's past pain. That was her secret. "You're worried the dog isn't trained? Give it a shot yourself."

Still pinning me with that wary expression a moment longer, Mama Jean shot a command at the dog. "Come."

Immediately, the dog disengaged from Jamal and trotted over to the older woman.

"Sit," she said next. The dog complied instantly, a serene yet intent expression on his face as if recognizing it was auditioning for his role.

Mama Jean rattled off as many commands as she could think of, including play dead and jump, and the dog followed every instruction.

Jamal's eyes settled on me after a while with a knowing look. The kid knew too much, and I could tell he was picking up that the dog might be extra special compared to the canines on the street around here. I ignored his intent gaze.

"Satisfied?" I asked when Mama Jean ran out of things to try with the dog.

"What's his name?" Jamal asked.

The dog met my gaze this time as we entered a silent conversation. "The dog had a name, but that was from his old life. I think he'd like a new one."

Jamal's eyes turned as big as saucer plates this time.

*   *   *

An hour later, I was smashing buttons on the handheld controller like my life depended on it alongside Mama Jean while Jamal stroked the dog and coached us from the sidelines.

"No, you've got it in reverse, press the left trigger—left trigger!" Jamal cried at me.

The dog let out a yip of encouragement.

"Ha-ha, you can't catch up now," Mama Jean cackled as her purple car on the television screen peeled away from me.

I gritted my teeth, hit the left trigger and got my virtual car on the track again. I couldn't believe she actually ran me off the road.

"I'm coming for you, old lady," I growled.

"Age before beauty, young man," she shot back, while sticking a tongue out the side of her mouth in concentration. "Know your place."

"What in the hell is going on here?" A voice cut through the din of game play. Mama Jean found the pause button before I did, and we all turned toward the front door.

"Hey Mom," Jamal chirped, as if he didn't notice her stormy expression or the way her hand gripped the door jamb until her knuckles turned a light color. "Xander got us a dog."

Either Miranda was having a stroke, or... well it didn't look like anything else could be happening based on her twitching expression.

Yeah, I was definitely getting stabbed.

Chapter Fourteen

THE BEAST

"You—" Miranda pointed at me.

"Me?" I gestured to myself.

Mama Jean shot me a pitying glance before getting to her feet. "I better check on dinner." I automatically reached out a hand to help steady the older woman, but she shooed me away.

"Come here," Miranda said between gritted teeth.

Jamal made an 'oo' sound that gave me the distinct impression he knew I was in trouble.

I dutifully set the controller down on the glass coffee table and crossed the distance to Miranda who yanked me the last foot onto the front stoop, shutting the door behind us.

As we made our way onto the concrete stoop, the intense heat of the sun immediately engulfed us. The angle of the sun's rays seemed to intensify the temperature, almost as if it were purposefully cooking us. The moment our feet touched the stoop, the searing heat penetrated through our shoes and into our skin. It felt as if we were walking on a bed of hot coals.

I was about to ask if we could go back inside, but Miranda's eyes snapped at me with an almost tangible whip of irritation. I shut up and took an involuntary step back.

Normally she had a protective shell around her, but right now it was as if walls shot from the ground to dizzying heights, protecting all parts of her, with a crocodile infested moat to boot.

"What are you doing here?" she asked in a hushed whisper, fist clenched on the doorknob. "We're not supposed to meet for hours at Sinopolis, and I come home to find you ingratiating yourself with my family."

A sharp pang of disappointment pierced through me, a physical ache that lingered. It was like a punch to the gut, realizing that she didn't want me near her family.

Not that I could really blame her. I wasn't exactly a stable, family kind of guy.

I tried to shake off her unwelcome demeanor. "Like Jamal said, I brought a gift."

Miranda opened her mouth but was cut off from whatever she'd been about to say.

"Hey Miranda," a deep voice off from the left interrupted.

"Oh, hey Michael," Miranda replied, suddenly distracted by the newcomer, giving him a slight wave and half smile.

A man wearing a suit and carrying a briefcase pulled out his keys as if coming home from work to the house next door. He toyed with them as he spoke.

"Whatever you're cooking over there has got me salivating," he said with a low, rich laugh. My eyes narrowed as a hot feeling flared in my body. "You keep cooking like that, and I'll be breaking down your door to get a spoonful of whatever that heaven is."

I waited for her to say if he came through her door, she would kick his teeth in, but it didn't happen.

Instead, Miranda pushed a braid behind her ear and her cheeks grew rosy.

The fuck?

"That's actually my mother-in-law," she explained. "She is an amazing cook. We're very lucky."

"You and your husband are very lucky," Michael the stupid-face neighbor said, his eyes briefly touching on me with disappointment.

My lips curved up in a smug grin as I embraced the idea that he thought I was Miranda's husband.

"Oh, oh no, no, we aren't married," Miranda corrected too quickly. A hand covered her chest. "I'm a widow. Have been for a while now."

Interest flickered in the neighbor's eyes, as if realizing he stood a chance with the goddess next to me.

My hurt was replaced by ire as I took in the man on his front porch next to Miranda's. The human was tall, fit, and what I'm sure most would consider to be attractive. And apparently so did she.

I grabbed Miranda's arm and pulled her closer to my side to show this guy where she really stood.

As soon as my hand encircled her, Miranda let out a sharp cry. Her body stiffened and flinched before she broke away from my grasp.

"What the—" the words flew out of me as she cradled her arm while putting a few steps between us.

Something inside me cracked.

"Hey man, let her go," Michael frowned, stepping off his porch and starting toward us.

"I'm fine, it's fine," Miranda rushed to say, holding up a hand to keep him back. "Michael it was nice to see you, but I have to talk with my... friend."

Now I was the one being grabbed and pulled off, around to the opposite side of the house instead of going inside. Thankfully, we were able to step into a shady area, though it was still over a hundred degrees out here.

Before she could speak, I said, "I hurt you." A part of me was mortified and the other side completely confused. "I didn't mean to. I must have excess power or don't understand my own strength—" I was babbling, my words becoming more panicked and disjointed as I considered that I could accidentally hurt her. I hadn't smashed the game controller? But what if I broke Miranda's bones?

The god-likeness roiled under my skin. The distress was ironically pushing it closer to the forefront despite that being the very last thing I wanted.

Miranda pressed a hand to my mouth, cutting me off midstream. I breathed her in, enjoying the warmth of her palm far too much. "You didn't hurt me," she explained, quietly. "Well, not the first time anyway."

Before I could ask her what she meant, she rolled up her T-shirt sleeve, showing me a bandaged arm where blood spotted and seeped through the white bandage. I reached out to gently hold her undamaged flesh around the bandage.

All emotion bled out from my body, leaving only rage.

"Who did this to you?" I growled, even as my hands remained gentle.

"Little fucker named Bes. He put up a fight but I got him. I got one, Xander." Her eyes gleamed with pride and excitement, overtaking her unhappiness at finding me at her home.

Unfortunately, I couldn't share the same sentiment.

"You went hunting without me?" I asked, my voice flat and cold.

She stepped back, pulling her arm out of my light grasp. "Well, yeah. You were gone, and I had to get a win."

For a minute, I couldn't tell who I was more pissed at. That little chaotic fuck of a god for touching my woman, or Miranda for deliberately going out on her own where she could have gotten killed.

Miranda's blatant disregard for her safety boils my blood to a dangerous degree.

Did she have a death wish, or was she determined to prove she didn't need me? She didn't understand the difference between flexing her independence and being straight up reckless.

I seethed with fury, torn between wanting to protect her and wanting to lash out at her idiocy.

"Had to? You couldn't have waited until this evening when we could have gone together? Do you know how dangerous that was? You should have taken me with you."

Her nostrils flared with defiance. "I handled myself just fine. I was going to tell you I'm taking the night off since..." she trailed off, but I knew.

It was mid-afternoon, and she hadn't slept yet, not even after we practically broke that bed.

Bringing her to the point, I gestured to her arm. "You got hurt. Who knows how much worse it could have been?"

As angry as I was, deep down, all I wanted was for her to be safe.

Still, my body reacted with visceral, primal energy. My brain kicked up a buzzing sound. Tendons and muscles flexed inside me, threatening to elongate and shift for the second time today. I was about to lose my cool and knew I should start working on getting control of myself before I did something I regretted.

"It was fine," she said, her voice like granite.

She was going to drive me insane. I mean, I was still half unhinged, but she was going to send the rest of me careening back over the edge of sanity.

Too furious to form coherent sentences, I took a deep breath and tried to calm the gears grinding against each other in my mind.

"Now explain why you gave my kid a dog," Miranda crossed her arms, fully on the defensive again.

It took everything in me to speak slowly, carefully. "I remembered what you told me about your dog getting hit by a car when you were young." I started.

I knew it affected her deeply when she pushed the words out to me, confessing that one day while she was playing in the yard and didn't want to watch the puppy anymore, she sent it away. That's when it got hit by a car.

Miranda dropped her arms, an unreadable expression coming over her face. Not quite blank, but almost a deer in headlights look.

"So I went to the underworld, tried to find him."

Her entire body tensed. "Find who?"

"Your dog. I didn't find him, but I found... someone else."

"You got me a dog from the underworld?" Miranda's voice seemed to come from a far away place. Like she couldn't comprehend what I was saying.

I wanted her to heal from her grief. To bring back what she lost so she could feel safe enough to let her guard down, to have fun, to love.

But she looked anything but elated.

Starting to grow uncomfortable, I stared past her to the browning grass. "Well, really, the Afterlife. So he's immortal. House trained, low maintenance. I thought it might be... fun?"

The dog rounded the corner at that exact moment. He immediately began to explore his new surroundings, his tail wagging like a flag in a breeze. He sniffed around, then with a sudden burst of energy performed an impossible leap, flipping over in mid-air before landing perfectly on his paws. It was a subtle hint of his otherworldly nature.

He was showing off for his new master.

Jamal's voice broke through as he rounded the corner. "Hey Mom, dinner is ready. Can we go get Heinz some dog food right after?"

"Heinz?" Miranda asked.

"He's like that Heinz 57 sauce," Jamal patiently explained, "where there are fifty-seven ingredients. He's all different kinds of dogs in one."

"I don't think that sauce really has fifty-seven ingredients," she said hesitantly.

Personally, that sounded like too many ingredients for anything, but the kid should do what he wanted.

Jamal shrugged. "He seems to like his name, dontcha Heinz?"

The dog barked in a clear affirmative.

Meanwhile, Miranda watched, her expression still an unmovable mask.

"We can keep him, right Mom?"

"I can't believe you did that," Miranda whispered the words, almost to herself. At the root of her words, I found accusation and disbelief.

It hit me then. I'd fucked up. I completely missed the mark. I thought this would be a welcome, thoughtful gift.

Of course, I knew it could go wrong, but I'd followed my gut.

The air hung thick between me and the woman next to me. I could practically hear Miranda's thoughts, her doubts, her fears. And worst of all, her disappointment in me. I had wanted to make things right, to bring some semblance of happiness into her life, but instead, I had only added to her burden.

"I'm sorry," I murmured, the words heavy with remorse. "I didn't mean to upset you."

Miranda remained silent, her gaze fixed on the dog—on Heinz—

who now sat at her feet, looking up at her with adoring eyes. I could see the conflict in her expression, the war being waged behind those guarded eyes.

As Jamal chattered away about Heinz's tricks, I turned to leave, the weight of my gesture—and its reception—heavy on my heart. "I'll see you tomorrow night for the hunt," I said quietly before slipping away.

Chapter Fifteen

THE BADASS

"He got you a puppy yesterday?" Vivien exclaimed from where she stood on a velvet pink pedestal, getting her dress measurements taken. "Oh my gosh, it will be like Cupcake has a cousin! Or a brother. Or a best friend," Vivien spiraled off as if the relation of her invisible reaper puppy to my stolen corporeal underworld mutt were a complex algebra problem.

I was at the Paris hotel with Vivien and Timothy to prepare for the upcoming event.

Bianca, the Oracle goddess, insisted on having her designers dress us for the immortal ball, so we were here, where the place was as Hollywood glam as the goddess herself. Something soft and fruity hung in the air, and everything around me was soft and feminine.

Basically, the opposite of me. Yet I enjoyed the uber girly atmosphere.

Timothy's even toned question cut off Vivien's squeal of excitement. "Did you *want* a dog?"

He sat across from me on a matching plush settee, drinking from a delicate China teacup. When you were rich as gods—literally—this is how you shopped for a dress. One was designed for you.

Or as Vivien called it, we were undergoing a *Pretty Woman*.

The fact neither of us are hookers didn't seem to make her back off that comparison.

I touched an empty spot on the chaise lounge next to me, my hand subconsciously reaching for Bob. I wasn't the only one getting a glow up today. My weapon was whisked away for a shine and sharpen by someone Timothy vouched to be the best of the best. While Bob seemed more than willing to spring for a spa day, it felt like I was missing a limb.

I'd been reluctant to hand him over and had to ask Bob why Bes hadn't been able to take him away from me during the fight yesterday. Xander had disarmed me many times during sparring. Bob explained I didn't give consent, that our bond was protected by my energies. So after a long assessment of the hotel maid who was to take Bob away for care and Timothy's assurances it would be fine, I relented.

Not that Bob would be any comfort in this uncomfortable conversation.

I answered. "No I didn't want a dog, but—"

What Xander tried to do, what he tried to return to me touched me deeply. It also brought on a tremendous amount of guilt.

Like a whale-sized canopy of guilt.

I had given Xander a partial lie about what happened when I was a child. There was a reason he couldn't find my pet, and the truth was much darker and more painful than he knew.

His gift forced the past to bubble up like hot lava, burning and churning in my gut with a near unbearable fervor.

"Do you not want the puppy?" Vivien asked, her tone carefully tiptoeing around me. Man, I must really seem fragile if Vivien was treating me with kid gloves.

"It is a big responsibility," Timothy added, pouring more tea into his cup. The woman taking Vivien's measurements whisked out of the room, presumably done with that task. I had yet to be poked and prodded.

Needing to do something with my hands, I picked up the flute of champagne from the glass table next to me and took a swallow. I shouldn't be drinking before going out to hunt tonight, but Xander had rattled me... bad. "The dog is pretty self-sufficient, actually. Jamal is instantly in love, as is my mother-in-law. But I just don't know why he would... do that."

"Get you a gift?" Vivien asked.

"To try and secure your affections?" Timothy guessed.

"But why *that*?" Frustration crept into my voice. "Why would he go to the underworld to try and find a pet of mine? Or Afterlife, or whatever." I threw up my hands.

Vivien and Timothy exchanged glances I couldn't read. Timothy put his cup down. "You know he is... fond of you." For a minute he seemed like he was going to choose a different word.

"He's hopelessly, head over heels, dead blind in love with you," Vivien corrected, stepping down to sit on the edge of the dais.

I sighed. "Xander's been trapped underground for so long, he doesn't know what he wants. I'm just the first person to show up who piqued his interest after lifetimes of misery and pain." I paused. "That, or he is super into the fact I stabbed him to death nightly for a while there."

Everyone had a kink. Death was his.

That or playing games with me. Both literally and metaphorically.

I went on. "But he's free of the cage and he's in the world now. He'll find out soon enough that I'm nothing special and figure out where he really belongs."

"Oh."

I glanced up to find Vivien's emerald eyes widening as if filling with some kind of understanding.

I furrowed my brows. "What?"

Timothy studied the tea in his cup a little too hard.

"*What?*" I asked defensively, suddenly on my feet, too agitated to be still a second longer. In fact, I was considering fleeing this place all together.

"You don't think you're good enough for him," Vivien said with a healthy dose of disbelief.

I squirmed in my seat. "That's not what I said."

Timothy set his cup down, his eyes meeting mine. "Miranda, despite my own reservations about your potential together, it's evident that Xander's feelings for you are... profound. His affection seems to stem from something deeper than mere whimsy."

I crossed my arms, uncomfortable with where this was heading. "He doesn't really know me. I get the sense he is a god trying to flex his power—that he just wants to conquer me as something to do."

Liar, liar pants on fire, a voice in my head chanted.

I felt slimy even saying the untruth out loud, but I was desperately trying to wriggle out of Xander's grip. It was slowly closing in around my heart, and I couldn't let it trap me for good.

Vivien chimed in, her tone filled with a fierce conviction. "Come on, Miranda. What if it's more than that? What if *you're* the something real he's never known before? Something he desperately needs? You are as real as it gets."

The truth about the dog situation jerked up into my throat. That story hadn't been entirely real. I swallowed the lump back down.

I'd never shared with anyone about that day. Not even my late husband knew.

"Hey," Vivien said, her face wrenching up in suspicion. "What the hell is this?"

"What the hell is what?" I asked.

"Don't you guys see this?" Vivien stood and backed up, her eyes darting all about her.

"See what?" Timothy asked, his eyes focused on his cup as he sipped more tea.

"The pillows, the pillows!" she cried out, flapping her arms around her. "There's dozens of them. They are all around me. I'm surrounded."

"She's finally cracked," I said to Timothy.

He continued to sip his tea a little too intently, which leads me to believe he might see exactly what Vivien does.

The whites of her eyes nearly swallowed her irises just before her face jerked to the side as if some unforeseen force collided with her face. Then her shoulder snapped back unnaturally.

"Timothy?" I asked.

"Mmm?"

"Did Grim assemble a bunch of ghost pillows to attack Vivien?"

His dark eyes met mine. "Are you suggesting the god of the dead, Anubis himself, would waste his time and energies on creating pillows from the ether just to torment his wife the way she has been doing to him?"

I matched his stare even as Vivien cried out and batted at empty air in futile defense.

Then I picked up my champagne and took another sip. Neither of us were inclined to get in the middle of the great pillow war. That would be the same as trying to stop a dog fight. It would only end in blood. Ours.

As Vivien cried out and tried to escape her relentless invisible attackers, I wondered why I'd shared such an intimate story with Xander.

I don't know what possessed me to even give Xander a small part of that story. It was like I was handing the ugliest part of my soul over on a silver platter to a man who'd lived nearly as long as time.

"Come on guys," Vivien cried out. "Help me."

But at the time, I'd felt a safety I didn't remember ever experiencing. It was like Xander and I could be torn up messes together and it would be okay.

Then he hurt me. And I hurt him when I flirted with my neighbor in front of him.

I was trying to convince both of us this thing between us wouldn't work.

"Argggh!" Vivien lay back on the pedestal, kicking and flapping her hands up in the air in defense. She'd literally been beaten to the ground.

But then Xander went into the motherflipping underworld to find my long-lost pet.

Aw crap.

Vivien was right.

I didn't think I was good enough for him.

Timothy's gaze was thoughtful. "Xander's experiences have been... quite severe. Through that, he might see what truly matters. And it seems, *you* matter to him a great deal."

I countered, my voice tinged with a mix of defensiveness and vulnerability. "But he's immortal. And I'm not. Why would he choose me?"

Vivien swept the champagne glass from my hand and downed it in one gulp. "What the hell guys?" Static-charged hair flew around her flushed face. She batted the strands back down with rage-filled swats.

"This is between you and Grim," I said with an arch of my eyebrow.

Ignoring Vivien entirely, Timothy went on. "That's the point, Miranda. To someone who's lived forever, the raw, genuine nature of mortal life can be irreplaceable. Your mortality doesn't make you less; it could be what he's drawn to."

"So he *only* wants me because of my mortality?"

Vivien's nose wrinkled even as she tried to calm her fly-away hairs. "Damn biatch, you are twisting Timmy's words around to prove that Xander's feelings for you couldn't possibly be real. Are you this cynical and mean to yourself in your head too? 'Cause, well... damn."

Timothy sighed, his expression softening. "You are my friend, Miranda, and you are enough as you are. Whether or not you're with Xander, don't doubt your worth."

My gaze fell to the ground, my heart wrenching at being found out. Timothy's words pierced through my façade, exposing the raw fear that has consumed me for far too long—the fear of never being good enough.

They dredged up all my insecurities, my deep-seated fears, and I could feel the weight of them crushing down on me.

Despite my constant efforts to compensate with hypervigilance and outworking those around me, it's never been enough. And lately, it seems to be getting me nowhere but deeper into this pit of self-doubt.

Xander thinks you're enough, my brain spits back.

But Xander doesn't know his own mind. He says he does, but I don't believe him.

"Wait," Vivien held up her hands as if to slow us all down. "Is all this uncertainty and fear coming up because of the immortal ball?" She tapped her lower lip, her hair still a wild mess. "Ball. Balls. It is so weird to say, much less go to one."

For being on the unhinged side, my friend was oddly perceptive. I reached down to re-lace one of my boots that was already perfectly tied.

"Oh, my sweet baby lambs," Vivien shot to her feet. "I'm right!" She did a little dance, shaking her hips.

I rolled my eyes and walked to the opposite side of the room, pretending to be interested in a painting of elegant women in a boat along a flower filled river.

I tried to keep my tone light. "This event is supposed to be a homecoming for Xander. He needs to socially rejoin his kind. He can take possession of one of the hotels, wear a sleek veneer, play twisted games out of sheer boredom, and indulge in ambrosia-fueled orgies."

Sure, Xander said he didn't want to rejoin them, but he couldn't put off going back to where he belonged for long.

A pair of hands found my shoulders and turned me around. Vivien's emerald eyes bore into mine, her expression serious and sincere. "Xander is *not* like the others. I've met enough of these a-holes to know."

"A-hem," Timothy said loudly and with great offense.

"You don't count, Timmy," she casually shot over her shoulder. Vivien picked my hand up. "It's okay to be scared. Letting someone in, especially someone like Xander, is terrifying. But sometimes, it's the broken souls who love the fiercest. Maybe you're what he needs... and perhaps he's the messiness, the passion you didn't know you were missing."

I lifted my gaze, meeting Vivien's. Inside, I was torn between the safety of my emotional barriers and the terrifying yet enticing prospect of a love that could easily destroy me.

Deep down, I knew my reluctance was about more than just Xander. It was about a lifetime of believing I didn't deserve happiness, not after what happened to my... dog, not after losing my husband, and certainly not after unleashing chaos on the world from the blade. How could I allow myself to enjoy anything when I was responsible for so much pain?

The weight of my past, the guilt—it was a secret burden I carried, always reminding me why I couldn't just relax and be happy. Happiness was a luxury I couldn't afford, not when every moment of joy felt like a betrayal of the memories of those I'd lost. And now with Xander, it felt like walking towards something I had long denied myself—a chance at love, at happiness, which... deep down, I feared I might never truly deserve.

Unaware how intensely I was processing her suggestion, Vivien straightened, her fingers tightening around my shoulders. "But yes, this event is going to be wall to wall with bloodthirsty sycophants who will treat you like the gunk between their toes. And since Xander won't be there to distract the masses with his glorious return, we had better arm you."

"She's right," another soft lilting voice added. Bianca strode into the room.

The goddess might have invited me here, but I hadn't forgotten that she'd begged me to stay away from Xander when I killed him nightly for weeks on end. She knew something terrible would come from it.

But I hadn't listened.

And we were all in danger now.

Chapter Sixteen

THE BADASS

Bianca's blonde hair was arranged in perfect curls. The Oracle's dress was a dreamy, white, form fitting number that showed off her curves.

If only I had believed her predictions, it might have stopped me from falling for Xander, from bringing him back, from unleashing all the evil from the blade.

Or it might not have.

Nerves and guilt had me rolling my shoulders back and straightening my spine in the goddess's presence. She had every right to despise me, and I deserved it.

Instead of voicing that, I said, "I'm not sure how the immortals will feel about me casually toting around the blade known as the 'god killer' at the party."

"There is more to me than just killing," Bob sniffed haughtily.

The maid from earlier rushed in and presented me with Bob, still in his sheath. I slid him out enough to see gleaming steel.

"Oh my gods, Miranda. I think I am in love. The blacksmith, her hands. I've never felt so cherished. The way she washed my blade."

I wanted to cut him off, but considering how many times Bob kept his mouth shut about witnessing my intimate moments with Xander, I didn't have a step to stand on.

Bianca glided across the room, her crystalline baby blues meeting mine. It was like staring into a cloudless sky, and my mood shifted into a lighter state. In that one look, she communicated more than should have been possible.

A brief flash of disappointment over how things turned out, deep empathy for me over Xander's death and now for the burden I carried.

Not sympathy, *empathy*.

It was like she cupped her hands gently to my heart with a loving aura that soothed my sins.

My lip trembled as the forgiveness flowed through me. Her divinity was like touching the softest ray of sunshine.

Her power over me ebbed as she wrapped her slender fingers around my shoulders, leading me to the platform Vivien was just on. Bianca nudged me to step up onto the riser and look at myself. "Vivien didn't mean arm you with lethal weapons. The gods will view you as weak simply because you are a mortal. When you walk into that ballroom, you need to be dressed in a different kind of armor. One that will teach them exactly who you are. A warrior. One worthy to protect us all. And rest assured, we can help with that." Her lips curled up in a mischievous smile even as Timothy and Vivien came up from behind me on the other side, a knowing glint in their eyes.

Viven added, "Oh, we guarantee you will knock 'em dead tomorrow night."

A spike of fear shot through me, but I was surrounded.

* * *

After the dress fitting, I was exhausted from the pushing, pulling, and sheer number of decisions that needed to be made. I had to pull Vivien back from her wild ideas until I curbed the design to something that would reflect me. Thankfully, Bianca was the voice of reason, keeping things from getting too out of hand.

Despite feeling like an irate pin cushion, I dragged my ass to the gym to get in a workout while I could.

As I reached for the free weights, I focused on the burn in my muscles, each lift a step toward becoming stronger and more capable. The wounds on my arm still burned and ached, a vivid reminder of Bes's attack, but I pushed through the pain. I needed to be prepared for what lay ahead. I killed one god, but I had countless others to go.

Sweat dripped down my face as I pushed through another set of shoulder presses. The clinking of weights and the buzz of gym equipment filled my ears, but a familiar voice cut through the noise.

"Working hard, I see."

I turned to find my neighbor Michael standing there with a towel around his neck, his gym attire accentuating his muscular physique. His presence was unexpected, yet not entirely unwelcome.

"So, you've joined my gym now?" I asked, setting the weights down.

Michael flashed a casual smile. "Seems like it. I've been looking for a good place to work out, and this one's close by. It's a bonus getting to run into you. Need a spotter?"

I hesitated for a moment, then nodded. "Why not?"

A little company couldn't hurt. Besides, I really did need a spotter.

There was something about Michael that was intriguing, a kind of gentle strength that was hard to ignore. His presence was comforting, a stark contrast to the chaos of the last couple days.

As I settled onto my back to do some heavy chest presses, he chatted about his life as a financial consultant, and joked about rising his way to the top where he would inevitably rule the world. He laughed low and hit a timbre that resonated through my bones with unexpected warmth.

He was everything that should appeal to me—handsome, stable, normal. Yet, as much as I recognized this, my mind kept drifting back to Xander. His wild, untamed nature, the way my body responded to his mere presence with a burning intensity I couldn't deny.

I went harder on the weights, trying to push out the confusion and desire swirling within me.

Michael was clearly interested in me and was the sensible choice—a man who could offer stability and maybe even normalcy. But my heart, my very soul, seemed entwined with Xander's chaotic essence. The thought of him ignited a fire in my belly, a yearning so visceral that it scared me. It wasn't just attraction—it was a profound connection that defied logic.

Michael and I worked out, side by side, while he politely kept the conversation light. Still, I could feel his eyes on me, appraising yet not intrusive.

Night was fast approaching, and with it the inevitability of facing Xander again. It sent a thrill mixed with dread through me.

Finishing my last set, I sat up, catching my breath. Michael handed me a water bottle, his touch lingering just a moment longer than necessary.

"You're quite impressive, Miranda," he said, his voice low and earnest. "Not just your strength, but your resilience."

I offered a weak smile, the weight of his words sinking in. "Thanks, Michael. I'm always just trying to get a little stronger every day."

He chuckled softly. "I have a feeling you're more than just a *little* strong."

I stood up, wiping the sweat from my brow. "I should get going."

Michael nodded, understanding in his eyes. "Well, if you ever need a break, or someone to talk to, I'm right next door."

I thanked him, grabbed Bob from my secure locker, and left the gym, my mind a whirlwind of emotions. As I walked away, I couldn't shake the feeling that there was more to Michael than met the eye.

But right now, it was time to focus on the hunt, on Xander, and on the next god I was going to kill.

Now if only we could keep our hands off each other.

Chapter Seventeen

THE BEAST

The Vegas Strip, with its neon-lit allure, stretched out around us like a carnival of the bizarre and colorful. As we maneuvered through the crowd, I couldn't keep my eyes off my hunting partner.

Miranda was a stark contrast to the glitz. I'd become convinced there was nothing more real than her. She moved with lethal grace, her eyes sweeping through the darkness, missing nothing. It was like watching a panther stalk through a flock of peacocks. My chest tightened, watching her. Every instinct in me wanted to draw her closer, to bridge the gap that stretched between us, yet I knew better.

I fucked up. Somewhere between her slimy neighbor and my gift, I'd made a number of missteps. All these years, I'd thought living in mind melting pain day in and day out was the hardest existence. I'd forgotten just how hard living was.

The uncertainty, the complexity. After all these years it felt like trying to speak a language everyone else knew that I barely mastered simple commands in.

"I still can't believe you got me a dog," Miranda said suddenly, her voice cutting through the noise of the Strip.

Something in her tone told me maybe I wasn't quite the massive screw up I'd been beating myself up for being.

"Yeah, well," I started, rubbing the back of my neck, "I figured you could use something less stabby in your life." I glanced at her, trying to gauge her reaction.

Miranda smirked, that dangerous little curve of her lips that always sent my thoughts into overdrive. "Less stabby, more fluffy. Got it."

"I thought you would like a canine companion. You know, someone to play with, to cuddle with when I'm not around..." I was pushing my luck, but I couldn't help it with her. I never could.

Her lips tightened as if she were trying to suppress a smile.

Maybe my gift wasn't totally off the mark.

"I did want to thank you properly, Xander," Miranda continued, her voice softer now, "But there's something I didn't tell you about my... dog. The real reason you couldn't find him in the underworld."

Her confession hung between us, poised on the edge of a knife. I could feel the shift in the air, a moment teetering on the brink of something important. Every fiber of my being leaned in, craving her truth.

Just as she opened her mouth to go on, her damn phone rang, shattering the moment like glass. Miranda's expression switched instantly from vulnerable to all business as she checked the screen before answering. "It's Echo."

I watched her, a mix of frustration and concern churning within me. The ringing phone was an intruder robbing me of the confession she meant to share.

As Miranda listened, her face hardened with urgency, and I knew her mind was back on the mission.

"What do you mean, scorpions?" she asked sharply, her body tensing like a coiled spring. "Which hotel?"

As she listened to Echo's response, I got the familiar itch of anticipation. Maybe I'd get to work out some of my extra frustration tonight, one way or another.

Miranda ended the call, her gaze meeting mine. "A goddess named Serqet has unleashed her scorpions in Fallon's hotel. He can't control her. We need to go. Now."

We raced toward the hotel, the city's cacophony fading into the background. As we approached, the scale of the chaos became apparent. People streamed out of the building in a panicked exodus, their screams and shouts filling the air. We pushed through the crowd, making our way inside.

The opulent lobby was in disarray, with scorpions swarming across the marble floors, their venomous tails raised threateningly.

Miranda's eyes flared wide and wild, her body recoiling. "I hate bugs," Miranda confessed.

"Technically, they are arachnids, like spiders."

The look she shot at me could have killed.

Okay, maybe not the time for a lesson.

"I got you," I assured her with a cocky grin. Walking straight toward them, they split for me, leaving the perfect trail for us to walk through. "Stay close," I told her.

Miranda was practically plastered to my back, her breath on my neck, causing goosebumps to rise. Despite needing to be on guard, part of me reveled in her closeness.

As Miranda and I edged closer to the epicenter of chaos, I couldn't help but marvel at the scene before us. "You know, for a goddess of scorpions, she's really got a flair for the dramatic," I quipped, eyeing the swarming arachnids with a mixture of disgust and fascination.

Miranda gave me a sidelong glance. "Dramatic? She's turned the hotel into a death trap."

"Oh, come on. You have to admit, it's kind of impressive, in a terrifying *we might not make it out alive* kind of way," I said, trying to lighten the mood.

I'd never let that happen to Miranda though. The goddess wouldn't lay a finger on my angel of death.

I led us to the main lobby where people stood like statues surrounding the massive obelisk at the center that glowed with purple energy. The humans' eyes were glazed as they murmured praises to their new master.

A towering figure of dark majesty loomed in the center of the chaos. Serqet was tall, her presence commanding the room like a queen of shadows. Her dress, a flowing garment that seemed woven from scorpion shells dripping in ichor, clung to her form, accentuating her menacing grace. On her head, a scorpion-shaped crown glinted in the dim light, each segment of its tail articulated, moving with a life of its own. Her eyes were a merciless cold, a black void.

Around her, the scorpions swarmed as if drawn by some invisible force, a testament to her control over the creatures of darkness. The air crackled with malignant energy, the power of the obelisk amplifying her already formidable abilities.

I glanced at Miranda, a sense of foreboding tightening in my chest. "Be careful," I warned her, my voice low. "Serqet doesn't just control scorpions. She gets inside your head, dredges up your deepest fears and darkest thoughts. She'll twist your mind if you let her."

Miranda's jaw set firmly, her grip on the Blade of Bane tightening. "Bob will protect me."

I could only assume the talking blade only she could hear had assured her of this.

Strangely, a stab of jealousy went through me at her having secret conversations with an inanimate object. For the millionth time in the last several weeks, I was reminded I was an outsider in this world in every respect. But I shoved off the self-deprecating bullshit for later when I'd inevitably brood alone.

"That obelisk," I nodded towards the towering structure in the center of the lobby, "It's not just a fancy decoration. It's a conduit for power, amplifying whatever energy it's fed. She's using it to bolster her control."

Miranda's eyes narrowed as she assessed the situation. "Great, so we're not just fighting a goddess, we're fighting a supercharged goddess."

Serqet's voice, cold and haughty, cut through the commotion. "Bow before me, mortals. Witness the resurgence of a goddess scorned. This city, this world, shall know the might of Serqet."

As she said those words, an ether of life force emerged from her followers, fueling the obelisk. She was going to drain them to death.

"Hey, goth scorpion lady," Miranda called out. "Let everyone go and maybe I won't stab you into your old prison."

Clever girl. We had no element of surprise here, and we needed to distract Serqet before she killed these people.

Serqet's gaze snapped to Miranda, her lips curling into a sneer. "A mortal wishes to challenge me? You are but a tool for my divinity."

With a flick of her hand, a wave of psychic energy surged towards Miranda, intent on ensnaring her mind. But the blade in Miranda's hand glowed, creating a barrier that repelled the attack.

"Thanks Bob," Miranda said quietly. "Pretty sure *you* are the tool," Miranda shot back at Serqet.

Tension coiled in my body, a mix of admiration for Miranda's bravery and a gnawing fear for her safety.

Amidst the chaos, I caught sight of a Black man laying slumped against a pillar. Fallon. His dark suit was rumpled and neither his blue nor his brown eye opened or so much as twitched. A wound oozed a purple liquid from his neck, a clear sign of Serqet's poisonous touch.

"You think you can defy me?" Serqet hissed, her form growing more imposing as she tapped into the obelisk's power. "I will crush you."

It was my turn. "Hey there, sis. I may have been underground for the last several thousand years, but I know a couple things you don't. We don't reveal ourselves to humans, we don't take followers anymore, and we sure as fuck don't throw tantrums for the glory of what, your ego?"

I held her attention as Miranda crept around to the side.

Serqet's sinister laughter filled the air as she raised her hands, the scorpions on the floor surging towards us like a living tide. Within moments, we were surrounded, the venomous creatures forming a barrier that held us in place.

I couldn't make them part to get to Miranda.

Fuck.

There came a knocking on my mind. Like the deep sonorous poundings against a massive castle door.

Serqet was trying to get in my head.

Panic rose within me as the walls of my mind shook under the strain of her power.

Serqet's eyes gleamed with malice as she turned her venomous gaze toward me. "Oh, Nun, once a mighty god, now nothing more than a deranged shadow, trembling on the brink of madness," she sneered, her voice a razor slicing into my mind like a scalpel.

My fists clenched involuntarily, and a cold sweat broke out across my skin. I told Miranda I would protect her, but Serqet was pulling my mind apart like a child with a pile of blocks. It had been a mistake for me to come. My mind was too weak, and I put Miranda in danger.

"Look at you," Serqet continued, her tone dripping with disdain. "Pathetic. Clinging to a mortal for some semblance of balance. Do you think she can save you from the chaos raging inside your head? She's a mere human, Nun. She cannot anchor a mind as fractured as yours."

Her words echoed my darkest insecurities—the fear that I was too far gone, beyond saving, beyond redemption. The fear that if I gave into my inner beast, I would never regain control, that I could not protect Miranda, the one person who had pierced the darkness of my existence.

"You're a ticking time bomb, Nun." Serqet's voice turned hushed. Her eyes locked onto mine, reading my turmoil. "One wrong move, and you'll unleash destruction upon those you claim to care for. How long before you turn on her, I wonder?"

Serqet prodded at the nightmare that haunted me—losing control and harming Miranda. That thought alone was unbearable. Whether I turned into the mindless monster I was, or simply crushed her fragile, precious heart, there were too many ways I could cause her pain and all of them felt inevitable.

"And you," Serqet turned her scornful attention to Miranda, "Do you realize the danger you're in? Aligning yourself with a god whose mind is a tempest of madness? How pitiful that you find strength in someone so broken and unstable."

Miranda's jaw tightened. "Xander, don't listen to her. She's wrong. You are in control, not her." Miranda's voice was firm, commanding. She was my lighthouse in this storm, but even her pull couldn't dispel the shadows clawing their way out.

Serqet's laughter echoed through the lobby, mixing with the hiss of her scorpions. "Let's see how long your resolve lasts. The broken god and his mortal crutch—what a tragic tale you both weave."

Serqet's hisses echoed in my head. "Feel the chaos clawing at your mind. Let it loose, Nun. Show your true self to your precious mortal."

The words were a relentless drumbeat, pushing me towards the edge. I could feel my darkness stirring.

It whispered at the back of my mind, a reminder of the depth and tempest of the powers I possess. *Let go,* it hissed, *Show them the might of Nun.* I clenched my fists, nails digging into my palms, a futile attempt to anchor myself to my humanity.

The monstrous part of my godhood that I had fought so hard to control threatened to break free. It was tempting, so tempting, to let go and unleash the fury and power that churned within.

A desperate laugh bubbled up from my throat, the sound more akin to a growl. *Is this it?* I wondered. *Is this the moment I become the monster?* But even as the thought crossed my mind, I knew I'd do anything, become anything, to protect Miranda.

There would be no telling what chaos or damage I would inflict if I gave into the monster inside. Not even Miranda would be safe.

In the reflection of the obelisk, I caught a glimpse of my eyes—no longer human, but deep pools of the abyss, swirling with unbound power and madness. The sight was both terrifying and exhilarating.

I would *not* be a monster to her. I would be a man.

Even as I insisted this to myself, the world narrowed down to those hissing whispers, each word a strike against the fragile dam holding back my madness.

A torrent of ancient power stirred within me, fighting against the chains I'd wrapped so tightly around it. My skin itched with the need to shift, to unleash the roiling sea trapped within my soul.

The air around me crackled with tension, thick with the impending release of chaos. My grasp on reality slipped, my thoughts fragmenting under the weight of her words.

Suddenly Serqet's words came from inside the cavern of my own mind.

"You are not a man. You are a monster, you always will be. Give in, Nun, to your nature. Give in to your chaos."

My control cracked, and bright blue ravines of power lit up at my fingers, traveling up my hands and forearms.

Power surged through me like a tidal wave, unstoppable and all-consuming. My bones shifted, my skin stretched, and for a moment, I was suspended between man and deity—a creature of water and wrath about to crash down on those who dared threaten what I held dear.

Chapter Eighteen

THE BEAST

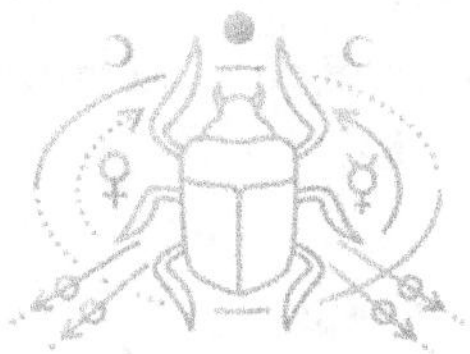

Electric blue sizzled off my skin with near atomic power that made all the cells in my body vibrate violently.

Taming the storm within me wasn't graceful. It was like trying to put a leash on a hurricane. Every attempt to calm down just ticked off the beast more. The power inside me was wild, gnashing and roaring for release. For a moment, it felt good letting it take the wheel, but then I caught Miranda's determined look.

"Xander, listen to me," Miranda called out, her voice a sharp blade cutting through the fog in my mind. "This bitch *does not* know you. Not like I do. And nobody can make you do anything you don't want. Not even burn those hideous Hawaiian shirts." The corner of her lips lifted, even as she pinned me with her intense stare, tethering me to her.

Don't you dare give up on me now, her eyes seemed to say. It was enough to make me wrestle back control. Hell, if Miranda thought I could do it, maybe I wasn't totally lost.

I met Miranda's gaze, finding an anchor in the storm. Her eyes were so clear, so trusting, so knowing. As if she had zero doubt I would pull myself together.

A reminder that I had something—someone—to fight for. That even in my darkest moments, when I felt most alienated from myself, there was a part of me that remained untainted, capable of resisting the descent into madness.

The wild, unbridled power that had been a breath away from over-taking me began to wane, my skin cooling and my thoughts sharpening into focus once again.

In that moment, something shifted between us. A bond, already strong, forged in fights, deaths, and the quiet moments in between, grew even tighter. It wasn't just about calming me down and pulling me out from my own destruction. It was about knowing each other's strengths and vulnerabilities and choosing to stand together regardless.

Serqet let out a furious hiss. "Listen to me, Nun. Your madness will consume you!"

But her words, once so potent, now seemed to lose their edge, blunted by Miranda's unwavering support.

What the hell had I done to earn it?

That didn't matter right now. What mattered was kicking this goddess' ass.

Serqet's face twisted into a snarl. "Insolent mortal! You're nothing but a plaything to the gods!" She extended her hand, a wave of dark energy pulsing towards us.

Again, the force of her power hit me, smashing against my mind, trying to unleash that which I kept caged.

With a roar, I pushed against Serqet's influence, the effort sending ripples of pain through my head.

"I'm more than just my madness," I growled, breaking free of her. Shooting a hand toward the wall fountain, I grabbed hold of my power and the water exploded from the pipes and into the room, sweeping the scorpions away and clearing a path.

Miranda lunged forward, her blade cutting through the air with deadly precision. Serqet countered with a burst of dark energy, throwing Miranda back.

"You are nothing but a speck to me, mortal!" Serqet spat, turning her attention to Miranda. She reached out, trying to ensnare Miranda's mind with her psychic power.

But the Blade of Bane in Miranda's grasp glowed brighter, repelling the attack. "Not today." Miranda charged again.

Together, we closed in around Serqet from different sides.

I threw myself at Serqet again and again, my fists meeting with her chin, her gut. Serqet absorbed my blows as quickly as I landed them.

A scorpion, larger than the rest, lunged at Miranda from the side. She rolled away, blade slicing through its body in a swift, clean motion, her focus never wavering from Serqet.

She had been training in my absence.

"You dare defy a goddess?" Serqet roared, her form growing larger as she drew power from the obelisk.

Something shifted from under the back of her dress and a massive scorpion tail emerged. The lethal stinger snapped forward like a whip to pierce me. I dodged, rolled, and dodged again.

That's right, you bitch, come after me.

The thrill of the fight coursed through my veins, but my heart raced with fear. One wrong move and the results for Miranda would be fatal.

Serqet whipped around, her tail aiming directly at her. Miranda ducked, the stinger grazing her hair, a breath away from a lethal blow.

With a burst of speed, I closed in on Serqet, my fists slamming into a barrier of dark energy she conjured. The impact sent shockwaves through my arms, but I didn't relent.

"Miranda, now!"

In that moment of distraction, Miranda found her opening. She leapt forward again, the Blade of Bane flashing in the dark purple light of Serqet's energy.

Miranda let out a fierce cry as she plunged the blade into Serqet's back. The blade cut through until the metal tip emerged out the front of her chest, dripping with thick, black blood. The goddess's scream echoed through the lobby, a sound of defeat and disbelief. Her form shuddered, then began to dissolve into shadows, her power ebbing away as her skin turned gray and flaked away into ash. The scorpions still scuttling on the edges followed suit.

Exhausted, Miranda stumbled back, her breath coming in ragged gasps. I rushed to her side, my own body aching from the fight.

"That's one less god causing havoc," Miranda said, her voice laced with fatigue but victorious.

I couldn't contain my admiration. "You are incredible," I breathed, my emotions raw and unguarded.

In a surge of impulse, I grabbed her and crushed her lips to mine in a fierce, fiery kiss. She tasted like adrenaline, citrus, and victory. She smiled into my mouth and the perfect moment imprinted on my ravaged and damned essence.

The remnants of Serqet's followers began to stir, their trance breaking.

Just as quickly as the passion flared, reality crashed back into focus.

"We need to wake Fallon," Miranda said. "He'll calm everyone down and use his power to wipe their minds, so they won't remember what happened here."

I didn't want to wake Fallon.

I wanted to throw Miranda over my shoulder and take her to my lair like a caveman with only carnal desires in mind. She was glorious, and the bastard I was, I wanted to drag her away and keep her all to myself.

Instead of saying any of that aloud, I only nodded.

* * *

FALLON WOKE UP CRANKY AS FUCK. NOT ONLY BECAUSE SERQET GOT the drop on him, but he now had a passel of people to brain wipe.

Then Bianca flew in on the scene in a particularly binding pink dress, her hair falling in beautiful, curled waves. Despite her looking put together, Bianca was practically frantic. She fussed over him like he was a baby.

Fallon's glower remained, but it softened as she tended to him, asking him if he felt dizzy or needed to lie down, or if she should use some of her healing powers on him. The imposing god only requested a stiff drink and a quiet place to relax after he dealt with wiping the minds of the human witnesses.

Miranda and I snuck out even as Bianca was trying to convince him it would do him good to let her run a healing bubble bath for him, using some of her tinctures.

Last I saw those two together, which was when we all lived among the pyramids in Egypt, they were at each other's throats over something stupid, like a differing interpretation of a prophecy or vision they both experienced. Now, the moon-eyed god could barely contain his raging affection for one of the most kind-hearted goddesses among us.

Heh, sucker.

My blood still rushed with adrenaline and I wasn't ready to call it a night. Judging by the glassy sparkle in Miranda's dark, cat-shaped eyes, she was of the same mind.

"We should celebrate," I pitched, practically bouncing on the balls of my feet.

Her grin spread wide. "I don't hate that idea." The smile faltered. "Though it might be wise to keep hunting. There are more threats on these streets."

I turned her shoulders to me. "You've killed not one, but two gods this week. At what point do you take a damn break, so you can celebrate your victory?"

"Our victory," she corrected quietly. Looking into her eyes, I expected resentment to swim there. She was so staunchly independent, and she made it clear on countless occasions that she didn't want my help. Instead, I found begrudging gratitude. We'd worked as a team.

"Fine," she consented.

It was like fireworks went off inside my chest. "I know the perfect place."

We started off toward my secret destination, but we'd only been walking for ten minutes when Miranda grabbed my hand, squeezing it hard as she tugged me in a different direction.

"Let's, uh, take a quick detour."

I raised an eyebrow at her. Miranda's eyes were wide, glassy, and she couldn't stop licking her lips.

Electricity zipped and danced along my skin as I felt her arousal, a palpable energy in the air.

I could only nod my consent with a lopsided smile. The truth was she could ask me anything and I'd agree. Pressure built up as she pulled me to a darkened storefront, the neon sign that read, *Arcadia Ba*r flickering sporadically, like a beacon calling us into the night.

"A little help?" she asked with a dare in her eyes, jiggling the locked door handle.

Someone was feeling naughty.

With a flick of my wrist and a murmur under my breath, the lock clicked open—a simple trick, but effective.

Miranda's grin was all the thanks I needed as we slipped inside. She closed and locked the door behind us before leading me into the darkness of the empty arcade bar. The air was thick with the scent of spilled beer, disinfectant cleaner, and the ghost of laughter, but now it was our playground.

The arcade machines stood silent, their screens dark, waiting for the touch of eager players. But tonight, they had an audience of two.

Miranda's hand found mine in the dark, her touch electric. "This is insane," she whispered, but I could hear the thrill in her voice, the excitement that mirrored my own.

Our bodies met, and the world narrowed to the space between us. I captured her lips with mine, the kiss deep and hungry, fueled by the adrenaline of our earlier battle.

Hands roamed, exploring, as we made our way down the rows of arcade machines, our moans mingling in the quiet bar. I backed her up to a pinball machine, the cold glass pressing against her back. Her legs wrapped around my waist as our kiss deepened, desperate and consuming.

The flickering neon lights painted us in surreal colors, casting long shadows that danced around us as I battled her hot, sweet mouth for dominance. Miranda clawed my shirt off like an unhinged animal. The sensation of being filled and engorged with desire was overwhelming. My arousal grew until it was almost painfully hard and throbbing in anticipation.

She bit and nipped at my lips, only stopping when I yanked her top off. Taking advantage, I dropped my mouth to bite and suck at her puckered nipples. The distinct taste of her skin filled my senses, ripping a groan from my throat.

Miranda cursed and moaned, her movements more desperate by the second. She shoved me away to kick off her boots and rip off her tight pants while I hurriedly tore mine off, so we were both naked. She only paused to gingerly place Bob behind the bar, as if he needed to be out of sight.

"I've seen these machines on movies and television, but I'm not really sure how they work," I confessed. I was doing anything I could to distract myself from the blood rushing south. My control was slipping fast, and I didn't want to scare her off.

"I can show you how to play," she said, her voice husky. With that, she pushed me back then dropped to her knees. She engulfed my cock in her hot mouth. My arm shot out to grip the counter of the bar.

"Oh fuck me," I groaned, panting. "You better stop or this is going to be over quick."

Her lips curved around my dick that felt more like a heartbeat about to explode. Deft fingers reached up and began to stroke my balls as she took me all the way down her throat. She let out a low sultry hum in her throat that vibrated up into my balls.

Oh fucking hell.

My abs flexed at the way she sucked me into the tight hot heaven of her mouth. A coil of heat and tension tied a string together from my spine to my testicles and drew upward too fast. My mind clouded.

I was going to lose it.

When I tried to pull away, she sunk her fingers into the meat of my ass, keeping me in place.

Control freak.

Fuck, she was dominating and playful and I loved every godsdamn second.

"Fuck sweetheart, I'm going to—"

Her nails dug harder into my ass, unrelenting in her wet sucking, taking me all the way in over and over.

I threw my head back. White sparks exploded in my body as I came down her throat. Miranda didn't stop, swallowing every last drop of my desire. My head was far too light and fuzzy, and nothing made sense except the woman on her knees in front of me.

"Oh shit," I breathed.

Miranda's nails grazed down the front of my bare thighs, and she looked up at me with a sultry gleam in those cat-like eyes. For a minute, I forgot she was mortal. Naked, on her knees before me, she was a seductive, otherworldly creature that I didn't deserve, but fucking hell if I wasn't going to take her.

The way her skin gleamed, so soft, over taut, long muscles made my fingertips prickle, and those seductive eyes and full lips had my chest wrenching in a vise.

She may be on her knees, but I worshiped this woman and always would. Eternity meant a very real thing to immortals, and as a god, I'd easily pledge it all away to her.

Pulling her to her feet, I teased and kissed her full lips and tasted myself, which sent twinges of desire pulsating back through my cock.

Her grip on me grew desperate.

Where I was floating, she was in need. And I sure as hell planned to provide.

My eye caught on an arcade game nearby and something absolutely wicked came to me.

"Do you trust me, my little badass?" I asked. My fingers swept up her slit. Fuck, she was so wet.

"No," she scoffed even as her eyes rolled back in pleasure.

I laughed darkly, and whispered into her ear, "Good."

That's when I picked her up and carried her over to a nearby game console. "Open up for me, sweetheart, so we can play a new game."

She barely understood what I meant before I lowered her slowly onto the joystick of the game. It penetrated her swollen slick folds, disappearing into her body.

Miranda's eyes flew wide, and she let out a sound of protest that she bit off into a moan of confusion and arousal.

Chapter Nineteen

THE BADASS

"Oh fuck," I groaned even as I bit down on my lip, feeling so exposed, strange, and way too turned on at being penetrated by a literal joystick.

I'd pulled us into the arcade bar because I couldn't wait another minute to attack Xander to work off my excited energy. Maybe it had been the subconscious relation I had to our playing games that had me acting so recklessly when I saw the dark sign of Arcadia.

But I hadn't expected this.

"Oh fuck, sweetheart," Xander echoed my words with breathy awe. He firmly held my hips even as he dropped to his knees before me. The game was low enough that it put him at the perfect height.

His tongue darted against my clit in a way that made me want to both push him away and pull him closer at the same time. He snaked a hand down and shifted the joystick inside me, and I couldn't help but arch my back and ride it out.

A half-cry escaped me. The object didn't go deep enough, but it was hard and shocking to my system.

"This is so wrong," I groaned.

"You fucking love it," he growled into me, continuing to lick and suckle at my sensitive bud, sending lightning strikes through my veins.

In the dark, I still saw the outline of his face between my legs. His eyes closed in concentration as his tongue moved intricately and insistently against my center.

The muscles in his arms flexed as he held me down, his entire body focused on giving me pleasure.

His hands rocked my hips on the joystick this way and that. My head fell back as unhinged, wild sounds escaped me.

So, so fucking wrong.

With the skill of a true gamer, he manipulated all the right buttons and triggers to drive me to the peak of pleasure.

His tongue pressed more insistently against my center. My body twisted and writhed beneath him as he built a vortex inside me. Swirling chaos swept away my thoughts until I was unable to comprehend anything other than the intensity of the sensations coursing through my body.

"Game over, sweetheart." His husky rasp barely cut through the noise in my mind. "Come for me."

Shudders wracked me and I broke into a thousand pieces, thighs shaking, gripping the sides of the machine for dear life.

When my body calmed, Xander stood, licking his lips like a wolf. "And here I was worried I wouldn't know how to play any of these games, but I think I just got the high score."

I swatted him even as he picked me up and carried me again, laying me down on the air hockey table.

"We both know you won that game." He playfully grinned, standing at the edge of the table, stroking his hard length in one hand.

I pushed myself onto my forearms. "Never thought I'd see the day when I'd be spread-eagled over an arcade game, let alone a fucking air hockey table," I panted, my voice slightly hoarse.

Xander's gaze landed on something beneath the table, and his eyes sparkled with excitement.

He reached for a small, red plastic puck and placed it between my slick, exposed folds. It was cold. The dark gleam in his eyes matched the evil smile on his lips.

"You having fun?" I asked, trying for my best scowl.

"Oh yeah," he breathed, continuing to stroke himself as he ran the cold, thin object down my sensitive swollen lower lips. He looked more sinfully sexual than was right, playing with me and the little object he picked up.

Something about him was so curious, so childish, but I guess that came with becoming reacquainted with a world he'd hadn't interacted with for so long.

"I fucking love seeing you like this," he growled, his voice low and thrumming with lust. "So hot, so wet, so ready for me."

I tried to act unaffected, but his words coupled with the puck pressed into me, sent a shudder of delight through me. My muscles clenched around the edge of the object.

"Give me that," I commanded in a huskier voice than I planned, while opening my hand. He handed it over then slid his naked body until it was settled between my spread legs.

Without warning, Xander surged forward, driving himself into me with a violent and unrelenting thrust. My body convulsed in pain and pleasure as I cried out, my hand clenching the puck so hard it felt like it might break, while the other dug into the edges of the air hockey table, struggling to hold on as it rocked violently under the force of his relentless pounding.

I was so full, I couldn't think. He reached places that turned my mouth dry and my mind inside out.

He pressed his lips against mine, and I could taste the lingering musky sweetness of my arousal on his tongue. I moaned softly as our tongues danced together, the warmth spreading through my body.

Sweat slicked our bodies as we writhed and fucked in long, hard thrusts.

Then I made my move, pushing the slickened air hockey puck into his mouth before I grabbed his hair, jerking his head back. He groaned either at the feel or the taste. I was below him but in complete control.

Xander surged forward, hitting me with a deep, powerful thrust, groaning, teeth gritted on the puck. He gripped my hips, pulling me closer as he slammed into me. Our bodies slapped together, the sounds of our fucking echoed in the arcade, punctuated by Xander's grunts and my breathy moans.

Xander's face was a picture of fierce concentration. His eyes, hooded and heavy-lidded with need, locked on mine as he continued to drive me higher. He turned his head and spat out the puck. He pushed my hands over my head, trapping them there.

"You're going to fucking come for me, Miranda."

"You'll have to work for it," I managed to choke out.

A devilish grin spread across his handsome face, his eyes never leaving mine. "It's always a fight with you, isn't it?" He leaned down, his breath hot and heavy in my ear, "And it's another challenge I'm willing to accept."

With that, he moved faster, his hips pounding into me with a fierce intensity that was both exhilarating and terrifying. I was being taken on a wild ride, one that I had no control over and yet, strangely enough, loved.

The hum of a machine turned on and air shot out of the table's tiny holes, penetrating my overheated body.

"What the hell?" I muttered.

"You got me too worked up," he rasped.

My brain was foggy with lust, but I realized Xander triggered the machine with his power. Whether consciously or not, I wasn't sure.

As his rhythm increased, my body responded. My muscles clenched around him, my breathing becoming ragged and erratic. I arched my back, trying to meet his every thrust, desperate for more.

The pressure in my core, the sensation building to a crescendo, threatened to consume me whole. I was close, so close, and I wanted him inside me when I came.

"Yes, Xander, yes!" I cried out, my voice hoarse with need. The intensity of his gaze bore into me, and I was swept away by his power over me.

The god's body shuddered with pleasure as he thrust hard and deep into me. His muscles tightened under my hands, and I knew he was close as well.

With one final surge, Xander's body convulsed, and he cried out as he came inside me, filling me with his warmth.

We lay there on the air hockey table, our bodies entwined in post-coital bliss. Only the hum of the engine and our loud pants filled the air.

"Did you turn it on, on purpose?" I asked, still trying to catch my breath.

He laughed slightly as he shook his head. "Nope, you're the only one I wanted to turn on."

The cool air of the table was a welcome feeling, cutting through the cloying heat we'd generated in the dark gaming bar.

My hands covered my face. "Oh my god, I can't believe we just did that. So much of that was so wrong." Feelings of horror and shock began to cut through the salacious things we just did.

He tugged my arm down so I'd look at him. "Can we not overthink this for once? Or at least, until tomorrow. I still have somewhere I want to take you. I promise you can regret all of this tomorrow, but not yet."

"We're a mess and look like we just had the kind of depraved sex we just had. We should probably clean up first, and definitely clean up in here. 'Cause if I didn't think about this being an adult hotspot, I'd say we need to get the place condemned."

Xander's thumb covered my lips. "Can you just be here with me for a little while longer? A complete and utter mess together?"

Something in his voice cut me to my core. It was the diverging point between us. My need to control and keep things in order and his inability to do so. A loneliness wavered in his eyes that told me if I didn't do this, he would be more alone than ever.

I took a deep breath and nodded. I could try.

Then Xander's face broke into a smile that made my heart skip and tumble all over itself in my chest.

I realized I couldn't deny him anything.

And for once, that didn't feel as scary as it should have.

Chapter Twenty

THE BEAST

We cleaned ourselves and the bar as best we could, then less than ten minutes later, we walked down the steps to my favorite bar, the Rusty Nail.

Stepping into the dive bar felt like entering another world, one far removed from the supernatural chaos that had become our daily routine.

The air was thick with the scent of aged whiskey and stale cigarette smoke, but the air conditioning from the loud, overworked A/C unit provided a stark contrast to the sweltering desert night. Neon lights buzzed overhead, casting a warm, inviting glow over the well-worn pool tables and battered bar stools. Classic rock hummed softly from a jukebox in the corner, the tunes a comforting backdrop.

Miranda moved beside me, her presence a constant pull on my senses. The way the dim light danced in her dark eyes, the confident measure of her walk, all drew me in like a moth to flame.

Even after fucking each other like the world was ending, the pulse of desire for her beat under my skin. She was everything, and the fact she didn't know it was frankly fucking insulting.

True to her word, she'd tabled all her reservations as we got dressed so I could bring her here.

"You... uh, like this place?" Miranda asked, giving the place a skeptical once over. "And don't worry about hepatitis?" She murmured that last bit, and I pretended not to hear.

I grinned at her. "It's completely off grid from the other immortals. This is an old-fashioned humans-only bar." There were only about ten other people milling about at the bar and at the high-top tables, making for a subdued environment as Chuck Berry crooned in the background.

The reservation on her face told me she didn't care for this as much as I did, so I proceeded to take her on a tour of the place. "See there are pool tables, and have you used one of these? It's a jukebox. I'd heard of them, but never got to use one until recently. And the drinks are..."

"Cheap and watered down," the bartender interrupted me.

A short man with gelled hair and olive green eyes, wearing a striped shirt smiled even as I leaned over to shake his hand.

"Nice to see you again, Xander. Can I get you the usual?"

"Yes, and whatever the lady would like."

"I'm Lester," the man introduced himself as he reached over and shook Miranda's hand. "What'll it be, madame?"

"Miranda." Then she asked me, "The usual?"

"Shirley Temple," I said, grinning. "Have you tried one?"

She shot a glance to the bartender who gave her a shrug. "You come here to *not* drink?"

I didn't exactly go into how drinking wouldn't help my mental stability so I told her the other half of the truth. "I'm here for the ambiance."

"I'll take whatever beer is good on tap," she said to Lester.

He clutched a cleaning rag over his chest. "A woman after my own heart."

"Be careful there, Lester," I laughed, though it was strained in my own ears.

"Don't put off my new boyfriend," Miranda mock accused me with a daring look, and set her hand on the countertop. Lester covered her hand with his own, playing into her antics.

"Yeah, can't you see we're in love?"

Miranda's eyes sparkled with mischief. "Yeah, we'll be getting married soon."

A possessive streak, dark and powerful swirled in me, making me want to yank his hand off hers, pull her against me and show her who she should be in love with. But I also rarely saw this relaxed playful side of Miranda. Tonight's win really lightened her mood, and I didn't want to ruin that. So I clenched my fists at my sides and gave a tight smile of warning.

"Which is why all our drinks will be on the house," she finished.

Lester removed his hand at that. "Sorry sweetheart, I think we should see other people."

Miranda laughed, in a full belly relaxed way I'd never seen. "Drats! Well, it was worth a try."

I grabbed her free hand and dragged her over to the pool table, knowing Lester would bring our drinks over. The way her hand felt in mine sent hot shocks up my palm and into my bones. Fuck, it felt so right to be near her.

Reluctantly, I let her hand go and picked up a couple pool cues. "Would you play with me?"

Lester silently dropped off our drinks with a wink before taking off again, leaving us to our private corner of the bar.

"Another game? I thought we'd had enough of those for one night."

I shrugged, hoping against hope. Just when I thought she'd shut it all down and walk out, she picked up one of the sticks. "Prepare to have your ass kicked, god of none."

"I don't care how you touch my ass, as long as you're doing it," I breathed, shooting her a leering smile. Miranda shook her head, even as she bent over to pull the ball rack out. My stomach jumped up into my throat before falling as her perfect rear was put on display for my view.

Memories of plowing into her tight body on that medieval bed in that theater came back in slow-mo technicolor, making my throat dry and my shorts instantly tighter. "How about we make things more interesting?" I asked, my voice a dry rasp.

Miranda lifted that perfectly arched eyebrow as she racked the balls.

"A little game called truth or dare. Every time you sink a ball, you get to pose a truth or dare to the other person."

Maybe I was pushing my luck too far. Miranda didn't want me poking around in her head, and as much as I didn't want my brain poked either, I was desperate to get past all those defenses.

Miranda licked her lips in a slow, torturous movement that made me want to capture those swollen petals into a kiss so hot her clothes would melt off. Instead, I gripped the pool cue with all my strength, doing my best not to crack it.

"Deal," she finally said.

There was something in her eyes that told me I might have made a massive mistake.

She leaned over, thrust the stick until the crack of balls broke the air and two solids disappeared into a corner pocket.

"Tell me about Aten, and how we can kill him."

Well, fuck, that turned on me fast.

Chapter Twenty-One

THE BADASS

Xander's relaxed grin twisted into a snarl, shoulders tensing and flexing. "You won't be going anywhere near Aten."

I resisted the urge to fight him. I knew by now that both of us were equally stubborn. If I wanted information, I'd have to take a different tactic.

"Fine," I lied. "But I still want to know. If I'm to be blamed for bringing back the biggest, baddest god of them all, what exactly has everyone shaking in their boots?"

Xander circled the pool table, examining the lineup of balls, his face still arranged in a grim expression. "He's not the biggest or baddest, he's just..."

He trailed off, and I mentally filled in for him, "...*the one who killed me.*"

That did put me on guard. The thought of Xander burning under Aten's power made me queasy anytime I thought about it.

"You should listen to him," Bob advised. He was fastened back to my hip and thankfully hadn't said anything about our detour.

I spoke to him with my mind. *It's my duty, my responsibility to put the cat—er, the sun god—back in the bag. No matter what either of you think, it is what it is.*

Xander picked up where he left off, "He's a sadistic bastard. Greedy, twisted, and I wouldn't let him within a thousand-foot radius of you if I could help it."

"So how was he killed?" I asked again, bringing my point back around even as I took another shot at a solid-colored ball. It sunk into the corner pocket. A smug grin curved up on one side of my face. I batted my eyelashes at him expectantly.

Xander shook his head, the unkempt hair swinging over his eyes with the movement. "I don't know. When I emerged from the cradle, I was out of my mind for I don't know how long. Grim and Timothy were able to sequester me for a time, but eventually they realized I was too close to the seas to be trusted. Egypt suffered floods and storms unlike any other until they moved to a place far from any open body of water."

"You're the reason all the gods are in Nevada?" I completed for him, the awe in my voice evident to my own ears. Xander was the very reason everyone had to pack up and move to a desert in North America.

I lined up another shot but missed. To realize the beast the Grim Reaper kept in the basement of his hotel all these years was the reason the gods resided in Las Vegas now was mind-blowing. From what I understood, most of the gods were not aware of what Grim had kept locked away, or rather *who*. They simply knew the portal to the After-life and the hub of all human souls was here, so they had to be here as well.

Osiris forbade them all from taking worshippers a long time ago because gods had become too powerful, domineering, and cruel. They could only stay powerful if they were near the well of souls that Grim reaped from this world.

I doubted Grim would love that I knew all this, but give Vivien a moisturizing face mask, some sliced cucumbers for her eyes, and two dozen pink frosted cupcakes at girls' night and she would spill anything.

Xander nodded. "Eventually, I came somewhat to my senses and Grim explained that because of my sacrifice the other gods were moved to action, and they took Aten out. But not without great cost.

Many were slain and sent back to the cradle of life. And of those, I believe few, if any, have reemerged." He bent over and his stick met the white ball with a loud crack. Three striped balls fell into two separate pockets.

"I still get another truth," I pointed out before he got ahead of himself.

That sly grin returned, making my heart flutter. It was that, or maybe the way his ass looked as he bent over to take his shot.

Xander shook his head. "Nuh, uh. You asked if I'm why the gods are in Vegas. That's your second truth. And if you keep pouting like that—" He slid closer to me, eyes still coolly scanning the pool table, though I could feel the heat of his body seep into my side. "—I'm going to kiss and lick that expression right of your gorgeous fucking face."

His words hit my spine like an electric shock, and I forgot to breathe. Sweat broke out between my breasts as my skin tingled and ached in anticipation.

I picked up my beer and took a generous swallow, trying to cool down.

"Truth or dare, sweetheart," he posed casually, rubbing the chalk on the end of his stick.

I never knew what a loaded question that could be until this moment.

"Dare," I said, trying to be nonchalant, but my insides quaked. I set my hip against the pool table, pretending to be unaffected. Pretending I wasn't anticipating him taking advantage of me.

How did he do that? A moment ago I was all consumed with pumping him for information, and now I wanted him to pump me in other ways. Again.

Xander took my pool cue and set both of them aside, turning to face me. "I dare you to close your eyes and not open them again until I tell you."

I frowned.

A spark glimmered in his eyes in response. "Ah, I knew you wouldn't do it."

My frown only deepened. I thought he was going to dare me to kiss him or something. Instantly, my hackles rose at the suggestion. We were in a crowded bar, well, semi-crowded. I wasn't super familiar with my surroundings, and it felt wrong to submit to Xander's dare.

He tilted his head. "I can almost see the smoke coming out of your ears from overthinking this."

I thought he meant it as a dig, but Xander merely studied my expression with open fascination. As if I were the most interesting person in the world.

"What do you think will happen?" he asked in a low husky voice. "Do you fear the second you close your eyes, one of these guys is going to spring upon us with a knife? That a god will pop out of nowhere and attack? That you won't be in complete control of your environment?"

I hated, absolutely fucking hated that exact scenario had run through my mind already.

"And you think I'd let anything or anyone remotely near you?" One of his brows arched in question. He wasn't touching me, but he stood so close I continued to breathe in his heat.

I narrowed my eyes at him, letting him know I wasn't happy with this before letting my lids flutter close.

"Now what?" I asked, deliberately sounding annoyed.

"Now..." he trailed off, and I could sense him watching me. I wasn't sure if it made me more nervous, or if I just felt stupid with my eyes shut in the middle of the bar. "Now you wait."

"I can't believe you're wasting a dare on this," I snorted. My skin prickled with unease. The sounds of clinking glasses, low chatter, and the jukebox in the background were all too indistinct and too acute at the same time.

While Xander stood in front of me, my back felt unprotected and exposed. I shrugged my shoulders a couple of times, feeling stupider and more vulnerable by the minute.

When he spoke again it was even lower than before. "You are perfectly safe."

I snorted.

My doubt did nothing to ruffle his quiet, even tone. "I would never let anything happen to you, Miranda. If you want, you can relax your shoulders."

"They're fine the way they are," I argued, feeling saltier by the minute.

Why didn't he just kiss me and get this over with?

"Okay," he replied smoothly, as if completely unphased by my thorniness. "Then keep them tense if that makes you feel better."

I hated how that immediately made them fall a couple inches.

His voice, rich and soothing, continued to flow over me. "But just know, you don't always have to be on guard. Not with me. I've got you."

There was a pause, a breath of silence that seemed to stretch between us, filled with the unspoken.

The memory of him after I brought him back from the blade slammed into my brain as it had done so many times in the last month, making my stomach tense and my throat to start to close.

A mask of betrayal and seething hatred twisted his features. I was sure it was for me. Even though Xander told me at the time he'd only been thinking of Aten, I didn't believe him. I deserved his scorn, his disappointment.

My throat closed up even more.

"Miranda," he murmured, and I could almost picture the gentle tilt of his head, the way his eyes would soften when he looked at me. "Whatever you're thinking right now, it's just a thought. It's not real. Whatever attack you are making on yourself, you don't have to."

I was about to open my mouth and tell him off for telling me what to do, but then he said, "But if you want to keep fighting yourself I'll just stand right here with you, and remind you to feel the floor under your feet, the way your clothes wrap around your body. Focus on the sound of my voice."

The angry, self-loathing thoughts began to slip away. Was I being hypnotized again? Had he been hanging out with Max and Alfonso, picking up tips?

I felt or maybe heard him shift his stance, though he came no closer.

"Trust is a hard thing to give, especially when you've been through what you have. But I want you to know you can trust me. I'm here, right in front of you, and I'm not going anywhere."

I bit my lip, the knot of tension in my stomach loosening slightly at his words. It was ridiculous how just a few sentences from him could start to chip away at the walls I'd meticulously built around myself.

"You can let go, even if it's just for now. Let yourself feel, Miranda. It's okay." His voice was almost a whisper now, a caress against the tension that held my body rigid.

And so, I tried. I consciously relaxed my shoulders, letting the tension seep out with a long exhale. The sounds of the bar seemed to fade into the background along with my wariness, leaving only Xander's voice, steady and sure.

"Good," he praised, and I could hear the smile in his voice. "How do you feel?"

"Vulnerable," I admitted, but the word didn't hold the usual weight of fear. It felt different this time—safer, somehow.

"That's okay. Vulnerability isn't a weakness, especially not with me. It's strength, Miranda. The strength to show your true self, to let someone in."

"And you? What does this make you feel?"

He chuckled, a sound that vibrated through the space between us. "Honored to be near. Fiercely protective. And... incredibly drawn to you."

The air between us seemed to spark with his admission, sending a thrill down my spine.

"Can I open my eyes now?" I asked. "You've used up a dare and a truth." He asked me how I was feeling. I was counting that against him. Even though he could do the same thing since I asked the question back.

"Not yet," he said, and I could hear him moving closer. "I've got one more. Truth or dare, Miranda?" A shiver ran up my spine at the way he said my name.

Seeing how he'd used the dare against me in ways I couldn't have anticipated, I knew what to choose this time. My breath hitched. "Truth."

"Do you love me?"

I opened my eyes though he didn't tell me I could. The world had somehow narrowed down to just him. Xander gazed down at me from under his long hair, eyes somehow piercing and vulnerable at the same time. His hand was on the pool table next to my body, but not touching me. He was as close as he could get to me without crossing any real line.

"Dare." There was no fucking way I was answering that.

A wry smile twitched at the corner of his lips. "I dare you to let me in."

He'd backed me into a corner. I either answered if I loved him or let him in. I didn't want to do either.

Though right now, in my relaxed state it felt almost too easy to do both.

He broke into a chuckle, taking a step back while shoving his hands in his pockets. My heart plunged into the space between us and it was like falling off a cliff.

His tone turned light and teasing. "You already owe me a date, but maybe I should use my dare to force you to pick the place and time."

The tension broke. As if he knew he'd crossed a line and went too far, he gave me space and room to breathe. Half of me was grateful. The other half of me wanted him to push me, force me to do what I wouldn't allow myself to.

"I'll take that dare," I said, quickly finishing my beer. "Tomorrow night, eight PM, the Florence hotel."

Xander's face shut down, all his emotions bleeding away from view. "The god's ball." The words came out flat and cold.

"Yes," I said, suddenly aware I was on unsteady ground.

"Why?"

He didn't just ask why, the betrayal stamped in his eyes asked *why would you dare bring this up?*

Tell him. Tell him he gives you strength.

Tell him part of you is afraid to face the hatred of all the immortals and wear your shame like a large red painted letter.

That he gives you strength, and you are starting to learn to love that.

That you're starting to learn to lov—

"Because I think you need it. It would be good for you," I blurted before I could finish the thought in my idiotic head.

Coward.

"Good for me?" he scoffed, picking up his pool cue again. He leaned over and took another shot at the balls. They clacked around the green felt but none of them found a pocket.

"You are one of them, Xander. You act... you act like you're alone, but you're not. You are one of the gods." A laugh of disbelief bubbled out of me. "I know it will take time to get used to this new world, but instead of taking your place above ground, you've retreated to another underground cave." I opened my arms indicating the dive bar. "You're hiding from what you are. From who you are and could be. Timothy told me you have the right to a hotel on the Strip, with wealth beyond imagining at your fingertips. And here you are, down in the muck, buying cheap Hawaiian shirts and acting like you're just another face in the crowd. But you're not."

His body tensed with every word, his emotionless face somehow becoming more distant and foreboding.

"You're telling me to join the ranks of my kind? What about you, Miranda?" He closed the distance between us again. Though he spoke softly in my ear, it felt as if he was yelling the words. "You either think you are invincible, or are willing to be a sacrifice because you deserve to be punished. And or what?"

I squeezed my eyes shut as his accusations hit me like physical blows. He didn't understand because I hadn't told him.

It wasn't a dog who died because I fucked up.

It was worse. So much worse. I never deserved to be forgiven for it.

"But let me tell you, sweetheart, I was the sacrifice for my kind. I warned them of Aten, and they didn't listen.

"Do you know when I asked for help, when I tried to warn everyone, they did everything from spit on me to kick sand in my face? They were more interested in fucking and feasting than helping me do what must be done. I gave up my life trying to stop him, and only *after* did anyone do anything about it. Do you think during the thousands of years I spent in the bowels of this desert—in agony, in unrelenting pain and imprisonment—I thought those arrogant narcissists were worth my life, my pain?"

So that would be a no.

"I'm not returning to the fold. I like being another face in the crowd. I like cheap T-shirts. I like spending my time with a human, which is something they would also sneer and spit on me for. Fuck them. Fuck that life. The only thing I want is you. I guarantee the second they think I intend on being with you without turning you into my sekhor, they will do everything they can to stop me or change you themselves."

I reared back. It was as if he slapped me, his confession snatching the breath from my lungs. "I would never choose to be a vampire."

His gaze dropped to my mouth with a cruel, knowing smile. I realized I was baring my teeth at him in challenge.

"You think I don't know that? That you would never abandon your child, your family to choose a life amongst the immortals?"

Something akin to grief or resignation glimmered in his eyes before it disappeared in his rage.

"Those assholes can burn for all I care."

With that, he turned and left the bar. He only stopped to throw some bills on the counter for our drinks. Lester barely looked up as he grabbed the green, knowing damn well how to mind his business.

I clutched the edge of the pool table, most of my weight supported by my arms as my legs felt like shaky noodles.

I didn't tell him I would be going tomorrow. That I would face them all alone. And that's how I felt now. Utterly and totally alone, and for once I didn't want that.

I wanted Xander by my side. Which didn't make any sense because this was messy and we were both fucked up and this would never work.

So why did my heart beat so hard, so painfully, pounding out his name over and over in my chest all the way home?

Chapter Twenty-Two

THE BADASS

I've been sleeping less and less. I can't tell if it's due to the insufferable heat that grows more intense by the day, or because Xander is knocking around inside my head.

Still splayed out on my bed above the covers, I rub my hands over my face. Jamal is at school and Mama Jean is out with her friends for lunch.

The bed shifts under the weight of someone new. A warm, fuzzy head drops on my stomach. I look down into big beautiful puppy dog eyes that seem to feel all of my pain, confusion, and uncertainty. The warm weight on my stomach instantly grounds me, and I feel my anxiety drop a couple notches. Which is confusing as hell considering Xander is the one who gave me Heinz.

Another wave of gut gnawing guilt plowed into me.

I still can't believe what happened yesterday. From killing a god, to the absolutely depraved things we did in that arcade, to Xander's sudden outburst and exit from the bar.

It feels like I'm living another life at night. Like I'm another person. But which one is the real me?

"Maybe both are you?"

I huffed. "Bob, could you pretend you aren't there and able to hear my every thought?"

"I could," he said carefully, "but I think you've been alone with your thoughts long enough."

"You're right," I said, sitting up. "I should head to the gym if I can't sleep."

Heinz sat up with me and firmly pressed his paws into my chest, forcing me back down.

"Heinz and I agree," Bob went on. "You need to be more forgiving of yourself."

My hand automatically went to Heinz's soft head, which was especially absurd because the dog just bullied me back down.

"What?" I asked. "You and the dog are conspiring against me now too?"

"Yes, but only in the most loving, supportive way."

"I liked it better when you were mute," I grumbled.

"Now we both know that's not true. Though I can't say I'm thrilled to be in the world, sucking down the blood of others. Blech."

Heinz let out a yip.

"Care to translate?" I said, dryly.

"Heinz thinks you should tell Xander the truth about your past."

Okay, I hadn't actually expected him to translate. I'd been joking.

"And the dog knows everything too? You been having a lot of time to spill the tea together?" I couldn't deny the sharp slice of betrayal that Bob told the dog about my past. Then I couldn't deny that this entire situation was fucking bonkers.

Bob sighed. "The dog is from the afterlife. Just assume he probably knows more than even me."

"And now he's a house pet, dining on kibble and named after a condiment."

"Heinz quite likes his name and when Xander went looking for your lost loved one, Heinz volunteered to come back to be with you and Jamal."

Emotion swelled in my chest though I couldn't name it. Grief, gratitude, guilt? Definitely one of the Big Gs.

"That's it," I said, lifting the dog with both hands before gently putting him on the ground and getting to my feet. "Enough therapy from supernatural creatures and objects today."

Despite my irritation with Bob, I took him into the kitchen with me. I put the kettle on, though I didn't really feel like having any tea. Heinz followed closely at my heels Apparently he felt he needed to be heard.

"This is crazy," I muttered.

"Of course it is," Bob said, though I really hadn't been looking for his input. "But what's making it more difficult is you aren't allowing it to be what it is."

"What does that mean?" I asked with a frustrated sigh, pulling at my braids.

I really should be resting. Tonight was the immortal ball and I would basically be put on trial in front of everyone. A piece of bait in a shark pit. I should be preparing my mind to be strong. Instead, I was unraveling faster and faster.

"It means you aren't just one thing. You try to put everything into neat little boxes, and you put the ugliest things in boxes, burying them six feet under and never pulling them out again. Xander is making you feel and be everything at once and it's confusing. Let it be confusing. You are not any one thing:mother, warrior, sinner, lover—"

"Have you been listening to Meredith Brooks?" I asked, cocking a hand on my hip with suspicion.

The sentient blade went on as if he didn't hear me. "You are all things at one time. It's messy, Miranda. Being human is messy."

I made a retching sound of disgust.

Heinz dropped onto my feet, looking up at me again with those big doleful eyes as if to say, *You should really listen to him. We both feel this way.*

"Xander is your equal opposite. He cannot control himself."

"That's not true," I snapped. "Serqet almost pushed him past the edge, and he came back to himself before he lost it." Not that I knew what that looked like anymore.

I suspected it had to do with him turning into his god-likeness, a monster of epic proportions that was out of its mind with pain and power. But Xander was divested of his excess of power.

"You pulled him from the brink, just as he pushes you out of your little tidy boxes that are slowly rotting and decaying in the ground."

The kettle whistled until I lifted it off the burner, making no move to make tea.

"Have you always been so keen to get a word in on your wielder's behavior, or am I just lucky?" I asked, suddenly feeling tired.

"I've never been wielded by a mortal before," Bob confessed quietly. "And I must say, it has been the best experience I've ever had by far."

I swallowed hard, the room suddenly feeling too quiet, too hot and heavy.

"Why's that?" I didn't really want to ask, but I knew he'd hear the question in my mind.

"I have been a weapon of destruction for thousands of years," Bob said solemnly. "But in your hands, I have found purpose beyond bloodshed. You are a wielder of compassion and strength, Miranda. It brings me solace to serve someone who values more than just power." Heinz nudged my leg with his nose, as if in agreement with Bob's words.

I leaned against the kitchen counter, feeling the weight of Bob's words settling around me like a heavy cloak.

"It's also why Heinz came along. He recognized Xander was looking for something in the afterlife, and once he learned of you, the pup realized he wanted to be with you."

My hand dropped to scratch Heinz's head, causing his tail to wag enthusiastically.

The reality of my situation—preparing for the Immortal Ball, navigating the complexities of my relationships, and coming to terms with my own identity—seemed even more daunting now. But a warmth spread from the center of my chest at Bob's words.

Suddenly being human didn't seem as bad as it had a moment ago.

I jerked when my phone buzzed on the counter. Grabbing it, I answered as soon as I saw who it was.

"Hey Timothy—" I started.

"I know we are to meet much later to prepare for the evening's events," he rambled in a hurried rush. "But there is a situation I feel you may be suited to—"

"Spit it out," I commanded.

He sighed on the other side of the line. "It's Xander."

Chapter Twenty-Three

THE BADASS

Xander was where Timothy said, standing in the Menaggio fountains. The god was completely naked, in the middle of the jets of water rocketing into the sky in time with music and lights.

The crowd surrounded the edges, entirely focused on the man standing waist deep in the water. Phone cameras were out documenting the crazy guy yelling and splashing in the water.

As I approached the edge of the fountain, Grim and Timothy stood side by side, their expressions a blend of concern and impatience. Grim, drenched from head to toe, appeared particularly irritable, water dripping from his soaked clothes onto the pavement, casting a dour shadow.

Steering clear of the pissed off and wet god of the dead, I sidled up next to Timothy. He was furiously tapping on his tablet. "What is Xander doing?"

Grim growled from the other side of Timothy.

Timothy paused, raising his head. "Losing his mind and making a scene I'll have to clean up."

A delivery man, uniform slightly askew and pushing a heavily laden cart, maneuvered through the crowd towards us. He locked eyes with Grim, an air of determination in his stride.

"Excuse me, sir?" he called out, pulling a small, oddly shaped package from his cart. "I have a delivery that requires your signature."

Grim glanced at Timothy with a raised eyebrow before turning back to the man with the cart. "This isn't a good time."

The courier shrugged as he chewed his gum in loud, open mouth smacks. The guy had no idea he'd chosen to face off with a god who could rip his soul from his body. "I can't leave until you sign and take your delivery, and I've got at least fifty more stops. The longer you take, the more people you'll be denying their important packages."

Grim snorted like a bulldog but acquiesced, stepping forward to meet the postman. He quickly scribbled his signature on the electronic pad, eager to dismiss the interruption and return his focus to the unfolding drama at the fountains.

However, as soon as Grim's signature completed the transaction, the delivery man, with a practiced motion that suggested he'd done this more times than one would expect, swung the small package directly into Grim's face. The package burst open upon impact to reveal it was, in fact, a pillow—a very soft, very non-threatening pillow.

The exchange was so out of context, it left me blinking in confusion.

The crowd that had gathered, initially tense with the anticipation of conflict, erupted into a mixture of laughter and applause at the absurdity of the situation. Grim, momentarily stunned, touched his face where the pillow had made contact, then looked at the courier with a mix of disbelief and outrage.

Completely nonplussed and shrugging as if this was just another day on the job, the man muttered, "My job gets weirder every day," before turning on his heel and walking away. He left Grim holding the pillow, a physical reminder of the unpredictability of his marriage.

"As if it isn't enough, I've been nearly drowned today." Grim shook his head as he turned his attention back to the fountain.

Determined not to get caught up in Grim and Vivien's ludicrous war, or newfound love language, I turned back to the person making a far bigger scene.

"Xander isn't doing anything godly that would draw suspicion," I pointed out. "He just looks like some crazy guy having a mental breakdown." Despite my dismissal, something inside me felt off kilter. As if my senses were telling me there was something very wrong that shouldn't be laughed off here.

"Oh?" Timothy raised an eyebrow as he pursed his lips. "What if I were to tell you those fountains aren't supposed to go off for another twenty minutes?"

I did a double take. "*He's* doing that?"

A jet exploded into the air like a geyser, far past what the Menaggio fountains were capable of. "Why don't you go in and get him?"

Grim flapped his hands at his own body with wet slaps as if to show he had tried.

Timothy snorted. "Oh we tried. *His majesty* blasts anyone who comes within striking distance of the edge. I'm working on getting a special tranquilizer gun delivered for our friend here."

"I'm going to lock his ass back up in the cage and put a collar on him this time," Grim muttered, more to himself.

I licked my lips, my heart pounding against my ribs, knowing what I was about to do. Slipping off my coat, I walked toward the edge of the fountain.

"Miranda, what are you doing?" Timothy called out in a panic.

I set my coat over the lip of the pool and shot back, "This is what you called me for. He won't hurt me." Throwing first one leg over, then the other, I dropped into the chest-high water.

"You don't know that," Timothy countered.

He won't.

"Miranda, think this through," Grim shouted after me.

Ignoring Timothy's and Grim's attempts to intervene, I knew it was up to me to reach Xander. As bizarre as the pillow attack was, it reminded me that sometimes the unexpected could break through the chaos. Maybe, just maybe, I could be Xander's unexpected moment of clarity.

Meanwhile, on the other side, more hotel security attempted to get into the fountain to pull the crazy naked man out. A strange cackling laugh, halfway to a hysterical hyena came out of Xander as he slammed his hands on the water. Shoots of water plowed through the men, hurling them back twenty feet until they crashed into the crowd of people watching. Screams and cries filled the air, but it was all background noise as I made my way toward Xander and keyed in on his strange chatter.

"It's no good, it's no good captain. This isn't your boat. You have no ship. You are lost at sea."

The strange cadence of his words reminded me of when he'd been in the cage, trapped and driven mad by his own power. My brows furrowed as something tightened in my chest. The madness he's exhibited should have been long gone after his rebirth from the blade.

The god turned as if sensing my approach. The crowd sucked in a collective gasp as if expecting him to blow me away next.

"Xander," I called out, wading my way slowly but surely toward him.

Turquoise eyes had turned stormy and unfocused, and for a moment he didn't recognize me. Xander's mouth moved as if he were still talking to himself in a jumble of nonsense.

My skin prickled with the realization Timothy could be right and Xander might view me as an enemy.

"What did I tell you about a shirt and shoes?" I called out in a taunt, hoping to snap him out of it. "And now you can't even be bothered with pants?"

Xander's eyes narrowed as he focused on me with all the attention of a predator, assessing if another being was adversary or prey. I stood my ground, unafraid.

"Miranda," he said my name with a growl, finally recognizing me. "You shouldn't be here."

My heart leapt in my chest upon hearing his voice, but it wasn't the warm, tender tones he would use when we were together. It was cold, distant, and filled with suspicion.

"Taking up the hobby of streaking?" I kept talking, keeping his attention on me. "Or is this another one of your ill-begotten attempts to seduce me?"

Xander's lips twisted into a smirk. "I don't need to seduce you,

Miranda. You're already mine." His words were laced with a possessiveness that sent a shiver down my spine.

I forced myself to remain calm even as my heart raced in my chest. "I belong to no one, Xander. You know that."

"Do I?" His voice was low and dangerous. "You're always finding your way back to me, no matter how hard you try to resist."

I swallowed hard.

"Xander, you need to come with me," I said firmly, still wading toward him. "You're scaring the guests and causing a scene."

He laughed, the sound manic and unhinged. "I'm not going anywhere, Miranda. Not until I've found what I'm looking for."

"And what's that?" I asked, treading carefully.

"My place." Xander suddenly looked stricken as he parted the water with his hands, looking down into the liquid as if he could find what he sought there.

"Your place?" I asked, stopping a few feet away from him.

"Yes, yes," he mumbled. "I've lost it. I belong nowhere. I've been lost in time and space, and I lost it, lost my place."

My lips parted as my heart cracked a little. "Xander," I said softly. In that moment, I wished I knew where he'd been staying. I didn't know where he was sleeping after being confined to an underground prison for so long. He needed something tangible—an address, something.

"You belong. I know you've been gone from the world a while, but you'll adapt. I promise."

Xander's agitation grew as he tunneled through the water more insistently. "No, no, no, no." Then his eyes squeezed shut as he clenched his fists shut. "It's not here. *I'm* not here. I can't find my place."

Those fists rose then slammed back into the water, causing a geyser to blast off. For a moment, I thought a bomb hit me. My hands clapped over my ears. I barely heard the screams and cries of the bystanders.

"Xander," I yelled. "You have to stop."

Cracking an eye open I found Xander's face contorted and mouth open in agony as the water continued to flow and explode all around us, but he never blasted me out. I wanted to cling to him, ground him in safety. So I did just that. Stumbling forward in water that was now only knee deep, I threw myself at him.

More water bombs went off.

"Xander," I yelled, plastered to his body. "It's okay, I'm here. You have a place with me. You're safe, everything is okay."

Underneath me, his body shuddered as if explosions similar to the water around us were taking place in his cells.

My hand gripped the hair at the nape of his neck, holding him to me, trying to ground him.

The silence that followed was deafening after the cacophony. Two strong arms wrapped me up and Xander held me to him until only my tip toes touched the ground.

In that moment, with Xander's form trembling against mine, a realization struck me like a bolt. He was a powerful god who commanded the elements, yes, but beneath that, he was achingly vulnerable. Here he was, lost and seeking a place in a world that had moved on without him. My throat tightened at the thought and a wave of tenderness washed over me.

His confession, raw and honest, sliced through the barriers I'd built around my heart. "I think I'm lost," he murmured, his voice a mix of despair and desperation.

Sharp pricks jabbed at the back of my eyes, emotion clogging my throat. "You aren't lost. I've got you." My voice was steady despite the turmoil churning inside me. Here, in the midst of the chaos he'd unintentionally wrought, I found a truth I'd been reluctant to admit—even to myself. I cared for Xander, not just as a god, or a fighting partner, but as the complex, fractured soul he was.

"I'm so sorry, Miranda. I'm sorry for everything." He clung to me like a lifeline, like his salvation.

The moisture in my eyes formed a tear, sliding over my cheek. I couldn't say it back, but I was sorry too. I wasn't even sure what for. For him? For me? For the pain he was in, for the mistakes I'd made?

That his apology was unnecessary because I found his flaws as lovable as his strength?

As we stood there, his arms wrapped tightly around me, I realized that his strength wasn't just in his godly powers, but in his willingness to show his vulnerabilities. In that vulnerability, I understood him more deeply than I had anyone else. And it scared me—how much I wanted to do the same. To let him see me as completely as he showed himself. Though it terrified me to my core.

After a long moment, when I was sure my heart wouldn'texplode in my chest, I said, "We need to get out of here." Side eyeing the crowd that had massively thinned out, I could see there were still phones held out, capturing our incredibly private moment. We needed to be anywhere but here.

Meeting Timothy's eye, he gave me a grave nod.

"Where do I go?" Xander's voice broke on the question.

"Where do you want to go?" I countered, letting him make the choice to find his own anchor.

"To where it's safe," he said, a note of hopelessness in his tone that clawed at my insides.

"Where is that?" I asked, my heart in my throat.

Was he about to tell me where he'd been for so many weeks after I resurrected him?

His eyes met mine, and in them, I saw a reflection of my own longing for acceptance, for a place to call safe. "Where we first met," he said, and the simplicity of his answer—the longing for a connection to a moment in time when things were less complicated, less burdened by the weight of the world—broke me.

Chapter Twenty-Four

THE BEAST

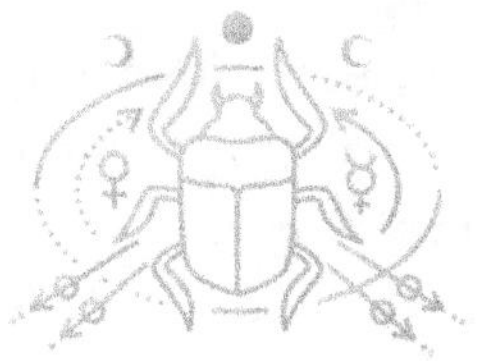

"Close the door, please," I asked, my voice hoarse. Bees and gnats still buzzed around my head.

Miranda pulled the massive cage door shut, but she closed it behind her, shutting herself in with me. I'd put some pants on that Timothy had at the ready when Miranda led me out of the fountains.

Instantly, the clank of my cage allowed me a sense of safety and assurance.

"You don't need to stay," I said more gruffly than I needed to.

Make her stay.

Make her leave.

Tell her to go away, not to look upon you like this.

Go drown in the ocean, drown,

drown,

drown.

"Hey," she said, snapping my attention to her. "Stay with me. I'm not going anywhere right now."

I grabbed my hair and yanked as I bent over, emotions and feelings drowning me in a confusing chaos, topped by a massive dose of shame. The sensation of fracturing from within is a constant companion, a reminder that I'm a mosaic of broken pieces, sharp and jagged, dangerous to the touch, even to myself.

"Xander, what's happening, talk to me," Miranda said quietly.

With every erratic beat of my heart, a new crack splinters through my psyche, widening the gaps where madness seeps in, whispering seductive lies of endless despair.

"I'm broken, sweetheart." That unhinged titter of laughter escaped me. "I tried... I tried to hide it. I tried to heal it. I tried to make it go away for you, you, you."

I blinked and found myself across the room, though I didn't remember moving. Miranda studied me intently and her gaze felt like razor blades slicing through my flesh.

It reminded me of all the times she killed me with the blade on her hip.

I wanted to taste it right now. It would silence my mind. I needed silence so badly. I needed to prove to her I could be still, be whole.

"I thought your powers weren't out of control anymore," she said quietly.

There's a hollowness echoing within me, each pulse a reminder of the chasm between who I am and who I yearn to be, a gulf filled with the debris of shattered dreams and unattainable peace.

Another hyena laugh tipped out of me. "It's not my power."

And even though I was still ancient and primal, and my mind was still racing with thoughts of the outside world, I knew in this moment, I was exactly where I belonged.

I paced to the far end of my cage and back again. Again and again. I did it for years. I'd continue to do it for years.

"It's not my power, it's my brain. It's broken. I'm broken. I didn't want you to see." A sob lodged itself in my throat, and I refused to let it out. If I did, an ocean would rush out behind it.

I wasn't making sense.

I'm never making any godsdamn sense.

"You thought I hated you. I could never hate you. That would be like hating oxygen. But I didn't deserve oxygen." Or was I supposed to say I didn't deserve her? "I tried to hide it from you. I didn't want you to see. So I hid away. I tried to be like you. I tried to control it. I tried to be steady. I tried to be what you needed, but I'm not."

My hands wrapped around the bars as I confessed all my dirty little secrets to her. "Outside of here, this world is too big. It's too bright. There are too many people. I don't understand what anyone is saying. They type on tiny devices and they don't look up. The lights up there are so bright they burn. The sounds of slot machines are machine guns against my brain. I can't, I can't, I can't be calm!" I was yelling now. Not at her. Never at her.

I was yelling over the pain and confusion in my brain as my stomach and chest constricted so tightly, I thought my organs would collapse inside me. But they wouldn't, they never did.

"But I practiced. I practiced so hard. Be normal, Xander. Be steady, Nun. Calm the waters inside, she needs calm waters. And I tried to calm them until I could come out. Come out to you."

When I turned to look at her, Miranda was still there. For some reason I expected her to be gone. My voice dropped to a whisper. I desperately didn't want to yell anymore.

"You have a name for this now," I said with another hysterical titter of laughter. "Crazy. I am crazy, Miranda. Things burn inside my brain, but I don't want to burn you." I slowly made my way toward her. She didn't move but her shoulders tensed.

"So, I come here and lock in all of my crazy." I needed her to understand. I failed, but I tried so hard, so very hard to be better, to be what she needed. I dropped to my knees before her.

Every attempt to tame my own traitorous brain was a battle lost before it began. My insides churned with a maelstrom of emotions, each one a sharp reminder of the fractured existence I couldn't escape. Miranda's presence here, in this space that represented my failures and fears, only amplified the turmoil. I'd spent countless moments, hidden in the shadows, trying to piece myself back together, to be someone worthy of standing by her side. The irony wasn't lost on me that in seeking to protect her from my chaos, I've only drawn her deeper into my storm.

The pressure to be what Miranda needs—a pillar of strength in her world of uncertainties—felt like chains around my chest, tightening with every breath. I wanted to come back to her, whole, healed, a beacon of stability in the tumultuous sea of her life. Yet, here I am, disintegrating before her eyes, a testament to my inadequacies.

The realization hit like a physical blow, leaving me gasping for air in the suffocating space between who I am and who I desperately want to be. For her. When my voice fractured the silence, it carried the weight of my brokenness as I confessed my deepest fears and failures in a raw outpouring I couldn't contain.

"I tried to be a man for you, but I'm not. I'm not a man. I'm not a god. I'm just pieces smushed together."

My arms wrapped around her strong legs as I buried my face in her stomach. I kept my hold light, as if she was as fragile as glass.

Fingers stroked the top of my head and I shuddered under her touch.

"I'm so sorry. I'm so sorry, Miranda." I needed her forgiveness so desperately, but I didn't deserve it. Yet I begged for it anyway.

"Shh," she hushed, continuing to stroke the hair on my head in a soothing manner until I sagged against her.

I didn't want to look at her face. I was too afraid to see what was there, and even more ashamed that I couldn't bring myself to face her.

She pulled at my arm after I quieted, bringing me to my feet, but I still couldn't bring myself to look at her face.

Thankfully, she didn't ask me. Instead, she drew me toward the back of my cage to where the light disappeared, and a hidden door lay. She pushed it open and led me down the stone steps into the rest of my enclosure.

I'd been to a zoo now, and I knew that's exactly what this was. An enclosure like the humans had for dangerous animals.

The humid air wrapped around me like a blanket as the reflection of my stone pools shimmered off the walls. The light was low down here and my shoulders lowered as my stomach stopped clenching. My senses calmed being away from the neon lights set at the front of my cage.

She guided me over to the largest pool and stopped us before yanking her own top off.

I was still turning my head away to keep from looking at Miranda, or maybe to keep her from looking at me.

She continued to undress, then reached for my pants. They dropped to my feet.

Strong, elegant fingers slipped between mine and my hand automatically gripped as if she were my only lifeline. With a tug, she backed into the pool, drawing me along.

The feel of the water along my skin made me catch my breath. It wasn't just any water; it was from the Red Sea. Imported from the shores of Egypt, from home. A place I wasn't allowed to be near again. Not when I made them boil.

Miranda had seen me do that before but this time the water remained blissfully calm. Another shuddering sigh escaped me as I crouched down with her, the water lapping against my neck.

"Look at me," Miranda murmured.

Despite the comfort of this place, I couldn't swallow around the lump still lodged in my throat.

Her hands found my face, forcing me to do what she said.

My heart pounded so hard against my ribs, my bones ached. When I looked into her eyes I saw a deep, cutting sadness that matched my own. Tears streaked down her cheeks.

Did she pity me? Was she sad I broke any chances of being the man she needed? My mind raced to fill in the space.

"I am so sorry," she said, her voice thick with emotion.

Of all the things I expected her to say, I hadn't expected that. I reached for her waist, pulling her over to me. Her legs wrapped around my waist, but she didn't release my face from her grip.

"I'm so sorry you felt you had to hide all the broken parts of yourself from me. I'm so sorry you felt you weren't good enough. The world is often too much for me, and I've been living in it all this time. I can't imagine what you must be going through."

My fingers dug into her sides as her words hit me almost physically.

I managed a small, pained smile, but the lump in my throat still wouldn't budge. "You don't know what you've done for me, Miranda. Without you, I wouldn't have made it this far. You didn't just give me a place to hide, you gave me sanity amidst the chaos." My voice wavered but I pressed on, trying to convey my gratitude.

"I made you feel you weren't enough," she rasped. I shook my head, but her fingers tunneled into my hair, forcing me to stop the motion. "You couldn't allow yourself to be broken with me, because I refused to allow myself to lose control around you."

"You've lost control around me," I countered, though it felt inappropriate to bring up our various sexual trysts. Even the thought of the bed on that stage, her writhing on that arcade game, the way her eyes turned glassy when she came apart under my touch, made my cock harden in the water. I couldn't help it.

Miranda nodded. "I did. I have. And it felt fucking incredible. Terrifying but incredible."

I gathered her closer to me. "I don't want to terrify you."

"I've been terrified of myself. Someone recently told me I should be forgiving of myself, let myself be all the things. Xander, you are *all the things*. The god, the man, you are steady when I need you to be, you are a mess when you have to be, and we need to stop punishing ourselves for all the messy parts."

She pulled back slightly, bringing her lips close to my ear. "And I'm here for you, Xander. I'm here to help you find your way back to yourself. If that means I have to stay in here with you when you need it, then so be it."

With that, her lips brushed against my neck and a jolt of electricity coursed through me. Her warmth seeped into every pore. The tension in my muscles began to dissipate as we held each other.

As we floated there, the darkness around us morphing into a million shades of blue, the sudden surge of relief that flooded through me was so intense and pure. I never knew such an emotion could exist within me.

"Miranda," I whispered her name, but it echoed gently in the cavern. "I love you."

Her response was a sharp inhale, and I wondered if I just undid everything all over again.

Chapter Twenty-Five

THE BADASS

My heart stalled in my chest, the beat replaced by a deafening silence as Xander's words sank in. He wasn't just confessing his feelings, he was handing over his soul to me, bloody pulp that it was, and in this place the declaration was so sacred, tears stung the backs of my eyes again.

Xander went on in a rough voice, "I don't need you to say it back, I just need you to know that in my entire existence I've never felt more alive, more anchored, more terrified, or had more fucking fun than when I'm with you."

My arms tightened around his neck.

"I need to tell you something," I forced through my constricted throat. It felt as though my body was physically trying to hold back the words that were begging to be released.

"The story I told you, about my dog, how I begged my parents for a dog because I would love it and take care of it? There is a reason you couldn't find him in the afterlife."

Self-hatred rose up inside me. My entire being recoiled at being forced to confront this deepest, darkest secret of my past. Every dark, twisted part of my soul curled up tighter at the prospect of being exposed.

To his credit, he didn't ask any questions, just gave me all the runway and space I needed to get the words out.

"It was a sibling I wanted. I wanted a little sister or brother. On my birthday they announced my mom was pregnant and gave me a picture to prove it. I was getting my wish… a little brother. I was more excited about being a big sister than anything and helped take care of him, but after a couple years, he started to get on my nerves and I started to push him away."

The guilt and shame washed over me like a hot wave, threatening to consume me. Knots twisted my stomach until bile rose in my throat. I could barely speak through the lump in my throat as I confessed to Xander. "I was supposed to watch him in the backyard, but I was annoyed and wanted to do my own thing. I wanted to *play*." I said the next part quickly. "He walked out into the street and was hit and killed by a car."

Admitting this truth to Xander felt like standing at the edge of an abyss, the ground crumbling beneath my feet, threatening to swallow me whole. Every word I uttered felt like I was excavating parts of my soul I had kept buried under layers of self-recrimination and denial. The weight of the confession pressed down on me, a tangible force that squeezed the very air from my lungs.

It's not just a secret I was revealing; it was a scar, deep and raw, a wound that never fully healed. No matter where I am, or what I'm doing, that moment always roils at the base of my every move, my every thought.

The silence that followed my confession was suffocating. It was everything about myself I tried to deny and outrun, but my mistake wasn't simply something I did. It was part of me. The vulnerability of this moment overwhelmed me as I laid bare the most broken parts of myself to the one person whose opinion mattered most.

"You were a child," Xander said quietly.

I shook my head, feeling like I had sliced my guts open and they were now floating in the water with us. "That doesn't matter. If I had watched him, if I did what I said I would… if I had been a good big sister, watched over him instead of playing, he would still be alive. He wasn't even three years old."

My parents did their best to keep what happened under wraps, saying they didn't blame me. But I knew the truth. At a young age, I knew my parents would always resent me on some level. It's why we kept in touch mainly via Christmas cards and a bi-yearly update call or email.

"Miranda," Xander's hands lifted from the water, dripping as they clasped my face, forcing me to look at him. "Where were your parents? What was the driver doing? You were a child. Of course you wanted to play."

I shook my head with a crooked smile. "I've tried telling myself all those things, but all I know, in the deepest parts of my soul, is that I wasn't vigilant and when I allowed myself to play, he died. Since then, I've known that every time I've given into that side of myself, the selfish side of myself, something bad would happen."

Shame coils tightly around my heart, a constant reminder of the irrevocable mistake of my past. It's a shadow that's followed me, growing longer with each passing year, a dark specter I could never outrun.

He let out a deep sigh. "When you brought me back, something bad happened."

I nodded. The shame burrowed into my heart, like worms eating their way through an apple.

"I love you, Xander."

He sucked in a breath as if pained, but I knew he was overcome with emotion.

"But I have to confess, I don't know how this works. I don't know how to do this even if I want to. Not to mention the whole other part."

The part I hadn't even allowed myself to entertain because I couldn't get past the first barrier much less the second.

"What other part?"

"You're a god and I'm a mortal."

His face wrenched up as if experiencing physical pain.

"You know I won't turn into a vampire. I have my son, who I love. I don't want to live forever. I want to grow old like Mama Jean. I want to see lines of age on my face. One day, I want to rest in the Afterlife."

Xander's nostrils flared, hands gripping me so hard to him though we both knew it wouldn't be enough to keep us together.

"I know," he said, his voice rough with emotion.

"I don't know how this can work," I repeated in a whisper.

Then he said something that made me feel like I wasn't alone for the first time in I don't even know how long. He ripped the walls down around me, clinging to me, and confessed, "I don't know either."

I wasn't alone, but being with someone I loved didn't keep me from feeling the deepest pits of sadness. So we clung to each other, unsure of what to do next. Or how to be better.

* * *

We moved from the pool to his massive bed, clinging to each other, kissing and touching even as our hearts broke together. As my emotional walls and Xander's big secret dissipated in that pool of water around us, I would have thought nothing could hold us back from each other, but it only seemed to solidify the hopelessness of our situation.

Xander eventually fell asleep, no doubt exhausted from fighting himself. I continued to lie there next to him, combing his hair back as his chest rose and fell steadily. Then I dropped a kiss to Xander's forehead, feeling my heart squeeze so intensely I feared it might implode. I stayed as long as I could before I quietly dressed, gathered my things, and slipped out.

I tried to remind myself there were still gods to hunt and Xander would be by my side as I did so. Instead of putting him off, I'd let him help me. But where would we go from here, him a god and me a mortal? It couldn't last forever. And unfortunately, I needed that certainty.

Xander had my whole heart, but sometimes love wasn't enough. I saw the two paths. One way led to me giving in and becoming a vampire. Vivien would no doubt help me. I'd bond to Xander as his sekhor and drink his blood for all eternity. But I'd resent him. I'd feel robbed of getting to grow old, of the promise of death.

Jamal would get older, he would graduate high school, then college, maybe get married. But as events continued on, I would eventually have to pull away from his life as age refused to show on me. I wanted to hold grandbabies in my arms, stay part of his life the way Mama Jean did with us.

Then there was the thought of outliving my own son, which sent ice cold fear flooding through my veins. No parent should have to outlive their child. Would I hate myself and eventually Xander for choosing a man over my family and how I wanted to live the rest of my life?

Then there was the second route. Xander and I kept things as is, we hunted gods together until I put all of them back into the blade. Even if I completed what seemed like an absolutely impossible task, I knew Xander would stay with me. But how would he feel watching me grow old? The thought of not being able to keep up with him, engage him with my youth and vitality, brought pain too. And one day, he'd be alone. Did that make it my responsibility to try and spend my days trying to nurse his mental state back to health so he could go on after me? Should I encourage him to rejoin the other gods? Help him open up to the possibility of loving someone else?

Selfishness curled sourly in my stomach. I didn't want him to love someone else. I was tired of playing the martyr, but maybe this was the only answer.

Everything in my body felt heavier on the drive home, as if I'd gained twenty pounds of emotional weight.

Pushing open Jamal's door, I found him sprawled on his bed, surrounded by textbooks and scribbling away in his notebook. It helped to know Mama Jean was there when he got home, but I realized I'd been distant lately for a number of reasons. But the kid never seemed to begrudge me for it.

The sight of him so focused and determined sent a wave of love crashing over me, grounding me in the present. Heinz was dutifully resting next to Jamal, receiving the occasional soft pet from my son.

"Hey, buddy," I said, keeping my voice soft as I crossed the room to sit beside him on the bed. "How's homework going?"

Jamal looked up, his expression lighting up in a way that eased the tightness in my chest. "Okay, I guess. Math's a bit tough today."

I glanced at the problems on the page. "Want some help?" I offered, knowing that these moments were the building blocks of our relationship, precious and fleeting.

"Yeah, actually," he said.

As we worked through the problems together, I was struck by the realization of how much I cherished these quiet, ordinary moments. They were a stark contrast to the chaos and danger of my nights, a reminder of what I fought for, what I lived for.

Jamal's laughter filled the room as we cracked a particularly tough problem, and in that laughter, I heard the echoes of a future I longed to be part of. A future where I could watch him grow, celebrate his victories, and support him through his defeats. A future where I could grow old with grace, surrounded by the family I loved.

The thought of becoming immortal, of stepping outside the natural cycle of life and watching from the sidelines as Jamal lived his life without me, was a cold, unfathomable prospect. No amount of time with Xander could compensate for the loss of these simple, human experiences.

My heart was going to break either way.

"You okay, Mom?" Jamal asked.

"Yeah, I'm good, why?"

"You seem sad."

I swallowed over the lump in my throat. My son, eleven going on forty.

"Is it because of Xander?"

"What makes you say that?"

"You were upset when he gave you Heinz." Even as Jamal said the words, his fingers curled protectively into the dog's soft scruff. As if thinking I might try to get rid of the dog. "You like him, but you don't want to."

I reached over and pet the mutt who lifted his head, closing his eyes under the ministrations. "I think Heinz is pretty great too." A little bit too much in my business, but Bob was worse. Until this moment I hadn't realized how the immortal dog made me feel like my son was safer with him nearby.

Jamal shook his head. "I don't mean Heinz, I mean Xander. You *like*, like him."

I tried to keep my shoulders from stiffening but it couldn't be helped. I couldn't reconcile the two worlds, my two selves with Jamal on one side and Xander on the other.

I didn't know what to say.

"Jamal," I began, my voice softer than I intended. "Liking someone... it's complicated. Especially when you're grown up. There are things to consider, decisions that don't just affect me, but us—our little family."

He set his pencil down and turned to face me fully, his young face etched with a seriousness beyond his years. "But isn't Xander nice? He saved me. And you smile more after you've been around him."

The mention of Xander's selfless act tugged at my heartstrings.

"He is nice, and yes, he makes me smile. A lot." I conceded, unable to mask the warmth that thought brought. "But being with someone like Xander... it's not just about the good times. It's about making choices that could change everything."

Jamal considered this, his brow furrowing in thought. "But don't you always say we should do what makes us happy? That life's too short to be scared?"

His words, a mirror of my own often-spoken advice, struck a chord. Here I was, wrestling with the fear of immortality, of a love that spanned the impossible, while my son distilled it all into a simple pursuit of happiness.

"I do say that," I admitted. "And I believe it. It's just... with Xander, it's not about not wanting to be with him. It's about figuring out how we can be together when we want such different things for our futures."

Jamal nodded, a maturity in his acceptance that made me wonder who was the parent in this conversation. "Maybe you don't have to figure it all out right now, Mom. Maybe just being happy together for a while is enough."

His insight, so pure and unburdened by the *what-ifs* and *buts* that plagued my thoughts, offered the clarity I'd been seeking.

As Jamal turned his attention back to his homework I leaned against his headboard, allowing myself a moment to just be.

Between the soft scratch of Jamal's pencil and the comforting presence of his room, life didn't feel so complicated.

That being said, the future did hold a weighty event I couldn't put off anymore. I kissed Jamal and reminded him of his bedtime before I headed out.

After the quick drive to the Strip, I stepped onto the elevator and hit the white button that led to the top of Sinopolis.

The sun set a half hour ago, so I wasn't surprised to find Vivien standing there waiting for me when the doors slid open. Timothy was there, handing her a massive frozen coffee piled high with whipped cream. As soon as he saw me he turned toward me, stretching out an arm with a large cup. An americano that was more espresso than water.

"I figured you ladies could use some fighting fuel for tonight."

Viven smiled at me. "Ready to get balls to the walls, pretty?"

I breathed in deep. "Ready as I'll ever be."

"Release the hounds," Vivien announced.

Chapter Twenty-Six

THE BADASS

Vivien did not mean literal hounds. She was announcing the unleashing of the hair, makeup, and dress stylists.

While Vivien groaned and complained the whole way through even as they dressed her in an extravagant red and black ball gown, I quietly submitted to whatever they wanted to do to me.

"How can you just sit there and take it?" she asked me with a scowl.

"I trust professionals to do their job."

Vivien blew a raspberry at me.

Out came my box braids, while creams were applied to moisturize and soften my face. They plucked and pulled at me the same as Vivien, until the job was done.

The room was filled with a weighty silence as I stood before the full-length mirror, my reflection a stranger adorned for war as much as for splendor. Timothy, Vivien, and Bianca had outdone themselves, weaving elements of the divine and the warrior into every thread that now clung to my form.

Hair cascaded around my shoulders in a torrent of loose curls that caught the light with a rebellious shimmer. The ensemble they'd chosen for me was an echo of the ideas we'd discussed, a perfect amalgamation that spoke of power and grace.

The top piece molded to my torso was a masterpiece of dark, burnished gold, sculpted to resemble the intricate carapace of a scarab, a symbol of eternal life which seemed almost a mockery considering the blade I bore.

A skirt of layered fabric, dark as the midnight sea, split along my thigh, offering freedom of movement and an unspoken promise of danger. It was trimmed in gold and dotted with blue accents that caught the light like the surface of water kissed by the sun. My arms were embraced by bands of gold climbing from wrist to elbow, a delicate balance of adornment and readiness.

As I turned, the light danced across the metal and fabric, casting a glow that seemed to ignite the very air around me. The effect was not lost on me—I was the only mortal who would stand among gods this night, the only one with the power to unmake them.

Timothy handed me a headpiece, a circlet that dripped jewels onto my forehead, the centerpiece being a scarab.

"The scarab is a sacred symbol to us," Bianca explained. "Just as the scarab rolls the sun across the sky, your actions can determine the fate of gods and mortals alike. You have been touched by the divine and are an agent of influence, pushing against the boundaries of your mortal existence to affect the divine realm."

I felt the weight of my own legend settling upon my shoulders. Tonight, I wasn't just Miranda. I was the mortal who held the Blade of Bane, the woman who had unlocked the gods' prison and who now walked willingly into their midst.

My hands itched for the familiar hilt of my blade but Bob was concealed, hidden beneath the folds of my skirt and strapped to my outer thigh.

In the mirror, I saw them standing behind me—my friends, my allies. And in their eyes, I saw what they had wrought—a warrior queen, fierce and unyielding. I would enter the Immortal Ball with my head held high, not just for myself, but also for Xander who couldn't bring himself to be there.

* * *

After a strange trip on a gondola down the canal of the Florence Hotel, our party ended up at an underground secret entrance. Vivien and Grim went in first, followed by Timothy, and then me.

As I entered, the hum of conversation and the soft melody of a live orchestra enveloped me. Everywhere I looked, there were wonders beyond imagining—jeweled goblets that filled themselves with ambrosia, mirrors that showed glimpses of alternate realities, and water canals that spanned the length of the football field sized ballroom. The ceiling itself was a mesmerizing display of shifting constellations, twinkling and dancing in harmony with the live orchestra's music.

The sheer opulence of the ballroom was like something out of a fever dream. Floating chandeliers? Check. Live egrets? Double check.

The smell of sugar and something lightly floral filled my senses. I scanned the room, taking in the glittering assembly of gods and other immortals.

One god wore a cloak made of shimmering starlight, its edges trailing along the ground like a comet's tail. His eyes glowed with an otherworldly power as he regarded me.

I had to admit there was something about a god in starlight couture that made my heart do a little flip. Not that I'd ever tell him. The last thing his ego needed was a mortal's approval. But seriously, if you're going to wear the cosmos, at least coordinate with your deity date. Clashing constellations are a fashion faux pas.

A goddess adorned in a crown of intertwining vines and precious jewels floated effortlessly across the marble dance floor with her stunning partner. Each step she took left behind a trail of blooming flowers, their petals swirling in an elegant dance with the music.

I felt out of place amidst this grandeur, the weight of the Blade of Bane at my hip a constant reminder of my mission. A mission that had turned me into a pariah in their eyes.

As I navigated the outskirts of the crowd I could feel their gazes upon me—eyes filled with a blend of curiosity and disdain. It wasn't long before a group closed in, their intentions thinly veiled behind polite, vicious smiles. They'd as soon slit my throat as smile upon me.

Bob chose that moment to interject. "If they lay a finger on you,

I'll... Well, I suppose I'll give them a very stern talking to. With lots of sharp, pointy words."

A goddess draped in gossamer fabrics with eyes like twin sapphires stepped forward. "Miranda West, isn't it? The mortal who dared to unleash Aten. How... brave of you," she said, her voice dripping with sarcasm.

I squared my shoulders, meeting her gaze. "It was a mistake. One I intend to fix."

A chuckle came from my right where a god with skin the color of the night sky and eyes like molten gold stood. "A mistake? You've endangered us all, human. Aten's return could be the end of us," he said, his tone laced with barely contained fury.

"I'm aware of the consequences," I replied, doing my best not to reach for Bob. If I did so they might see it as a move to attack them. "And I'm here to face them."

Timothy caught my eye from across the room for a moment. His expression was tight with concern and I knew he wanted to intervene.

When we'd been getting ready, Timothy and Vivien had vowed to be by my side all night to make sure this exact thing wouldn't happen, but I ordered them in no uncertain terms not to interfere. If I were to be put on the chopping block I would handle it myself. I didn't need these immortals to like me, but I needed them to respect me, and hiding under the power of someone else would only make me look weak.

Despite Timothy and Vivien's protests, Grim agreed with me.

Their circle tightened around me, a suffocating ring of divine judgment.

"You don't belong here mortal."

"You should be scrubbed from the earth for what you've done. Damned to Amit's belly."

An icy drip of fear started in my belly. Maybe I'd been wrong. Maybe they would try to kill me right here, out in the open. No one besides my few allies would do anything to stop it from happening either.

"I'd stop them," Bob said encouragingly, followed by, "Well, I'd at least make a very cutting remark. But don't worry, I've got your back. Metaphorically speaking."

A hush rolled over the room. The atmosphere shifted. The gods paused their verbal smackdown to see what was the cause.

Xander strode in.

He was near the grand staircase, his presence unmistakable and overwhelming. The unkempt, wild man I knew was replaced by a figure of poise and power. His hair, usually a wild mane, was now neatly swept back, framing a face that radiated an unearthly aura. Dressed in a blue suit that seemed woven from a stormy ocean of silk, he was every bit the deity of deep waters.

"Is that who I think it is?" a goddess whispered from nearby.

"It can't be. No one has seen him for thousands of years."

"I heard he was dead."

"I heard he'd lost his mind."

More murmurs and interest raced through the room, a live wire.

So everyone knew I released Aten, but they didn't know why it came about. I imagined I had Grim and Timothy to thank for their discretion. I was suddenly as grateful to them for keeping those details private as I was for Xander drawing all the attention away from me.

Despite getting cleaned up, Xander lacked a refinement everyone else in the room possessed. It was as if an ancient savagery clung to him, pulsating in his muscles, the tightness in his jaw, in his shoulders.

I could only imagine everyone else felt it too.

A true god amongst house trained pussy cats.

Our eyes locked and a jolt of electricity shot through me. The room, with all its splendor, faded into an inconsequential blur. I was unprepared for the intensity of my reaction—Xander's appearance not only stunned me but set flame to that deep, raw attraction only he inspired.

I was acutely aware of my mortality, of the blood rushing through my veins and the beating of my heart.

As he neared, the immortals closest to me murmured, "He's coming this way."

"I heard he'd gone crazy."

Another god nudged them hard in the ribs. "Shut your mouth. He is one of the first gods among us."

Only in that moment did I realize how much the gods craved to bring Xander back in the fold. They revered him. Like some past savior coming to life, the gods around me gaped, some even misting at the eyes.

And I knew he absolutely fucking hated it.

Xander would rather be wearing a barely buttoned Hawaiian shirt while sipping a Shirley Temple in that dirty dive bar than be here in this glittering realm of sophistication and power.

As Xander neared, I couldn't help but notice the transformation was not just in his appearance—there was a newfound purpose in his stride, a sense of belonging. He was a god who could orchestrate the vastness of the oceans, yet all his attention was fixed on me.

Xander studiously kept from meeting the gaze of anyone else, his entire being locked on me. His presence transformed me from a soldier on a mission to a woman acutely aware of her own desires and vulnerabilities.

"Do you think he's coming to ask me to dance?"

"Dream on, Jocita."

The murmurs grew louder as Xander sauntered through the crowd, a mix of surprise and speculation rippling through the gods and goddesses.

A goddess draped in shimmering silver with a midnight-blue cascade of hair eyed Xander with open interest. Even her outfit complemented his.

"Nun, the elusive god of primordial waters," she cooed, stepping into his path. "Your absence has been... noted. What tempts you back to our midst?"

Xander's lips curved in a half-smirk, not slowing his stride. "It's a *crazy* story." He emphasized the word crazy, an inside joke between us. I hated how that warmed me by several degrees. "Let's just say I'm here for the view," he replied, his voice laced with a hint of mockery. His gaze remained fixed on me, as if the goddess was no more than a fleeting shadow.

Undeterred, a god with the sheen of polished bronze on his skin stepped forward, offering a hand. "Xander, perhaps you seek new alliances? Or new... conquests?" His eyes flicked up and down Xander's body, suggesting an unspoken offer.

Xander's reaction was immediate and dismissive. He sidestepped the offered hand, his eyes rolling slightly. "Alliances? Conquests? Don't you have anything better to do?" he asked, his tone dripping with disdain.

A murmur of laughter and whispers broke out among the immortals, their intrigue piqued by Xander's blatant disregard.

The god's face tightened, a mix of embarrassment and annoyance flashing in his eyes.

Then, with the ease of a predator ignoring lesser beasts, Xander closed the distance between us. His eyes were alight with a mischievous spark, the kind that told me he was fully aware of the stir he was causing.

"Ms. West," Xander's voice cut through the tension. "May I have this dance?"

Shocked expressions turned toward me, as if trying to gauge if this was a joke.

At first I'd been relieved he'd shown up. He'd become the focus of everyone's attention but just like that, he threw the bullseye back on me.

Damn him.

His presence radiated confidence and power, the very essence of the god he was. But I didn't need his rescue.

"That isn't necessary, *Nun*," I said in a cold, clipped tone, making sure to let him know this was very much a professional setting for me.

He smirked, but his eyes flickered with something when I used his ancient god name.

"Not necessary, but a pleasure," he practically purred. "Can you blame a guy for wanting a dance with the most intriguing and powerful woman in the room?"

More immortals bristled around me, as if his asking me to dance over any of them was a direct insult.

In for a penny, in for a pound.

Despite myself, a tight-lipped smile tugged at my lips. "Just one dance," I conceded, slipping my fingers into his large, warm palm.

As we moved to the dance floor I felt the eyes of everyone on us, their whispers growing louder.

But in Xander's arms I found an unexpected comfort. His steps were sure, his hold firm yet gentle. For a moment, I allowed myself to lean into his strength.

From the corner of my eye, I saw Vivien giving me the thumbs up next to Grim, who firmly had an arm around her waist.

"You shouldn't have done that," I said in a low voice, somehow keeping up with his lead, though I'd rarely danced.

"Why not?" his low voice grated against my skin in a far too seductive manner.

"Because I need to show them I can, and will, stand on my own."

He scoffed. "Whose genius plan was that?" He went on before I could answer. "You should never truly be alone or at the mercy of others." His tone was so bitter, so angry.

"Xander." His name came out with all the emotion built up in my stomach.

"You should be surrounded by those who would back you up, so no one even thinks they can touch you."

"Hurt me?" I corrected.

"That either."

I chewed on my lower lip to keep from smiling or laughing. "No one wants me like that."

"That's not true."

The solemnity in his words hit me at my core, and I found myself drowning in his intense gaze until I couldn't feel my feet.

"Even your neighbor can't seem to resist you."

"You're jealous." It was a statement. I knew it, but he hadn't said it before.

The side of his mouth kicked up though it didn't reach his eyes. "Of course I am, sweetheart."

I didn't know what to say to that. Casting a look around, I found varying expressions of shock, awe, and disgust peppered the room.

"I didn't realize how much they all missed you."

Xander's jaw tightened.

"They think a lot of you, for what you gave up for them. They treat you like their savior."

His lips peeled back from his teeth. "They're all idiots."

"But you did save them."

"In symbol alone. I died, Miranda. I didn't beat Aten. He killed me. And even after death he managed to contort my existence into a personal hell. They think I can save them again, but what does that mean? I need to die for them to get off their asses and do whatever it was they did the last time to put him away?"

The dance ended and I stepped back, putting distance between us. "Thank you, Xander, but I need to show them all I can stand on my own. I need you to keep your distance." That last part was hard to get out because I didn't want that at all. The deepest parts of me wanted him glued to my side, touching some part of me to share his strength. But this was how it needed to be.

He nodded, a complex emotion crossing his face. "Understood. But just know I'm here if you need me." Then he couldn't help but add with a smirk, "Sweetheart."

"Thank you for coming," I whispered.

He turned and stalked away but not without a little wink.

The gods gave me a considerable berth after that, only a few bold enough to pass by me to drop a scathing insult and even fewer who would stop to ask me a genuine question. Even the hostess of the party, Isis, approached me. The wife of Osiris and the matron of the gods. A goddess who appeared to be in her forties, she wore a pearlescent dress and exuded energy in a way that tingled my skin like a thousand raindrops.

I barely remembered anything of our interchange, other than she blessed me with luck in my endeavors.

Xander sipped on something that suspiciously looked like a Shirly Temple as a crowd of gods hung around him, flapping their mouths and fawning all over him. Even from across the room I could see something in him I'd never seen before—his eyes were cold and dead.

I thought if... when he rejoined the ranks he would feel like he belonged and he would allow himself out of his self-imposed shackles to embrace his new life, but my heart cracked like a rock under too much pressure as I saw him dying in front of me.

I wanted to go to him. I wanted to save him, but I knew I would cause more problems than I would solve. Instead, I explored until I found a set of stairs to a balcony that overlooked the ballroom.

This ballroom made Buckingham Palace look like a budget motel. If I weren't so busy being so in awe of its beauty, I'd be calculating how many lifetimes it would take to dust this place.

Note to self: *if reincarnation is real, do not come back as an immortal housekeeper.*

"So this is where our guest of honor is hiding," a male voice came from behind me.

I turned to find myself facing a god I didn't know. He was tall and imposing with piercing pale eyes that seemed to see right through me. There was an air of arrogance about him, a sense of superiority that made my skin crawl.

His silver hair cascaded down his back in intricate braids and his cloak shimmered with a strange purple iridescence.

"I don't hide," I replied, trying to keep my voice steady despite the unease creeping up my spine. "I simply wanted a new view of things."

The god's lip curled in a smirk and my blood ran cold. "A brave mortal, aren't you? To speak so boldly to a god." His voice was like velvet over steel, smooth yet dangerous. I resisted the urge to step back, holding my ground even though every instinct told me to flee.

He took a step closer, his presence overwhelming. "Do you think it's wise to be alone up here? Where no one can protect you?"

Danger flashed in my mind like a big neon sign.

I was feeling very out of my depth. But if he pushed me, I'd do what I had to. "I don't need anyone to protect me," I assured him.

"And she's not alone," another voice answered.

Chapter Twenty-Seven

THE BEAST

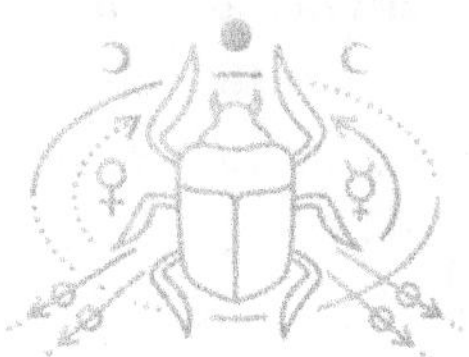

I came upon Miranda cornered by the god Min and every part of me wanted to rip him into shreds once I saw his threatening body language.

The god's face eased into a smile. "Nun, so glad you are back. Now you can help me teach a lesson to this dirty little mortal."

Lifetimes ago we had been friends. We drank, we partied, we even got involved in some sexual exploits that were worth their weight in gold. But I wasn't the same god Min knew. And he'd fucked with the wrong human.

"Don't... don't talk about her like that." My tone was airy, a half-smile pulling at my lips as a finger wagged in the air. One of those hysterical yelping laughs vibrated at the base of my spine, threatening to bubble up. If it arose and popped, so would the thin hold on my self-control.

The god laughed, his head turning back and forth between me and Miranda, as if he's in on a joke I'm telling.

He didn't understand what I was fighting to keep down. If I let it out, it was definitely going to ruin the party mood.

"You're joking right, Nun? This worthless human thinks she's special because she carries a big toy."

A long groan rolled out from my chest as I rubbed my chin. "Ah, but is that any different from you?"

Min's eyes clouded with confusion before my gaze darted to the place between his legs.

Miranda stiffened, watching me carefully. This god didn't know me, but she did. All of me is dangling off the cliff except for the one hand hold I had on the sanity and decorum these events called for.

The god's brows furrowed, his upper lip pulling back in a sneer. "Oh, I see. Your brain has softened to shit after all these years. What a pity." He sniffed. "You were as formidable as Anubis once. And now you're just a broken little demi, who found a safe little toy to play with." He jerked his head in Miranda's direction.

Before I could react, his face blanched. The tip of Miranda's sword tapped at his balls. "You got a thing about toys, don't you?" she asked, with cool assessment. "Maybe I should take yours away. After all, you're a god, right? It'll grow back. Give you a chance to think with your head instead of your little sensitive prick, since it's clearly turning you into a dick."

The god's eyes bulged as his Adam's apple did a dramatic rise and fall down his throat. He stupidly looked to me for help.

I shrugged as my lips split into a sly smile. "You shouldn't mess with a girl who carries lethal weapons."

"Or any self-respect," Miranda added with an absolutely vicious grin.

My chest swelled with warmth and pride.

That's my little badass.

Miranda stepped closer to him, hissing in his ear. "I've never chopped off anyone's bits with the Blade of Bane before. As it truly takes the life of an immortal, I wonder if it would permanently claim your balls as well."

A human cut his ego down to size and it awoke a hungry ferocity in me for her. She was so alive and amazing. I wanted to run my tongue along her skin to taste the electricity I saw sizzle in her eyes.

The god's face twisted and flexed. He wanted to say something but knew better than to open his trap while in such a precarious position.

"But as long as you don't fuck with me, I won't investigate that particular feature of my *toy*." Miranda turned on her heel and was out the door, leaving an imperious air in her wake as if he wasn't worth another moment of her time.

The god made to leave, pulling me from my thoughts, but I clamped a hand down on his shoulder, and yanked him back before he could get out of reach.

"Whoa there, hold on just a minute," I said, my voice dripping with delight and malice. "We're not done here."

A flicker of uncertainty crossed his face, and for a brief moment I saw glimpses of the arrogant façade crumbling away. The tables had turned and now it was his turn to feel the weight of someone else's dominance.

With a swift motion, I released him from my grasp. The god stumbled. He glared at me with wariness.

"You don't speak like that to her ever again, do you understand?" Then I laughed lightly as my hand clamped on his shoulder again, crushing the bone underneath.

He cried out and fell to a knee, his face turning a mottled red. I paid his reactions no mind and instead thoughtfully added, "Actually, you don't speak to her at all. You don't even look at her."

The false levity dropped like a hammer as I drilled into him with what I knew must look like the eyes of a demon. The crazy clawed at the side of my brain, begging me to paint the walls with his blood for being too close to Miranda.

"You don't even think of her, do you understand? If you do, I will make what she threatened to do look like a day in the park compared to what I'll do to you. Because I've had an eternity to know what pain really is and how the true torture is never knowing when it will end or *if* it will end at all. And I'd be happy to share my life lessons with you."

Blood gushed from where my fingers brutally penetrated his flesh like a strip of flattened bread dough. His cries and groans for me to stop drowned out my words. I shook his shoulder forcing a shriek of pain to escape him. "I fear you aren't listening. Are you listening?"

"Yes, yes," Min practically yelped. "I'm listening. I'll never look at her or think of her again." With a final wicked grin, I released him. The god fell backward, crumpling into a protective ball. I lifted my hand and licked my blood covered fingers. "Add a little more salt to your diet while you're at it. You taste a little bland."

I strolled out of the room.

THE NIGHT PROCEEDED AND MIRANDA CONTINUED TO MINGLE WITH those who despised her, though I watched her make a few allies who mentioned her unique bravery and success over Bes and Serqet.

I noted their names and faces for later. As much as the other gods tried to draw me out, I dodged their attempts to be drawn into conversation or dance. I eventually caught Miranda's eye and jerked my head in the direction of an adjoining room. Understanding my motion, she excused herself.

Casting an eye about to make sure no one was watching, I closed the library doors behind me.

"What is it?" Miranda asked. "Are you okay?" Worry etched lines between her eyes.

"No, I'm not okay." I closed the distance between us and cupped the back of her neck, pulling her against me and kissing those irresistibly full lips. A mix between a sigh and a groan escaped me. "Do you know how fucking hard it is to keep my distance? To not kiss you, touch you? When you look like this? You are the most dangerously beautiful creature alive, and I can't fucking stand not touching you a moment longer."

"We have to get back out there," Miranda said, even as her hands clawed at my suit and her tongue invaded my mouth with a hot slick lick.

My dick hardened painfully. "Five minutes. Please, fuck, give me five minutes, Miranda. If you don't, I'll fucking die."

The woman was irresistible. Her dress had been made to kill me. All her strength and softness was on display in equal measure and I had to have her, had to claim her.

The need to bite into her flesh and leave marks behind so everyone knew whose she was, possessed me with a vengeance.

But I could control myself. I was a man, not a monster. And I'd show her I could be trusted with her body, her heart, and her soul.

Her lips curved into a smile under mine before I continued to trail kisses down the column of her dark golden brown throat. Miranda's unique scent and taste filled my senses.

"What if I need longer than five minutes?" she countered, breathlessly.

My lips and tongue traced over the swells of her breasts, pushed up by the carved golden armor molded to her torso. "Oh, you won't need more than ninety seconds."

That's right sweetheart, let me have control for a little while. You can enchant the others, but let me amaze you.

She scoffed. "Well don't you think you're hot shit?"

I lifted my head, licking my lips. "Do you doubt it?"

That eyebrow arched.

"Challenge accepted," I said. I picked her up by the backs of her thighs and carried her over to the tufted settee. I sat down, placing her on top. "If I win, I want the date I've already won to be at your house for a family dinner and I want *you* to cook."

Warning, or maybe fear, flashed in her eyes.

"And if you win..." I prompted.

"You owe me Perkatory drinks for a month."

It was weak, but it would do. I nodded quickly.

I walked over to a counter with a jug of water.

"What are you doing?"

"Making good on my word," I said, throwing a wink at her. Bringing the jug, I hovered over where she sat. "Do you trust me?"

"No," she said, eyeing the jug fearfully. "And if you fuck up my hair, I'll stab you with Bob."

"Don't worry, sweetheart. I would never."

Then I poured it out. Miranda recoiled, anticipating the fall of the water to hit her. It took her a moment to realize the water hovered over her, mid-air. Only when her eyes opened, did I allow a few droplets to hit the tops of her breasts.

She gasped.

I smirked. She had no idea what was coming.

But she *would be* coming, in less than ninety seconds.

Water droplets rolled down, disappearing beneath her armor. They sluiced over the tips of her breasts, and through my connection to the water as they circled the dark tips there, I could feel them harden.

Oh, fuck I wanted to wrap my lips around those pretty buds and suckle her into a frenzy, but I wanted her to experience the lighter side of my power for once.

Some of the water diverted from the frozen mass hanging in the air and dropped to her bare thighs. Instead of following gravity downward, they streaked upward, under her skirts and armor.

Ten seconds.

"What are you —" Her words cut off as the water beads found her center.

With a flick of my wrist, the droplets multiplied, coating her in a fine mist. Each droplet danced along her skin like a thousand tiny hands, massaging her sensitive nerve endings. She let out a low moan, her eyes fluttering shut.

Twenty seconds.

My finger twitched and the mist of water intensified, some of the droplets joining together to form a single, powerful stream. It cascaded between her legs, parting the armor as it went, revealing her throbbing core. She gasped, her hands flying to her chest as the stream filled her, causing her to thrash beneath me.

I smiled. "How does that feel, Miranda? My power caressing you like this?"

I focused my power, urging the remaining droplets to increase their intensity. No longer did they simply graze her skin, but now they swirled and twirled, each one a surge of cool, electric pleasure. The warmth between her legs built as her climax approached.

Forty seconds.

I created a small concentric circle to surround her clit as another small wave of water rolled up and down her slit. Then I increased the pressure and speed slowly but steadily.

Right now, I felt every ounce the god I was and Miranda was my plaything. Perhaps claiming my abilities wasn't so bad?

"How are you doing this?" she whimpered, her voice hoarse from the tremors that had taken hold of her body. But I couldn't resist any longer. I needed to see her crumble before me, to know the power I held over her.

Because she owned me unequivocally. It made me desperate to prove my worth to her. To show her that there could be advantages to being with an unhinged, mentally unwell god who put her pleasure on a pedestal.

Sixty seconds.

As the water continued to stimulate her, her breaths became ragged, her moans echoing through the empty library. She was close. I had her on the edge.

It was time to give her the final push, with a few seconds to spare.

The water surged and vibrated in triple time against her.

Miranda's eyes rolled back as her body convulsed, her hips bucking against the settee. A cry of pure ecstasy escaped her lips as the apex of her release washed over her.

Aw fuck yes, that's my little badass.

Pride swelled in me. She'd seen me fractured, lost, and broken, but now she knew I could control myself too. I'd fought hard for it, for her.

Her aftershocks were slow to subside. Face flushed and breathing ragged, her eyes were alive with desire. At the same time, I pulled the water away, wicking it off her skin and directing it back into the water jug before setting it aside. Miranda frowned and cursed.

I couldn't help but laugh. "When are you going to learn to stop taking bets against a god? That was only a minute."

"Shut up and fuck me, Xander."

That sobered me. "Whatever you say, sweetheart."

My demonstration of control was over, and I'd gladly hand the reigns over to her.

I pinned her to the couch. Our tongues tangled while our hips bucked at each other with the intense need to interlock. In no time, she had me seated, my pants unzipped so the air could hit my hard cock. Miranda lowered onto me, pushing her panties to the side, and I slid home.

We both made a strangled sound. Miranda rode me steadily, driving me to madness.

"Your trick is cool and all, but I think I prefer this," she said in a breathy tone.

"You and me both," I agreed, my hips surging up into her tight wet heat. She bucked and fucked me like a goddess, and all I could do was let her lead.

My warrior. My goddess. My everything.

She wasn't afraid to face the immortals out there though I'd been terrified. I shamelessly borrowed strength from her, but I planned to give it back to her tenfold.

We had to return to the ballroom, but right now I couldn't give a flying fuck. There was only the angel of death, riding my cock like she owned me, which she did.

Miranda arched her back, her nails digging into the flesh of my arms as she reached her climax. The second she let go, her inner walls clenching and milking me, my release overtook me.

I drew her to me, burying my face in her breasts, covering up the groans of pleasure as I emptied myself in her.

"Can we not agree that you technically keep winning our bets too?" I said, breathing heavily as if I'd run halfway around the globe.

"No, we cannot," she said, standing. "Even if it's true," she muttered.

It didn't take long for us to clean up and take turns exiting the library room to return to the party.

I tried to keep the smug smile from forming on my face, but it seemed damn near impossible. But I'd barely been able to enjoy my post-coital bliss when a male voice boomed through the ballroom.

"Well, well, well, did you all miss me?"

"Ah, fuck," a woman next to me muttered.

I turned to find Vivien standing next to me, her face a dark stormy cloud, her fangs elongating in response to the newcomer.

A man with deeply tanned skin and silver streaked hair, wearing several gold chains against an expensive, white snakeskin suit, waltzed in with a martini dangling in one hand.

"Who is it?" I asked, though I had a suspicion even after not seeing my brethren for so many years. I remembered only one who had such a hold on his own slimy charismatic nature to foster his own massive fucking ego.

"Seth," Vivien said through gritted fangs.

Chapter Twenty-Eight

THE BEAST

Yep, that's the fucker I thought it was. Seth, or Set. Brother of Osiris. At one time, he tried his hand at usurping Osiris to become top god.

He was also one of the gods who'd been released from the Blade of Bane.

I glanced across the room, finding Miranda slipping backward into the crowd while surreptitiously pulling Bob out.

Well, the party was fun while it lasted.

"What? You aren't all happy to see me again?" Seth asked at the top of the stairs.

Vivien growled next to me. A dark mass was suddenly there at her back, steadying her with hands on her shoulders. Grim.

"Can I get the cliff notes of his most recent crimes?" I murmured when Timothy sidled up to my other side.

Recorder that he was, Timothy rattled them off. "Conspiracy to incite another uprising, this time against Anubis. Captured and held a god against their will. To say the least."

"You are saying the least," Vivien growled again.

Grim spoke to her in low warning. "Most gods have committed sins and returned to join the ranks after a time. If he'd gone to the cradle instead of the blade, we would have had to deal with him eventually."

"Too soon," Vivien muttered. "*Way* too soon."

"Regardless," Grim ground out as if he didn't like it either, "If he wishes to play nice, he gets to stay."

"Oh look," Seth announced drolly, with a wave of his martini. "It's Grim and his bitch."

"Guess he's not playing nice," I pointed out the obvious while sticking my hands in my pockets and stepping away as all the attention turned toward Grim and Vivien.

"Why are you here?" Grim asked, his voice suddenly as resonant as Seth's in the massive ballroom.

I couldn't shake the feeling that this was all about to go horribly wrong. The tension in the air was a tangible thing, a live wire sparking and ready to ignite. Seth's presence alone was enough to set everyone on edge, but it was the look in his eyes that had me feeling the real danger. It was the look of a predator that had just cornered its prey.

Seth raised his arms and the murmur of the crowd hushed in a crescendo of suspense. "My dear friends," he began, his voice a melodic poison, "I thought it was time for a grand reunion. You've been hiding from the world, wallowing in your own self-pity and fear. It's time to remember who we are!"

As he spoke, the edges of the room darkened, shadows shifting and coiling like living things. A chill ran down my spine as I realized what was about to happen. "Miranda," I breathed, my eyes searching frantically for her in the crowd.

As if summoned by Seth's words, the gods and monsters released from the blade began to appear. They materialized from the shadows, grotesque and terrible, their eyes alight with bloodlust and chaos.

A monster slithered from the shadows with its many heads weaving through the air, each one bearing a crown of venomous fangs. Another creature that could only have spawned from the darkest depths of fear itself, moved on all fours, its body a grotesque amalgamation of wolf and serpent. Its sickly yellow eyes scanned the room with a predator's interest.

Next came a goddess, her beauty terrible to behold. Her eyes burned with a furious light, her gaze alone enough to ignite the very air. Flames danced around her, not providing warmth, but a cold, consuming fire that sought to incinerate all it touched. Her laughter echoed, the sound of delight and destruction, turning blood to ice.

The air became a cacophony of roars and hisses, the elegant ballroom suddenly a stage set for a massacre.

It was an ambush.

I pushed through the crowd, my heart pounding in my chest. "Miranda!" I called out, my voice drowned by the burgeoning chaos. I had to reach her, had to get her out before all hell broke loose.

I spotted her then, moving with a grace that belied the deadly purpose in her stride. She was making her way behind Seth, unnoticed by the preoccupied god. My breath caught in my throat as her hand gripped the hilt of the Blade of Bane as she maneuvered through the throng of deities.

Seth, too caught up in his moment of glory, was blind to the mortal danger approaching him. "We will rise again," he proclaimed, "and under my leadership, we will—"

Miranda lunged, the blade piercing through his back before it split through his front. Seth's eyes widened in shock, the crowd gasping in unison as the god of chaos was skewered by the only mortal in the room.

And then the impossible happened. The tip of Miranda's blade emerged from his chest, and the exit wound caught fire.

Like an ant under a magnifying glass, Seth began to burn.

Chapter Twenty-Nine

THE BADASS

The smell of charred flesh assaulted me as Seth burned on Bob like a shish kabob on a barbeque. His chest was a pulsing beacon of light, somehow sucking the air from the ballroom.

Light erupted from Seth's chest in a blinding, pure, brilliant white that seemed to radiate from within him. It shot out in thick beams, hitting each dark god and monster with precision.

It spread out in every direction like a burst of energy. It seemed to target the dark gods and monsters that had surrounded the ballroom. They burst into flames, their screams and cries filling the air as they all burned alongside Seth. Flames danced and flickered across their writhing bodies.

The smell of burning flesh and hair filled the room, a pungent aroma. The mixture of sulfur and charred meat was suffocating, filling every corner of the ballroom with its putrid stench.

Then the panic exploded amongst the immortal guests in the ballroom. Half of them began to shift into their god-likeness, while the others tried to flee. They turned on each other in the confusion.

As chaos enveloped the ballroom, Vivien leaped into the fray with a ferocity that was both exhilarating and terrifying. She moved like a shadow among the flames, her figure a blur of motion as she dispatched dark gods and monsters. Her laughter, wild and unrestrained, echoed above the turmoil, a testament to her unhinged nature as her fangs gleamed with menace. But when a dark god landed a lucky strike, wounding her, the atmosphere palpably shifted.

Grim's reaction was immediate and visceral. His form blurred, and for a fleeting moment, the fearsome visage of death itself flashed across his face, a skull wreathed in shadows. With a roar of outrage, he extended his hands, telekinetically hurling assailants away from his wife with the force of a tempest. His power, dark and implacable, swept through the room like a scythe, clearing a path to Vivien's side.

Timothy, ever the tactician, didn't leap into physical combat but instead orchestrated a battlefield of his own making. His fingers flew over the surface of his tablet, glyphs and symbols dancing in the air around him. With a few swift taps, barriers of light snapped into place around allies, deflecting attacks and sealing wounds with precision.

Fallon transformed into his monstrous likeness of Horus, his eyes glowing with a fierce, blue light. The transformation was both terrifying and awe-inspiring. With a roar that seemed to shake the very foundations of the ballroom, he positioned himself in front of Bianca, his massive wings unfurling to shield her from the chaos. His sharp talons glinted dangerously, ready to tear apart anyone who dared come near her.

For her part, Bianca stood calm and serene behind Fallon's protective form, her hands glowing with a soft, golden light that pulsed with power.

"Bob?" I asked audibly, shock turning my limbs numb.

"It's not me," he confirmed, his tone filled with revulsion. "Now get me out of here. It's disgusting."

I pulled him out of Seth and stumbled back, only to be caught by a pair of strong hands. I didn't have to look to know it was Xander who held me.

Seth turned even as flames licked the flesh off his body. "You." His raspy voice was monstrous and tortured as he locked eyes with me. "*He's* going to take away what you love most until he is the only one left."

And then with a hideous grin, or maybe his lips were just burned away, Seth collapsed into a pile of broken burning limbs.

"Xander," I said, my voice failing me.

"We need to go, now," he said, then yanked me out of the ballroom before I could protest.

I came to my senses and ran alongside him.

"What's happening?" The wild look of terror and pure rage in his eyes was one I'd never seen before.

"It's Aten," he said.

"What?" Sun god, burning other gods. It somewhat computed in my brain but it also didn't. "He wasn't in there," I protested.

"He must be close." Xander grabbed my arms and hauled me up for a fierce kiss. "And you are getting out of here."

"The fuck I am. I'm the only one who can kill him." I raised Bob as if to prove my point, though even Bob was shaken into silence.

It was one thing to slice through a god, another to do so before they burst into flames. He already hated blood, and I could tell skewering a burning body was beyond him.

"Listen to me," Xander said carefully. "It's all of the gods against him. I went up against him alone. Together we can subdue him. But I can't focus or help if you are around. I'll be too worried about you. If Aten doesn't get you, surely one of the other gods might take their shot at you. I can't protect you against that many."

"I can protect myself, Xander," I practically snarled at him.

His lips tightened as he looked back in the direction of the ballroom we fled. Screams and shouts kicked up higher. "But can you protect Jamal and your mother-in-law?"

The atoms in my body stilled all at once, and I couldn't hear anything else but his words. "What are you saying?"

Xander's voice lowered, and it suddenly felt like I was under water. My ears were clogged, and everything was moving too slowly, including my mind. "He's going to take what you love most away. Seth was talking about Aten. You need to get home. You need to protect your family."

The water I was under crashed over in a breaking wave and my heart nearly exploded from my chest in violent beats. "No." Even as I denied it, I knew it to be true.

The gods had powers and were already congregated to fight together, while my very mortal family was at home, alone and unprotected.

I gripped Xander by the back of the neck and kissed him just as hard as he'd done to me, until a coppery taste filled my mouth. I didn't know if it was his blood or mine.

"Don't die," I commanded.

That devil may care grin spread on his face. "Only you are allowed to kill me, sweetheart."

With that, we rushed off in two different directions, and I swore my heart split in two.

As I ran out of the hotel, I managed to unhook my skirts, leaving me in a bodysuit, albeit a very fancy, armored bodysuit. I'd made clear to Bianca and Timothy in no uncertain terms that I didn't want to be bogged down in fabric if something went down.

Maybe I jinxed the whole night by adding that detail.

Driving home, I was like a bat out of hell, and god help anyone who got in my way.

The tires screeched as I pulled up to my house, my heart hammering against my ribs. The street was eerily quiet, the only sound the rapid beat of my own pulse thrumming in my ears. I didn't bother with subtlety, bursting through the front door, Bob gripped tightly in my hand, ready for a fight.

My hand trembled as I reached for the light switch, but no matter how many times I flicked it the room remained shrouded in darkness. Suddenly, my eyes adjusted to the dim light and a scene straight out of a nightmare greeted me. Mama Jean and Jamal were on the living room floor, bound and unconscious with heads lolling lifelessly. In a corner, Heinz lay silent and still.

Waves of panic crashed over me, drowning me in horrifying thoughts. Each one worse than the last.

Am I too late?

Are they dead?

Please don't let them be dead.

Terror constricted my throat, leaving me gasping for air. My mouth went dry and my tongue turned heavy and useless. I was simultaneously sweating and shivering, my stomach churning into knots. My heart thumped rapidly in my throat, threatening to choke me.

Desperation clawed at my chest as I fought back tears. Muscling it all back down, I forced myself to stay calm and keep my cool.

I rushed forward to untie them when the *click* of a firearm shocked me still and a figure emerged from the shadows. "I wouldn't do that just yet."

My heart thundered in my chest, threatening to burst through my ribcage. But I couldn't let panic take over.

"Sunny," I hissed, recognition flaring as I took in the sight of her, her gun not trained on me, but on my kid. Thankfully, I was close enough to spot the slight rise and fall of his chest. Both Jamal and Mama Jean were breathing.

My knees nearly buckled at the knowledge I wasn't too late.

I was finally face to face with the one who tricked Aoiki and me into releasing everything from inside the Blade of Bane.

She was no longer the teenager adorned in a school uniform. Now, the fae girl was all seriousness, her sleek black bob framing a face that was a mask of concentration. Her square features and thin eyes were cold and calculating.

"Seems your family is just as compliant as you are when it comes to my dream weaving," she said, tilting her head to the side.

Sunny had been responsible for my dreamwalking that nearly resulted in me killing my own child. I'd suspected, but she confirmed yet another reason I had to take her down. And I'd do so with extreme prejudice.

"What do you want with my family?" My voice was a low growl, barely containing the fury boiling inside me. Bob felt alive in my grasp, vibrating with a shared desire for retribution.

Sunny turned to face me, a small, mocking smile playing on her lips. "Just ensuring Aten's plan goes smoothly. Don't worry, your family is unharmed. And they can stay that way if you accept *him* into your heart and mind." She pressed a finger into her chest then her temple.

I wanted to shoot back a mouthy retort, but with Jamal in the crosshairs, I couldn't risk it.

"What makes him so great?" I asked instead, trying to draw her attention enough to let her guard down.

She smiled, eyes lighting up as if I'd asked her the only question she ever wanted to be asked.

"What makes him so great?" Sunny repeated. "He is the one true god. He is the one who bathes the rest of us in his warmth and glory. No one has power like him."

I thought of the gods—Grim, Timothy, Bianca, and Vivien—back in that ballroom, fighting Aten. Surely they and Xander could take him out.

I forced my voice to sound genuinely intrigued, suppressing the revulsion bubbling inside me. "Why go through all of this? Why me? Why my family?"

Sunny's eyes gleamed with a fervor that made my skin crawl. "Aten wants *you*, Miranda. He sees your strength, your power. And he admires it. But he also knows you're loyal to those you love." Her gaze flickered to Jamal and Mama Jean, then back to me. "He wants to show you he can protect what's dear to you, make you part of his new world order."

I had to bite the inside of my cheek to keep from lashing out. "And you believe him? That he's going to just let us live peacefully?"

"Of course," she said, her conviction unsettling. "Aten's world is one of order, not chaos. Under his rule, we'll all thrive. You, your family... All under his benevolent gaze."

I took a step closer, feigning interest. "And what about those who oppose him?"

Her grip on the gun tightened. "They'll learn. Or they'll be removed. It's for the greater good, Miranda. You'll see."

At that moment, a floorboard creaked behind Sunny, but her attention was so fixed on me that she didn't notice. A shadow moved, a figure approaching her with silent determination. Someone had come in through the back door, silent and stealthily.

They crept closer, but I never took my eyes off Sunny. I couldn't chance alerting her to the new presence.

"But you are more important than any human, Miranda. You have the power to slay immortals alongside *him*, bring order to the chaos that is these self-involved spoiled gods." She practically spat the words.

The man who crept up behind her now held the rolling pin Mama Jean used for making her famous pies. With a swift, precise movement, he swung it, connecting it with the back of Sunny's head.

The fae girl crumpled to the ground, unconscious before she knew what hit her. The gun clattered harmlessly to the floor.

For a moment I could only stare, a mixture of relief and confusion swirling within me. Michael met my gaze, his expression one of concern and urgency.

It was my neighbor who had come in through the back and to our rescue. His light green eyes were in earnest as he explained, "I heard yelling earlier, and saw her with a gun when I went by the window. Are they okay?" He gestured to Mama Jean and Jamal.

I nodded, still processing the turn of events. "Yeah, thanks to you." My words were sincere.

Moving past him, I went to tie up Sunny before she came to. I didn't know how long it took for fae to recover from injuries. Michael caught my shoulders in his strong hands and kissed me.

What the holy hell?

I wrenched away from him. "What are you doing?"

Why in the fuck nuggets was my near stranger of a neighbor pulling a move when my family had been attacked? It came from left field and made zero sense.

But maybe I'd lost my mind somewhere between Seth burning in fire and my family being in danger.

His hopeful smile faded only slightly. "I guess I'm just glad you are okay."

"Cool, well maybe don't show your gladness with your lips. It's called consent, and you don't have it." My words came out harsher than maybe they should have. Apparently he thought we were something more, but I didn't have time to molly-coddle him. Shit right now was far bigger than his apparent crush.

"Miranda," Michael said, stepping closer, his voice turning husky. "You must know how I feel for you."

I must have entered some kind of twilight zone.

A sun god was attacking my immortal allies, a fae gunwoman lay on my floor, my family was tied up, and my neighbor was trying to make a move on me in the midst of it all.

Everything felt a little too surreal. Like a puzzle with big chunks missing from its picture.

My brain couldn't catch up to some important fact, even though I knew it was in grasping distance.

"Thank you but I need to tie—Shit!" I cried out.

I stepped around Michael and my gaze landed on the spot where Sunny collapsed. It was empty.

I cursed some more.

"Don't worry, I'll protect you if she comes back," Michael announced with far too much certainty. He rubbed my shoulder, but I shrugged him off.

My fury that she'd gotten away because of him simmered like bubbling water on a stove. "That won't be necessary."

Michael's smile faltered as I stepped back, creating distance between us. His eyes, once filled with concern, now sparked with a new intensity. "Miranda," he pressed, his voice carrying an edge that sent a shiver down my spine. "Why can't you see we're meant to be together? I saved them." He gestured towards my family, "For you."

I shook my head, feeling Bob's vibrations as a silent warning in my hand. "Saving my family doesn't give you a claim over me. I don't owe you anything."

Heinz, previously subdued and silent, erupted into a cacophony of barks and growls, his body tensed and hackles raised, directed not at the darkness outside, but at Michael.

My relief that the dog was okay was chased away by his outburst.

"What's gotten into him?" Michael feigned confusion, but the dog's reaction was unnervingly clear.

"Bob?" I whispered in my mind, seeking understanding from the only creature who could translate the immortal dog's alarm.

"That is no man." Bob's voice was grave. "Heinz can smell his immortality."

Michael's olive eyes narrowed, as if realizing I knew too much.

The air in the room shifted, growing thick and heavy as if charged by a storm. Michael's demeanor changed and the neighborly façade melted away to reveal a being cloaked in blinding light.

His eyes blazed like twin suns, searing into me with an intensity that made my heart race. The air crackled with electricity as he extended his hand towards me, fingers tipped with glowing embers.

His skin shimmered like liquid gold, adorned with intricate patterns of hieroglyphs that seemed to writhe and shift with a life of their own. Beauty and fear melded inside me in an impossible collision of desire and revulsion.

A god stood before me, and everything inside me trembled before him.

"You think you can reject me?" His voice boomed, no longer Michael's but something otherworldly and powerful. "I am the greatest. I am the best. I am Aten."

Heinz's barking crescendoed, a desperate attempt to warn, to protect. But it was too late. Aten's transformation was complete, his figure now a beacon of light that filled the room, casting long, ominous shadows.

The room seemed to shrink in his presence, every corner touched by his incandescent glow. His voice returned to a more natural timber, but it somehow sent a shiver up my spine. "You will learn to worship me, Miranda. Either by choice or by force."

Chapter Thirty

THE BADASS

The air was thick in the charged silence following Aten's reveal and declaration, electric with the tension of a brewing storm. Heinz's barking had subsided into a low warning growl, his body tense and ready. He put himself between Aten and my family, guarding them.

Bob's presence in my mind was a cold comfort, a reminder that I wasn't entirely alone in facing the god before me.

"So you're the big bad," I said, my voice steady despite the adrenaline coursing through me. "The one who has everyone shaking in their boots."

I might be too if I were wearing them, but I wore sandals and a bodysuit, like some kind of ancient gladiator.

"I am more than a god," he replied in a silky voice.

There was a reason I was innately drawn to my neighbor. Divinity was wildly attractive to humans. I should know. I felt it whenever I was around Grim, Timothy, or any other god. I'd been so stupid not to recognize it only a couple feet from my door.

"I am your helpful, handsome, knight in shining armor just next door." He swept a hand out in the direction of his house. "Stable, pleasant, strong, and supportive. Everything you've ever wanted, Miranda."

They were things I'd told myself I wished Xander was, or claimed to have wanted in the past, but aside from that divine glimmer I felt from "Michael," everything fell flat.

"Why waste your time pretending to be my neighbor?" It didn't make any sense.

"Because we were falling in love. I wanted you to love me as a man, not just blindly fall for the brilliant god I am." His lips tilted up in a half smile that screamed, *aw shucks, didn't we just?*

But we didn't, and what an absolutely deluded creep.

"You think a couple interactions would have me falling at your feet?" Disgust filled my words.

His smile slipped and despite his near-blinding glow, his eyes went flat and cold.

"We've barely spoken or interacted. You know nothing about me." I stiffened, my hand anticipating slicing the sword at him.

In less than a blink, Michael—Aten—was right there beside me. "I'd wait to hear what I have to say before you try slashing me down," he cautioned. "If not for the sake of your family, then because there is the very real possibility of you and I talking this out to a reasonable solution."

His warm breath puffed over my skin, and warmth seeped into that side of my face and body. Knowing it was a trick of his power made it easier to compartmentalize now.

"You are special, Miranda. You wield the Blade of Bane. You're a mortal knowingly walking amongst gods, knowing how undeserving and how entitled they are. Whether you realize it or not, we are perfect for each other."

Aten moved to stand behind me, his presence radiating heat that seemed to seep into my bones. It was tempting to give in to the comfort he offered, like a warm blanket on a cold night.

But my disgust for his lies and presumption kept me glued to my senses.

Not to mention, here he was, all shiny and godly, making his pitch while Mama Jean and Jamal were tied up like it was some twisted hostage negotiation.

"Together we can bring order to a world that needs direction and unquestionable leadership."

"You mean a despot," I corrected.

Aten's laughter filled the room, a sound that seemed to vibrate with power. "I prefer to think of myself as a necessary ruler. One who brings order. Humans already ordain so many to manage themselves, from presidents to prime ministers down to managers at the local fast food restaurant. I can effortlessly become part of this natural order to give humans what they need."

I turned to face him, not shying away from the brilliant shine of his eyes. "And what exactly do humans need?"

"To believe in a higher power, to have faith and direction. I can provide both."

"After you kill all the other gods?" My tone was flat and judgmental. "You think I want that?"

"Humans don't always know what is good for them until it's too late," he said with a knowing smirk. It made him more devilishly handsome.

His words hammered at me with both specific and nonspecific guilt. It was as if he took all of my regrets and turned them inward, beating me with hammers until I could barely breathe from the weight of self-loathing and remorse.

"But in my presence, I can melt away the uncertainty," he added. The internal onslaught disappeared, and I sucked in a breath, my body now weightless and free.

"You're quite the salesman. But I've seen infomercials with more subtlety."

Aten's smile didn't falter, but his eyes—they flickered. Not with less power, but with something more human. Annoyance? Frustration?

In case he didn't think I understood, I spelled it out. "You want me because of the weapon I wield."

"Miranda, you misunderstand. This isn't about salesmanship. It's about destiny. Your destiny is to be alongside me."

"Oh, destiny," I ground out between clenched teeth. "That old chestnut. I get it. You're all-powerful, sun-shiny, and apparently, into kidnapping. But you're missing a crucial piece here."

"And what would that be?" he inquired, genuinely curious, or so it seemed. Gods were hard to read.

"Consent. You're missing my yes. And here's a fun fact about me—I don't do well with coercion."

Aten's radiant façade dimmed just a smidge, but it was enough. "This is about Nun, isn't it?" Before I could answer, he went on. "He always did have a knack for interfering."

I nodded, keeping my stance relaxed though every muscle in my body was coiled tight. "Yeah, what can I say? I got this thing about guys not annihilating their peers or enslaving humanity, and he's weird like that."

Aten chuckled, a sound like warm sunlight. "Nun... Xander... he's always been a thorn in my side. Even back when the world was younger, he opposed me out of principle."

"Principles are pesky things, aren't they?" I nodded. "They can really get in the way of a good dictatorship."

I began to shuffle ever so slightly in the direction of Jamal and Mama Jean. I had to get them out of here.

He leaned closer, forcing me to freeze. Heat radiated off him until it beaded on my skin. "You jest, Miranda, but think of what we could achieve. No more petty squabbles among the gods. A unified world under a single, guiding light."

"What if people—and gods—don't want to be micromanaged by a giant celestial lightbulb? What if they like their free will?"

Aten's smile wavered, and for a moment I thought I'd pushed him too far. But then he sighed, a sound like the wind over the desert sands.

"Miranda, I'm beginning to believe you don't even appreciate my gift," he said, exasperated. "Did you not like my gift?"

"Your gift?" I asked, uncomprehending.

His lips curled up in devilish glee. "Seth was easy to talk into making a move when the rest of the gods were gathered. And he brought the ranks of gods and monsters with him for the coup against the others. I gave you the perfect opportunity to display your power in front of the others, and then took your burden from you."

"My burden?" I whispered.

"You needed to kill all those that you released, correct? I solved your problem in one quick go."

The way Seth burst into flames and then they reached out and set all of his fellow dissenters aflame.

"And the other gods?" If he could burn all the baddies, did he kill Grim, Vivien, and Xander?

My throat went dry as my stomach tightened at the thought.

"They are also enjoying my hospitality." Aten's twisted smile revealed his enjoyment of my suffering, and my heart thudded with fear at what he could do.

My throat constricted as I imagined the fate of Grim, Vivien, and Xander—all imprisoned by Aten and trapped in this hellish realm. The thought alone was enough to make me physically ill.

The realization hit me like a punch to the gut—I was truly alone. No allies, no backup, just me and the cruel god who held all my loved ones captive. The weight of isolation pressed down on me.

"Perhaps in time they will see the wisdom in accepting me as the god of gods, setting a good example for the rest. But Miranda, the more of them I kill, the more I send back to the cradle, the more that will rise again over time and try to defy me again and again. I need your assistance in a more permanent solution."

"The Blade of Bane. That's what you really want." He can't take Bob from me, not without my allowing it.

"No, Miranda, I need *you*. Help me," he urged. "And there will be a place for you, in this new world order. A world without chaos, without needless defiance. A world under one god and his right hand." He held his out to me, an offer.

His plan came into focus. Aten thought he could move in next door and make me fall in love with him. Then I'd either gladly hand over the blade or do his bidding willingly. Except he was a god playing human the way children play with Barbies. He had no true conception of what it was to be a mortal or how to connect with others. In his eyes a human dressed in a suit, went to work, engaged in activities like working out at the gym. Sprinkle in some pleasantries and everything would just fall in line.

What an absolute simpleton. But this simpleton had an insane amount of power at his disposal, which made him even more dangerous.

Xander had been so far removed from the world and yet he had more emotional intelligence in his pinky than this dude had in his entire being.

"And if I refuse?" I asked, already knowing this game had no winner.

Aten's smile turned predatory. "Then I suppose we'll have to see how hot the sun can really get."

I weighed my options, none of them good. Outright defiance wasn't going to cut it, not with Jamal and Mama Jean in the balance. I needed a plan, and I needed it fast. "Give me time to think about it," I said, stalling.

"Time is a luxury, Miranda. But for you, I'll make an exception. You have until tomorrow's sunrise."

Sunrise. How fitting for the sun god to set a deadline.

As Aten vanished as quickly as he had appeared, leaving a trail of warmth in his wake, I exhaled slowly. I had until this evening to come up with a miracle. Or, failing that, a really good plan B.

"Bob? How did you kill Aten the last time?"

He hesitated. "The gods and fae put their differences aside and worked together. Many lives were lost, but there was an opening and my fae wielder took it."

"Well that sounds like a plan to me," I said, realizing exactly what I needed to do next.

Chapter Thirty-One

THE BEAST

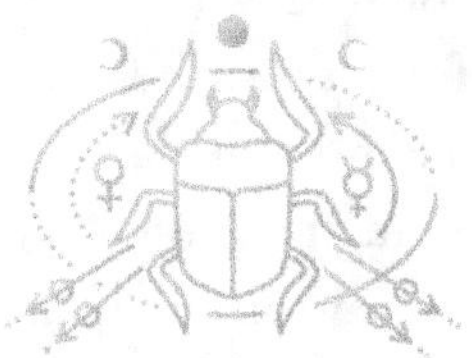

"Didn't take any time to redecorate, did it?" I asked.

The god I'd feared and despised for thousands of years sat on a golden throne. In fact, the entire level now sitting atop the Illusion hotel was bright yellow with gold embellishments. Art of him was everywhere—friezes, paintings, even statues filled the room until my eyes were bursting with the image of Aten.

Even the chains holding me to the wall were a golden hue, but they were made of far stronger materials. Materials that wouldn't melt before my flesh did.

The irony wasn't lost on me—a creature of water, now a prisoner of flames.

Aten cast a look around as if noticing for the first time. "Yes, well I missed that 'at home' feeling and thought some nesting might make me feel more in my element."

"Yeah, it's gaudy and an absolute masturbatory ode to you. Did you put a big picture of your face on the exterior of the hotel as well?"

Aten calmly surveyed his nails.

"I was right?" I couldn't help but break into snorting laughter. "You are such an egocentric asshole, you know that?"

Aten rose from his throne in a sweep of robes. He lifted a hand and my already blackened fingertips lit on fire for the countless time.

Heat blasted my body like a sandstorm from hell. I gritted my teeth and cried out as the searing pain engulfed me.

Even as the flames licked higher, scorching flesh from bone, I clung desperately to my humanity. Because to give in, to let the monster out, would be to lose the very thing that made life worth living—Miranda's love and her acceptance of me not just as a god, but as the flawed man who loved her beyond reason.

Yet part of me yearned to let myself become that ancient wrath.

Miranda's love and belief in me as a man and not a monster, became the only things keeping me from losing myself to the darkness.

Aten released his hold on me and I collapsed, gasping for air as my body trembled from the aftermath of his power. Every breath was a struggle as I tried to regain control and composure after being subjected to such intense pain. But even as I recovered, the fear of feeling that searing pain again lingered in the back of my mind.

The thought of Miranda facing Aten sent spikes of ice through the inferno of my torment. I'd endure a thousand lifetimes of this agony if it meant keeping her safe.

Aten unleashed another wave of torture, and as my body convulsed under the onslaught, a part of me realized the cruel irony—in trying so hard not to become the monster for Miranda's sake, I was enduring a hell few could fathom. Each flame that seared my skin, each bolt of pain that wracked my body, was a testament to my love for her—a love so profound it anchored me to my humanity even as I teetered on the brink of oblivion.

"The people need to know the face of their god and master," Aten said evenly, but the twitch at the corner of his eye and his need to punish me told me I hit him in a sore spot.

"And how is creating a cult going? I've seen some documentaries, and you are no Charles Manson."

Aten cocked his head to the side, his eyes alien and blank.

I landed a good hit, and no one was here to witness it. That's the real tragedy here.

"I'll amass all the followers I need soon enough." He drew a phone from his robes. "Have you learned of these fascinating little devices? People congregate with their minds and astral selves, pouring their energy—all their feelings and attention—into this little... *thing*."

"Can't say I've bothered to pick a provider yet," I said flatly.

He tsked. "You really are missing out. In no time, I've not only created an online church, but so many seeking guidance and a benevolent force to help them have flocked to the church of Aten, where the sun always smiles upon them." He matched the words with a grin that spread too wide on his face yet didn't reach his eyes.

Nausea roiled through my gut.

I couldn't be sure if it was from Aten's ability to gain power and influence so fast, or if it was from the stench of my own charred flesh.

"Sunny." Aten snapped.

A young Asian fae woman with black bobbed hair rushed forward.

"You've been watching Miranda— make sure she doesn't go to ground with anyone. I want her completely alone."

Any teasing humor bled out of me. "What do you want with her?"

Thousands of years have taught me how to endure pain, but the fear of what Aten might do to Miranda carved deeper than any flame.

Panic shot through me. Sunny was going to make sure Miranda was completely alone.

I needed to come up with a plan, and fast. I couldn't let him get to her. But for now, all I could do was grit my teeth and endure the pain as Aten's power once again engulfed me. My body trembled and every breath was a struggle, but I refused to give in.

As Sunny scurried away, bowing backwards, Aten turned an amused look on me.

"I want her to realize how special she is. Don't you?" He quirked an eyebrow.

Absolutely no fucking way will I believe we have the same intentions for Miranda.

"In fact, we have more in common than you think," he said, settling back into his throne. With a flash of his eyes, the soles of my feet began to sizzle and burn. I tried to resist. I rattled in the chains trying to escape the heat, but there was no getting away from it.

"I'm just like you," Aten said, running his fingers back through his golden hair. "I want her to love me."

I struggled to focus on what he was saying as the pain slowly ate away at my senses. Words came out through my clenched teeth. "If there is one thing I know about Miranda, it's that she can't be forced to do anything. She may be mortal, but she has a steel will, more powerful than yours."

Part of me wanted to see her spit on his offer, just to see his face. She asserted her own independence and strength like she wielded Bob. But another part of me feared for her safety, knowing full well the consequences of defying Aten.

He flicked a wrist as if it was of no consequence. "It's not about will. It's about leading her to the only inevitable conclusion."

The fiery burn had traveled from the soles of my feet up my shins and over my kneecaps. Aten was only toying with me.

"What conclusion is that?" I asked, still doing my best to focus on the conversation, and not the agony slowly but surely engulfing me.

"That if there is no one and nothing else for her to love, then she must love me."

The audacity of his statement fanned the flames of my anger, the intensity of my emotions almost as searing as the burn crawling up my legs. The very idea that he could engineer Miranda's love, as if it was something he could isolate and manipulate, repulsed me.

Alarm surged, sharper than any flame.

He wasn't just targeting me. The realization chilled me to my core before a blaze of protectiveness roared to life. The thought of anyone touching them, hurting them because of me... It turned my stomach, leaving a metallic taste of dread in my mouth.

"Oh, don't worry," he said, noting my response. "It may not come to that. Her family is safe... for now."

The veiled threat, so casually delivered, was meant to unnerve and destabilize.

Instead, it crystallized a resolve within me, a burning need to protect and preserve what was most precious. Not just Miranda, but her family.

In that moment, amidst the searing pain and the struggle against the chains that bound me, a strategy formed, born of desperation.

"You think she'll love you? I've got that woman wrapped around my little pinky. She spends most of her time with me. Who do you think she really cares about?" I forced out, my voice a blend of mockery and defiance, aiming to provoke, to distract Aten from his darker designs. Every word was a battle, a conscious effort to keep talking, keep taunting, despite the agony that threatened to consume me.

Could I really convince him that Miranda loved me more than her own immediate family? Probably not, but fuck all if I wasn't going to try. This vain prick hated any kind of rivalry, and I planned to press every godsdamn button until he forgot about Jamal and Mama Jean.

"And you think she'll want you? Over me?" I snorted. "Please. You may have used your little cheat code with the internet, but we both know I'm older and stronger than you where it counts."

Fire literally flashed in his eyes.

"Soon Miranda and all the world will see how superior I am." That spot under his left eye twitched with annoyance.

I knew what I was about to say would really be a stick in his craw and it would come with a lot of pain, but he needed to forget about going after Miranda's family.

A wheezing laugh escaped me even as the burning blanketed my torso, eating me up like thousands of fire ants. "She won't think you're superior if she finds out your dick is smaller than mine. Not to mention, I've always been the prettier of the two of us."

Aten's nostrils flared, and that spot under his eye twitched double time.

Bullseye. I'd hit my mark.

At that, the rest of me went up in flames. My screams were eaten up by the fire around me until consciousness eventually left me.

* * *

WATER. OH FUCK, I NEEDED WATER, LIQUID, HYDRATION, anything to replenish my body. The drought inside me was worse than any pain fire could inflict.

Metal clanked, and my sore limbs moved under the heavy, yet shifting chains.

Forcing my eyes open, I gazed upon the most beautiful hallucination I'd ever seen.

"Miranda," I rasped over a bone-dry throat. "I won't let him get them. He'll have to kill me first."

I wanted to say more, but I couldn't speak. I couldn't tell the beautiful mirage that I promised even if Aten sent me back to the cradle, I'd force myself to revive as soon as possible to protect Jamal and her mother-in-law.

"Shh," she hushed, eyes tense with worry as she unshackled me from the wall. I dropped. The beautiful Miranda mirage caught my arm over her shoulder, but the impact knocked all the air from my lungs. My body crunched like a dry husk.

Aman came to my side, catching my other arm. He was short, Mexican, with a thin black mustache over his mouth. His dark brown eyes were serene and serious, as if he'd never heard a joke in his life.

"I've been away so long you got another boyfriend?" I complained to my fantasy woman, my words crackling like my lungs.

"Shut up, beast boy," Miranda said, using her old nickname for me.

It wasn't an illusion. She was really here. She came for me.

She went on, "Be nice to Javier, he's working overtime to help us out. So say thank you and be quiet."

"Thank you, Javier," I repeated dutifully, but meaning it. Then I did as she asked and shut up. Though it was easier to comply when all the energy had been burned from me.

Somewhere between my consciousness wavering in and out I found myself laying on something soft that smelled like potpourri.

Miranda's face and other unfamiliar ones appeared and disappeared over me in blurry halos. When I finally came back to my senses, I was lying on a floral couch in a warehouse where one massive wall was covered in television screens. An IV stuck out of my arm next to a pole with a bag of liquid, and I realized I didn't feel like a dried husk of a being anymore.

Though I desperately needed a dip in the water of my grotto.

"You're awake," Miranda's tense, silky voice said from nearby. My angel of death seated herself next to me on the couch, her warm dry hand covering my forehead as if to check my temperature. I closed my eyes, drinking in her touch. So soft, so perfect, it was like heaven on earth.

Dark circles clung under Miranda's beautiful brown eyes, and I reached out to wipe them away with my thumb. She leaned into my hand, still blackened and a bit on the charred side. She dropped kisses on the abused fingertips. "How do you feel?" she asked softly.

"It probably looks worse than I feel."

A line drew between her brows. "You look like you've been barbecued and then thrown in a fruit dehydrator."

"Oh shit, that's exactly how it feels." I tried to push up onto my arms, panic lacing my voice. "We can't stay here too long. Aten will come for us. For me."

"He won't find you," a brusque voice interrupted. I followed it to the swiveling computer chair that turned around to reveal a rather short, stout woman with a close crop of dark hair, and a wide face. An ethereal glow surrounded her. Some of her essence stretched out in thin bright strings to all of the monitors lining the wall and to the pieces of tech surrounding her. The woman was an immortal, fae if I had to guess.

"I like your muumuu," I said. It had a lot of bright colors on it. Aten long ago incinerated my Hawaiian shirt. Bastard.

Miranda introduced us. "Xander, this is Echo."

Ah yes, the elusive tech support for our hunts. Then what the woman said sunk in. "He can't find us, you say, because of technology or magic?"

Echo's lips thinned so much they disappeared back into her face.

Okaaay, I guess we weren't in a sharing mood.

"I'm glad you are awake," she huffed like a bulldog, which made it difficult to believe her. "This one was a nightmare," Echo jerked her head in Miranda's direction. "Barking directions and pacing all around you while you slept and healed."

"Aww, you do care, honeybuns," I crooned at Miranda. I was feeling particularly mushy since my rescue.

"Well shnookums, someone had to rescue the damsel in distress," she cooed back though there was a flinty gleam in her eye.

A pretty, teenage girl strode in from an adjoining room wearing an expression that was far too severe for the schoolgirl outfit she wore and the pink pom-poms that held her hair in pigtails.

"She's ready to talk," the girl said grimly.

I looked between the three women. "Who's ready to talk?"

Chapter Thirty-Two

THE BADASS

"Since you love talking about Aten, why don't you tell us a little more about him," I suggested.

Sunny sat bound to a chair in what seemed to be a cleared-out storage room. Aoiki had captured her when Sunny came poking around to find me.

Sunny had planned to kill Aoiki, Echo, and Ryuki to further isolate me. And since she'd previously posed as Aoiki's girlfriend, Sunny knew all the weak points of their warehouse hideout.

But Aoiki and her family counted on that. Sunny walked right into a trap and was now going to answer for her lies and tell us what we needed to know about Aten.

If we knew more about his movements, his plans, we could anticipate them and catch him off guard at just the right moment.

"You should join the church of Aten," Sunny answered, not sticking to her previous role of strong and silent. "You too can feel the glory of his warmth. Feel exalted in his presence."

Aoiki shifted near me. She was playing this off well, but I couldn't imagine how she felt. Sunny had posed as her girlfriend for a hundred years, both of them fae. But Sunny did it only to use Aoiki and her ties to find the blade to free her sun god.

No, that's not true. I could see Aoiki's heartbreak had cost her. It had turned parts of her hard, parts that might never turn soft again.

"Yeah, I'm more spiritual than religious," I said to Sunny. Then I realized. "He made a church?"

"The wonders of the internet," Xander croaked from where he leaned against the wall. My heart still swelled at the sight of him. He'd been broken, burned, and bleeding, but was still alive.

Echo and I hadn't been able to locate where Aten had restrained the other gods, but he had Xander on display in a makeshift throne room at the Illusion hotel he'd commandeered as his own and had been torturing him. It's almost as if he wanted Xander's pain to be on display, as if it were a piece of art for his own sick amusement.

It was hard not to go to Xander even now—to touch him, feel his heartbeat, make sure he was okay.

"It's how he's become so strong and was able to overpower the rest of us," Xander explained. "He'd been eliciting humans to worship him again, and based off the power I've seen, the church must have gained quite a following."

"The church of Aten is great." Sunny tipped her head and closed her eyes as if she were bathing in his presence right there.

"If I'd known you were such a religious zealot, I would have dumped your ass decades ago," Aoiki snarled. "I should have known you were trash when you kept saying my father didn't know how to brew a proper pot of tea."

She said *what* about Ryuki?

Well, now I wanted to slap her face right off her head.

Aoiki's father was precious beyond all measure and should be protected at all costs. That man was always there with a cup of tea and a kind word.

God, I hoped Jamal could spot the red flags before he ended up with a nightmare of a partner like Sunny.

Whoa Miranda, one trauma at a time.

Sunny straightened, meeting the angry stare from Aoiki. "It wasn't all a lie. You too can join me, Aoiki. We can be together, in his divine light. His love can strengthen ours."

A crazed, almost goggle of her eyes had me wondering if she'd been taking any drugs.

Aoiki's face twisted into a sneer as she crossed her arms tightly across her chest, her fingers digging into her biceps. It was clear she was trying to restrain herself from slapping Sunny across the face.

A dark look passed over Sunny's face, a malevolent spark of darkness in her eyes. "You can't deny him. He will take his place as the rightful god of this realm and remove all false gods." Her hate-filled glare turned on Xander. "And there is nothing you can do to stop him."

I lunged forward and grasped her wrists tightly, the ropes cutting into my palms. I leaned in close, my face inches from hers, effectively blocking her view of Xander. "We'll see about that. Because Aten won't get his hands on Xander again, and he sure as hell isn't going to make me *love* him." I filled that last remark with as much disgust as I could.

"I love when she gets all territorial over me," Xander tossed lightly to Aoiki.

Instead of wanting to deny or punt his remark, I easily let it stand now. I knew he felt the same for me, and though we may not have our shit figured out, neither Xander nor I would let anyone hurt the other.

With that, I turned on my heel and walked out, Aoiki and Xander behind me.

Back in the warehouse, Ryuki was just setting down a fresh pot of tea and beautiful Japanese tea cups. Echo sat on the floral couch, flanked by her rabbit familiars who were snuggled in.

"Think she'll do it?" Echo asked.

"Oh, she'll do it," I affirmed.

"Do what?" Xander asked, slowly lumbering behind us.

I walked over to a backpack I left on the ground. I pulled out a brand new teal Hawaiin shirt and handed it to him.

"While you were sleeping, we made a plan."

I couldn't tell if he was more shocked by that news or the flowery garment he held between his fingers now.

"What do you mean, a plan?" His expression darkened as he stepped closer. "You should get as far away from him as possible, Miranda. He's coming for you. We need to get your family to safety."

I nodded, keeping myself from running my hands along his carved chest. "I know. Javier took Jamal and Mama Jean out of harm's way." Heinz was with them too. I'd trust my old army buddy with my life, and my family was my life. "But that's why we need to take care of this now."

His jaw flexed. "This isn't a game, Miranda."

Unable to stop myself, I smoothed a hand over a sculpted shoulder. "All the same, I plan to win." A smile quirked the edge of my lips.

Xander blinked.

"*We* plan to win," Aoiki corrected.

"See?" I chirped. "We are all playing on the same side."

"You lose all the time," Xander said.

"As you've pointed out in the past, I usually win in a different way."

From Monopoly to our billiards game, I'd won in a very physical sense. I didn't want to admit it before, but I could now. I threw all the games. For a woman who was fiercely independent, I kept handing over all the power time and time again to the beast in the cage. I'd been too afraid to admit what I was doing to myself, even as Xander teased me about it.

But I wasn't afraid anymore.

And I was wondering what would happen if we played on the same side for once.

He was about to find out.

✶ ✶ ✶

TO PREPARE AND GET XANDER'S STRENGTH BACK, WE STOPPED BY Sinopolis so he could immerse himself in the pools of his primordial water. He tried to tempt me to join him but I had other plans.

"I want to take you somewhere," I explained, keeping out of his reach and splashing zone.

After he'd thoroughly bathed, he emerged with healed skin, dripping wet. I had to turn away and focus very hard on the rock formations so as not to be deterred from my plan.

My plan didn't involve licking the droplets of the Red Sea off of his chiseled abs. Not right now anyway.

My grip on his hand was unwavering as I led Xander back through the neon-lit chaos of the Strip. Echo assured me we would be scrubbed from Aten's radar and that we could move freely as long as the god didn't set his eyes directly on us.

My heart pounded until we crossed the grand entrance of the Atlantis hotel and were no longer out in the open.

I wondered if Xander sensed my intentions. His shoulders stiffened and he tugged at the barely buttoned Hawaiian shirt.

The lobby sprawled before us, vast and opulent, yet I didn't pause. I led him to a secluded set of elevators, retrieving a small ring of keys from my pocket. "It closed hours ago, but I used to help with security here so I still have a key," I explained, unlocking the private access to the elevator.

As the doors sealed us from the world outside, I caught Xander's gaze, his breath quickening, mirroring my own racing heart.

"How did you know?" he asked.

"Timothy told me," I said, wondering if Xander would turn volatile. I wouldn't leave him if he did. But this was something he needed to face, needed to own at the very least.

The elevator's chime signaled our arrival and we stepped into a dimly lit corridor that opened up into an awe-inspiring room. The glass walls and ceiling revealed the expansive blue of a vast aquarium. Fish glided overhead, their vibrant hues blurred by the curved glass, bathed in a serene, underwater light that enveloped us in an ethereal ambience.

I carefully studied Xander's reaction. His eyes glazed as his mouth softened and parted in awe. I could feel a soothing thrum over my skin, as if I could get a second hand feel for the way the water seemed to call to him, harmonizing with his soul.

"It's yours if you want it," I pointed out.

"I know," he said airily, eyes still fastened on the giant aquarium surrounding us. His reaction tugged at my heart. Here was Nun, the god of primordial waters, visibly moved by the semblance of his elemental realm.

"I thought you might like it," I murmured, closing the distance between us and slipping my hand into his. Fingers squeezed back around mine. His reaction to the aquatic surroundings confirmed I'd made the right choice. This felt like a rare moment of connection, a bridge to the divine part of him he so often kept guarded.

"If you step up amongst the gods and claim your inheritance you would own this place. You could move out of Grim's basement and live here. Play with the sharks in your downtime."

I expected him to laugh at my joke but the way he stared at the life teaming in liquid told me that might be a very real pastime for him.

When he still didn't answer, I asked, "Why don't you take what's yours?"

Xander turned to face me, his eyes filled with longing. "I have no right to take anything. I have to earn it."

His fingers trailed down my cheek, igniting a fire within me as they traced their way down my neck and over my collarbone. His touch was filled with reverence and longing, leaving me breathless.

Xander wasn't talking about the hotel.

"Have you?" My question came out barely above a whisper. "Earned it?"

He slowly shook his head. "No, but I'm still hoping."

The quiet fell around us like a blanket and there was only the intensity of his gaze. Gratitude, pain, and raw emotion were tangled inside him, and he wore it all out in the open. Whether he could choose it or not didn't matter. For once, I let my defenses down and joined him, letting him see me. The real me.

Reaching up, I traced his jawline, my fingers weaving into his hair, grounding him to this moment, to me. His response was immediate, pulling me closer with a longing that mirrored the depth of the seas surrounding us. Our kiss was a confluence of all the tension and passion that had been building between us.

In that moment, with the gentle glow of the aquarium illuminating us, everything else faded. It was just Xander and I, and the vast, uncharted waters of what lay between us.

Our breathing was harsh in the calm quiet of the empty aquarium. I unbuttoned and pushed Xander's shirt down over his shoulders, revealing the carved muscles. Running my hands over his flexing abs, I could feel them turn to grating washboard.

Finding Xander burnt and bloodied did something to me.

Years of trying to keep my emotions locked away, shielding myself from any romantic attachment, came crashing down when I saw him hanging there.

His incoherent mumblings about saving my family sliced into my fleshy organ. It made me not want to waste what time I had denying what I already knew I wanted.

Xander's hand wrapped around the back of my neck and his face contorted as if he were in pain. "Do you understand how beautiful you are? How fucking irresistible you are to me?"

"Why?" I shook my head, breaking away. "You're a god."

I should be better than needing his reassurance, but I stopped fighting it. Instead of building a steel box around my insecurities, I handed them over to Xander, trusting him not to crush them in his bare hands.

Xander's grip on my neck tightened, his eyes burning with a fierce intensity. "Because you see me, sweetheart," he whispered, his voice husky with desire. "You see the god *and* the man within me. You don't worship blindly; you challenge and inspire me. That's what makes you irresistible."

His words ignited a need in me, a craving for this man who saw every part of me and accepted it all without hesitation. In that moment I surrendered to him completely, trusting him with my insecurities and vulnerabilities. And as his lips met mine with a fierce passion, I knew I had found my equal—a god who worshiped me just as much as I worshiped him.

Xander's head dipped to kiss down my neck, even as he picked me up. My legs wrapped around his waist, and I notched onto the hardness growing in his cargo shorts.

We both moaned at the contact. My need for more ratcheted upward immediately.

"I need you." The words came out of my mouth before I could stop myself.

Chapter Thirty-Three

THE BEAST

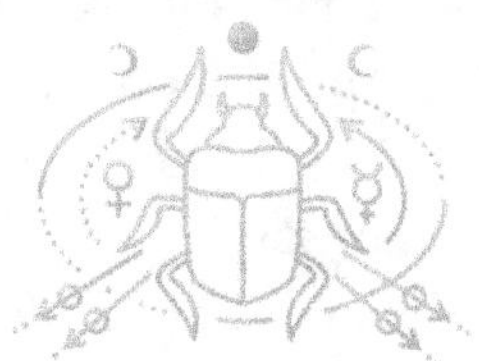

In the serene silence of the aquarium, our ragged breaths were the only sound, a stark contrast to the peaceful environment. As Miranda's fingers worked the buttons of my shirt, exposing my chest, I felt a rush unlike anything else. Her hands traced over my abs, igniting fires deep within me.

This place was sacred, this moment with her was sacred.

When we entered the aquarium I'd forgotten to breathe. The water called to me, sang to me in a voice as old as time, resonating with the very essence of my being. I was Nun, god of the primordial waters, and this... this felt like coming home.

Miranda's touch was a balm to the chaos that always threatened to engulf me.

The moan that escaped us both was a sound of pure need. Her admission, *I need you*, was a call to every instinct I possessed.

A large, silver shark glided by. Its dark eyes watched us with an almost eerie curiosity before leaving us behind. I set her down gently on the black leather bench and stepped back.

In her eyes, I found a reflection of who I could be—not just a deity bound to creation and destruction, but a man capable of tenderness, of love. This realization, this acceptance, filled me with awe. Here, in the dim, underwater glow of the aquarium, with the serene world of water around us, I felt the divide within me narrow. She didn't just tolerate my complexities; she embraced them and in doing so, showed me that perhaps I could too.

She didn't waste any time removing her clothes. I hurriedly did the same until we were both fully naked and exposed under the glimmering streaks of blue light from the waters.

Miranda reached for me and the heat of our skin pressed against each other in a conversation of hard and soft, want and need.

Her hands moved with purpose and tenderness over my chest and my pulsating heart. Miranda had shown me that to be loved in all my messy, chaotic entirety was not just a possibility, but a reality. In her presence, I was not Nun, the ancient god of primordial waters. I was simply Xander, man and god, loved and loving, wholly accepted. It was beyond anything I had dared to dream, and for that, I was eternally grateful.

Our lips met, a slow and tender kiss that sent shivers down my spine. My body trembled with ecstasy as the heady mix of passion and vulnerability overwhelmed me, leaving me gasping for air and craving more of her intoxicating touch.

As our lips met again and again, I realized that this moment was a departure from every encounter we'd had before. There was no struggle, no attempt to best one another. Instead, there was an unspoken agreement, a mutual surrender to the connection that had always simmered beneath our surface interactions.

She was a woman allowing herself to be seen, to be vulnerable. And in that concession, I saw her strength, her courage to stand as my equal, not just in battle but in love. It was a revelation, a gift of trust that she offered me, laying bare her heart without the armor of sarcasm or the shield of defiance.

As I wrapped my arms around her, feeling her heart beat against mine, I realized the significance of what we were doing. We weren't just sharing our bodies—we were sharing our scars, our fears, and our dreams. Miranda, in her openness, was teaching me that to love and be loved in return was the greatest power of all.

My hands explored the curves of her body, feeling the soft skin and the warm flesh beneath my fingertips. Her lips parted, inviting me in, and I took advantage of the opportunity, deepening the kiss and angling her head to taste more.

As our kiss deepened, I tasted the sweetness of her lips, the heat of her breath against my mouth. And when my lips trailed down her neck, I tasted the saltiness of her skin mixed with a hint of sweat.

I kissed down her neck, my teeth gently grazing her sensitive skin as I made my way to her breast. I took her nipple into my mouth, sucking gently, eliciting a gasp.

Her body was a masterpiece of curves and contours, her skin glowing in the soft light, beckoning me to explore. Her parted lips were full and inviting, her eyes dark with desire.

Too far gone, words clung to my throat. Unable to speak, my fingers dug into the soft curve of her ass and I hoisted her up. Her legs instantly wrapped around me as I pressed her against the cold glass. She hissed and bucked her hips, grinding into me. The wet heat where our bodies met told me she wanted this as badly as I did. The water glimmered in the soft light and I could see the reflection of our bodies.

I thrust into her slick entrance, her heat wrapping around me. She let out a soft cry, her eyes wide with pleasure. I groaned. Her walls squeezed tight, hugging my hardness to perfection. I wanted to touch every part of her at once.

I thrust deeper, letting her tight heat engulf me.

"Xander," she breathed, her voice hoarse with need.

Her hands gripped my back, pulling me even closer, her nails digging into my skin and leaving small marks that would fade with time. Again and again, I slid into her heat, coming home every time.

I didn't belong in this world. I wasn't right in the head. But I found my home and my sanity right here, safe in Miranda's embrace. With her legs wrapped around my hips as I drove into her, she couldn't possibly know she was actually holding *me* up in every sense.

Our gasps echoed in the glass tunnel as sweat dripped down our faces. Our breaths turned ragged and desperate as our bodies found the rhythm that drove us higher and higher.

Miranda's eyes locked with mine, a mix of ecstasy and vulnerability that took my breath away. I could see her without the defenses, without the walls. It was just Miranda, every messy little imperfectly perfect piece laid bare to me.

As I thrust harder, my body shook. The rush of pleasure and power overwhelmed me. The muscles in my thighs and buttocks tensed, as waves of pure ecstasy threatened to consume me. I was moments from losing it.

Miranda whimpered, her body convulsed around me, shaking violently as she succumbed to the sensations that washed over her. Her body tightened around me, pulling me in deeper.

I groaned, the force of her climax pushing me over the edge. I released myself into her, our bodies shuddering in unison as the orgasm tore through us.

We collapsed back onto a wide viewing bench, our bodies still intertwined, our breaths ragged, hearts beating wildly. I gazed into her eyes, seeing the reflection of our passion and the connection that bound us together.

Then without a word, we dressed and left the tranquil sanctuary of the aquarium, stepping back into the world. The sun was coming up, and we were either going to kill a god or die trying.

Chapter Thirty-Four

THE BADASS

The nights had grown too oppressively hot, and even the pre-dawn light streaked through the sky in red spirals like hellish spikes.

Aten wanted his answer at dawn, and I was ready to give it to him.

Xander's hand held mine with a death grip as we neared Kaleido-Quest Experience Center. The wacky museum experience was all the rage, and when we let Sunny go I told her to pass on the message this is where I wanted to meet Aten.

She was to get him exactly where we wanted him.

"I don't want you to go on your own," Xander growled next to me.

I squeezed his hand to reassure him. "I'm a badass, right? I've killed you so many times, this will be a piece of cake."

That didn't mean my insides weren't sloshing around in worry about what could happen.

"Besides, I'll feel better knowing you're nearby," I said as we stopped by the museum entrance. I leaned up and kissed him and Xander pulled me into him, turning a brief kiss into a long, exploratory one that left me dizzy.

Despite his reluctance, he let me go.

We navigated through the fake grocery store with its meticulously placed shelves and plastic produce. Next came the hall of endless self-ies, an Instagrammer's paradise with all kinds of floral backgrounds to choose from.

Finally, I came upon the entrance to the maze of mirrors. The walls shimmered and twisted in every direction, reflecting my own image back at me. Taking a deep breath, I positioned myself at the start and prepared for Aten's arrival.

The ceiling stretched impossibly high, adorned with an intricate web of rafters. Later on in the exhibit, visitors would be able to watch others make their way through this same maze of reflections from above. It was like a never-ending funhouse, full of secrets and illusions waiting to be discovered.

I longed for Xander to be up there with me, but he had to remain at a distance. I didn't know where he took up his post, but I was sure he was moments away. His nearness made me feel less alone, less exposed to danger.

After what felt like an eternity—but was really fifteen minutes later—door opened. My breath cut off halfway on an inhale.

Aten's image filled the mirrors.

The air shimmered around him, particles of light dancing in his wake, casting reflections that dazzled and mesmerized. Every mirror caught and multiplied his image, creating an endless sea of his perfection. The sight was so captivating it almost made me forget the danger he posed.

Almost.

His divine nature had been amplified by the countless prayers funneled through his church.

"Where are you, my god killer?" the sun god asked in an intrigued voice. His new nickname made me cringe. Though I didn't care for being his right arm either.

Aten was at the entrance and he could see my reflection though I was farther in.

Despite the dread pooling in my stomach I steeled myself, forcing my legs to stand firm, my hands to stop shaking.

"You have to come to me," I said evenly.

His love for his own image was evident in the way he paused to admire his reflection, a smile playing on his lips—a god completely enamored with himself.

A strange sense of resolve settled over me as Aten drew closer.

In his eyes, I was nothing but a mortal, a minor inconvenience to be dealt with. As I steadied my breathing, I prepared to face him.

Aten made his way through the maze slowly but steadily. I paid sharp attention to how he navigated, noting that he spent more time looking at his own reflection than focusing on the route to me.

Aten loved his own image, so I gave him as much as I could of what he loved most. It was already distracting him whether he realized it or not.

I did everything I could not to tense when the heat of his body preceded his entrance into the corridor where I stood.

Finally, he came to stand in front of me. We stood there a moment appraising each other. Thankfully, I'd mastered the poker face long ago, and the sweat sliding down my back and under my breasts could be attributed to the actual heat he cast into the maze.

Aten broke our silence. "Why here?"

"I spoke to Sunny."

"I'm aware," he said, raising an eyebrow.

"She told me about the church, the glory of following you."

"Yes, and..." he drawled expectantly.

"At first, I thought she was full of bullshit, but I wanted to experience it for myself."

He tilted his head and took a step forward, his mouth curving into a lascivious grin. "Experience what exactly?"

"What it was like to be surrounded by you," I said, gesturing to the mirrors around us.

Again, he caught his own eye and couldn't help sending a reciprocal smile to the hundred other Aten's in the room.

It was just distracting enough, just enough to put him off guard, and it was exactly where I wanted him.

If I were Vivien, I'd have something pithy or punchy to say in the moment to let him know the tides were about to turn. But that wasn't my style. I was a woman of action.

Slipping my hand into my pocket, I pressed the little red button.

A massive bin opened overhead. My nostrils burned at the terrible stench that permeated the air. His cry of outrage was garbled as rotting seafood and sticky pancakes came down on him in an unexpected torrent.

Though it happened quickly, time slowed to a crawl for me as I pulled out my sword.

"You bitch," Aten hissed, wading his way through the mountain of trash I'd buried him in with significant help from Echo and Aoiki.

His heat turned white as rage swept over him. My death burned in his eyes. Aten wouldn't suffer humiliation and he would make me pay.

I had seconds before he blasted me into fire and ash.

But taking him down in a specific type of garbage was only half the plan.

A hungry growl resonated in the maze of mirrors. Aten paused.

Then a mass of muscles and fur leapt from the rafters and directly onto Aten. Sheshem and Aten went down with a chorus of hungry snarls and angry yells.

Looking up, I searched the rafters for Xander, but he wasn't there. I wished he'd join us now, but he'd come when he could.

The plan was to lead Sheshem here. Aoiki explained she was great with cats, though I didn't even know what the hell that meant in this case. But she'd delivered.

I did what Xander taught me. I couldn't outmaneuver or use power to defeat Aten. I had to be smarter.

And delegating the fucking up to a massive hungry cat god seemed like a great idea.

Now all I needed to do was find the opening to leap in and run Aten through with Bob and finish this.

The two gods fought but Sheshem had the upper paw so to speak, and was currently trying to gnaw on Aten's head even as the sun god let out a stream of curses.

Just as I saw my opportunity and was about to spring into action, a massive metal hoop fell over Sheshem's head.

"I've got him Max," Alfonso cried.

Oh, no. Oh, *fuck* no.

Why were they here? Or rather *how* were they here?

Xander should have seen them and stopped them.

Max stood behind Alfonso as they both gripped a massive pole attached to the metal loop. They began to tighten it around Sheshem's throat, but the god spawn let out a bloodcurdling roar, shaking his head and backing away from the two idiots.

Before I lost my chance, I lunged between the bucking Sheshem, sword poised to plunge into a bloodied Aten.

A force like a cannonball slammed into my side, knocking me off course.

The moment slipped from my fingers in slow motion as I careened sideways, away from my mark.

The heavy weight of Sunny held me down in a sticky puddle. The sharp edge of a knife bit into my jugular as she stared down at me with a wild gleam in her eye. "You will not hurt my god."

Sheshem let out another displeased roar before knocking directly into a wall of mirrors, pushing it right over. The rest of the maze went down like a line of shattering dominoes in the wake of Sheshem's retreat.

"Hurry Alfonso," Max cried, wasting no time chasing after Sheshem. Max's portly magician friend hurried after him as well.

Shit, my trap hadn't just attracted Sheshem. It'd drawn the attention of Max and Alfonso. The two bumbling idiots had chased off my ace in the hole.

Shock had me by the nuts. If I had nuts.

Did I have nuts?

Control of the situation slipped from my grasp so quickly I didn't know which way was up or what kind of genitalia was attached to me.

Aten lumbered to his feet—a stinking, horrific monster that looked more like a bloody, chewed up piece of bubble gum.

"Get off him," Aoiki screamed. Now that the maze had fallen, I caught sight of Aoiki and Xander fighting off a hoard of people. Their eyes glowed with bright light and they moved stiffly as if zombified.

Aten's followers swarmed the place. Xander and Aoiki were trying not to hurt anyone while keeping them at bay.

"No," I rasped. Everything was spiraling into chaos.

My plan crumbled to ash and there was nothing I could do about it.

"I've got her, Aten," Sunny said, her teeth bared in a vicious grimace.

An incoherent sound gurgled out of Aten's mouth. He reached out toward Sunny, and she instantly grabbed his hand with her free one.

"I'm here, my god! I will serve you however you need."

A blazing inferno erupted from their intertwined hands, engulfing her in scorching flames.

She thrashed and writhed, desperately trying to break free, but Aten's grip was unrelenting.

The flames traveled like a runaway train along her body, melting her. Sunny's screams of agony bounced off the rafters as Aten inhaled the fumes of her essence into his own body.

As his faithful servant burned, Aten regenerated, until not a single hair was out of place on his golden head and Sunny was no more.

Once he'd regained his composure, Aten turned his livid gaze to me. Bob groaned under the pressure of Aten's magic, and I knew he was trying to take my life force too.

When he realized it wouldn't work, Aten dropped his power.

"You won't help me?" he snarled. "Then I'll do it myself. Sending the rest of my brethren to the cradle will be a massive pain in my ass when they all begin to emerge and challenge me again, but you won't have the blade forever, Miranda. If nothing else, you'll die and the blade will go to someone else. Someone more amenable to my offer."

With that, he disappeared in the direction Sheshem and the two idiot magicians went.

"I got it," Aoiki said, successfully locking the doors against the swarms.

Xander was suddenly there at my side, bleeding profusely. His body was peppered with stab wounds and slices to his skin.

"I tried—I tried to get to you, but they would have killed Aoiki." Even as he said it, I saw the self-hatred raging in his eyes.

I wanted to assure him he did the right thing, that it was what I would have done. But the truth was, she might be in more danger now. We all were.

I ran out the back way without explaining as nasty feeling churned in my guts. Once outside, we found all Aten's worshippers. They all stood before him, still as traffic cones, eyes glowing.

"Give me your love," he announced from atop the building next door.

Now the sun god stood atop his perch, drawing the attention of all of Vegas. They raised their hands up, as if to welcome the warmth and favor of their new god. Aten glowed brighter and brighter under their worship, becoming more powerful with each passing moment.

Then the collective essence flowed out of all of them as Aten inhaled the power of their souls.

Fuck, fuck, fuck.

Xander's fierce expression let me know he also realized we were royally screwed.

With Sheshem gone, my whole plan had fallen apart. I needed that chaotic element to give me the opportunity to strike Aten down. Now he was more powerful than before and definitely pissed.

Wait... a chaotic element.

I had been overlooking the biggest chaotic distraction I had.

"Xander, I need you to give into your god-likeness."

Chapter Thirty-Five

THE BEAST

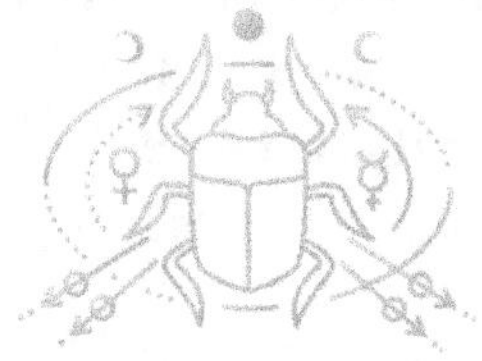

"What?" There's no way she said what I thought she said.

"I need you to change," Miranda reiterated.

She was saying the words, but none of them made any sense.

"I need you to change and distract Aten." She motioned with her hands for me to hurry up.

"I can't do that, Miranda. You don't know what you're asking." I won't risk it. I won't become the monster. With my shattered brain, who knew what I would do if I gave into my power. I hadn't since I was revived, and I had no intention of abandoning Miranda in a critical moment that could get her killed. For crying out loud, I could be the one to hurt her or worse.

The thought alone instantly made me blanch.

"Xander, I trust you." Miranda's pleading eyes bore into me as she asked the impossible.

A dry scoff escaped me. "Well that's a fucking first."

I've asked her a dozen times if she trusted me and the answer had always been no, and that's how it should be.

"Xander." My name snapped out of her mouth as she pleaded with me. "I trust you," she repeated in earnest, taking my hand in hers and squeezing it. "I always have. But I need you to trust yourself. Do it."

I splayed my hands open to show her I couldn't give her this. "Miranda, I don't know what I would do if I let that much power rush into my broken mind."

Something in her face softened and her fingers slid up the side of my jaw. "You'll be perfect. Just as you are. You are perfect."

What she's saying doesn't make any sense. It's all wrong. She can't mean that. I'm the furthest thing from perfect. I'm a mess—a tangle of power, crazy, and usually out of control with lust for her. But there is something in her soft touch that tells me she means every word.

And if there is one thing about Miranda I know for certain, she doesn't bullshit.

I closed my eyes and reached inward to the part of me I'd been holding at bay for weeks, the part that had been trying to claw its way out. There were barriers there, walls I'd fashioned to stay in control after what I observed in Miranda.

It was not with a deafening roar or a battle cry, but with a sigh that I let them all come down and the inner power flooded me.

My body elongated, the sensation akin to stretching muscles I never knew I had. My skin turned a deep, iridescent blue, reminiscent of the darkest depths of the sea.

As I yielded to the power I had suppressed for so long, the transformation overtook me like a tidal wave crashing over a ship, dragging it down into ocean depths that never end.

Veins of glowing aquamarine light traced across my form, illuminating me from within as if I had become one with the bioluminescent creatures of the deep. My eyes morphed into deep pools of water, swirling with untold power and ancient secrets, reflecting the vastness of the ocean itself.

I was losing myself and I might never come up for air again. A distant, weak cry of fear begged me to come back to my senses—there was something worth remembering. Then it was gone.

A cascade of waterspouts erupted from my back, each one writhing and twisting like a living entity, a manifestation of my tumultuous psyche. The massive, fluid appendages undulated like the tails of whales and the tentacles of a kraken, a testament to the primordial forces that made up my essence. With each movement water seemed to materialize out of thin air, swirling around me in a mesmerizing dance, responding to the call of my reclaimed power. The air crackled with the energy of a storm unleashed, my presence commanding the very essence of all waters in this earthly realm.

The only thing I was aware of was the burning entity before me that threatened everything.

I surged forward, my form colliding with Aten's radiant brilliance in a clash of elemental forces. In that moment of impact, the very fabric of reality seemed to tremble, the clash of our powers unleashing a cataclysmic storm that swept across the celestial expanse. As I grappled with the sun god's divine fury, I felt the primal surge of the ocean driving me.

Each searing beam of light he threw at me felt like a blade of fire slicing through my watery essence. They left behind a trail of blistering wounds that smoldered with searing pain. Yet even as I writhed in agony, the icy depths of my power surged forth, a tidal wave of determination.

We clashed again and again, and slowly but surely, I was wearing off some of his excess power. He burned away my liquid extremities, but we were still evenly matched.

Two ancient, powerful gods, and while he was relatively young compared to me, he was fueled by pure prayer and the undying worship of thousands.

It was just like the last time we battled. Except this time I had a whole can of crazy that just cracked open and now that it was unleashed, it wasn't going back in.

Aten finally broke away, his face contorted in outrage. His light had dimmed and I was just getting started. I'd known nothing but pain thanks to the god across from me.

He may burn me, but I welcomed the end of Miranda's blade for so many nights. I'd died more times than he knew, and I had finally embraced the pain of living.

The world suddenly crystallized as I accepted my own nature. The very thing I'd been keeping at bay was part of what made me whole.

I was still a fucking mental mess, but it all came together in balance as I let all of myself free. I had claimed the beast and now I raged with a power unlike any I'd ever known.

"You think you can stop me?" Aten raged. "You think you can send me back to the cradle? Well perhaps it's best to start this world over from scratch. This world will be good and pure, birthed in my life-giving light, and it will be perfect with me as the only god and being left in this realm."

Aten sounded like a childish brat having a meltdown. I half expected him to fall to the ground and pound his fists on the floor until he got his way.

But as his anger reached a fever pitch, fiery tendrils of energy writhed and twisted around him and coalesced into a swirling vortex of incandescent power. The ground beneath him trembled as though it was unable to withstand the sheer force of his rage.

He wouldn't.

He wouldn't actually attempt to scorch this whole world until he was the only living being left, would he?

Aten's form warped and distorted, the very fabric of his being unraveling at the seams.

Fuck.

This narcissistic piece of shit.

Aten's eyes widened and the veins in his forehead pulsated. A blinding white energy emanated from his body. His muscles tensed and his skin seemed to vibrate with an otherworldly power.

My mind raced for a way to stop him as he began to shrink in stature, but the light around him intensified, almost blindingly so. The only idea that sprang to mind was terrible, reckless, and certified suicide.

With a look at Miranda, the mortal woman who would give up everything to do what was right, my choice was made for me.

Sinking into the depths of my power, I swelled and expanded until I washed over Aten, engulfing him in the center of my watery being.

The pain.

Oh gods, the *pain*.

I'd known pain and even death, but this was a new level. Aten seared through every fiber of my being as he dissolved me from the inside out. Steam hissed from my melting body as I fought to maintain my form.

"Xander!" Miranda cried out.

My angel of death stood before me. She reached out to touch me, only to hiss and pull her hand back, her fingers an angry red. I was nothing but a volume of boiling water.

It took all my concentration to form coherent sentences.

"I'm sorry to do this to you again, sweetheart. You deserve more. You don't deserve to keep choosing between love and loss."

"No..." She shook her head.

"It's okay," I assured her, the word ending in a pained grunt. "If you didn't know this about me, I've gotten really good at dying."

Ah, that scowl. One of my favorite Miranda expressions because it pushed out that bottom lip.

"Just when I got a good crack at trying to live," I said wryly. "And I was getting kind of good at it too."

I bit off the last word as my head snapped back, and the pain doubled everywhere at once. I was slowing him down, but Aten was going supernova no matter what I did.

"You can't bring me back again," I warned her, my voice raspy and hoarse from holding it together. "You can't let him out again. If you do, he'll come straight for you. For Jamal and Mama Jean."

"I know," she whispered, reluctant acceptance shining in her eyes. Both our hearts were breaking with the weight of the impossible choice. It was either the entire world or me. And she had to fulfill her duty. It's what she did. It's who she was. And I wouldn't have her any other way.

Maybe I'd have her on that arcade joystick one more time though. I made strange, cracking sounds as I amused and aroused myself in my last moments.

"I wish we had more time," she confessed with a trembling voice.

I struggled to maintain any semblance of levity as my body threatened to implode from the intense pressure raging inside me. "Time is overrated."

I'd had a near eon of it and it was wasted without Miranda in it.

Timothy's warning had sunk into my bones. My future was borrowed time with Miranda and it would have never been enough. The prospect of walking this earth for all eternity without her was too unbearable to comprehend. It was better this way.

"You're going to be okay," I said with a lopsided smile. "Afterall, you are a badass."

"Truth or dare," she said, tears streaming down her face as her body shook almost violently.

That threw me. "Truth?"

"I love you."

If I weren't already burning from the inside out, I would be now. "I love you, too," I managed to whisper. "But the game is over, sweetheart."

The steam only thickened and molten fingers reached out from my inside. Aten was making his way out of me.

I wanted her to shut her eyes. I didn't want her to watch what she was about to do, but in true Miranda form, she stared straight into my eyes as she plunged the blade through my body and into Aten's.

A different, sharper pain sliced through me as death blackened the edges of my vision, and the bright burning sensation went out like the flick of a light switch.

Chapter Thirty-Six

THE BEAST

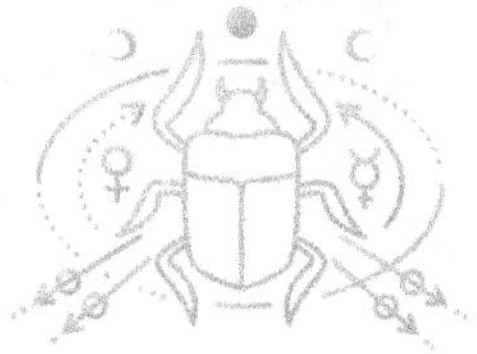

Death felt a lot like living, or so I thought as my eyes fluttered open in Grim's penthouse. Someone had a death grip on my hand and I felt strange, different. Like my senses had been muted and I no longer held that internal thrum of power I'd always known.

"Welcome back," I heard Grim's voice from over my shoulder.

I didn't turn to look at him. Not when a certain cat-eyed goddess sat at my side, staring at me like I was some kind of miracle.

"Miss me, sweetheart?" I grinned.

Then Miranda threw herself on me. I wrapped my arms around her even as I sat both of us up on the couch.

"I thought I killed you." Her words were muffled into my shoulder.

Vivien gave me the thumbs up and dragged Grim out of the room, leaving us alone.

I held Miranda, rocking her back and forth, giving her soothing hushes even as I inhaled her scent like it was oxygen.

She pulled away to meet my gaze, tears shining in her eyes. I brushed away a tear that trailed down her cheek with my thumb. I was awed to see her vulnerable enough to cry not only in front of me, but over me.

"Is Aten..." I was still dazed and confused by waking up.

"He's dead," she assured me. "Or rather, he's trapped in Bob again."

I let out a sigh of relief. "Good. I wouldn't have wanted to die for nothing. That being said," I patted my chest. "How am I alive?"

Miranda gave me a lopsided smile. "It was a gift from Bob."

"Oh really?" Now this I had to hear.

"Instead of taking you whole, he took your godhood." Her face twisted in distress and worry, her eyes searching mine as her voice dropped to a whisper. "You're mortal Xander."

I stiffened.

"What?"

"I'm so sorry," she rushed to say. "He didn't ask, he just did it, and I know it's probably not what you wanted but—"

I jumped to my feet and took Miranda with me, twirling her around in my arms. Her laughter filled the room, infectious and pure. I felt lighter than air.

Mortal.

The realization washed over me like a wave crashing onto shore. It was both terrifying and exhilarating.

As I stood there with Miranda in my arms, I became acutely aware of the dullness in my senses. Colors were less vibrant, smells less potent. And when I reached for my powers within, they were noticeably absent.

But that also meant the harsh lights no longer pierced my eyes like vengeful lasers and the noises no longer drowned out my inner thoughts.

In this mortal form, I could finally experience life without constant distractions and overwhelming sensations. "Okay, okay, I get it. You're not mad about it. Now put me down, you psycho."

Dropping to the couch, I nuzzled her neck. "Oh, but I'm *your* psycho, sweetheart."

"Is it safe to come out now, or are you guys humping like rabbits?" Vivien called out from the hall.

"It's safe." Miranda extracted herself from my grip though I refused to let go of her hand.

"*Is* it safe?" I waggled my eyes suggestively. I got a smack on the chest for that, but I caught her fingers and dropped kisses on them.

Grim and Vivien entered the living room again, he with a serious gait while the auburn-haired vampire practically bounced on her feet.

She threw her arms around us. "Come here you guys." She squeezed until I actually couldn't breathe.

"Viv, too much," Miranda squeaked out.

"Oops! Sorry."

I rubbed at my throat. "Is this what all mortals feel like?"

"Annoyed by overly affectionate vampires?" Miranda said dryly. "Not all of them, but I imagine some."

"You love it," Vivien tossed back before wrapping her slim arm around her big, tall, and dark husband.

"How are the others?" I asked Grim. All of the gods had been taken hostage by Aten, and I didn't know if they'd survived.

He nodded. "Everyone is fine. I can't say I'm thrilled that all of the dark ones from the Blade of Bane are in the cradle now, instead of Miranda's weapon. Eventually they will rise again and may have to be dealt with."

"Try not to be so dark and cynical, honeybuns." Vivien patted Grim on the chest. "There's a lot to celebrate! Being released from prison, Xander's new mortality, and a brand spanking new magic show on the Strip."

I shook my head, not understanding the significance of that last bit.

Miranda answered. "Apparently Sheshem is happy to star in a show with Max and Alfonso as long as they feed him all the shrimp and syrupy pancakes he wants and promise not to interrupt him when he feeds."

My mouth opened, then closed. "Okay, then."

Miranda's lips pursed as she shook her head like she didn't get it either.

"So..." Vivien turned to me. "What now?"

"Give him time," Grim said with restrained impatience. "He just learned that he's mortal."

Vivien pouted.

"No need to put her off, Grim. I do, in fact, have plans."

"You do?" Miranda said, looking up at me.

I swung an arm over her shoulders with a grin. "I have a dinner date."

* * *

THIS WAS THE WORST BET I HAD EVER WON.

I did get Miranda to invite me over for that dinner, and she did in fact cook. But I also did not realize she lacked any culinary talent. The chicken was dry and the spinach was overcooked, and it took a lot of soda to wash it all down.

And yet, I was the most fantastically happy man on the fucking planet.

Not god. Man.

I was Miranda's man, and she was my woman.

"What's for dessert?" I asked.

Miranda raised an eyebrow as she set her napkin on the table and got up. "What makes you think I made dessert for you?"

I encircled her waist as she walked by, drawing her onto my lap. "Because you always treat me to a little something sweet."

"You," she poked me in the chest, "are ridiculous."

"And you," I said, punctuating kisses on her full luscious mouth, "love it."

I kissed her deeply, angling her head back to get deeper. She moaned and came away breathless. "You couldn't have worn a nice shirt?" She flicked one of the buttons on my Hawaiian shirt.

"This is the nicest shirt I own," I said. "My girlfriend got it for me."

Girlfriend.

If you had told me a couple months ago I would end up mortal with the most badass woman with a built-in family, I would have laughed myself to death that night.

"You sure Jamal isn't going to ask to come home?" I moved to kiss down her neck, enjoying the silky delicate skin there. When I found the right spot, her fingers dug into my arm.

"He's good to stay at his friend's for the night." Jamal and Heinz both went to one of his friends' houses for a sleepover, and Mama Jean was back at her own.

Thankfully, Mama Jean only thought they'd been attacked by house looters and had no idea there was a supernatural element to it. As it started to really shake her and affect her sleep, I went and asked Fallon if he could do something to ease her mind. He was gruff and appeared reluctant, but he did so.

Which meant everyone was safe and sound, and we were alone for the night.

"I lied and I cheated," Miranda said from where she writhed on my lap. "Dessert is in the fridge. I got Mama Jean to make a chocolate cake."

"Later. I need something sweeter first." With that, I hauled her up and carried her to the bedroom, laying her down on her lavender quilt.

Our clothes were soon discarded, forgotten in the growing heat between us. Miranda's skin was soft and warm under my touch, her breath coming quick as she pulled me closer. There was a hunger in her eyes that mirrored my own, a need that had been building between us for far too long. We hadn't been alone together since she defeated Aten.

"I love you, Miranda. And if you let me, I'm going to grow old and die with you."

Half her mouth quirked up. "Kind of romantic, kind of dark."

"Dark," I pushed hair back from her face, "would be having to face an eternity without you."

At that she pulled me to her and kissed me, reassuring me we were together in this moment.

"What's irritating is you'll still probably look hot with wrinkles."

"Oh, you bet your sweet ass I will. And wait until you see how good I look with a mustache."

All humor fled from her face. "No mustache."

"Oh, come on," I tickled her sides, but she slapped at my hands. "It will really complete that Magnum PI look I've got going."

"You're crazy."

"You love it."

Before she could fight me anymore, I gently stroked her breast, brushing my thumb across her nipple until it hardened under my teasing. Miranda moaned into my mouth, her hands threading through my hair, holding me closer. I slid my hand over her body, slipping my fingers down until I found her hot, ready, and wet for me. My finger parted her lower lips and sunk into her, making her gasp, sending blood to my fast-stiffening cock.

"You can't imagine how good this feels, being with you in your bed like this. Like we are just two people." I added a second finger and stroked faster.

"We are just two people," she said even as her breathing turned ragged and she fought to keep her eyes open.

"Oh god, that's so hot," I said, pulling back.

She giggled even as I removed my fingers, but she stopped as I dropped between her legs and licked up her slit slowly. Her breath hitched as I continued to lap at her, my tongue swirling and twirling around her sensitive areas. I could feel her pulse quicken, her desire for me becoming more desperate. It was in this moment that I felt truly alive, that I knew I belonged to this woman, that I was home.

Fingers wrapped around my hair as she held on for dear life, nearing her breaking point. I didn't realize how much I needed this connection, this moment of pure intimacy with Miranda, until I felt my tongue dancing over her most intimate places. She tasted sweet and salty, her skin warm and soft against my touch. I licked and suckled, savoring every taste and every moan she let out, drinking in her passion like nectar.

Her moans grew louder, and I knew she was close. I slipped a finger inside her, matching the rhythm of my tongue, and she let out a scream, her body convulsing as she arched against my face. I drank in her climax, savoring every drop, every sensation.

I continued to gently lap at her until she recovered, and then she rolled us over, so she was on top.

Gazing up at her beauty, I found my rock, my North Star—and I would do anything to keep her safe, happy, and content.

Straddling my hips, her gaze met mine. Slowly, she lowered onto me, surrounding me like a hot velvet glove. I threw my head back and dug my fingers into her hips.

Being mortal didn't make sex any less mind melting, as it turned out. She rode me like she owned me, which she absolutely fucking did. We came shaking and crying out together until all the pleasure had been wrung from our bodies.

In the end we lay naked, sweaty and satisfied, limbs curled around each other.

"I still want that cake," I said into her neck.

"Perfect. You go get it and bring it back here with a couple forks," she said, with a contented sigh. "And a big glass of water while you're at it."

"What do I have to do to get you to do it?" I said, feeling too boneless to get up.

She held out a fist. "Rock, paper, scissors. Loser gets the cake."

"Game on."

EPILOGUE

2 years later - The Badass

"You can play video games when you guys are done with the dishes," I said, stopping both Xander and Jamal from creeping away.

"I made dinner," Xander pointed out with more than just a little too much smug pride. He had, and it was ridiculously delicious. Rustic lamb ragu and pasta. Xander was more than a fast learner and had become something of a chef in short order.

"Fair enough. You're off the hook."

Xander dropped a kiss on my cheek, then took my hand and dropped a kiss right on the knuckle next to the diamond ring he'd put on it a couple weeks ago.

He would have done it sooner, but I insisted we take things slow. Xander disappeared to the living room where Mama Jean was already waving a controller at him, ready to race some cars.

Heinz barked excitedly beside her. He loved when everyone got riled up in front of the television.

Xander hadn't been wrong. That dog made life more fun with loving licks, simple requests for treats, or for me to throw a ball. Playfulness and lightheartedness had been growing and expanding inside me in more ways than one.

Xander moved out of Grim's basement and in with Jamal and me. And while I didn't need as much help with childcare, Mama Jean came over even more now.

Neither Xandar nor I figured out how this would work, but it turned out the answer was one day at a time. And our family grew even more close knit.

While his powers and immortality were gone, Xander still had a lot of mental health issues to deal with. Living in isolation for so long had really caused a disruption in his mind, but we found resources to help him learn how to deal with any attacks of anxiety or confusion. When he worried he didn't deserve me or he was more trouble than he was worth, I reminded him he had to deal with my fiercely independent nature and my tendency to stonewall. We were perfectly imperfect together.

I was still working on being vulnerable and taking life a little slower. Which of course still included morning coffees at the Perkatory with Vivien and Aaron.

"Looks like it's you and me on dish detail, kid," I said, ruffling a hand on Jamal's head. He flapped his hands to get me to stop. At thirteen, his limbs had shot out and elongated from his body until he was almost as tall as me.

"Rock, paper, scissors for it?" he suggested hopefully.

"Not on your life."

"Why can't we just hire someone to do the dishes?" He dragged his feet all the way over to the stack of dirty pans.

"Xander is rich, not us," I said. Xander may be mortal, and lived with us, but he still owned the Atlantis hotel and had exorbitant funds from living for so long. I only asked that he split rent and utilities, though he splurged and spoiled us every chance he got.

"But after you get married—" Jamal tried to reason.

"Hey, you better cool it on the Christmas list this year, you hear me? Do not ask him for jet skis again."

"Aw, come on, you know he would love them," Jamal said, his eyes sparkling.

My phone buzzed so I just shot him a warning finger as I picked it up and walked into my bedroom to take it. "Hey."

"Hey my bestest, best, best friend in the whole wide world," Vivien's voice poured over the phone like butter and sugar. Looks like someone needed my help mediating a dicey situation between some gods and vampires. It sometimes helped to have someone there as back up, especially when that person had a weapon that could inflict some real damage to immortals.

"I'll be right there."

"Thank you, thank you, thank y—" I hung up, cutting her off.

Going to my closet, I retrieved my sword. Drawing Bob from his sheath, I asked, "You're always going to be here with me, right?"

"It's very likely that one day you'll turn around and I just won't be there. I come and go according to the magic that dictates where and when I'm needed. But that could be tomorrow, or it could be in ten years."

I didn't like the idea of Bob not being there. He'd changed my life in both good and bad ways, but I had a lifetime to spend with Xander now and I could never thank him enough. Though he certainly enjoyed it when I tried.

When I stepped into the living room, Xander saw I was dressed to go out and handed the controller over to Jamal—who had already abandoned dish duty.

"Vivien needs some help."

"I'm coming with you. You okay to stay with Jamal for a few hours?" Xander asked.

Mama Jean waved a hand in consent before trying to ram Jamal off the racetrack. Heinz trotted up and gave us a sincere look as his tail wagged wildly, as if to tell us he also understood the assignment before heading to Jamal's side.

It was hard to let Xander come along knowing that he was mortal now and our time could be cut short in other ways. But Xander did have eons of fight training and knew about the politics of gods. I nodded, and he was right there with me, locking up the house.

Maybe there will be a time when we will switch to a totally normal life, when my job didn't entail threatening with a god killing blade with my badass fiancé who didn't let anyone fuck with me.

But today was not that day.

* * *

Want to experience an unexpected turn? Get a bonus with favorites Timothy and Aaron.

Head to www.hollyroberds.com and check out the bonuses to read!

BONUS CHAPTER

Jamal

"Are you sure you're going to be fine while I'm gone?"

Mom stood by the front door with her duffel over one shoulder and her hand on the knob like she half-expected to walk back in and find the place smoking.

I sprawled across the couch with the TV remote, wearing the most dead-eyed teenager expression I could muster. "We'll probably just sit here. Stare at the wall. Cry, maybe."

Xander lounged in the armchair like a very tired jungle cat who'd been rehomed to a mid-level tax bracket. He nodded solemnly. "Might alphabetize the spice rack. That's the wildest I can handle without supervision."

Mom didn't laugh. She narrowed her eyes with suspicion.

With the rise in chaos between the vampires and the ancient Egyptian gods coming out of the sarcophagus to all the humans, things had been tense.It activated what I privately called *Helicopter Mom Mode*." Secretly, because I would never say that to her face. I would like the privilege of leaving the house again before I turned eighteen. A mere two years away.

At least Xander kept her from barring the doors and windows. He added a steadying presence to our weird little family.

Heinz laid his head on my leg, eyes rolling between Mom and me like he, too, was pretending not to care. I scratched the scraggly fur on his head.

"No frozen pizza," she said, leveling her gaze at Xander in particular. "He needs protein. Greens. Vitamins. Real food."

Xander blinked, slow and innocent. "What are these 'greens' you speak of? Sounds dangerous."

She looked at me instead. "If he passes out from sodium overload, call 9-1-1. Tell them to pump his stomach."

"Copy that," I said to Mom, snapping a salute.

"Or," Xander added with enthusiasm, "I could finally get one of those colonoscopies." His attention swiveled to me. "Turning human? Best decision I ever made. So many cool medical procedures to look forward to."

She muttered something about regretting everything and kissed me on the top of the head. Then she turned to Xander, hesitating.

He stood. She didn't reach for him, but he pulled her in anyway, hand gentle at her waist. They kissed—not gross or anything, but long enough that I became deeply invested in the news broadcast.

Mom was going to meet Aunt Vivien and Grim to kick some immortal butt. Something about a scorpion god? I'd offered to help, but Aunt Vivien keeps saying I'm too young. Mom insists I'll *never* help. Apparently, I'm supposed to focus on getting into a good college and becoming a brilliant scientist or engineer.

Both sound solid. But lately, I've been thinking about a third option.

"I'll be back Sunday night," she said into Xander's shirt. "Keep things calm."

"Always," he replied. Bold-faced liar. Which is part of why I like having him around.

She gave us one last suspicious glance before disappearing out the front door.

The second it closed, we both launched into action like we'd been shot from a cannon.

"GO GO GO!" I shouted.

"TO THE PANTRY!" Xander bellowed.

Within five minutes, the kitchen counter looked like a vending machine exploded. Pizza rolls, Takis, Gushers, soda, those tiny cinnamon rolls that come in foil packs. Heinz barked once and immediately got a slice of bologna tossed his way. Thankfully, he's an immortal dog Xander *stole from the afterlife,* so his digestion is basically indestructible.

Xander stood in front of the microwave like a general, arms folded, watching his cheesy empire spin. "This," he said with reverence, "is what heaven must smell like."

"I think that's the inside of your arteries disintegrating," I offered helpfully.

"Don't care. Worth it."

We settled in for a full-blown gaming marathon. Heinz curled at my feet while Xander tried—and failed—to beat me in *Street Kombat VI.*

"I used to command armies," he muttered.

"Yeah, but can you parry the Blade of Neon in a crop top skin? Didn't think so."

We were four hours in when my phone buzzed.

I ignored the first alert—too busy launching Xander's avatar off a rooftop—but the second came with a banner from a live news feed.

I opened it. Froze.

Grainy security footage—Fremont, probably. A cloaked figure stepping off the curb. The camera glitched as they turned their head. For a split second, their face looked... wrong. Too symmetrical. Too still. Their *shadow* peeled away from their body, moving in the opposite direction.

"Whoa," I said. "You seeing this?"

Xander leaned over to watch. His face was unreadable.

"You miss it?" I asked. "Being in all that?"

I wondered if this was the same guy Mom had gone to fight.

He took his time answering.

"You're always drawn to what you grew up with," he said. "Those were the gods I ruled beside for centuries. But I've spent more time in a cage. So while I love a good brawl, I'd rather be here. With you."

"Bullshit."

Xander turned sharply. I didn't usually talk like that.

"You want to be out there too. Mom stuck you with me to protect me. You've been benched because of me."

I knew it was true—and it burned.

Compared to Mom and her friends, I felt fragile. A little caged, too, if I'm being honest.

I'm smart—everyone tells me that—but I could be *helping*. Or at least not sidelining one of the best players on the team. Xander may be mortal, but he's still got combat instincts. Plus, he's *phenomenal* at pissing off the other gods.

Xander shrugged and popped a pizza roll in his mouth. "Maybe I *asked* to sit this one out. Besides, we've got those little cinnamon rolls in the fridge that come with frosting."

"Don't bullshit me," I said again, quieter.

He paused, brushing crumbs from his hands, and squared off next to me on the couch. "Fine. I'm benched. But no one *made* me, Jamal. You're the most important thing to your mom and..." He squirmed. "To me."

A little shock went through me. I guess I knew that, but we don't usually say it out loud.

The closest we came was when Xander married my mom in a fast, private ceremony in the desert two years ago. There'd been a lot of heavy back pats and throat-clearing.

He'd been in my life six years. And in this moment, I finally had the courage to try something I'd been holding onto for a while.

"You're important to me too." I cleared my throat. Fidgeted with the controller. And added that last final syllable. "Dad."

Xander's eyes widened, just a fraction—but he schooled it fast. Suddenly, we were both deeply focused on the game again.

Yeah, uh, good talk...son."

I had to keep from laughing. It sounded so awkward out of the both of us, but it kind of felt right.

* * *

LATER, AFTER WE'D *SORT OF* CLEANED UP AND I WENT TO MY ROOM, I heard the front door open.

"Miranda?" Xander called.

"Still standing," she replied. I heard her drop her keys into the bowl and stash Bob in the front closet.

From my doorway, I watched her move through the kitchen, brushing a kiss across Xander's cheek as she passed. He turned toward her like gravity had shifted, and they disappeared into the bedroom, taking the night's battle recap with them.

For a second, the house was quiet. Warm. Safe.

I stood up and went to the closet. Heinz lifted his head.

"Don't look at me like that," I told him as I reached for my mom's sword. "We're just securing the area. Not starting anything."

Bob—now sheathed and slung across my back—buzzed with what I could only describe as *judgment*.

"Be cool, Bob. Snitches get stitches. Or dull edges. Your choice."

He didn't reply. Obviously. But if he didn't like these little sneak-outs, he would've tattled by now.

I slipped out the back door, shadows stretching long across the street.

The TV still hummed in the background.

Time to see what was creeping back out of the dark.

* * *

Want to experience an unexpected turn? Get a bonus with favorites Timothy and Aaron.

Head to www.hollyroberds.com and check out the bonuses to read!

Timothy and Aaron's story is coming 2026!

A LETTER FROM THE AUTHOR

Dear Reader,

Thanks for diving into *The Beast and the Badass* duet. Whether this is your first trip to Vegas or a return visit, I'm so damn glad you're here.

This world—full of gods, monsters, and messy, powerful love—has a special place in my heart. Miranda and Xander's story may have ended, but the Immortals aren't done with me yet. I left Timothy and Aaron in a heap of emotional wreckage, and you better believe I'm coming back for them.

If you loved these books, leaving a review is one of the most powerful ways to help other readers discover my stories.

Want more magic, chaos, and exclusive content? Join **Holly's Hotspot**, my newsletter, and I'll send you a **FREE ebook** just for signing up.

Want to make sure you never miss a release or any bonus content I have coming down the pipeline?

Make sure to join Holly's Hotspot, my newsletter, and I'll send you a FREE ebook right away!

You can also find me on my website www.hollyroberds.com and I hang out on social media.

Instagram: http://instagram.com/authorhollyroberds

Facebook: www.facebook.com/hollyroberdsauthorpage/

And closest to my black heart is my reader fan group, Holly's Hellions. Become a Hellion. Raise Hell. www.facebook.com/groups/hollyshellions/

Cheers!

Holly Roberds

TASTING RED

Enjoy Holly's unhinged heroines, broody heroes, and spicy side? Come to the tatted, goth side of badass fairytale retellings with spice that will leave you panting and page flipping like a machine.

"Why did you call me here?" I ask, though I know perfectly well why the grizzled old son of a bitch sent for me. I spin the titanium ring around my forefinger with my thumb.

He frowns under his thick beard, across from me at the wooden table. He pushes a pint of ale over before grabbing his own. I don't pick up the mug, but the man shrugs and takes a swig.

How did I end up here? For most of my life, I've lived on my terms with no consideration for anyone else. Not even the women I sometimes let in my bed. I follow the jobs that bring the most money and that has served me perfectly well until now.

"It's been a long time, Brexley," he says.

Nineteen years, if one were counting. And for nineteen years, I've felt the ghostly shackle, tying me to someone else. Nearly two-thirds of my life, waiting for the shoe to drop.

"Not long enough," I say gruffly, finally grabbing the mug and taking a healthy swallow of the stuff. I hate to admit the shit is good. So I don't.

I've done everything I could to be free of social ties. There is no place for me among mage, man, or fae. But today is the day my only marker is called.

I owe one being a favor in this entire world and he has summoned me here to the musty backroom of his tavern. Boxes pile high around the room, surrounding us. He named the joint *Sam's*, though his name is Jameson. I never asked who he named it after, and I still won't ask.

The drizzle kicks up a heavy mist that clings to the windows. The cold seeps its way into my bones despite my knit sweater and leather jacket. On a shitty day like this, I'd normally be at home by the fire with a book. But this old son of a bitch has me by the balls.

"You owe me, Brexley," Jameson starts, as if he expects a fight.

I wipe my mouth with the back of my hand. "I'm aware, you old bastard. Just tell me what you want so we can get this over with."

His calloused fingers drum on the manilla folder next to him before sliding it over. "I need you to take care of her."

His tone tells me he doesn't mean take her out for lunch and shopping. He must have been keeping tabs on me to know what kind of business I'm in now. Or maybe he's just a sadistic son of a bitch, and I could be a florist and he'd still give me the same mission.

I push the mug away, despite wanting more. Drinking won't make this problem disappear. But once my only debt is paid, I won't have anything hanging over me. I'll truly be free.

I flip the folder open to a picture and a single page of details: name, occupation, home addresses. But I didn't need any of that info. I instantly recognize the older woman in the photo. I've seen her many times—on billboards, commercials, packages of food, enamel pins that people stick on their jackets.

A dry snort escapes me. "You've got to be joking."

The old bastard doesn't crack a smile, doesn't move a muscle.

Fuck me.

I run a hand through my already unruly silver hair. "Grandma. You want me to go after Grandma from 'Grandma's House?' The face of the most popular household brand, and one of the most powerful witches known to the world?"

Jameson repeats himself in slow, steady words. "You owe me." Coiled tension is locked up behind his dark eyes and in the set of his broad shoulders. Blood lust shines out from his face. This is business from his past. But I don't ask questions, and I'm not about to start now.

I study him, observing how he's changed since I last saw him. Even more gray strands pepper his black hair and beard. His scowl has only deepened with the years, multiplying the lines at the corners of his eyes. He must be nearing his fifties, but under his flannel shirt vest is a body still packed with the sturdy muscles of a heavyweight boxer.

Once upon a time, I considered this man to be like a father to me. He quickly dispelled me of that notion with an unholy vengeance. He taught me the truth. Dependence is death. Don't buy into the lie. You don't need others to survive in this world. It is a gilded lie that ends with getting stabbed in the back.

Or, in my case, a set of claws raked across my face.

But finally, I'm given the opportunity to dissolve my last tie to another being, and this is my chance. As one of the most beloved celebrity icons, this also may be my chance to get killed.

My fingers wrap around the cold handle of the mug, suddenly thirsty. "She won't be easy to get to. And afterward, I'll be hunted like an animal."

His chair creaks with a loud groan as he leans back with a smirk. I've already accepted his terms. "Good thing you're used to it."

So he does know my business.

I shoot him a cutting look over the edge of the mug as I swallow the rest of the amber liquid.

"After all," he folds his arms across his chest, "you are the Big Bad Wolf."

My grin is half-grimace. "And that is very bad news for grandmas right now."

* * *

Head to Holly's website https://hollyroberds.com to find out what happens when Red and the Big Bad collide at grandma's house

*Available on Audio and Kindle Unlimited

WANT A FREE BOOK?

Start your Lost Girls obsession for FREE!
Hooking Tink—my sizzling novella starring Tinkerbell and Captain Hook—is part of my bestselling Lost Girls series... and you can download it free right now! Visit my website https://hollyroberds.com to grab your copy now!

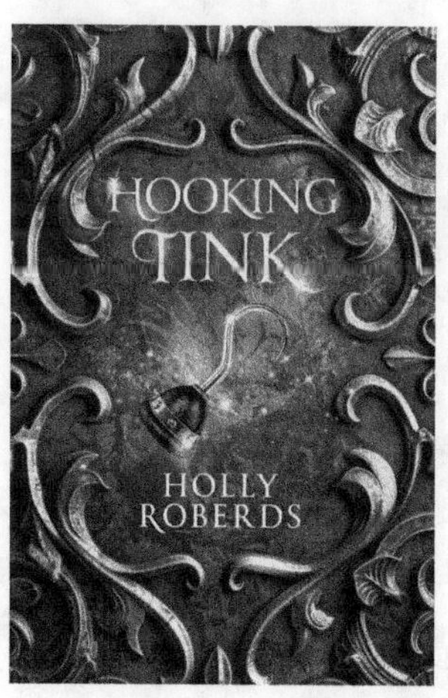

Even better? It comes with 53 more fairytale retellings, but only for a limited time.

Holly Roberds is an Amazon Top 40 Bestselling Author of the Vegas Immortals and Lost Girls series, known for badass heroines, gut-busting laughs, and spicy romance. When not writing, she's playing Dungeons and Dragons, sinking her teeth into her husband's very bite-able arm, or enjoying a "Holly Happy Meal" (prosecco and espresso) at a vibey coffee shop.

For more sample chapters, news, and more, visit www.
hollyroberds.com